CW0055B469

The Sicilian Novels

I: The Chemist of Catania

II: The Nymph of Syracuse

III: The Feast of the Dead

The Feast of the Dead

Alexander Lucie-Smith

Chapter One

'How sweet love is,' said her husband in a low voice.

How sweet indeed. The children, both children, little Cristoforo, and the new baby, Maria Vittoria, were miraculously asleep, and there were no visitors, there were only themselves, snatching at long last this surely deserved peace and quiet, the first for such a long time. She was filled with delight and contentment.

Her entire family had passed through the doors of the flat in the last three weeks since the birth. Not just her mother and father, her sister Pasqualina, and her grandparents, but also all the aunts, all the uncles and all the cousins, and even, surprisingly, some of the second cousins. Some lived locally, in the Purgatory quarter, and some lived in the city of Catania and its province, but others had come from as far away as Caltagirone and Syracuse. She had not expected this level of attention. Indeed, given that her family had been furious at her association with Traiano when it had started, she had expected that the business of childbirth and marriage would be lived out principally by themselves alone, without the involvement of the wider family. She had prepared herself for that. After all, they had come to the wedding but had kept themselves at a distance. They had ignored the birth of Cristoforo (which had occurred before the wedding) but they had made up for this earlier slight by their pronounced attentions now. It was as if they were straining to correct their earlier mistake. She was inclined to forgive them. After all, it was an easy mistake to make. When, at the age of fourteen, she had been impregnated by this Romanian boy of the same age, they had, she supposed, been right to be furious. But now time had passed and they had seen in him certain things that they had not seen before. He was the close and trusted collaborator of don Calogero di Rienzi, the property owner and businessman; he was rich, richer than any of them, with their poor but honest pose. Their house was nicer, bigger, airier, better furnished. Their children were undoubtedly extremely beautiful. Traiano had a more confident and successful air about him than any of the male members of her family. They admired him, were wary of him, and feared him a little, she could tell, while the women noted his good looks, his fine clothes, his bold stares.

But Traiano, she had been glad to observe, was gracious in victory. He received them all with great politeness, with a touch of warmth which they did not deserve, in order to signal that he had noted their past lack of appreciation but was very happy to overlook it now, though they should bear in mind that this was a favour that would not be repeated. In the kitchen, he poured drinks for her father, grandfather and uncles, glasses of beer, of limoncello, of amaro, and of wine. He called his father-in-law and his grandfather-in-law, as well as all the uncles and older cousins, 'sir' and the older women 'signora', as was only proper. He poured coke for the children and for himself (he rarely ever drank, and even when he did, it was only Cinzano) and he listened politely to what they had to say. He deferred to the opinions on the matters of the day that the older men expressed. He answered questions from the younger men in a way that deflected them from being too curious. Some of them, she could tell, were itching to know what exactly he did for don Calogero, or to ask how it was that don Calogero had become so rich. Some too were anxious to gather crumbs from the table, to find work for themselves or friends as waiters at the pizzeria, or barmen, or personal trainers at the gym that don Calogero had recently opened. But she knew that her husband saw the currency of favours as something that needed to be conserved if it were not to lose its value, and that though perfectly friendly, he was determined to keep all these newly found relations at a slight distance. She did not blame him. After all, what had they ever done for him?

She knew, better than anyone else, except possibly don Calogero di Rienzi, that under his quiet and polite exterior, her husband felt deep resentment towards many of the people whom he imagined had injured him in the past. This she knew too was all connected with his mother, Anna the Romanian prostitute, now living in Syracuse. His mother's profession caused him deep shame, compounded, quite possibly, by the fact that she had taken it up in order to provide for him, and because she had supposedly had no other means of living when she had fled Romania and her abusive, indeed murderous, husband. But still, to know that your mother did that, to have witnessed it, to have known too that the men of the quarter had all, by and

6

large, slept with her, these things, she imagined, things he never talked about, even to her, must have haunted him, and must haunt him still.

There was the question of his nationality too. He had not had a passport or an identity card until he had married her, and there had been some difficulty establishing that he was an Italian in the legal sense, which had emphasised the feeling that he had always had that the Sicilians did not like foreigners even when they spoke their language, ate their food, and had lived among them for years. In this he was mistaken, she was sure, but he had constantly assured her that he was not. Perhaps don Calogero saw him as a member of the family, but the people in Palermo, the ones who really counted, saw him as someone who, though he could pass for a Sicilian, would never truly be one. Even Calogero was not averse to reminding him of this from time to time: that Romanians were thugs, thieves, crooks, pimps and drug dealers. Of course, Calogero liked to tease his favourite. But sometimes the tease went too far, and anger would surface. Traiano was the only one who could be angry with the boss, who could swear at him and who could rebuke him, and sometimes even get into a fight with him; though when this happened, he was always careful to let him win.

Under his black curly hair, which he had allowed to grow long and more Caravaggesque of late, there were various lumps and scars, souvenirs of past fights. Occasionally, at moments like this, she would run her finger along the tracks of ancient cuts, but he did not like to be touched in this way; the reminder was painful even if the pain of the cuts was long gone. He had, as he put it, been patched up on several occasions by Doctor Moro, a man whom he heartily disliked, but who provided a discrete medical service to the fighting men and the prostitutes of the quarter. His most recent trophy was the scarring on his chest, where Calogero had poured boiling coffee on him.

She had known, when younger, that boys got into fights, and that this was something they grew out of; then she had met Traiano, and become aware

7

of don Calogero, and realised that some boys never gave up the fighting spirit. Traiano's deep devotion to her and the children, and a small number of other people, was matched by his distrust of everyone else. He had a collection of knives, which were kept in a safe place – she dreaded the children getting hold of them – and even a gun, and he never left the house without one or the other, sometimes both. She disliked weapons of any sort, but she accepted his explanation that they were an insurance policy. Because he was armed, because he was strong, he would always be safe, for no one would dare attack him. His job, she knew, was to guard the empire that don Calogero had built, and to guard Calogero himself. There might be people who would want to harm him or his interests. But it was best not to think of this. Why rush to meet that which you should most avoid?

Of course, they were both young, and that meant that things would develop and change. She stroked the back of his neck, brushing aside the long tendrils of hair.

'When can I get my hair cut?' he asked.

'When you are forty,' she said.

He giggled. Calogero wanted him to get his hair cut, but she had countermanded this. He was her husband after all. He would always be hers, but he might not always work for Calogero. One thing was certain. Their son never would. Cristoforo would be a doctor or a lawyer. He would be educated. Like Rosario di Rienzi. Hadn't Rosario said that it took three generations to sanitise a family? Rosario's father had been a criminal, but Rosario himself was an honest man, a lawyer, and his children would be good people too. Her husband, she knew, worshipped Rosario, just as he worshipped the priest don Giorgio. Apart from his family, they were the only ones he cared about.

She carried on playing with the curls on the back of his head, which would soon perhaps reach his shoulders. The softness of his young face was buried between her breasts, but eventually their mouths encountered each other once more, and she felt the blood stir in him, heard the quickening of his heartbeat. The children, thank God, were still asleep. Then, suddenly, the front doorbell buzzed, with three long, shrill notes.

'Ignore it,' he said.

They ignored it.

The three notes came again. And, after a few seconds, again. He groaned in frustration, jumped out of bed and ran into the hallway. She heard his voice speaking to the intercom, his voice harsh and annoyed, but immediately softening.

'Sorry, sorry,' he was saying. 'I was in the shower and Ceccina was asleep. So are the children. But just give me a few seconds and I will be right down to bring you up.'

He came back into the bedroom.

'It's Anna,' he announced hopelessly. 'Just turning up unannounced and assuming that we have nothing better to do that to see her. I am sorry.' He began to hunt around for his clothes. 'You take your time. I said you were asleep.' As soon as he was dressed, he bent over to kiss her. 'She will guess what we have been doing,' he said with a rueful smile.

She watched him go, and then listened for the sound of him re-entering the flat with his mother. There was someone else with them too. Gradually, she got up, and then, because she was to meet her mother-in-law, took particular care with her appearance, especially her hair, which was long and dark, and required little attention except to be tied back in a pony tail. She examined herself in the mirror, and then went into the sitting room.

Traiano was there, with his mother, Anna the Romanian prostitute, her two-year-old son Salvatore, and a third adult, a man who got up as she came in and looked at her with a radiant smile. He was about fifty years old, tall, slim and had a mane of glorious white hair. He took her hand and greeted her with a look of complicity.

'This is Alfonso the photographer,' explained Anna. 'Fofò,' she said, 'This is my dearest daughter-in-law, Ceccina.'

'Perhaps we called at a bad time,' murmured Fofò, who, she was immediately aware, was the most charming of men.

Her husband, Ceccina noticed, was looking most uncomfortable, sitting there on the sofa, his cheeks flushed, an air about him of interrupted marital passion, something to which Fofò's seemingly innocent words had drawn to her attention, though, she hoped, not Anna's. She stifled a little giggle.

'It is such a lovely surprise to see you,' she said, meaning Anna, 'and to meet you,' she added, meaning Fofò. 'Shall I take you to see Maria Vittoria?' she asked. 'She and her brother are asleep still.'

They went in to admire the sleeping children. This was something necessary. Maria Vittoria had been born three weeks previously, and this was the first visit by her grandmother. Needless to say, Traiano had told her of the imminent birth, expecting her to come at once; had phoned her once the child was born, and then, despairing, had heard nothing. And now she had turned up just like this. He did not like his mother, and she could

10

see why: she treated him like this, holding off, pretending she did not care about the birth of his second child; then, just when he despaired of any attention from her, she turned up at the least opportune moment. And why had she come? To inspect the baby, but perhaps more importantly to ram home the reminder that she had this ability not to disappear from his life and that he would never be rid of her. And perhaps to show off her new acquisition, the divinely handsome and cultured Fofò.

The mane of white hair, the clear blue eyes, the retro glasses, the wonderfully made suit that fitted him like a second skin, the shirt with its cufflinks, and the perfect shoes – Ceccina decided that if she had acquired someone like Fofò she would be very inclined to show him off too. She left her husband to talk to his mother, who, she noticed, had certainly taken care of her appearance, perhaps under the impulse of keeping up with Fofò – they were certainly a handsome couple. But Ceccina could sense something more than the glamour of mature good looks. There was something else about Alfonso, this man called Fofò. He was someone important, someone she pictured living in beautiful interiors, the sort of person one saw in television advertisements for luxury goods. He was not from their world, a world where everyone knew or was related to someone in prison, a world where few were properly educated. That was it: he was educated. She herself never felt her lack of education, interrupted as it had been by early pregnancy and marriage; she did not feel, as she thought Stefania did, that there was some catching up to do. She had everything she wanted, for she had no unfulfilled ambitions. But here was this man, new to them and new to Anna, who, she assumed, had entered her life and transformed it.

He explained how they had met. It had been in church, in the Cathedral in Syracuse. He had seen Anna there, praying in front of the shrine of Saint Lucy, her child, pretty little Salvatore, with her. He had been struck by the sweet nature of the scene. On leaving the Cathedral she would cross that wonderful square and go to the bar opposite for a cup of coffee, and there he had seen her again. They had spoken. He had said he had seen her praying; she admitted that she had sensed him looking at her, she had felt his eyes upon her. But he was an artist and liked looking at things. She was the ideal model, the sort of woman who knew that she was made to be

11

looked at. He had asked to photograph her. He had done so at night, at the fountain of Arethusa, and quite a crowd had collected to admire the beautiful nude woman. His photographs, he thought, had transformed her, brought out her inner beauty, and though she was not native to the island, had been particularly Sicilian. He now had the idea of taking her to classical sites around Sicily – Agrigento, Segesta, Selinunte – and photographing her against these wonderful backdrops. He took out his phone and showed her some of the pictures of Anna; Ceccina was struck by her brazen nudity, her wonderful beauty. It had only been after they had got to know each other, he continued, that he realised that his widowed father was one of the gentlemen whom Anna saw in the afternoons. Every Tuesday, his father, who was approaching eighty, came to see Anna for an hour. It gave him great pleasure, indeed, joy, and he, Fofò, was deeply grateful for that.

Ceccina reflected that if she were a prostitute, she would at least have the shame to lie about it; but not Anna. Anna made a virtue of being honest about things that would be better kept quiet. But she did it to make her son uncomfortable, she thought; she did it to punish him for his extreme conservatism, his complete devotion to his wife, his unspoken and furious disapproval of his mother's way of life. Or so she thought. But - and there was always a but, - Traiano was a hypocrite in his mother's eyes as the bar and the pizzeria in the quarter, which he oversaw, were places where prostitutes met clients, and men and women bought cocaine. It was hard to understand, but what one could not tolerate in one's mother, one could perhaps tolerate in oneself.

Fofò, perhaps because he was of a different social class, did not seem to mind that Anna was a prostitute and sleeping with, among other men, his own father. Ceccina did not dislike her mother-in-law, but she knew that they were very different. She herself could not even think of anyone apart from Traiano in that regard; but no doubt Anna, in running away from her husband, in taking up with Salvatore's father, in prostituting herself, had perhaps established her unmistakeable credentials as a revolutionary in the sexual field. All she herself wanted was her husband, and Anna's attitude seemed like an unspoken reproach. She did not dislike Anna; in fact, in

12

many ways, she was a little frightened of her; but she wished she did not make Traiano so unhappy.

Anna was now approaching her, to talk, no doubt about the children, bringing little Salvatore with her. But no, as they settled on the sofa, it was other things that Anna wanted to discuss. How was Traiano? Was he well? Was he happy? Her eyes looked across the room to where her son was speaking to her friend Fofò, and her glance seemed to indicate that her happiness depended in great part on the welfare of these two human beings.

'And how is my old friend don Calogero di Rienzi?' she asked, still not taking her eyes off her son and Fofò.

Her smile conveyed a pleasant irony.

'I have known him since he was a teenager, younger than you are now. In fact, we met when he was thirteen. I believe that story is well known. Boys will be boys; and then they grow up into men. But who would have thought that he would have become so important and so successful? But it is the women behind him, you know, who have made him what he is, or so I think. There is me, of course. Whenever he thinks of me, and I am sure he does so often, he becomes the little thirteen-year-old who is desperate to prove himself. And Stefania, she has made him too. She has reinforced his social ambition, made him want to get on in society, to compete with all the important lawyers and businessmen; and she has given him children, and he is desperate that his three children should have a better life than he ever had. Little Renato, he hopes, will grow up, and no one will point him out as the grandson of old Renato, the Chemist of Catania, the man who murdered all those people, the man who founded the family fortune. And no one will point out that Calogero started life as a thief of car radios. All his crimes will be forgotten, because money has no smell and is the best disinfectant of all. Stefania was once the same as the rest of us, but look at her now. So beautiful, so fashionable, so blonde the last time I saw her. I am glad that you have not dyed your hair, my dear. You look lovely, by the way.'

'I need to lose weight,' said Ceccina.

'I was not going to mention that, but one always does after a birth. I am almost forty, so will have no more children. I have your husband and I have this little darling, and I have two grandchildren, so it is not as though I am short of descendants. Fofò adores little Salvatore, which is very nice, and little Salvatore adores Fofò. All we need now is for Traiano and Fofò to decide they like each other. I think it certain that Fofò will like Traiano, and as for Traiano liking Fofò, I rely on you to bring that about.'

This was flattering.

'Of course, I will. He is so charming.'

'They both are. Perhaps I will marry him.'

'But aren't you married already?'

'Ah,' said Anna, as if remembering something she should have mentioned earlier. 'That is something else you can do for me. I know you have a large family, and my poor boy only has me in the whole of Italy, and Salvatore too. But there is a large clan back in Romania, a grandmother, uncles, aunts and of course his father. I hear from some of them from time to time. They told me that his father, whom he never asks about, I might add, is dead. He was in prison, as you know. They killed him in the prison showers. He was stabbed in the chest. How this will affect my son, I do not know. But you will, and you will know the best time to tell him.'

Ceccina was silent.

'They have knives in Romanian prisons?' she asked in a low voice.

'The same question I asked. They have metal detectors. There are no knives. He was stabbed with a toothbrush handle. They held him down and banged it into his chest. The prison guards were all looking the other way. Whom my late husband offended I do not know. It may be best to say nothing as yet, or to wait till he asks, which he may never do. The thing is that we do not want him wondering who was behind this, do we, and doing something stupid.'

'But we cannot not tell him, if we know,' said Ceccina. 'We cannot keep secrets from him.'

'Doesn't he keep secrets from you?' asked Anna. 'Does he tell you about his work?'

'Not everything,' admitted Ceccina.

'He is still going away regularly to Donnafugata?' asked Anna. 'There is no need to look so guarded, my dear. The whole of Sicily is talking about it. Anna Maria Tancredi is six months pregnant, and everyone is wondering who the father is. She has kept the pregnancy secret, but the secret cannot be kept forever, mainly because she is so huge, and she is staying in Donnafugata, too tired to go into her office in Palermo. She is working from home, to the frustration of her clients. That is a considerable number of people and they all talk. That is how Fofò heard all the rumours swirling around. The most ridiculous one of all is that her child was fathered by the Cardinal Archbishop himself. But Fofò tells me that this is because Tancredi was always such a devout woman, handling a lot of the

Church's money; His Eminence has never been one for the ladies, or so Fofò says, and he also says that if I were to meet the Cardinal we would get on like a house on fire. Well, the truth of the matter is that Calogero has been seeing her regularly, with Traiano, and now she is pregnant, so you can work it out, can't you?'

'If don Calogero is the father….' began Ceccina.

'If!' said Anna.

Ceccina knew he was, but did not like to admit it, because to admit he were the father would be to admit something else: that Traiano had told her about his trips to Donnafugata, and indeed told her that the boss had made Tancredi pregnant. For all the talk of the trips to Donnafugata being for business, this matter of the new child was difficult and dangerous. She knew that Tancredi had made the boss's fortune, and the fortunes of all who worked for the boss. But had the boss now ruined everything by creating a huge public scandal? And his wife, Stefania, did she know? And if she did, what would she do? The potential for trouble was surely enormous.

'Does Stefania know?' asked Ceccina, abandoning the pretence of innocence, overcome by curiosity.

'She must know about Tancredi. She is not stupid. Does she know about the child? If she does not already, she will do soon enough. It is bound to get back to her. Some kind friend will tell her. One person will not and that is her husband. He is a terrible coward when it comes to dealing with women. Men, he has no problem with. Women… well, look at his mother, and his sisters. They all terrify him. If I had gone to university, I would have liked to have studied human nature, something like psychology, or maybe literature, and learned about what it is that drives men like him. And I would look them deep in the eyes when they were at their most

16

vulnerable and say to them 'Tell me all about your mother.' These dear old men who come to me, all they want to discuss are their long-dead mothers. Can you believe it?'

'I can believe it,' said Ceccina. Of course, Traiano never spoke about his mother. It might do him good if he did, she reflected. But what a mother she was.

Anna smiled. 'Get him to like Fofò,' she said. 'But Fofò is doing that already, I see. Of course, Calogero is fearful over what he has done. It means that he is now in Stefania's debt. She will be quite pleased by that. She will be able to exact a high price from him.'

'Hasn't she already?'

Outside, it was getting dark, even though it was not late, a sign that winter was beginning. It was in fact Monday 1st November, the day of All Saints. Tomorrow was the feast of the quarter, the feast of the dead, All Souls. They had been to Church on Sunday, as usual, and they had been to Church that morning because of the feast, and they would go to Church tomorrow, to pray for the souls in Purgatory. All day, people would be coming to visit the Church of the Holy Souls and to hear Mass, which would be celebrated by numerous visiting priests every hour on the hour, culminating with the High Mass in the evening, which would be celebrated with the entire Confraternity of the Holy Souls in attendance, one of the members of which was don Calogero di Rienzi. One of the earlier Masses was for the repose of the soul of his father. It was a long weekend, Ceccina reflected.

The unannounced visitors showed no sign of wanting to depart, so Traiano suggested that they should all go to the pizzeria and have something to eat. The children were waking up, and he and Ceccina announced that they would get them ready and tidy themselves up at the same time.

'I hope he likes you,' said Anna, when they were gone, and they were alone in the room. 'He hated Salvatore's father. He was so jealous. But I am sure he will like you. Especially as ours is an amorous friendship and no more.'

'You like that phrase,' he remarked. 'I liked him. He is very handsome in a rather unhealthy way. You never told me that. He has inherited your good looks. The wife is delightful too.'

'He is full of murderous rage,' said Anna.

'And whose fault is that? Can you blame him?' said Alfonso with a smile. 'Is it that big a deal? The Greek gods did it all the time, well, not all the time, but some of the time.'

'You are wrong. They disapproved. I know about the story of Oedipus.'

'Well, as long as the gods don't kill you or me. After all, you have slept with my father.'

'But I am not proposing to sleep with you, thank God. I am sick of all that. Calogero di Rienzi, don Calogero, might not like it, but he will soon have his hands full. He won't have the time to have you murdered, what with his mistress having a baby, and his enraged wife.'

'You exaggerate the danger.'

'Hardly.'

Traiano was brushing his teeth. His wife stood behind him and put her arms around him. He stopped brushing. He knew she wanted to tell him something. He looked at her in the mirror, then turned round.

'What has she said?' he asked, getting to the point.

'Your father is dead,' said Ceccina.

He said nothing for a moment.

'He was in prison.'

'They killed him in prison. She has the details if you want to ask. And there is something else. She talked of marrying this Alfonso, and she wants you to like him.'

'I do like him. He seems interesting. And he is well dressed. I like his suit. And his shoes. Did you notice his shoes? But has Anna noticed that he is perhaps not the sort who is that interested in women?'

'I think that is the whole point. And another thing. She is going to create trouble between the boss and Stefania. She is going to tell her about Tancredi being pregnant, unless she knows already.'

'She said that?'

'No. I worked it out. She thinks the boss will try to stop her getting married. Why I am not sure. But she wants to give him other stuff to worry about.'

'He wouldn't give a damn,' said Traiano. 'But she thinks that every man she has ever met is in love with her, including the boss. Especially the boss. It is her vanity. Now she has the photographer. I hope she enjoys himself. Perhaps they are made for each other.' He paused. 'What exactly happened to my father?'

He wrapped his arms around her as he said this, and did not look at her. She knew she had to tell him. He had asked because he wanted to know; and he wanted her to tell him, gently, to cushion the blow, rather than hear it from the far less sympathetic lips of his mother. So she told him. She felt him flinch slightly in her arms as the manner of his death sunk in.

'I suppose she was glad, was she?' he said, meaning, of course, Anna.

'No, not really; but she was not sad either,' she replied. 'What about you, what do you feel?'

'I don't know. I will have to discuss it with the boss. And I will have to discuss it with Saro. And perhaps don Giorgio. He was my father, and yet he was not my father. So, I do not know what to feel.'

'Will you talk to your mother?'

'No. I wish we were alone.'

'The sooner we get this over with, the sooner we will be,' she said. 'And tomorrow is the feast of the dead,' she added with a sigh. 'Another busy day.'

'It will be a busy winter,' he said. 'Lots of projects,' he said, in answer to her questioning look. 'And lots of money coming in, and even more in a few years, you'll see.'

They went to the pizzeria - Traiano, Ceccina, the two babies, little Salvatore, Anna and Alfonso. There was a private room at the back, which was always kept reserved for the owner and his friends, so they walked past the queue that was waiting in the street and went straight in. The room had a long table, and the two men sat at one end, the two women at the other, and the children in between. But it was not long before another party entered: Calogero di Rienzi and his wife Stefania and their three children. There were now six children at the centre of the table; Stefania went to the women's end, and Calogero to the male end, with a wary greeting and a look at Anna who dominated the other end of the table.

He was introduced to Alfonso; he remembered the night on which Alfonso had photographed Anna at the fountain of Arethusa, creating a useful distraction while the body of Michele Lotto, the wild Romanian, was dumped in Syracuse harbour. He looked at Alfonso with guarded respect. He admired artists, educated people, cultured people, and regretted his own missed education. He heard with interest that Alfonso's widowed father was a client of Anna's.

'Those of us who have enjoyed Anna have never ever been able to forget it,' he said ruminatively, his hand resting on Traiano's shoulder as he spoke, giving the boy a slight squeeze. Traiano frowned at the enunciation of this truth. 'But if she belongs to your father, she does not belong to you,' he said.

21

'Correct,' said Alfonso with a smile.

'But they are talking of getting married,' said Traiano. 'Though I imagine it is going to be what is called a white marriage. Correct?'

'Correct,' repeated Alfonso. 'I am glad you have brought the subject up. Because it means that I can solicit your approval.'

Calogero appraised him.

'Our approval? Of yourself? Of your marrying Anna? Of white marriages in general? The latter is easy to answer. I greatly approve of white marriages, now that I have had a chance to consider the concept. My own has not been so in the past, as you can see, as I have three lovely children. It might have been better had it remained white. It certainly is white now. If I had to marry again, which I never shall, I would ensure that any future marriage would be white, stainless, pure. I can't tell you how tedious a matter copulation is. I wish I had your ability to live without it.'

'Ignore the boss, Fofò. He is joking,' said Traiano. 'But he has a strange sense of humour. He screws everything that moves. I know. I have to drive him to Donnafugata.'

'I know about Donnafugata,' said Alfonso.

'You do? Is nothing secret in the province of Syracuse?'

'Donnafugata is in the province of Ragusa, boss,' said Traiano sourly.

'What do you know?' asked Calogero.

'It is where Anna Maria Tancredi lives, and she is about to have a baby. Who has not been fathered by the Cardinal Archbishop of Palermo.'

Calogero smiled.

'And they are saying I am guilty?' asked Calogero.

'He's guilty,' said Traiano. 'Look at Anna right now, deep in conversation with Stefania. They are discussing your guilt.'

'What can she tell her that she already does not know?' asked Calogero.

Stefania had in fact been delighted to see Anna the Romanian prostitute, who had kept away from Catania for some time. She liked Anna simply because Anna was one of the few women – her mother-in-law and sisters-in-law fell into the same category – who made her husband uncomfortable. She could see Calogero right now, at the other end of the table, watching them in conversation, and she hoped he was suffering. While Ceccina fussed with the children, the two older women were in close conference.

'Of course, there is nothing you can tell me that I do not know,' said Stefania. 'He has been going off to Donnafugata or some other place every few weeks since last winter. He has been taking Traiano with him, as some sort of alibi. But it was not hard to guess what was happening. He has got someone. And do I care? Not really.'

'Do you know who?'

'He has admitted he has been seeing Anna Maria Tancredi. For business. And that part is true. We have made a lot of money through this association. A great deal. I can't hide the fact that I am glad about that. We are rich, or at least richer than we were. One can never be rich enough, that is his way of looking at things. And if he is screwing her, that does not bother me in the slightest. I shall get my revenge. Indeed, I have already had it. I am squeezing him.'

'By the balls?' asked Anna.

'No, by the wallet, by the bank account. It is far more painful for him, and more satisfying for me. My dear Ceccina,' she said, turning to the younger woman, 'Make sure you get as much cash out of that young husband of yours as you possibly can. He has got tons of it these days. But you get it off him and go into business with it when the children are older. It was my sister-in-law Assunta who alerted me to this. She always thought I was extravagant and greedy. What a joke. She squeezed a fortune out of him for her wedding, and he gave it to her because he felt so guilty about defrauding her of what she should have had from her father. His sense of guilt is useful to me. I know about Tancredi. I know she is not young. I know he must have gone to bed with her to please her and not to please himself. Caloriu was never a great one for the bedroom, you know, even when he was younger. Power and money, they are what he really likes, and now he has to share them with me.'

'Good,' said Anna. 'Then you will be glad to know that she is pregnant, and will give birth in a few months.'

'At her age?' remarked Stefania calmly. 'Good for her. No wonder he has looked so shifty these last few months. He has been wondering if I knew. Ceccina, did you know?'

24

'No. Traiano never mentioned it. He is too discreet.'

'How did you know, Anna dearest?'

'Fofò told me. The whole of Sicily is talking about it. But they think it is some very important cleric who is responsible. Tancredi herself is not saying anything, she is letting people say what they want.'

'She is very rich, and now she has someone to leave it to,' said Stefania. 'Her child will be richer than my children perhaps. Oh well. You know this new building that he has bought and done up? The basement is a gym, and the upper floors are all offices; the top floor will be for me. We are having everything set up, and there are lovely views over the city and a roof terrace. That is the headquarters of the new company, Catania Developments Limited. And the person running that is me. All the properties he owns are being transferred to the company, and he has shares, I have shares, Traiano has shares, and Saro too, and some of the other boys, Alfio and Gino and the rest…'

'How is Saro?' asked Anna. 'Pity he is not here. I love him so much.'

'You do?' asked Stefania. 'How nice for you and for him. I too am quite fond of Saro.'

'Traiano loves him,' observed Ceccina. 'You watch, at some point tonight he will go off to see him, and perhaps bring him back here for an ice-cream.'

'You may not know this, Anna, but Saro has at long last got a girlfriend. She is the daughter of the lawyer Petrocchi. They met in the summer, when Petrocchi invited him to stay in their house in Zafferana Etnea. She is the last of three daughters, still unmarried, not very attractive, but attractive enough. But Petrocchi has always liked Saro. He is not so very attractive either. But he is good son-in-law material in the lawyer's eyes. His wife may have different ideas, as she is more socially ambitious. The girl is in Rome, finishing her degree, but she is nice. I have not met her, but I have squeezed Saro for details. Just right for him. Very holy. Likes going to church. Well, we all like going to church, but she as much as Saro. So, they are well suited. They may well marry. Of course, Caloriu cannot make his mind up. On the one hand it is a great step up for the family. She is a middle-class girl, the daughter of an important lawyer. They are rich. Which means that we cannot admit to being less rich, and Caloriu will give him a fortune if he marries her. But at the same time, he sees what I see, that this has been engineered by Petrocchi and that Petrocchi will use the relationship to squeeze Caloriu for favours. He is not sure whether he should resent this or be flattered by it. But, of course, this has something to do with the new company, because to impress Petrocchi, he is going to be very generous to Saro. But there is plenty to go round,' she added hurriedly, noting that Ceccina was listening intently. 'He knows who his most important friends are. He knows he needs Traiano more than anyone else.'

'He said that?' asked Ceccina.

'No, he never talks about his work. But I know it. He needs money to invest. Traiano guarantees the income coming in from the bars and from this place. And your husband is quite often round at our place late at night, discussing things with my husband. What, I am not sure, as I do not listen at the door. At least, what details, I am not sure. But he is planning to buy up property on the far side of the airport. That I know. Because that is the bit that I am handling. A farm here, a flat there, a petrol station there, and any bits of land going. The idea is to buy it all up, and then develop it. But the whole thing will take years. It is a horrible area and it is all going cheap. And for this, we need Tancredi. You know, I ought to meet her.'

'You should,' said Anna.

26

'Tell us all about this gorgeous man you have brought with you, dearest,' said Stefania. 'He is so beautiful you would think he was English. Those eyes, that hair, the glasses, oh my goodness, those glasses, and what a lovely suit. I wish I could see his shoes.'

Ceccina had seen his shoes, and described them.

'I am thinking of marrying him,' said Anna. 'Did I mention to you, Stefania dearest, that my husband was dead?'

'No, you did not mention that. How did your son take that?'

'It is hard to say,' said Ceccina.

'He did not know him,' said Anna. 'He cannot mourn him. I knew him, and I cannot mourn him either. My second husband will be very different.'

She smiled down the table towards Fofò.

'And you will give up work when you marry, my dear?' asked Stefania.

The pizzas arrived, which precluded an answer. The waiter who brought in the pizzas was not the one who had taken their order, Fofò noticed. He was about twenty years old and dressed in black chinos and a red checked shirt, the standard pizzeria wear. He noticed how this young man leaned over to give the women their pizzas and paid particular attention to Stefania, who seemed flattered by his smile. Gradually he moved down the table, giving their pizzas to the children, who seemed enchanted by him. As he arrived at the male end of the table, Alfonso noticed the way the young man became less attentive and at the same time more tense. He was sure of his popularity with women and children, but he seemed to realise that the only people worth impressing were at this end of the table. In particular he seemed at pains to make a good impression on Calogero di Rienzi, while aware of the eyes of Traiano on him; and at the same time feeling himself to be under the scrutiny of Alfonso himself.

'Your brother has been working on the office?' asked Calogero, as the pizza was placed before him.

'Yes, sir,' said the boy, in a tone of deepest respect.

'And he is coming round to the house?'

'Yes, sir. He will come again. He is not quite sure of the wiring and the best place for the router.'

Calogero waved a hand, as if batting away an insect.

'It is for my wife, not for me. I have never looked at a computer in my life, and I do not intend to start. But I can't stop her having one anymore; and in the office, I am told, it is essential. I don't even have a mobile phone,' he explained to Alfonso.

'Maso,' said Traiano, 'How are you feeling now?'

'Fine, boss, thanks for asking.'

'Have you had a cigarette since then?'

'No, boss, I have learned my lesson,' he said with eyes downcast.

'Because next time you will not be so lucky. You'll be in hospital.'

'Understood, boss,' said Maso. 'Boss, did you like the mobile phones I got for you?'

'Yes, Ceccina likes hers and the other she gave to her sister Pasqualina. Thanks.'

Having put down the pizzas, Maso stood as if awaiting some other order. He was standing next to Fofò, and his thigh almost rested against the elbow of the photographer.

'You can go now, I have not forgotten,' said Traiano. He watched him go. 'Smarmy little shit,' he remarked.

'What was it you had not forgotten?' asked Calogero.

'He asked me to ask you whether we would give him a job.'

'He has got a job. Waiter.'

'You know what he means....'

'Yes, I do. I gave his brother a job, now he wants one. Strange family. Enzo gives me the creeps. Remind me why I hired him?'

'Because he is useful.'

'Oh yes,' said Calogero, losing interest. 'Perhaps useful to others, not me. Use the brother if you want. Not my concern.'

He turned away to look at his children.

Alfonso looked at Traiano questioningly.

'Would you like some cocaine?' he asked. 'That boy Maso will bring you some if you ask for 'white pizza'.'

'I'm fine without it,' said Alfonso.

'I have never tried it myself, but half of Catania, it seems, cannot live without it. So we provide it. And girls. And boys for those who like that. But that is my side of the business. The boss is a respectable property magnate. I am just the Romanian pimp who does the dirty work. That boy Maso is from a good family; he got thrown out of school for being lazy and for fighting; he made his parents despair. But he thinks this sort of life is the better sort of life to the one that could so easily be his. His brother Enzo fixes computers and phones. He is a genius, but he is not normal. The boss does not like him, but he likes to keep things in the family, so he hired him, because he would not talk. He can't talk.'

'He is dumb?'

'He chooses not to talk. Only the brother can communicate with him. They have a sort of private language. This has been a big worry for the parents. Enzo went to school with Saro, the boss's brother. Saro recommended him. Saro does not know, but Maso is a thief, he steals phones and computers, and Enzo wipes them clean for resale. We help with that. Now Maso wants to get up the ladder, do bigger things, work with me. Perhaps I will let him, if only to show that this is not a game. Are you sure you want to have anything to do with people like us?'

The children had wolfed down their pizza in record time, as they always did, and little Salvatore was now ready to sit on his half-brother's lap and go to sleep. The first course over, the adults moved around. With the heavy two-year-old pinning him to his chair, Traiano was unable to move away when Stefania approached him.

'When are you next going to Donnafugata?' she asked.

'When the boss says,' he replied. He knew outright denial was impossible. 'Probably Wednesday.'

'Business meeting?' she asked.

'Of course. The banker, the boss, people from Palermo maybe.'

'I want to be there.'

'What has the boss said?'

'I think he needs time to get used to the idea. That is why I am telling you, and you of course tell him everything. And I know. About everything. Anna has told me. So you can tell him that. And tell him he is going to pay for all this. I mean in money. I want a piece of the action. Me. Not you, not Saro, not Elena, not his mother, not Assunta. Especially not Assunta. Me. The mother of his children.'

'What exactly has Anna said?' asked Traiano. 'Just so I do not make a mistake.'

'About Tancredi, about the child. Things you did not see fit to mention to me, even though you must have known I would have liked to have known.'

'It is my job to keep secrets, Stefania,' he said. 'And you have spent the last ten years enjoying the fruits of his work and my work. I have got my hands dirty for you.'

'And that is a secret you must keep. But the clean side of the business will make even more. I am not going to make trouble with Tancredi. I see her as he does, a business partner. She is going to make us a lot of money. So tell him what I have said.'

He nodded.

'My father is dead. What do you know about that?'

'It is sad news. But what should I know about it? Do you mean....?'

'Anna would stop at nothing,' he said bitterly.

32

Calogero was sitting with Anna.

'So, congratulations,' he said, knowing that this was what she wanted to hear. 'You have got what you want, I assume? He is very charming. And intelligent. An artist. I like that. I think now we are settled, don't you?'

She looked at him with a mixture of scorn and loathing.

'We will never be settled,' she said. 'Look what I did for you, in covering up the aftermath of what you did to Michele Lotto.'

'For which I was grateful,' said Calogero coldly. 'Please remember the house you live in is my property.'

'You want it back?'

'I bought it for you. It would be nice if you could be a bit more reasonable. I do not ask you to be grateful, that is not in your nature. Just reasonable. I had to call in quite a few favours and spend quite a lot of money to arrange for your last request. I did my best to persuade you to let it go, but you would not listen to reason.'

'I don't let anything go, ever. It's my nature, as you would say,' she said.

'You have alienated your own son, and you have alienated me. One day you will run out of friends.'

'You are no longer the sweet little boy you once were.'

'I was never a sweet little boy,' said Calogero. 'And you know it.'

'True,' she admitted. 'You want to control everything, but you cannot control me. You cannot control your own wife. You will find that you cannot control Tancredi. And you are frightened of your mother and your sisters. But I am the one who has enough information to have you put in jail forever.'

'Yes, you do. Information you will never use. Without me you would have no money, and without me you would have no cause to live. I know that I am absolutely safe with you. And you are sure that you are safe with me. I am never going to murder the mother of my very best friend, am I?'

'You killed his father.'

'No, you killed his father. I merely arranged it. How is he reacting?'

'I don't know,' she said. 'He seems happy enough for now.'

She gestured down the table, where Traiano and Alfonso were busily exchanging telephone numbers.

'And is he impressed by your history?' asked Calogero, motioning towards Alfonso.

Now Anna looked cross. He had scored a point. Calogero smiled.

The party broke up early. The children were tired, and tomorrow was the feast of the dead, when they had to go to church to mourn the late Renato di Rienzi, a day that was difficult for many of them. They poured out into the street and walked towards the square. Stefania disappeared with her three children, and Ceccina with her two babies, while Traiano hung back to say goodbye to Alfonso, his mother and his half-brother. Calogero watched. He watched him shake hands with Alfonso and kiss his little brother, and peck his mother on the cheek. Then they got into the car and drove away.

It was the night of All Saints, and tomorrow was All Souls, a Tuesday, a working day, and the square was empty. Calogero stood there is his large expensive overcoat, the one Stefania had bought for him. His highly polished shoes gleamed in the light provided by the street lamps. Traiano stood next to him, in his expensive jeans, his leather jacket, his expensive shirt, his hair reaching over its collar. It was cold. Winter had come.

'I know what you have done,' said Traiano.

'What have I done?'

'You know.'

'You speak in riddles. Has Anna said something?'

'She did not need to. Her finger marks are all over it. I know the way she works.'

'She has me in her power,' said Calogero. 'You too. She was a witness to the murder of Lotto. That could land us in grave trouble with the police and with the Romanian people. The police are not hard to deal with, but the Romanians… Of course, she will not betray us, but… It is best to keep her onside. Besides, Antonio Santucci agreed that it would be a good way of sending a message to the Romanians, just to show them that none of them were safe, that we have a long reach. Naturally I had to clear it with him.'

'But not with me,' said Traiano. 'But I understand why you had to do it,' he continued gravely. 'He was a stranger to me, he meant nothing to me. He meant something to her, clearly. But you should be careful. One day she may get someone to kill you. She blames you for everything.'

'She should blame herself,' he said.

'Yes,' agreed Traiano.

'So, you do not care?' asked Calogero.

'My family is here now. It has always been here. You, and Saro, and Ceccina and the children and don Giorgio. He was not my father. You are.'

'But don't you like Fofò too?'

He gave a low laugh.

'I think I will love him as much as she does; we are going up in the world. Fofò, and of course Tancredi. Rich people, cultured people, who have money and talk of art. Next time we see Tancredi…'

36

'On Wednesday.'

'On Wednesday, I will not be left in the garage or in the kitchen and have to endure the sound of you screwing her, will I?'

'It is a business meeting. You will be there for the business part at least; and the social part. I haven't the slightest intention of doing anything with her you cannot witness. She is six months gone.'

'Ceccina and I were at it until the day of the birth.'

'You dirty little rat. I hope you will continue to be so happy. What did Stefania want?'

'You miss nothing.'

'Ah. So, she did want something. Tell me when the day of the dead is over. I want to have as little on my mind as possible tomorrow. Tell me when we are on our way to Donnafugata the day after tomorrow.'

'Sure, boss.'

They embraced, and parted. They always embraced on parting and meeting; it was a sign of their closeness. Usually Calogero kissed his cheek. With the others, it was always a handshake: the kiss on the cheek was, in the case of adults, a special privilege. With his brother Saro, uniquely, he kissed the lips. But now, as he walked away, Traiano knew, from the kiss he had received, that he had been brought to a greater degree of closeness.

Chapter Two

Their routine was always the same, ever since the first child had been born. Ceccina would put the children to bed and then go to bed herself shortly afterwards. Traiano would go to bed with her, and then, after an hour or two, get up and go out to work. He would then come back early in the morning, get into bed and wait for her to wake up. After making love to her, he would sleep on, while she roused the children, and then get up at some time in the late afternoon. Sundays were different, because on these days the bars and restaurants of the quarter were closed. On such days, he would spend the day with the family, go to bed at night and sleep through the night, though, as this was a change to his routine, he never slept well. On Sunday nights she was accustomed by now to knowing that the man next to her was lying awake, staring upwards, or perhaps just pretending to be asleep. That Monday had been a public holiday, the day of All Saints, though everything in the quarter had been open, but she half expected him to come back and go to sleep. She drifted off, knowing he would not, and then, just before dawn, she felt him get into bed with her, felt his warm body next to hers.

She placed her arms around him, knowing that he was disturbed by the news of his father's death, and by his mother's visit, feeling from the touch of him that he was not as he had been. She sensed his unhappiness, the way that on this day, the day of All Souls, the feast of the dead, the fact of death had touched him. He was in mourning, not for the man he had never known, but for himself. He was so young, and he was confronted by the fact that what had happened to his father might well happen to him, she knew. He was not fearful, not frightened and trembling, but nostalgic for what might have been, and this communicated itself to her. A lifetime together was what she hoped for, but it might so easily be cut short. How much time did they have left together? How much longer would she have him close to her? When would she be condemned to the cold bed of a young widow? When would her children be fatherless? When would his warm presence be taken away from her and leave just the cold shell of memory?

She held him tight, knowing that he would not want to speak, and she felt the heat of his breath against her and the smoothness of his cheeks. Gradually, the greyness of dawn filled the bedroom, and he fell asleep. To her relief, he slept on, while she and the children awoke, got dressed and had breakfast. The children, young as they were, somehow seemed to know not to wake their father. At eleven, she roused him. The Mass was at noon. He promised her he would be at the Church in good time and that he would meet her there. Shortly after that, she descended to the street, with both children, and made her way to the Church. As she expected, there she saw Saro. He was standing by the door talking to don Giorgio. Seeing her with the children, he said goodbye to don Giorgio and came over to her immediately. He kissed her, he kissed the two children. taking the heavier one, Cristoforo, from her, and carried the boy. They crossed the square and went into the bar, taking a quiet table, and ordering coffee. The bar never shut, but at this time, mid-morning, its clientele was at its most respectable. It was also quite sparse, and perhaps would fill up when the Mass, which was about to begin, ended.

'He told you?' said Rosario.

'He didn't need to tell me anything. I know,' she said. 'I know that when he feels upset, he goes to see you. He talks to you when he can't talk to me.'

'He does not want to worry you,' said Rosario.

'I know, I know,' she said. The coffee arrived, and with it a sense of hopelessness. How was she to help him? She looked at Rosario, who looked back at her, as if wondering whether to speak.

'Do you really want to know?' he asked. And because she did not reply, he knew she really did want to know. 'Your husband,' he began, and immediately paused. 'I have never seen him like that before now. He was, as you have worked out, very upset. He spent a good hour in tears, crying, saying that no one must ever see him like that. You know, big tough man, has no feelings, certainly no pity. He is supposed to be hard. Well, last night he was not. But then he pulled himself together, he toughened up. That disappointed me. You see, he knows who killed his father, and he has decided to let it go and to use it for his advantage. He has made a conscious decision to go along with it; to agree to the murder retrospectively, if you like. Your father-in-law, whom you never met, the grandfather of these children, whom they will never see, was murdered. You know that. Someone asked for it to be done, and someone arranged for it to be done. I think you pay out a certain amount of money to people in Romania, and they do it for you, wherever the victim is - in prison, in police custody, wherever.'

'They wanted to stop him talking?'

'Oh no. This was revenge. Of the worst type - delayed revenge. Or so Traiano says. And he is certain of it. Because, you see, Calogero organised it, paid for it, gave the order, and told Traiano he had done so last night. His best friend paid for his father to be murdered. So, no wonder he was so very upset. But it is his best friend, so he has to overlook it; indeed, he can go further. Now Calogero owes him something. Calogero is about to make his fortune.'

'I thought he had already done that.'

'He has. Now he is going to do it again. What he is going to do will make him one of the richest men in Sicily, or so he hopes.'

'Something illegal?'

41

'No, something wonderfully legal. Though there will be bits of illegality too. That is where Traiano comes in, and the other boys. As I say, a huge amount is to be made; and Traiano can use this incident to ensure he gets a bigger slice of the cake. That is how it works.'

'But it can't be true,' she said. 'I don't mean you are lying to me, but that you are mistaken. Why on earth would Calogero have Traiano's father killed? What is he to him?'

'Nothing. But he was something to Anna.'

'And what has Anna to do with Calogero?'

'She blackmails him. She knows his secrets. Secrets serious enough to make sure that when she asks him to kill her husband, he cannot dare refuse. People may fear him, but he fears her. He has to do what she says. So he went to Palermo, saw the bosses there, got their agreement, then they asked the bosses in Bucharest, after which payment was made, and the deed was done. As simple as ordering a bunch of flowers. And he did not tell Traiano in order to spare him. Reckoning, correctly, that Traiano, after an initial sense of anger and grief, would rapidly recover at the thought of the money and power that was coming his way.'

He looked at her, and he thought for a moment that she too might now burst into tears. She certainly felt the tears well up inside her; and she knew that they were like the unseen tears of her husband, tears provoked by the pity of knowing what one had to sacrifice for the pursuit of money and power.

'I have asked him to give all this up and go to the police, but…'

'He would end up dead in a police cell,' she said. 'Before the day was out. Besides, he loves Calogero too much.'

'But he loves you more,' said Rosario.

She knew what he was asking, and she was almost angry that he should ask her. He loved her, she knew that, but she also knew that when he was alone with her and the children, those were the only moments he had of pure happiness. And when they were alone together, then he was able to forget for a moment about 'work', the euphemism they used for the terrible things he had to do for Calogero. To take that away from him, to take that away from herself, would be impossible.

'I cannot judge the man I love,' she said. 'You will see. If you did anything wrong, would you want Carolina to hold it against you? Or would you want her to love you more than she loved truth and justice itself?'

He acknowledged defeat.

'Think,' she continued. 'All he has got is me and the children. He hasn't got a mother. Well, he has, but she is the sort of mother he would be better off without. She is a monster, if what you say is true. And I have no doubt it is true. She murdered her own husband, and if Calogero had not arranged it, someone else would have done so. So you see how important it is that he has something normal in his life? He needs to be loved. Can you imagine what it must have been like being brought up by her?'

'I was there, I saw it, and what I did not see, I guessed,' said Saro. 'I know he can never talk about it. There are some things you cannot talk about. That is how Calogero controls people.'

She noted that he said Calogero and not Anna.

'He makes us do horrid things, witness terrible things, and then he does not let us forget. So we belong to him forever.'

She noticed he said 'we'.

'You should have been there last night,' she said, changing the subject. 'Anna and Stefania are curious about Carolina. I am curious about Carolina.'

'I saw her yesterday. I was at her parents' house for dinner. Today they have gone to Caltagirone or was it Caltanisetta to visit the family tombs. His family tombs. Not hers. They alternate each year. Hers are in Catania somewhere.'

'Are they very grand people?'

'The lawyer Petrocchi is not. His family are ordinary people, and he has done well for himself. Signora Petrocchi is a little more socially distinguished, in her own eyes at least. He is very nice. I have known him a long time now. She is very nice too, really, though a bit guarded. But the daughter is the one who really matters. Why should Stefania be so curious, I wonder? You will meet her. I was thinking that I would bring her to the baptism, if that is alright with you. She will be down that weekend. She is going back to Rome tonight. It will be nice for her to meet you and my goddaughter, and, well, see the family. At least see Calogero. And to see all this…'

All this was the Purgatory quarter of Catania. Carolina had grown up less than a kilometre away, in via Tomaselli, but she had never been here, never seen all this. The sun was out, shining on the square and the façade of the Church; a figure in a suit appeared in the doorway of the bar. It was Ceccina's husband.

He kissed his wife and children, and then turned to Rosario and kissed him. His manner was merry. He had alighted on all the people he loved together in one place, his manner said. He caught the eye of the barman and ordered a café latte. The other two declined more coffee on the grounds that they were going to Holy Communion.

'What do you think?' he asked, meaning the suit, which she recognised as being the Prince of Wales check that they had bought together in the via Etnea. 'I thought I would try it out before the baptism.'

'It is very nice,' she said, glad to see him so happy. 'It looked nice when you tried it on in the shop and it looks great now.'

'What do you think?' he said, turning to Rosario.

She watched, waiting for the verdict, knowing how much this meant to him, Rosario's approval.

'I like it. Is it English? Anything English always looks so smart. And your shoes look good too. I have never seen you in a suit before, except when you got married. Did Caloriu tell you to come in a suit today?'

'As a matter of fact, he did mention it,' said Traiano.

Ceccina knew her husband was lying.

'Your suit is nice,' said Ceccina hurriedly. 'Is it new too?'

'No. I wear it for work. But Caloriu said people will be watching us, and therefore I ought to dress a bit more smartly than I did last year, since it is a Mass for my father. I remember the funeral. I can't remember what I wore for that. Not the suit I was given for my confirmation, because that was later. I was twelve. And you were about six or seven.'

'I was preparing for my first Holy Communion,' said Traiano. 'The night your father died, your brother came and hid in our house. He thought the police were after him, but they weren't. He read my Communion book with me, until it was safe to go home. That was the place with the leaky roof. I think it has been done up now.'

People were coming out of Church, meaning that the Mass was over. Traiano sipped his coffee and was pensive. He had hated that place where they had first lived in the quarter, the place with the leaky roof. Thank God things were better now, and would get much better. In his jacket pocket was an envelope with a single five hundred euro note inside, which he would give to don Giorgio to have Masses said for the repose of the soul of his father, the man his mother had had murdered, and whose murder had been facilitated by Calogero, his best friend.

The cheek of signora di Rienzi, that both her sons had to kiss, was cold, hard and rough, like granite. Her eyes narrowed at the sight of both of them, and she said nothing to either, as they took their places in the church. She knelt in prayer, dressed in back, with a daughter either side of her. The daughters too, Assunta and Elena, had extended cheeks, but uttered no word of greeting. The atmosphere was heavy with feminine fury, and there was no mistaking the way that it was directed at both young men, Calogero and Rosario. Moreover, so perfected was this skill the signora had of projecting disapproval, that it was clear to all who troubled to look that she disapproved of both of them for completely different, in fact contradictory, reasons. But at present, in the silence of the church, whilst they waited for Mass to begin, and as the Mass rolled on, she was content to say nothing, to make no direct accusations or insinuations, but to leave them both to suffer the discomfort she generated.

In the row behind her were her son and daughter-in-law and their children, and nearby was Rosario. Both Rosario and Calogero could sense, just from the attitude of their mother's broad back, that today was to be the hardest of days. In addition, there was Stefania present, clearly enjoying herself at this display of feminine anger. Her husband, the adulterer, was pretending that nothing was amiss, but his pretence was futile. As for Rosario, he too was uncomfortable, and, of course, as adulterous as his brother, having, despite his holy poses, slept with not just a married woman, but his own sister-in-law. Was it only last summer that he has gone to bed with her, responding to her invitation with an alacrity that had betrayed very little moral struggle? And since then, he had avoided her. That was unforgiveable. As if it had been her fault – well, it had been her fault, or at least her choice - but if he'd had any gallantry, he would have shouldered the blame himself. And it was not as if he had been so innocent, having, he told her, managed some sort of act of sexual intercourse before that with the girlfriend of one of Calogero's employees, that gorilla-like man from Agrigento, the one they called Gino. She had not forgotten that. If Gino were to find that out, then the fact that Rosario was the boss's brother would not save him.

After the Mass was over, the family was to gather in signora di Rienzi's flat, the childhood home that Calogero and Rosario had once shared, and which they both now visited infrequently. The signora was a good cook, and the lunch on All Souls' Day was always a good lunch. There was pasta alla Norma, then there was roast lamb, with potatoes cooked with rosemary, and there would always be some alcohol-laden cake at the end to go with the coffee. When she had been married to the Chemist, her late husband, whose soul had been prayed for this day with such solemnity, neither of her sons could remember her devoting much time to the kitchen; but, in her widowhood, she had taken much care in only producing the best type of food. Food, after all, was a weapon. Though Calogero hardly ever ate in his mother's house, she wanted him to know that the food here was better than anything Stefania could create. Stefania had taken him away when he was seventeen, and it was important to her that he should know that his leaving the maternal home, so soon after the death of his father too, had been, in culinary terms, a mistake. As for Rosario, who had left the nest in his mid-teens to go to school in Rome, he too should be reminded that his defection was likewise an error. Indeed, why didn't Calogero come back every day to his mother for his lunch? And why didn't Rosario eat with his mother, live with his mother, instead of choosing to live in a very small flat two streets away, and eating, goodness knew what, which he cooked for himself?

Both her daughters were, in her humble estimation, plain girls, though thank goodness they could both cook and clean. Assunta had managed to get a husband, the fat but reliable Federico; Elena was still unmarried, which was a shame, and her own fault. She had never really cared much for her daughters. But Calogero, as he came into the dull, lightless flat, as he entered the kitchen, filled the place with his beauty. Tall, broad-shouldered and strong, with clear wide apart brown eyes and close-cropped hair, this was the only person she had ever truly loved. But had he loved her? If he had, why had he preferred to marry so young, and marry such a girl as Stefania? And look what she had done with him! She remembered the old Calogero, before his wife had got hold of him, put him into a suit, made him wear such expensive shoes, bought him such a collection of shirts and cufflinks. His father never dressed like that, and Stefania herself with her high heels, the tight-fitting dresses, her blonde hair, why had she chosen to transform not just herself but Calogero as well? And, in the end, she had not made him happy. Yes, she had heard. He had a mistress in Donnafugata, a rich woman almost twenty years his senior. Being old-fashioned, the signora had contradictory feelings about mistresses. She did not admire over-uxorious men (she despised her son-in-law, the reliable Federico). She was glad that Calogero seemed to be freeing himself from the shackles of Stefania. A wife should turn a blind eye from time to time. But at the same time, a wife should turn a blind eye when that was possible. The idea of this woman in Donnafugata was one thing; that everyone should know about it was quite another. Scandal was never good. Men got up to things, but it was always best not to know about it, and thus

48

not to think about it. So, she sympathised, for once, with Stefania. And she condemned the woman of Donnafugata for taking him away from his family even more than Stefania herself had done.

In discussing this matter with her daughters, who had told her the news, she had been distressed by the thought of the child to be born to the mistress, a child she was confident she would never see. The woman was rich, influential, powerful, known to many, unmarried, not by any means the sort of woman the signora had ever met, or known or admired. By wandering off in this way, her dearest Calogero had made a worse mistake than even Stefania. For neither Stefania nor Tancredi were good women, she was convinced, by which she meant, if she were honest, they were not women like herself. Stefania had led him by the nose; Tancredi would do the same, only more so. Men were so stupid. They listened to women, when they should listen to their mothers, the ones who had their best interests at heart.

As for her younger son, as she watched him take up a position in the corner of the room, his defection, his disobedience, his rebellion was the worst of all. The eldest had found two women, the younger none as yet. He had left her, and he had done so because she had forced him away. It was, she knew, her fault. Calogero had bullied Rosario, and she had never interfered, thinking boys must be able to look after themselves. But he had never forgiven her for this. This infuriated her. She knew his sisters disliked him; his sister-in-law seemed not to like him either, and even Calogero held him in a sort of amused contempt. But as she looked at him, she felt, not guilt, rather a sense of miscalculation. She had pushed him away, and he had gone. She had never expected him to go. She had never expected the elastic to snap, the tie to be broken so definitively. Her younger son, whom she hardly ever saw, looked on her as a stranger. For this, she blamed him, naturally, for being so unfilial; but she also blamed Calogero for not forcing Rosario to be a better son.

She felt an overwhelming bitterness at the way the men in her life had deserted her: her husband, killed by that stupid accident in the hotel room in Milan, her eldest son not caring for her any more, and the dull resentment of past wounds that her youngest son carried around with him. They were both there, not because they wanted to be, but because they had to be. And, for this, she was resolved they should suffer.

The pasta alla Norma was served, and they sat around the table.

'Why are you wearing a suit?' asked his mother, addressing Rosario. 'You never wear a suit except for work. Is this work, being here with me?'

'Caloriu told me to, mama,' he replied politely. 'Caloriu, why am I wearing a suit? You never explained.'

'I wanted him to look smart, mama,' said Calogero. 'For the sake of the family. All those people in church were looking at us.'

'You imagine it,' she said. 'Anyway, he does not need to look smart. No one will ever look at him.'

'But mama, they have,' said Elena, the nicer of the two sisters. 'He has got a girlfriend. At last,' she could not help adding.

Rosario hunched his shoulders, felt his cheeks burn, and said nothing. He felt Calogero looking at him. And he knew that Stefania must be looking at him too.

'The lawyer's daughter,' said Assunta with great hauteur. 'Well, she is rich. Or, at least, her father is. He will be glad to see her settled, and he must know you, as you have worked for him for some time now. He looked around his office and he found you. You must be flattered.'

'It is not an arranged marriage,' said Rosario. 'In fact, it is not a marriage at all. We only met in August. And I can find someone for myself without the lawyer Petrocchi to help me, and so can she.'

'Yes,' said Stefania. 'Of course you can. Who was the girl you were seeing before the August holidays?'

Rosario now became completely scarlet, and began to sweat under his shirt.

'Stefania, there is no need to mention that at all,' said Calogero smoothly. 'If you mean what I think you mean. After Traiano's wedding he took that girl back to his flat, but nothing happened at the time. There was a little trouble, with Gino, and with her cousin, Alfio, but it was established that she was just there because, well, because, I have forgotten why. You girls should stop tormenting my poor brother.'

'Your father was married at eighteen; your brother was married at seventeen; that Romanian was only sixteen; that is the custom in this quarter. And you are not married at all,' said his mother sternly.

Accused of being a Lothario one moment, now the opposite, Rosario was taken off his guard.

'We will get married next year,' he said. 'When she has finished her degree.'

There was complete silence round the table. Everyone had a look of consternation on their face. His mother looked furious. This had been arranged without her consent or knowledge, and she did not even know the girl. Moreover, the girl was a lawyer's daughter, hardly likely to be overawed by a widow from the Purgatory quarter of Catania. She would not be dominated by anyone, she imagined. Assunta too felt a pang of jealousy, given that the family of the lawyer Petrocchi was clearly a cut above the family of her own husband. Stefania seemed displeased too at the thought of a social rival. As for Calogero, he contented himself with observing the female reaction, and saying:

'I did not realise it had gone so far. You need to speak to me before you make any definite plans.'

Rosario looked at him without replying.

Calogero saw the defiance in his look.

'If you are marrying the lawyer's daughter, you can be sure he wants you as a son-in-law because, among other things, you are my brother. It will bring him advantages, and it may bring us advantages too. If you inherit that law firm or a controlling interest in it, that would be useful to me. And Petrocchi, you can be sure, will want to make use of me. Naturally, he and I will have to come to an understanding. He is rich. I am not letting him have you for his daughter without paying. How much will he give her?'

'Oh, you want him to pay so you do not have to?' asked Elena.

'You want Petrocchi to shell out, so you can spend your money, well, we know where,' said Assunta.

Stefania raised her eyebrows.

'Whatever Petrocchi pays, you have to match. Simple,' she said. 'Do we want Petrocchi and his wife, particularly his wife, to think that we are mean? Or that we are poor? He has got to be the one who brings more to the marriage. Whatever Petrocchi gives her, you double it.'

'We are not even engaged,' said Rosario.

'Federico, how much did I give Assunta when she married you?' asked Calogero.

Federico, who had said nothing so far, mumbled something. Assunta snorted with rage. Elena was white with anger.

'You must give me the same,' she said.

'If you get married, I will give you whatever you ask,' said Calogero. 'I can make that promise safely.'

Rosario said, leaning towards his brother, in a low voice: 'Neither I nor any woman I will ever marry would take a cent from you.'

They all heard him. There was silence. Calogero stood up, looked at his brother, and delivered a blow to his cheek. Then he sat down. The silence was total. The two elder children, Isabella and Natalia, looked puzzled and horrified. Only the baby, Renato, not yet nine months old, seemed not to notice.

The pasta alla Norma was taken away. The two brothers stared at each other. Federico wished he was anywhere but where he in fact was. Signora di Rienzi brought in the roast lamb and broke the silence. Looking at Rosario, she said: 'You must obey your brother.'

Stefania, watching this, seeing the reaction of the children, realised that her husband was a monster.

'He is the one getting married,' she said. 'He can do what he likes. You can't force him. Well, you can kick him downstairs and break his ribs, which is what I am sure you are thinking of doing right now – you see, I know you, Calogero. But in the end, unless he gives in to your physical threats, there is nothing you can do to stop him. He can get the train to Rome and never come back. Remember he has done that once before.'

'But he did come back,' observed Calogero. 'And I am sure he wants to marry her, after all, he has to marry someone sooner or later, as he seems to have given up the idea of being a priest. And I am sure she doesn't want to marry a poor man. And the man with the money is me. As you all know,' he concluded, looking round the table.

'You have the money, you have the power, but you cannot control our minds,' said Stefania calmly. Her sisters-in-law and her mother-in-law looked at her with surprise. 'We are, in a certain sense, free. And you hate that.' She smiled. 'You own this quarter, but you do not own me, or your brother, or your children.'

The children looked up at their mother as she spoke, not understanding. Calogero remained calm, and took up a forkful of roast lamb, remarking how delicious it was. But this was little consolation. He could see just how he was being challenged by his wife, his mother and his sisters. He wanted to be a great man? Well, they were certain in their eyes that he would never be respected, never be loved, at least not by them. But their victory, he was determined, would be Pyrrhic. They would not prosper.

Lunch was very good, but it was necessary to leave at last. There were various goodbyes and kisses among the women, and Calogero found himself standing at the head of the stairs with Rosario next to him. His brother looked deeply uncomfortable.

'Are you coming to the procession this evening?' asked Calogero, by way of conversation.

'Of course,' replied Rosario.

'You seem jumpy. Do you think I am angry? Do you think that I might throw you down these stairs, and then administer a good kicking? And then, when you groan pitifully, piss all over you? That is what Traiano does to tenants who do not pay their rent. Did you know that? He does not have to do it very often, or at all, these days. His reputation, my reputation, is enough to ensure compliance. One encounters very few rebellions these days, but you, you and my wife, the two people to whom I have given so much… You have been unfaithful to me. Do not look puzzled. Your greatest loyalty should be to me, and you have betrayed me time and again. As has she.'

Once more, Rosario went deep scarlet. At this very moment, Stefania joined them. The children were still being hugged and kissed by their grandmother and aunts.

'I gave you everything,' said Calogero.

'You owe me everything,' she retorted. 'You and your whore.'

'You will both of you do as you are told,' said Calogero quietly. The children emerged, and he picked up Renato, and took Natalia by the hand while Isabella trailed behind, and led them down the stairs.

'Does he know?' asked Rosario, when he had disappeared.

She gave him a contemptuous glance and shook her head, and then followed her husband.

There were about six hundred members of the Ancient and Noble Confraternity of the Holy Souls, but never more than twenty or thirty ever gathered to process through the streets of the Purgatory quarter on the day of the Commemoration of the Holy Souls in Purgatory. The lawyer Petrocchi never missed the occasion as he was head of the Confraternity, and Calogero was always there as he lived within sight of the Church, from where the procession started and at which it ended. The route had been fixed since some time in the seventeenth century, and in recent times, ever since the restoration of the Church and the supposedly miraculous return of the stolen Madonna, the procession had attracted the attention of more people than had previously been the case. Some years the Archbishop came, and the canons of the Cathedral, which added colour to the scene; there were even tourists taking photographs. But it was a tedious matter, this shuffling through the narrow streets following banners, dressed in a dark ceremonial cloak decorated with a white cross, though Calogero liked it, knowing that he was the most important person in the quarter and that most of the onlookers were in some way connected to him. This evening he found his position next to Petrocchi, and rather enjoyed the sensation that this made the respectable lawyer uncomfortable. The hypocrisy of lawyers was something that Calogero believed in with fervour.

'Your wife has not come? Nor your daughter?' he asked.

'They are tired. Today we went to Caltagirone. To visit my parents.'

Calogero nodded, he knew he meant to visit the graves of his parents.

'Business is good?'

Petrocchi nodded, wondering where this was going.

'You know I am setting up a new office, and my wife will run it? It is very kind of you to give us Rossi.'

'You are welcome to him,' said Petrocchi with a touch of asperity. He had never valued Rossi who dealt with all Calogero's property matters, but he had resented the way Calogero had poached him.

'And Anna Maria Tancredi is sending me someone too, to work there. My wife thinks she will be in charge, and I am sure that she will pick things up very quickly. Perhaps one day my brother will work for me too. I know he likes working for you. He is a good boy.'

'He is a good boy,' echoed Petrocchi.

'I know he likes your daughter. And she likes him.'

'We all like him,' said Petrocchi noncommittally. 'As you say, he is a good boy.'

'I am going to Donnafugata tomorrow where I am having a meeting with don Antonio Santucci. We are contemplating a joint venture which will be vastly profitable to both of us. I know that you do not like the thought of people like Santucci. Neither do I. That man sails a little close to the wind for comfort or safety. But Catania is not Palermo. Still, we have to do business with Palermo as Palermo is the path to Rome, and everything depends on Rome, and Rome depends on Brussels. I know that my brother is a good boy, but he is not handsome or charming, and he does not earn very much at present. But he is my brother. Certain people see that as an advantage perhaps, and others a disadvantage. Our family is not like your family; and in particular not like your wife's family. We have dirt under our fingernails, and we may have tried to wash it off, but much remains. But, if you were to overlook this, and if the two of them want to do so, I would be glad to see them marry. The poor boy needs a good wife.'

'There would be no objection from me,' said Petrocchi quietly.

Calogero understood. There might be from the wife, whom he had never met.

'It's possible my wife and I may move house, in which case I would give them my current place. It is quite large. Nice view of the square. Four bedrooms. That would be my little wedding present. You might consider giving your daughter a dowry. I don't know how much that would be, but I would give them, in cash and in shares in my company, double the value of anything you gave her. On top of the flat, which would not enter these calculations.'

Petrocchi's brain whirred. He had been thinking that if Carolina married, he might give her at most sixty to a hundred thousand euros. Now he realised there was more at stake. There was a very good chance of making Carolina and her husband rich. He would have to speak to his wife. He would have to persuade his wife. He would have to speak to Carolina.

'You are very generous,' he managed to say. 'But does he want to marry her?'

'Of course. He can't hide such things from me. Does she want to marry him?'

'These are things she discusses with her mother,' said the lawyer with a sigh.

'The only thing is that I want them to live here when they are married,' said Calogero. 'I don't want to lose my brother. And you have two daughters abroad, don't you? You do not want to lose her either, do you?'

'I don't want her to move away,' he said. 'Neither does her mother.'

Calogero smiled.

Signora Petrocchi frowned. She had just got a text message from her husband saying that he would be bringing Rosario di Rienzi back home with him for supper. But Rosario, the murderer's son, as she tended to think of him, had been with them only last night. What was he thinking of? And she noticed, before she replied, that he had copied Carolina into the message, which was a sign that he knew how to head off any possible objection. She thought carefully what was in the fridge. They had had a huge lunch in Caltagirone; no doubt Rosario had eaten well too; but there was Parma ham, some speck, some fruit, some cheese, and some cake. All of the very best quality. She headed towards the fridge to check. It would not do to give the impression, in front of Rosario, that they did not eat well, that she was unprepared for visitors, nor that she was inhospitable. If fault were to be found, she would find it with him, not he with her.

She was prepared to concede that he was a likeable boy, polite, intelligent, well-behaved, with good conversation, devout, one who never missed Mass, hardworking and dependable, indeed, as her husband had hinted, perfect son-in-law material. It was true that he was slightly awkward and not in the least good-looking in her eyes, though she was prepared to admit that her daughter thought differently, and she was also prepared to admit that Carolina herself was not so very attractive, certainly not as attractive as her two elder daughters. (If only they had had a son!) It was always possible that, after she finished her degree next summer, Carolina could come home, and live with them, and stay with them. But the idea of an unmarried daughter. Would she find someone? Or would this Rosario be the best chance she had?

Her objection to Rosario was the family he brought with him. The brother. The late father. Their origins in the slums of Catania, the slum that had been Purgatory. These people were the worst, they were criminals, they were the people who had ruined the reputation of Sicily. Yes, she knew that Rosario was not responsible personally, and that made her feel guilty for disliking him so much. But he was one of them, and he made her middle-class soul shudder. And one had to be so careful as to whom one chose to marry. Her two elder daughters had made excellent choices, and so one lived in Verona and the other in Turin. They had escaped the squalor of the south. She herself, in marrying her husband, had made a marginal choice, but the years had passed, and no one remembered, luckily, that her husband's family were of no great account. But the fact that her husband was nothing special meant that one had to be particularly careful in choosing a husband in the next generation. One could not afford another marginal or bad choice. And yet, and yet, she felt sorrow for her daughter: if she liked him, if he were the only chance she would get, could she dare interfere?

Carolina came into the kitchen as she closed the fridge door. Her mother noticed at once that she had brushed her hair, put on her makeup and changed her clothes. Her mother spoke of what they would eat, and what they might drink. Carolina went into the dining room to set the table. After this flurry of activity, they both settled down in the sitting room to wait. There was silence between them. Carolina realised that her mother was not best pleased by the thought of Rosario joining them, and at her father's invitation too. But the message was clear. The lawyer Petrocchi was marking out Rosario almost as a member of the family. He approved, and her mother did not; her mother did not approve that her father approved. But what this told her was that her parents realised that Rosario was a serious matter, not some transient phenomenon; they both knew that they were in love or teetering on the brink of love. In fact, whatever her parents thought was now irrelevant, for she was in love, had been in love from their first meeting in August, and was determined to marry him. She and her mother had discussed the family connections he brought with him; she had realised that this was an attempt to put her off, but her mother's objections struck her as snobbish nonsense, for Rosario was not like that.

They arrived. Rosario's appearance created both surprise, concern and hilarity. He had a black eye. It was more than just black: around the lid it was more or less purple. He assured them that, though it looked terrible, it did not hurt. He had hit himself in the face with a cupboard door in his flat earlier that day. Carolina was all sympathy. Petrocchi, having entered the room, announced he had to comb his hair. His wife retired to the kitchen to see to the supper. They realised that they were being given a few moments alone. They kissed.

'Sure you are feeling all right?' she asked, referring to his bruised eye.

'Yes,' he said.

They kissed again. He felt her warm soft bosom pressed against his chest. She felt his arms around her, and the delightful sense of the blood pounding though her veins and through his. Their intimacies had not strayed into the territory of mortal sin, and they were both determined they should not, though she could feel the flesh stirring within him.

They withdrew to opposite ends of the sofa.

He looked at her seriously.

'You know how I feel,' he said. 'Tomorrow, at work, I am going to speak to your father.'

'Tomorrow, I am going to be back in Rome,' she said. 'I am taking the 11pm train, don't forget.'

'I hadn't forgotten. I was going to surprise you at the station but as your father surprised me by inviting me to your last supper...'

In the kitchen, the lawyer Petrocchi had told his wife the substance of the conversation he had had with Calogero. She had listened in silence and said nothing. But he could see that his words had had an effect. Now she called them all into the dining room.

She smiled broadly at Rosario. It struck her that the black eye made him more attractive. She remarked on their trip to Caltagirone.

'Were you at your brother's today?' she asked.

'No, at my mother's, signora. She always invites us for the feast of the dead.'

'Where does your brother live?' she asked.

'On the northern side of the square,' he replied artlessly. 'There were several apartments on the penultimate floor that my brother knocked together, and they all look over the square and face south. They all have a very nice view. My sister-in-law had the whole place more or less rebuilt. It wasn't very nice before.'

'But it is nice now, I am sure,' said signora Petrocchi, picturing her daughter living there. She beamed at him. Rosario had always found his future mother-in-law a little stand-offish. But not now. She asked him numerous questions about his family, his mother, his sisters, what his brother-in-law did; this level of interest struck him as meaning only one thing, that the signora was sizing him up as a prospective son-in-law, and had overcome her previous hesitations on the subject. He was elated.

Supper ended. Carolina's mother went to pack certain things she wanted Carolina to take to Rome. The lawyer Petrocchi retired to his study. The two young lovers were left in the sitting room, silently looking at each other, their elation knowing no bounds, for it was infectious. To the sound of her mother rattling plates in the kitchen, they kissed again. His hands touched her smooth cheeks. He smiled, and then was serious.

'I want to marry you, and I want to marry you next year at this time,' he said. 'But you need to know that I don't have much money saved up. I only have what your father pays me, and that is not very much, not that I am criticising him. I do not own the flat I live in. Would you marry a poor man? Or rather a man who has only what he can earn in the future?'

'Yes,' she said. 'I want to marry you. Papa might help. You must be due for promotion.'

'We could live in Rome, or Naples,' he said.

'It is cheaper here and here you have a job and I can get one too,' she pointed out. 'Besides, my sisters have left, and so I should stay for my parents' sake.'

Once more they kissed. She longed to touch him. But this time next year they would be married.

Chapter Three

He awoke late and stumbled to the bathroom, knowing that today, the day after the feast of the dead, would be important. Gradually, he revived himself by brushing his teeth and then standing under the shower. It was the very best sort of shower available, and the water thundered over his head and shoulders in a way that he always found comforting. The bathroom had been arranged according to Stefania's instructions when they had first moved in, and, at the thought of that, he groaned at the memory of the previous day, the sheer misery of that lunch at his mother's, the way all the women had turned against him, and the way that Rosario had defied him once more. But there was nothing he could not sort out or deal with; he had worked through worse problems. By the end of today, he ought to be on the way to making a huge amount of money.

He switched off the water and stepped out, reaching for his towel to dry himself. His wife was there, having entered on silent feet. They had not spoken yesterday evening at all, and he had slept on the sofa. He hated being looked at without his clothes on, even by her, especially by her, and he knew that she knew this, and that she had chosen her moment accordingly. But he did his best to deny her this tactical advantage. He ignored his nudity, and dried himself slowly.

'Are the girls at school?' he asked. 'Is Renato at the nursery?'

'Yes,' she replied.

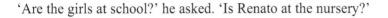

'I want to have another child,' he said.

'You are having another child, with Tancredi, remember?' she said.

'I want to have another child with you,' he said. 'Tancredi's child is Tancredi's child. This would be our child. With my surname. A full brother or sister to our three children. We are rich, we can afford it, and we are going to be richer.'

'To have a child you need to....'

'I know, I know, and we have not, since August. I am sorry. I have neglected you.' He wrapped the towel around his waist. 'I have to be away today, and I am not sure when I will be back, but when I am...'

'That is very romantic,' she said.

'You know me,' he said.

'I do,' she replied.

He went the mirror and began to shave, then to rub his face with moisturiser; then he went into the bedroom to look for his clothes and to pick out a suitably smart suit. As he did this, he felt her eyes upon him constantly.

'I want to buy a new house, bigger, better. Suitable for four children. Could be near here, or could be elsewhere. You could look at what we already own and have several apartments knocked into one, as we did with this one. Or buy something nice on the Etnea itself. Or perhaps outside the city. Or perhaps buy a new apartment in the city, and a house outside, somewhere nice, for summer, perhaps on a beach. Spend as much as you like. I have decided to follow your implied advice. I am giving this place to Saro and his future wife when they get married, whenever that will be.

Well, you said we do not want to look mean. We have lived here long enough, haven't we?'

'You have told Saro?'

'No. But it will be a handsome apology for slapping him in the face, don't you think?' He was looking through his suits. 'I can afford it. You know I cannot talk about my work, but, very soon, you will get the hang of what we are going to do. Our new company. The way it is going to expand. The direction of travel. And you will want to be on board. We are going to make a lot of money for ourselves and our partners.'

'What are you planning?'

'A vast housing complex in the suburbs. It will take time and ingenuity to buy up all the land we need, but we can do it. You will see. That nice office of yours is where it will all be co-ordinated from.' The doorbell rang. 'That is Traiano. Either he is early or I am late. Do you want to let him in and make us some coffee?'

She left him, but when he got to the kitchen, putting the finishing touches to his immaculately knotted tie, it was not the faithful Traiano who was there, but Maso and his brother Enzo. Maso had been provided with a cup of coffee, and Enzo was drinking coke. Maso adopted the very deepest attitude of respect for the boss; he stood in silence and stared humbly into his coffee, as if this drink was something he had not, could not possibly deserve; Enzo ignored him utterly. Stefania rarely saw her husband interact with his employees, and now watched the three of them.

Calogero said nothing, but his look was questioning.

'Enzo is here to finish the installation of the computer,' explained Maso. 'And he cannot work on his own, so I am with him.'

'He can't?'

'No, sir. He doesn't speak or look at people, but he speaks to me. If the signora wants something done, then I can tell him and he will do it; and if he needs to tell her something, he tells me and I pass it on. I understand him. I can communicate with him. I am his gateway to the world. Apart from me, it is just electronics that hold his interest. He can't work with people without me.'

'And what does he do when you are at the pizzeria?'

It was odd to be discussing someone who was present as if they were absent.

'He works at home, sir.'

Maso looked a bit embarrassed. Calogero looked at Stefania, and she took the hint.

'Doing what?' he asked, after Stefania had left.

'I steal phones and computers, and things like that, and he works on them to clean them up, and then I sell them on.'

'How?'

'I give them to Alfio, and he arranges it with people who work in a shop in the via Etnea. They repackage them and sell them as new. Alfio gives me the money.'

Calogero nodded.

'I am sure he takes his cut,' he said. 'But all that is his affair,' by which he meant any criminal activity. 'You can get phones that cannot be traced?'

'There is no such thing, sir. Every phone leaves a trace. But I can get you clean phones which you can use once and then throw away.'

'I am cautious about these things,' said Calogero. 'I never ever say anything that could be used against me. I expect others to do the same. And none of us ever talk. You understand that?'

'The others told me. I do not talk. Enzo cannot talk. Except to me. And I do not talk.'

'How did you meet Alfio?' asked Calogero, curious. 'You are not from the quarter, are you?'

'No, sir. I live with my brother and parents near the Borgata station. I live in the same block as Doctor Moro. I have known him a long time. One day I saw Alfio going to see the doctor, and we got talking, and I offered to give him a phone.'

'Did he take it?'

69

'He did, but not for himself. And he said if I had others....'

'I see,' said Calogero. 'I don't allow my men to have phones. As you say, they leave a trace.'

'I understand, sir,' said Maso.

The doorbell rang. That was clearly Traiano. It was time to go to Donnafugata. He nodded towards Maso, he ignored Enzo, and when he saw his wife, he gave her a cold kiss on the cheek. Then, in the hallway, he put on his very elegant (in his eyes, and, he hoped, in the eyes of others) dark green overcoat. Traiano, he noticed, was wearing his suit, the new one, and brightly polished shoes. He caught him in the act of putting back the brown leather flying jacket that was hanging there.

'What did you find in his pockets?' asked Calogero, once they were in the car.

'What I expected to find. Mobile phone, wallet, stuffed full of fifty euro notes, a knife - a nice one - and what I thought was a pack of cigarettes but turned out not to be. I promised him a beating if I ever caught him smoking again.'

'The youth of today,' said Calogero. 'But he is not stupid, clearly; he did not dare risk another beating from you. Good. I presume you taught him a lasting lesson?'

'I am not sure I trust him,' said Traiano, ignoring this. 'He has certainly wormed his way in. Alfio says he is OK. I don't know him very well. He is not one of us. He was not brought up in Purgatory. His mother is a teacher, his father works for the government. They are respectable people. And he wants to be a criminal. You watch. He will get himself killed. Not that that bothers me. But he might get us all killed.'

'He's enthusiastic, that is all. We all were once. We can use him, in that he can provide us with phones, which you may need. He won't give us any trouble. He knows who is in charge. As for boys not from this quarter, we took Gino, didn't we? Alfio recommended him. If he recommends this one…. And another thing; the brother may be useful, and he cannot talk. That is important. Whatever he sees or overhears, it goes no further. With all these people sniffing around….'

'But the other one, Maso, he can talk,' pointed out Traiano.

'He's protective of his brother,' said Calogero shortly, settling the matter.

They drove out of the city in silence.

'Boss,' said Traiano, as they made it onto the motorway, 'When you have a chance to see Santucci on his own….'

'I know what you want, just leave it to me. Santucci is a bastard, but I will be able to handle him, if anyone can. And if I can't, Tancredi can.'

In Donnafugata, everything was arranged. But when the first car drove up, and she saw Calogero di Rienzi emerge, perfectly dressed as ever, allowing herself to be distracted for just a moment by the perfection of his shoes (surely English, handmade, very expensive), and she saw the Caravaggio boy, as she called him, emerge, also dressed in a suit, and perfect shoes, with a tie as well, she knew that her arrangements would have to be adjusted and immediately so.

Calling the maid, Veronica, who had come from Palermo to join her mistress in Donnafugata for these last few months of her pregnancy, she told her carefully what needed to be done. Four places at lunch not three. And a guestroom to be made ready as well. Then she went to the door to receive the delegation from Catania. She extended a cheek to Calogero, who told her how well she looked. She wondered how sincere this was. She felt enormous, dragging around this huge bloated womb, weighted down by the prospect of another three months until birth and liberation came. Today was the third day of November, and the delivery (never was a word better chosen) was pencilled in for the second day of February, the Madonna of the Candles, the feast of the Presentation of Our Lord in the Temple. This struck her as lucky, for she was growing more superstitious or perhaps more religious as pregnancy advanced. The 2nd February was associated with the Madonna and the prophetess Anna, and she was called Anna Maria, which made it doubly significant. It was also the day of the prophecy of Simeon, and she was half tempted to call the child Simeon, though her heart was set on calling him Sebastiano, simply because it was such a beautiful name and associated closely with Syracuse. Years ago, she had been in Syracuse in January, on the 20th, and, wandering the narrow and deserted streets of Ortygia, she had been overtaken by the procession of the martyred saint, and suddenly found herself in an alleyway, surrounded by young men shouting 'Long live Saint Sebastian!' That experience had stayed with her for some reason; the 20th January would be the earliest possible date for the birth, the beginning of the end of the pregnancy, and this an auspicious saint to invoke and to give as a patron to her son.

She told Calogero, as he kissed her cheek, that he too looked well, and no one could question her on that judgement. His youth put her own lack of glamour into cruel relief. There was nothing nice about wearing maternity dresses, she now knew, and all this talk of expectant mothers looking so well was rubbish, or so she felt. Such sacrifices! And now the Caravaggio boy was coming into her hallway, in a smart suit, clearly now not in the servant class, not to be exiled to the garage with Muniddu and his shotgun.

How lovely he looked. She complemented him on his long hair, and she decided that she would kiss his cheek as well. His cheek was as smooth as a girl's. It reminded her of her nephew, Fabrizio; how smooth his cheeks had been. She felt a brief stab of sadness, even though she had long ceased to love Fabrizio.

They went into the drawing-room, a large, almost cavernous space, full of antique furniture, old prints and a few well-chosen, very large oil paintings. The maid Veronica approached and asked what they would like to drink. They settled on the chairs waiting for Santucci to arrive; the Caravaggio boy had his usual Cinzano on the rocks; Calogero had a dry vermouth, and she restricted herself to a Virgin Mary. There was a lot of business to discuss, and this was the only moment before the tide of business rushed in, before Santucci arrived. She had news for Calogero, but she was not quite prepared to tell him just yet. She had mentioned that she was having a scan, but she was determined to make him work for the information that she would give him. She looked at the Caravaggio boy, who was examining one of her paintings. She had brought it with her from her flat in Palermo, she explained, wanting to have it here with here, knowing she was going to be in Donnafugata until the birth. It was a picture of the Immaculate Conception, dating from the eighteenth century, by a follower of Murillo. He remarked that it reminded him of the Madonna in their church in Purgatory, which she thought was an intelligent comment, as they were both of similar date and provenance, even if this were a far less accomplished piece. But the Madonna was not there because of her obscure connexion to the great Murillo, or because she was the finest thing Anna Maria possessed. She was there to protect the house, to protect the expectant mother, to watch over them all. She knew that Traiano understood this. As he held his glass and looked at the painting, he had the reverential air of someone in church.

A week previously, the Cardinal Archbishop of Palermo had come to call. That had been a great honour. His Eminence made few house calls, and those he made never stretched such a distance. Two hours in a comfortable Mercedes with a driver was something of an undertaking. But, of course, she knew His Eminence, and insofar as one could be friends with a Prince of the Church, they were friends. She knew, it was true, all about him, as she handled a lot of the finances of the Palermitan Church, and, more importantly, the personal finances of His Eminence. She kept his secrets, but she had not in return divulged her own. The Cardinal had clearly wanted to know who the father was, though he had done nothing as vulgar as ask directly, so instead they had discussed her picture, which he had greatly liked. He had never been to her house before. They had had a delicious lunch, and then she had watched him depart. And so with all the other visitors who had called unannounced. (The ones who had asked to come were all graciously put off.) But the important people felt themselves entitled to turn up without warning. It was interesting to see who was curious enough to come all this way to fish for information about her pregnancy.

'All they need to do is ask in the streets of Purgatory,' said Calogero, leaning back on his sofa with his vermouth. 'There, everyone knows: my wife, his mother, my mother, my sisters…'

'And who told them?' she asked, surprised.

'A man called Fofò,' said Calogero.

'That is what my mother calls him,' said the Caravaggio boy. 'He is called Alfonso Agostini. He is a photographer from Syracuse.'

'I know him, very slightly. His late mother knew my mother, I think. I think I have some of his books. He takes architectural photographs. There is one about the reconstruction of Noto Cathedral. You know, the place where we all met. I think it is over there. I am rather surprised he should be so well-informed.'

'He is a gossip,' said Calogero disapprovingly. 'One day it may get him into trouble. But everyone now knows, though they do not know for sure. It is not necessarily a bad thing.'

A car was heard. It was, of course, Santucci. He was shown into the drawing room, apologising for being late, and was served with a drink. There was a young man with him, whom he introduced as his nephew Renzo, the son of his recently deceased cousin and brother-in-law Carlo. While Renzo looked round the room with curiosity, Antonio congratulated Anna Maria on how well she looked. He kissed her cheek. Then he turned to Calogero, and congratulated him, and also kissed his cheek and hugged him. This, she could tell, was utterly insincere. They were not friends, they were rivals. Moreover, Antonio Santucci was a rival who felt his competitor pulling ahead. He owed his position, not to his talent, but to his uncle and father. He had pulled ahead a little in the summer when his brother-in-law and other competitors had been written off in the attack on the yacht off Favignana. How convenient that had been, even if there had been a price to pay in the tears of his wife, his children and his mother-in-law. But now, Calogero had pulled ahead, not just by screwing the financial lynchpin of the organisation, but earning her undying gratitude by giving her a child. She could see that he wished he had thought of that himself. He called his nephew forward, and the young man came and shook hands with her, then with Calogero and finally with Traiano.

Anna Maria watched first Antonio, then Renzo Santucci, greet the Caravaggio boy. Clearly, they were surprised to see him in the drawing room and not over the garage, but determined not to show it.

'Hi, handsome,' Antonio said, kissing Traiano. Renzo, by contrast offered a slightly disdainful handshake.

The arrival of Renzo was unexpected, and she whispered to the maid that yet another place was needed at table. A short while passed. Renzo, sipping his drink, felt himself scrutinised, first by Anna Maria, then by Calogero and finally by Traiano. He knew all three of them by reputation. He had insisted his uncle bring him to this meeting, as he wanted to secure the place that had once been his father's, and had no desire to let his uncle have a free run of the family business, despite his youth. He was older than Traiano and slightly younger than Calogero, but he knew he lacked experience. Until now his life had been passed in matters that had nothing to do with business. He was there to look, to watch and to learn. His uncle had not wanted to bring him, but he had worn him down, and won the argument that he should come. He could tell that his uncle resented this. There was something febrile about Uncle Antonio, and the way he dealt with these people. It struck him, for he was not stupid, that Uncle Antonio's authority in Palermo was something of a front, and that when he was with Tancredi and with these thugs from Catania, he seemed somewhat less sure of himself.

Lunch was announced, and they went through to the dining room. The opening course was pappardelle with hare, and all the requisite sighs of appreciation were made. The bottle of red wine was passed around and Anna Maria allowed herself the tiniest sip. Once the maid withdrew, business was discussed.

'We will look at the maps when we have finished lunch,' she said. 'But I have had various people look at the area that interests me and will interest you too, and the plan is a good one, as I am sure you will all agree. First of all, Catania is a hellhole of traffic and crowded apartment blocks and crime. Finding a parking space is a nightmare, everyone agrees, and we all know how people like driving, how they long for green spaces, how they long for fresh air. So, a vast new complex, a new town in effect, will make us all a fortune. The land we have identified is cheap, largely because it is degraded by abandoned factories and run-down apartment blocks as well as some pretty much uncultivated farm land; and it is too close to the airport, far too noisy for human habitation. The other problem is that the vast territory we need belongs to several hundred people. Quite a few dozen have already sold to us, taken the money and run, and more will follow. But in the end, after we have collected the low-hanging fruit, the last few stubborn holdouts will be hard to bring in. I do not deny that. But that is the nature of investment: identifying an opportunity that others have missed. Now you can see what we need here, I hope. Three things. Ready cash, which my bank will provide should you run out. That is easy. Liquidity. No problem. Then political clout. That is the role of myself and Palermo. People who will grant us a change of zoning, from industrial to residential, from agricultural to residential. And people who can change the flight path of the aeroplanes from the airport. And as for getting rid of the present owners, that is the job of Catania. One requires influence, the other requires muscle. I lend you the money, and the proceeds are split between Catania and Palermo.'

'The muscle part is relatively simple; it is not easy, it is not clean, and it will not be swift, but one knows what to do, and it can be done. And I know just the person to do it,' said Calogero with a smile directed at Traiano. 'One who will enjoy doing it too. But the political part…. We do not know who the government will be in a few months' time, let alone a few years' time.'

'This government will collapse, and soon,' admitted Santucci. 'The bankers will pull the rug out from underneath our dear Prime Minister by refusing to service the national debt for a reasonable price. Sooner or later, the bankers will impose one of their own on us, a technical government, to steer us through the financial crisis. And then, after that, some politician will come back to power. But does this matter? The faces change, but the people behind the new faces all remain the same. When the application for zoning changes appears on someone's desk, they will know that they have to sign, and the same thing with the flight path; and they will sign because not to sign will be too difficult. We have helped them too much in the past for them not to be grateful, and our men are at every level of the machine of government. Besides, something that Anna Maria did not mention, and which is my own brilliant idea, I have to say: we manufacture a crisis for which this project becomes the solution. With our friends in Libya to help, and they are very keen to help in this, we arrange for clandestine immigrants to set up camp in the empty spaces and to squat in the empty properties. Then when the place has been taken over by them, which will cause a storm in Catania, particularly in the city hall, we get rid of them, and we create a beautiful new suburb, and let them take credit for that.

They will be so pleased. They will have the glory, and we will have the money. A beautiful plan, I am sure you all agree.'

Everyone murmured their appreciation. Even Renzo, who had tried to look detached and sardonic, seemed impressed. Anna Maria rang the bell, and the maid came in and took away their plates. In came the Milanese cutlets. The maid withdrew.

They began to discuss the architects and the contractors, and the huge amount of work, and the corresponding influence that this would generate. There was of course a list for architects, and contractors, and, at a lower level, a list of men who could be employed. None of these lists were written down. The lists existed in Santucci's head, in his prodigious memory, of all the people whose favour he, his father and his uncle and Carlo had enjoyed, and all those who longed to gain his favour. Every contract, every job offer, however small, would bring with it a tie that bound, a pledge of loyalty, an undying friendship. But this was a Catania project, and this meant that he was handing to don Calogero an enormous opportunity, that of gaining the gratitude of so many local people. The value of the combined contracts would be split fifty-fifty, but every bricklayer and earth shoveller in Catania would now become a potential best friend of don Calogero di Rienzi. This was far bigger than giving out jobs in the pizzeria and the bars of the Purgatory quarter. Traiano saw that everyone he had ever met would now want to gain his favour. He took a tiny sip of wine and felt it go at once to his head. His wife's relatives would love him so much.

Then conversation ceased for the removal of the plates and the arrival of the zuppa inglese. Then they fell to discussing the new office that Calogero had opened up, where his wife would preside but where the real work would be done by one of Anna Maria's men, and the lawyer Rossi.

In Catania, in the Purgatory quarter, in the flat belonging to the boss, his wife was looking at her bedroom floor. Between the door and the bed lay her shoes, one close to the door, another closer to the bed. Maso still had his shoes on, but his trousers were round his knees, and she could see, by raising her head, his pale and hairy legs reflected in the mirror on the front of the wardrobe.

'Are you sure?' she asked.

He raised his head, and nodded breathlessly. He grappled with his shoes and his trousers, while she pulled the rest of her dress over her head. A moment later, it happened. Very slowly, Maso began to move. She caught sight of her raised knees in the mirror and then shut her eyes.

Over the zuppa inglese they were discussing risk. If they did not manage to persuade all the current owners to sell, if the government zoning laws did not fall into place, if, above all, the flight paths were not moved, what would happen then? Anna Maria was amused by this. If any of these things happened, then they would not make their huge profit. It was as simple as that. But though there was a risk of failure, the probability of success was huge, and the latter far outweighed the former. When the plates were cleared, the coffee was brought in, along with the post lunch drinks – sambuca and limoncello and amaro – and the maps were laid out on the table. Would the development be walled? Would there be one way in and one way out, or several? Would there be a direct access to the motorway? Would it be served by bus routes? Would the residents use buses? No, but their servants would, the cleaners and the gardeners. Would there be a supermarket? Would there be a lake? How many children's playgrounds would there be? Would there be a leisure centre? Would there be a church?

How many units of housing would there be? How many would be high-rise and how many low-rise? All this boiled down to the architects. When could they talk to them, under conditions of greatest secrecy, of course?

But more important than the future map was the present map, she warned them. The thing to think of was the low-hanging fruit. The abandoned factories and agricultural land would surely sell easily, given the right price. If one of those abandoned factories were to go up in smoke – difficult, not much to burn – or become the haunt of clandestine immigrants from Africa, that would be a huge help. The actual residences were all vulnerable, to fire, to squatters, to other disasters. The roads were poorly lit and in a bad state of repair. The Caravaggio boy nodded. He understood. Youngsters drove their cars out there for peace and quiet and unobserved assignations. That would have to stop, and the place gain a reputation. There was a petrol station in the middle; he would check it out. Anna Maria looked at him with appreciation. Antonio Santucci expressed the desire to smoke and said he would step outside for a few minutes. Calogero accompanied him. The Caravaggio boy watched them go, knowing that his boss was going to speak to Santucci about what they had mentioned in the car.

She observed his anxiety as they left the room. Renzo Santucci also excused himself. They were alone now.

'You do not like Santucci,' she observed. 'I am not surprised. Very few people do. He inherited his position; he did not earn it. There is an air of entitlement about him. And the nephew: I confess I was not expecting him. His arrival, his quiet but observant presence, tells me a great deal. I can tell too that Santucci stands between yourself and something you want. That is unwise of Santucci. I would not like to have you as an enemy. Tell me, when we have gathered in the low-hanging fruit, and when we still have just a few holdouts to deal with, people who will not listen to reason, will you do whatever is necessary?'

'Of course, how could you doubt it? Whatever is necessary.'

'Without remorse?'

'Without remorse. They would all have been warned in advance, and if they are too stupid to take the warning and get out in time, in that case they deserve what they are going to get.'

She looked at him and smiled, and then was serious.

'You may remember my nephew. He was a policeman. A silly boy in many ways, but I was once fond of him. He has not been seen since August. That was the time when there was a spate of murders. The fact that he has disappeared leads to only one conclusion. My poor sister, his mother, is desolate. She was very fond of him.'

'The Romanians must have killed him,' said Traiano. 'They would have buried him somewhere in the lava fields of Mount Etna, or dropped him into the sea. That is what happens to bodies that are never found.'

She nodded. She knew he was dead. Who killed him? Did it matter now? The younger Santucci, who had been snorting cocaine in the downstairs loo, now rejoined them, and the subject was dropped. He noted that his uncle was still outside talking to Calogero, and whatever it was that they were discussing was taking time. He smiled at Anna Maria, paid her a compliment on the beauty of the house and the garden, and then looked at Traiano uncertainly. He was about to speak, when don Antonio Santucci, having smoked at least three cigarettes outside with Calogero, come in to say goodbye. There were more kisses, a particularly warm one for the Caravaggio boy, and then he was gone, talking Renzo with him. Anna Maria then announced, with meaning, that she would lie down for an hour or two. Calogero nodded. She went to the kitchen to thank her maid, told her that she was not to be disturbed, and disappeared up the stairs. Once in her bedroom she took off her clothes, and rested her weary self on the bed, idly picking up a book that she had been reading. After a few minutes, she laid the book aside, watching Calogero enter the room, take off his jacket and tie and kneel at the foot of the bed. She moved down the bed, feeling the mountainous weight of her pregnancy, and surrendering herself to the touch of his warm hands.

'What were you talking to Santucci about?' she asked.

'Traiano wanted me to talk to him on his behalf,' he said, concentrating on what was before him, sensing her appreciation. 'He wants a reward for all his hard work, all that he has done. He wants to join the honoured society. Santucci says he is too young. I said that will change. Santucci says you have to be Sicilian to be a member, and that the Americans won't like it. I said that is stupid and that he is, to all intents, a Sicilian already. Of course, Santucci fears anyone with talent as he has so little of his own. He is sly, of course. His last argument was that if he supported Traiano's application, he would have to enable the nephew to enter as well. He does not like the nephew. He senses trouble from that quarter. He admitted it. The nephew is a useless, spoiled kid. I told him that Traiano is a completely different case, and has done more for the honoured society than anyone else.'

'What has he done?'

'You know I cannot tell you that. I am telling you too much as it is. You are not a member, my dear. How does that feel now?'

'Wonderful. You have lovely fingers. But do not stop. Carry on.'

He carried on.

'Who killed my nephew? His mother wants to know. She cannot let it go.'

'The Romanians. The same lot who shot the man at Cefalù in front of my wife and brother, and blew up Carlo, the brother-in-law of Santucci, the father of Renzo. The body is buried at sea or on Mount Etna, I reckon. I think I will stop talking right now. My hands are getting tired.'

She exhaled deeply.

Stefania awoke, knowing she had been deeply asleep, but only for the very shortest time. The boy Maso still had his arms around her, and his warm face was close to hers, his cheeks flushed, his smooth back and shoulders sweaty. Her legs were still wrapped around him.

'Will he kill me if he finds out?'

'Yes, though not because he cares, but because he would think it expected of him. But he won't find out. Are you going to tell him? I am not.'

'Most certainly not.'

'Oh God, your brother. What has he been doing all this time?'

'He has been at your computer screen. He does not talk, he does not know how. He only talks to me. He is safe. He is silent.'

'Does he have a girlfriend?'

'No.'

'Does he understand sex?'

'I think so. He looks at things on the Internet and you know…'

'Masturbates?'

She was amused that he was embarrassed by this.

'Yes. I catch him at it. We share a bedroom. But he has no self-consciousness. If I walk in, he carries on regardless. It upsets my mother. She cannot understand him.'

'But you do?'

'Yes. Part of his brain is highly developed and another part not at all. He would have heard us but paid us no attention at all.'

'Do you have a girlfriend?'

'I do now,' he said. 'When will he be back?'

'Not for hours.'

'Let me just go to the bathroom, and I will be right back.'

'I have to pick up the children,' she said with a touch of anxiety. 'In an hour's time.'

He stood at the door and turned, and gave a little shrug of the shoulders.

'We'll be fine,' he said, smiling.

'Take off your clothes and come and lie down next to me,' said Anna Maria, when she was able to speak.

He did as he was told. She felt his hot breath on her ear, and she turned to kiss him. Their lips met for a moment. He held her hand. She could feel his body extended next to hers.

'How much leverage do you have with Santucci?' he asked quietly.

'Plenty. Why? Is this about little Caravaggio?'

'Yes.'

'I'll fix it. Though it won't happen overnight. He will have to wait until he is older. But it will happen. You can rely on me.'

'Thanks.'

Her mind had worked rapidly. To have the Caravaggio boy in the organisation, with him knowing that he owed his position to her, would be greatly to her advantage. She would grant the favour. But there was something else she wanted to know.

'Are we going to tell the world that the child is yours?'

Her skill in reading him told her that this was a genuinely difficult question, one that he had considered but to which he had no answer.

'What is best for the child?' he asked. 'What do you want?'

'What do you want?' she replied. 'What does your wife want? What will your other children want?'

'Do we know....?'

'Does that make a difference?'

'No.'

'I have had the scan and it is clear that it is a boy. Do you like the name Sebastiano?'

'Very much. Sebastiano di Rienzi. That is his name. Stefania will be furious, but to tell you the truth, I think her fury has peaked. None of my family can be furious with me forever. I have the one thing they all want. Money. And in a few years, I shall have more and more, thanks to you.'

Downstairs, Traiano had dropped off to sleep on the sofa in the drawing room, with the book of photographs by Alfonso Agostini in his hands. The photographs had been architectural in purpose, and apart from various buildings in Syracuse and Catania, as well as a few in Noto, he had recognised none of them. How little he knew, how little he had travelled in Sicily, or anywhere else for that matter. He fell asleep reflecting on the way early adulthood, marriage, children, the business of enforcement and murder, had precluded so many of the other things that people of his age did. Perhaps he should get on a train with Ceccina, leave the children behind with her sister or her mother, and go to Palermo and see the Palatine Chapel, or the Cathedral at Monreale, both of which, judging by the pictures Fofò had taken, were marvels of the world. To take a holiday might be nice. He had never been on holiday. Not even to Taormina. Had he even slept a night outside the Purgatory quarter, apart from the nights spent in the eerily quiet countryside of Donnafugata? He could not remember. Would he die before seeing Palermo, let alone Rome, Florence, Milan or Venice?

The stupid thing was that he was rich. Lots of money flowed through his hands, all going to Calogero, and lots of it flowed back, for Calogero paid him well. He was, 'in white', as the expression was, paid several thousand a month as the overall manager of the pizzeria and the bars; on top of this, 'in black' were the rewards he was paid for the occasional but lucrative jobs he did for the boss. He could not remember now just how much the boss had given him for killing Michele Lotto, the wild Romanian, but it had substantially paid for the house he and Ceccina lived in. So much money, and even more to come. With this new project he could ask for, and surely get, a percentage, and that would set him up for life, and set the children up for life as well. And then, when the huge struggle to escape poverty was over, what then? Would the terrible gnawing worry ever go away?

He felt himself drifting off to sleep on the comfortable sofa, whilst the dull November light coming through the windows soothed his mind. He stirred himself and put the book of photographs aside and went in search of the kitchen. The maid, Veronica, seemed surprised to see him, but he smiled, thanked her for the superb food, and settled in a chair while she made him a cup of coffee. She had worked for the signora for over thirty years, first being employed by the signora's parents, and she lived in Palermo, but had come to Donnafugata because of the signora's interesting condition, as she called it. It was not good for her to be alone, at her age. She was, Traiano could judge, devoted to Anna Maria, less so to the boss, who was responsible for putting her mistress in this interesting condition. Yet she seemed well disposed to him, looked with great interest at the photographs he took out of his wallet of Ceccina, of Cristoforo and Maria Vittoria, exclaiming over the beauty of the children and their mother. Traiano was keen to stress his working class credentials, realising that Veronica had to deal with a series of visitors who gave themselves airs to which, in her eyes at least, they were not entitled. It was important to him, he felt obscurely, to have an ally in the house, and Veronica would fill that role, just as Muniddu did.

The boss came in, drawn by the sound of their conversation, and looked at his watch; it was more or less five in the afternoon. He ignored the presence of Veronica entirely, and she looked at him with less than glad eyes.

'I have fixed it, I have fixed it,' he said happily, and ordered him to get his coat, so they could go for a walk in the orange groves and get some fresh air.

From an upstairs window, as she prepared to take her bath, Anna Maria watched them go. She knew what they were discussing. No doubt the Caravaggio boy would be very happy. She watched the father of her child, and inside herself she felt Sebastiano di Rienzi stir.

Chapter Four

It was not considered auspicious to celebrate a baptism in the month of November, which was dedicated to praying for the dead, and which was the month when the Church of the Holy Souls in Purgatory received the most visitors and when the Spanish Madonna, in her glory, above the high altar, found that the most fervent prayers were addressed to her. For this reason, the baptism of the infant Maria Vittoria, daughter of Traiano and Ceccina, had been put off until the first Sunday of December, which fell that year on the sixth of the month, just two days before the feast of the Immaculate Conception. On the Friday, there would be a gathering of the female relations and friends at the house, where they would admire the child and her clothes and each other's clothes as well; and on this Friday, Traiano thought it a good idea to invite the male friends and relations up to the gun club at Nicolosi, which was, of course, the property in all but name of don Calogero di Rienzi. Usually, the gun club was shut at this time, but it could be opened specially for the occasion, and the barman would be in attendance. They would shoot, they would drink, and then they would go home. The gun club was open to women, but none of their wives and girlfriends were ever interested in guns.

Traiano would have liked Calogero to have come, but the boss never frequented such gatherings these days. The gathering in the gun club was technically illegal, as some of the guests were not members, and some were too young to shoot legally; some of the guns they used were not kept in the club, since they were unlicensed. In addition, the club was one of two places where they planned operations. So the boss, even though he controlled the place, never went there, just as he never went to the gym, which he actually owned, and which was also a place where the men Traiano controlled planned their operations. It was as if he were planning his defence in some forthcoming trial, and setting clear ground between himself and crime. But he would come to the baptism. A baptism was only a baptism.

The other person he wanted to come was Rosario, though he invited him thinking he would refuse, but to his pleasure and surprise, Rosario accepted the invitation with alacrity, claiming that although he did not like guns, he nevertheless wanted to see what the gun club was like. And so he came; all the other guests treated him with reserve and respect, as if unable to forget that he was the boss's brother. They all shook hands with him. It was Traiano's privilege alone to hug him and kiss his cheek. He was, after all, the leader, though one of the youngest; he was the boss's friend and confidant; he was also the friend of the boss's brother. This public display of affection was also a public display of power. But the truth was - and it was an uncomfortable truth - that he had strong feelings about Rosario in reality; it was not just an empty show. If Calogero was like a father to him, Rosario was like a brother, a brother he had known all his life. It was to Rosario, he had gone for comfort, on the night he had discovered that his father had been killed. Rosario was the only person who had ever seen him in tears, the only person to whom he had revealed his weakness. And, of course, Rosario was to be godfather of little Maria Vittoria. He would protect her and look after her, and ensure she was properly brought up. It was a sign of his absolute trust and his deepest friendship, asking Rosario to be godfather. Moreover, he was surrounded by people like himself, and he knew few people who were good: his wife, don Giorgio, and Rosario. That all three cared about him, in their different ways, was very important to him.

As for Rosario, now visiting the gun club for the first time, he found himself surrounded by men he knew, though not well. These, he saw, were the people his brother employed, the people Traiano habitually frequented. There was Alfio and there was Gino, the one from Agrigento, with whose girlfriend Catarina, Alfio's cousin, he had been briefly and embarrassingly involved before he had met Carolina. There were various men he recognised as waiters at the pizzeria, barmen from the bars. There was Maso, and rather surprisingly, there was Enzo. He had not expected to see them.

Maso explained to Rosario that he had been invited and asked to bring his brother with him, because he could not leave Enzo behind, partly because Enzo always had to come with him, and it was really too much trouble to leave him behind. Besides which, Enzo liked guns. The two boys shared a bedroom, and Maso had caught Enzo examining his recently acquired gun;

91

the older boy liked the technical perfection of the weapon, he liked the way it came apart, and could be put together again. Maso had read about soldiers who were trained to disassemble and reassemble their guns blindfolded and in the dark, and he was sure that Enzo could do this. Of course, he was frightened his brother might have an accident with the gun, so thought it best that he try shooting, whilst at the club, to satisfy his curiosity.

Rosario was shocked that Maso had a gun, but tried not to show it.

To everyone's surprise, Enzo, when given his turn, was a good shot, a natural. He never spoke, he never looked at anyone apart from Maso, but he seemed to have a natural affinity with mechanical things. Maso seemed content with this. All the boys spent time shooting at the targets and comparing them later, all except Rosario, who, though he tried shooting a gun, derived no great pleasure from it. The targets were compared with great interest, to see who was the best shot.

'Of course, the whole point of having a gun is to make sure you never have to use it,' said Traiano, when he and Rosario sat down with a beer each after the shooting was over. 'Unless of course you want to shoot birds, which I do not. Your black eye has gone, I am glad to say. It made you look awful. Have you seen your brother recently?'

Rosario laughed.

'Carolina liked it, funnily enough, and she believed me when I said I walked into a door. No, I have not seen my brother, not to talk to, only in the distance. I have heard about Tancredi and the child. Everyone seems to know about that.'

'He says he does not care if everyone knows. That was what he told me the other day. And he has decided, and he has promised her, that when the child is born, he will be called Sebastiano di Rienzi. His name will be on the birth certificate. Well might you look at me like that. He is doing this to spite Stefania. It seemed that she might be on the point of getting over her annoyance, and that they would eventually iron things out, but it has all gone wrong again. He was sleeping on the sofa in his office, but now he has taken to sleeping in another flat altogether, and he just comes home when the children are there. They have stopped talking. It is very awkward. I know she is annoyed, but… well, she is not helping herself or her children. I know what you will say. I always take his part. And I do. He was always faithful to her until he met Tancredi. And Tancredi was hard to refuse, shall we say. She is a big player. I know she is a banker, and that sounds harmless enough. But she is the banker to lots of important and dangerous people. She has friends. She is probably more important than anyone I have ever met. And though not in her first youth, she is attractive. If Caloriu had chosen some girl from the quarter, Stefania would not have minded so much. But how can she compete with Tancredi? You should see the house: books, pictures, silver, orange groves. This time I got to stay in the house. It was pure luxury. You would like it. Perhaps he will take you there one day. I wonder what will happen when the child is baptised, who will be there? You will, of course; perhaps I will be too. She likes me, funnily enough. She may well like you. But you, of course, may well choose to stick to Stefania, and your mother and your sisters, all of whom disapprove so much.'

'I feel sorry for my brother,' said Rosario. 'I feel for him in his situation. It is awkward. It is going to be a boy? I feel sorry for Stefania as well. Though she has not been a good wife to him, in my opinion. She is too worldly.'

'When are we going to hear about your engagement?' he asked.

'Soon. I mean, it has already taken place. We have agreed to marry. I proposed and she accepted. So we are engaged. But I am a sufficiently shy person not to want to have all the attention. I would like to get married quietly.'

'Well, you can't. You will have to have a big party and spend lots of money and have lots of people looking at you and speculating about you and poring over the details. Don't look horrified. It is the right of the public. Besides, you are the brother of our boss. Your wedding is our property. You will be the centre of attention and you will enjoy it. Someone wants to talk to you,' he observed, with slight annoyance at the thought of their private conversation being interrupted.

It was Maso. But Maso wanted to talk, not to Rosario, but to Traiano. He approached nervously. Hands were shaken. Enzo was in the background, and feeling sorry for him, Rosario beckoned them both forward. They took seats and Maso sipped his beer, while Enzo, also holding a beer bottle, merely stared at his. Rosario had known Enzo for some time, as they were the same age, but had never spoken to him. He had remembered a rather sad figure at school, very clever, but without friends. Since then, Enzo seemed to have got worse, become more isolated, more remote.

'Enzo,' said Maso, addressing Traiano, 'would like to give you a laptop. The very latest model.'

Traiano was polite but cool in his refusal. He had no need of a computer, and would never use one. Neither would Ceccina, he could answer for her too, when he was asked if she would like it. Disappointed, Maso turned to Rosario, who explained that his work provided him with a laptop. They discussed whether the one he had was as good as the one Enzo could get him. Enzo could also give Rosario a mobile phone, indeed two, one for him and one (this detail was added shyly), for his girlfriend. Rosario admitted that she was in Sicily this weekend, currently with her parents for dinner, though they would see each other tomorrow, and a new pair of mobiles would make a nice present for her. Maso brightened at this, and immediately produced from the inner pocket of his leather jacket two slim mobile phones. He began to demonstrate all the things that the phones could do. Traiano paid attention, recognising that these phones were similar to the ones that Ceccina and her sister Pasqualina had, which had also been presents from Maso. They now had Enzo's attention as well, for as soon as the screens were lit, he was looking at them, no longer only looking at his feet or the beer bottle.

'Show us yours,' said Traiano.

There was the slightest pause, and Maso explained that he no longer had one, but had disposed of it, just as he had been told to do so. His brother of course still had one, and he gestured to Enzo to take it out. He passed it to Traiano.

'I hope there is nothing on this,' said Traiano, 'That could ever get you into trouble.'

'Nothing, boss. It is all quite innocent. Text messages from my parents, texts and calls from the pizzeria about when to work there, as they know they can get me through Enzo, and texts and calls from people who want Enzo to work on their computer systems and their websites. Nothing that would ever interest a curious person.'

'Does he have any friends?' asked Traiano.

'No,' said Maso. 'He has just got me.'

'And you?' asked Traiano.

'Boss, I have my brother with me all the time, more or less. If I leave him, he gets anxious. If I spend time with someone else, he gets very jealous.' He paused. 'Of course, I can leave him at night if I explain I am off to do something important.'

Rosario, who had been rather sympathetic to the Maso's obvious lack of ease, wondered what these nocturnal activities could be.

'Like what?' he asked.

He saw Maso and Traiano exchange looks. Business was not to be discussed in front of outsiders, and the boss's brother was an outsider. But Traiano's mind was working. There was more than business in Maso's mind. There was something that he could not tell Traiano.

'Like…. Working at the pizzeria,' said Maso defensively. 'We are always together, so it makes it hard.'

'Are you seeing a girl?' asked Traiano.

'Not at present, boss,' said Maso, after an almost imperceptible pause, which Traiano noticed.

'Is he seeing a girl?' asked Traiano of Enzo.

'Of course not, boss. He cannot communicate, as you must have noticed,' he added with a touch of asperity. 'He will never have anyone but me.'

'And your parents,' put in Rosario.

'He hates them. They made him go and see lots of doctors when he was younger and sent him to various hospitals, to make him normal. But he likes being the way he is.'

'I don't blame him. We all like being the way we are,' said Traiano. 'Have you been in lots of fights?'

'At school. Before they chucked me out.'

'You got thrown out of school. And your mother a teacher? And your father working for the government?' said Traiano in mock disbelief.

'I don't like my parents, boss,' said Maso. 'And they don't like me. I don't like living at home either, and, as soon as we can. Enzo and me will live somewhere else.'

'And don Calogero will help? You think he runs a service for runaway boys?'

'Boss, I am twenty, and Enzo is twenty-two. We are old enough to live on our own.'

Traiano extended a hand and felt Maso's arm through his jacket and his shirt.

'You seem strong,' he said. 'But are you brave? Could you challenge one of these guys here to a fight? Could you challenge Alfio? Could you fight

Gino? I don't think many people have beaten him. Could you fight Gino? Look at him. Just fists, mind you, no knives. What do you think?'

Maso knew that this was a test. It was one he was determined to take, and to pass. He looked directly at Traiano.

'What about you and me, boss?'

Traiano had not been expecting this. It conformed his dislike of Maso, not that one should let that colour one's decisions. But he had walked into this and there was no way out.

'Why not?' he said.

He called over Alfio and Gino, one of whom would have to be the referee.

'Are you crazy?' asked Rosario. 'Your daughter is getting baptised on Sunday.'

Traiano waved a hand in dismissal of this.

Maso had gone pale, but there was no going back, and he was determined not to show that he was in any way frightened. He spoke to his brother, who seemed, at least so far, unperturbed. The whole crowd of them, once the word was out that there was to be a fight, now poured out of the club into the carpark, which was brightly floodlit. There was a buzz of excitement.

Traiano went to one end of the open space, and Maso to the other. Maso was accompanied by Alfio, who was, in a sense, his sponsor, the man who had introduced him; Gino, by default, accompanied Traiano.

'You have got to let him win,' said Alfio in whisper. 'Put up a fight, and make it look as if he deserves to win, and that you are not a walk over, but he has got to win. Gino and I might be able to get away with beating him, but he would never forgive you. But make it look natural. And don't hit him in the face, as he has his daughter's baptism this Sunday and he has to look presentable.'

Maso nodded. He could neither retract nor withdraw; he had to go on and fight, and he had to put up a good show, in order to prove himself, but he could not possibly win if he wanted to be part of Traiano's crew.

All the others had seen similar situations, for they all loved fighting, and many of their evenings in the gun club ended like this. No one had ever beaten Traiano, just as no one in the old days had ever beaten Calogero di Rienzi. But the whole matter was interesting even if the outcome was more or less certain. How badly would Maso lose? He was after all a tough boy. How badly would Traiano humiliate him? Would Maso acquit himself sufficiently well to win respect?

One of the boys went around collecting fifty euro notes from the others, though Rosario refused to contribute, and stood with Enzo next to him. This would be the prize money. Alfio whispered further advice to Maso. Traiano casually stripped to his shoes and his boxer shorts, even though it was cold, to show that this was fists only and not knives. Knives were kept for enemies, and this was friendly. His muscular flesh was pale and smooth in the light of the carpark. The various scars which disfigured him were now on display, like badges of honour, like signs of past fights won or defeats. Trying not to tremble, Maso did the same, revealing a pair of unfashionable y-fronts, a precociously hairy chest and very broad shoulders. The preliminaries were begun. They regarded each other with deep hatred and exchanged insults of the very worst kind. Obscene gestures were made. Both preened like fighting birds, grinning confidently. The onlookers goaded them on.

After some hesitation they charged each other. Traiano grabbed Maso by the neck and punched him repeatedly in the ribs. Each punch brought a cry of appreciation from the crowd and, Rosario could sense, a surge of anxiety in Enzo. Maso freed himself and managed to land a few punches on Traiano, but they were not sufficiently strong to do any great harm. Recovering himself, Traiano grabbed his opponent, placed his neck under his arm and pummelled him repeatedly. The small crowd roared. Traiano let him go and acknowledged the applause. The jeering and goading of Maso became intense. Rosario held onto Enzo, frightened that he would intervene. Just then Maso recovered himself and landed a powerful punch on Traiano's stomach, which temporarily winded him, and then two further strong punches to the shoulders. For a moment Traiano staggered. The fight now seemed more equal. Traiano took several swings at Maso, which he deftly avoided. They grappled once more, and Traiano landed several very powerful punches on his opponent's back, chest and thighs. The crowd was now completely silent, the only noise being the sound of fist hitting flesh. Rosario had the strange impression that he was witnessing some sort of ritual, some piece of ceremonial, in which each had a part to play, and followed a set pattern. At the same time, the pattern might be disrupted, and something could go wrong.

Maso, his face now contorted with pain and with a fury that could not possibly be assumed, as if he felt deeply his humiliation in front of the crowd, and knew he had to reverse it, managed to get his grip around Traiano's neck and squeeze. Only a tremendous kick from Traiano made him let go. The two opponents stood back from each other for a moment. Alfio rushed forward to advise Maso to give way, to surrender, and that he had put up a good fight and could now concede with honour. He shook his head. He knew that every minute from now on that he could endure would be crucial to his final reputation.

It dragged on. It was clear to Rosario that perhaps Maso was a better fighter than Traiano had realised, and that this was a tougher fight than he had bargained on. Of course, there was no possibility of Traiano losing, that was unthinkable, but it was equally clear that Maso would emerge as a tough opponent, a worthy conquest. Maso managed to land several punches, several kicks, and get Traiano in a hold on a few occasions, pulling him by the hair and beating him on the back. But, though Traiano was by no means the stronger, he was the more well practiced in these matters. Gradually Maso weakened. It seemed to Rosario that the fight was never-ending. There was blood, a lot of it, from a split lip, that might need the attention of a doctor. Naturally enough, Maso had taken this injury without daring to inflict it on Traiano. After a terrible pounding from the triumphant Traiano, Maso slid to the tarmac.

There was now complete silence, for much would depend on what followed. Rosario sensed that the key moment of the ritual was about to be enacted. Traiano, standing over Maso, looked around for guidance, like a victorious gladiator looking up to the Imperial box. The spectators looked to him, though, wanting a sign from him as to what he wanted them to do. Traiano, red, sweaty, held out a hand. Gino rushed forward with the prize money. He took it, and put the notes in the waistband of his shorts, having nowhere else to put them. Still Traiano did nothing, waiting for a sign, but no one moved. By this time a bad opponent would have been subjected to the humiliation of a group kicking as he lay on the floor, or else they would all have watched Traiano lower his shorts and piss on him. But it was clear Maso was not a bad opponent in the eyes of the crowd, and their judgement was final, though Rosario could sense that Traiano somehow wished it was otherwise. Nevertheless, he bent down and hauled Maso to his feet. Then he took the money, and gave it to him, stuffing it into his waistband. Then he held him in a tight embrace and felt the blood and sweat up close.

In Catania, Ceccina was entertaining the females of the family and friends. Stefania had come, along with her sister Giuseppina, and so had Elena di Rienzi, the boss's sister, and Catarina, the cousin of Alfio and the girlfriend of Gino, the one from Agrigento. Also present were all Ceccina's female relations: her mother, her sister Pasqualina, her cousins and her aunts. (Several of the male relations were up at Nicolosi, in the gun club, invited by Traiano.) The flat was a large one, though by no means as large as that of the boss himself. Stefania, Ceccina, Elena and Catarina were able to seclude themselves in one room. Luckily, Anna had declined the invitation, and she had not had to invite the boss's mother or his other sister, Assunta, whom she barely knew. But she had invited Elena, the nicer and younger of the two sisters, who had come to see the baby shortly after the birth and had brought a present. She was a little surprised, and awed, that Elena had accepted the invitation. It was the first time she had ever come to the house. In addition, Ceccina was overawed by the presence of Stefania and taken aback by her acceptance. Neither Elena nor Stefania had ever met Catarina before now, except in the distance, and it was nice for the four women to catch up on matters of mutual interest, though Ceccina noted the way Elena held back from the conversation.

They were talking about Alfio, his dreadful teeth, and his proposed trip to Hungary to have them fixed there. It seemed Hungarian dentistry was very good and very cheap, and one could have a holiday at the same time. Neither Alfio nor Gino had ever been out of the country, nor even crossed the straits of Messina. Catarina worried about the holiday aspect, but the others assured her that Alfio would be in too much pain with his teeth to enjoy himself too much. However, it was not her cousin that worried her, but her boyfriend, who was going to keep Alfio company. Everyone knew about eastern European women, who were so beautiful, several of whom worked in the quarter as prostitutes. Catarina did not have much confidence in Gino's ability to keep away from temptation.

Gino was something of a problematic boyfriend. The other women listened sympathetically. She had met him through Alfio, who was a problematic cousin, as far as her parents were concerned, having been in Bicocca, and being the son of her uncle by marriage who was in Piazza Lanza. And of course, Gino had been in Bicocca too, and they all knew what for. Could one trust a man like that not to lose his temper? Men could be so unreasonable and so jealous without cause, and even when there was cause, they were very bad at overlooking things. That summer past they had not been together, and she had become friends with Rosario…. At this, the others were all interested. She could not resist telling them all about it. If only she had not been so stupid as to have gone off on holiday and left him, and he had not gone on holiday at the same time to the lawyer's and fallen in with his daughter. She might have hooked him. He had been keen. Of course, Gino was not to know this. She had almost hooked him, and what a catch that might have been. He was so nice.

Ceccina agreed. He was so nice, but she found him very ungainly and unattractive. The way he wore his clothes, the shape of his face, the way his hair grew. He was not handsome like the boss. Strange that they should be brothers. But he was a very nice man, and would make an excellent husband. Her husband Traiano adored Rosario, she had to say. He scarcely talked of anyone else. They were very close. She sometimes accused him of being in love with Rosario, a phrase that had annoyed Traiano.

Elena heard all this in silence. It had never occurred to her before now that people looked on her brother, her younger brother, as a man, as a marriageable prospect, as someone who could be found attractive. It was a curious experience, to think that her brother Saro might have this sort of life, be the centre of this sort of speculation, that some women might look at him and want to sleep with him, or even marry him. It was even odder to think that Traiano liked him so much.

Catarina opined that Rosario was not so ugly. She had seen him without his shirt on, and well, it was not so bad. In fact…. Stefania admitted that she had seen him in his bathing suit on the beach at Cefalù, and there was no denying… he was neither good-looking nor attractive, though his wife would have her consolations. But the really interesting thing was what had happened between him and Catarina, and was the pure and holy Rosario not as pure and holy as one imagined? Catarina was able to set matters straight: Rosario was completely inexperienced. (Elena his sister felt some relief at hearing this, she was not sure why.) But though inexperienced, perhaps because inexperienced, he was very nice. And quite passionate. And now, said Ceccina, he had the lawyer's daughter, or she had him. There was a feeling amidst the four of them that he should have gone to one of their own. After all, Ceccina had numerous friends and relatives; so did Stefania; and Catarina thought that she could have, should have, had him herself.

Even Elena felt that her brother catching the lawyer's daughter was a piece of luck he did not deserve. This had nothing to do with money. Her sister Assunta had married the fat and reliable Federico, the sort of marriage that made one think that perhaps marriage was not the bed of roses one was led to believe. Even so, in her heart of hearts, Elena longed to be married more than anything else. To be married, not to have to live with one's mother, to have one's own place and the attentions of a nice man. Of course, her mother warned her that men were only after one thing, and that was certainly true and, also true, was that women, at least this woman, was only too willing to provide that one thing to the right person. He just had to be reasonably nice. The trouble was the shortage of nice men. The office in which she worked was full of women, and she had the feeling that the men there were put off by the realisation whose sister she was. She felt resentful of this: Calogero, who seemed to regard her as worse than useless, put people off, whereas if he had had any fraternal regard, he would have pushed men her way. There must be someone in his orbit who would do for her.

They had now moved on to discussing was how rich the lawyer was. The answer was that he was considerably so, but that whatever he was worth was nothing compared to what Calogero was making. But his money was older, more respectable. The bars, the pizzeria, the other businesses, the properties, these all brought in a lot, but that sort of money was not the same sort of money as the fees a lawyer got. Nevertheless, as a very junior member of the office, Rosario was not paid much, though with Petrocchi as his father-in-law, he was bound to be promoted. He might end up very rich. But their money was as good as his, in Stefania's opinion, and she had persuaded her husband - she did not say how – to be very generous to Rosario if and when he married Carolina Petrocchi. They might well marry next October or November; Calogero would give them his flat, and they would move somewhere bigger and better.

This was of great interest. Elena knew that, whatever Calogero gave to Rosario, he would have to give to her too, if she ever made it to the altar. The current flat the boss had was large and well fitted out, easily the best in the quarter. That would be a very handsome wedding present. Ceccina frowned, because she had always assumed that if the boss ever left it, it would come to her and Traiano. Rosario's present place was essentially one room, too small for a married man, but a little bit better than the place Gino lived in, in Catarina's opinion, and if ever she were to marry Gino, a nicer flat than his present one would be essential. If the boss were giving his own flat to Rosario, in order to impress the lawyer, what would he give to Gino, to Traiano and the rest? They were not family, but they were more important than family. What did this Carolina expect? Had she made demands? And why would the boss leave? Where would he go?

Stefania spoke of the possibility of a villa in the suburbs. It was also possible that they would have another child, and thus need more room. A fourth child was not certain, but a possibility. He wanted a fourth child, and she was considering it, but under her terms, her conditions. These things had to be negotiated. After the insult represented by Tancredi, which no one dared mention, but everyone knew about, he had to earn his way into her favour once more. He could not assume. But both Ceccina and Catarina thought that it was a good thing that the boss was so paternal, that he wanted a fourth, legitimate, child, which would make five altogether with the child Tancredi would have. Men who wanted children were nice. This was a belief shared by Elena too. She badly wanted babies. To Ceccina her husband's best quality was his love of his two children, and his desire to have more. For Catarina, Gino's huge drawback was that he showed no sign of wanting to get married and no sign whatsoever of wanting children. In fact, quite the opposite. One thing was sure. If Rosario married Carolina, they would have their first baby within a year.

The other female relations now discovered them, and the conversation became more general. The relations of Ceccina were now full-throated in their love and admiration for Traiano. One of her old uncles had been recruited to manage the car park under the office block that Calogero had recently bought and reconstructed. Several cousins had got jobs in the gym, and several young relations, male and female, were working on the front desk. What heaven, what bliss, in a city where jobs were so scarce.

Maso had refused Rosario's offer to drive him to the hospital to get someone to look at his lip. An early exit after his triumph would not look good, he felt, nor the admission that he needed medical attention. When Rosario had insisted they leave at once, he was quite firm. Nor would he admit to being in any pain, even though the bruises hurt a great deal. When people clapped him on the back in congratulation, he tried not to flinch. He gave the prize money, which was over seven hundred euros, to his brother to keep. There were several more beers to be consumed as alcohol dulled the pain. Several more of the boys wanted to fight each other, and bets were taken. Some of these fights were short and sharp, others long and involving, all leading to cuts and bruises and other badges of honour, and money changing hands. The finale of the evening was watching Alfio and Gino, both very evenly matched, engage in a wrestling match. Both were immensely strong, and the aim of the match was to gain points by pinning the opponent to the ground on his back, until such a time as one conceded the match. Rosario was a little surprised that he found this worth watching. It lasted over forty minutes, and ended with the monstrously huge Gino conceding, admitting defeat at twelve points to nine. Rosario had even put on a bet, winning ten euro. He had been shocked, horrified, yet impressed by the way Alfio had lifted the struggling Gino up and then thrown him to the ground, and how Gino had seemed not to feel any pain on being flung onto the tarmac.

'You see,' said Traiano, giving him his ten euro winnings. 'You are one of us really. You might even like to take up fighting yourself. But this is just fists. You should see it with knives. That can be nasty. Your brother was an expert with a knife, until he gave it all up. Hey,' he said to Maso. 'How many fingers am I holding up? Good, just the one. That means you do not have brain damage. What are you doing now? Going home? Or are you going to see some girl?'

'I told her not to expect me, boss,' said Maso.

He nodded. They all began to get into their cars and onto their motorbikes. Rosario prepared, at last, to drive Maso and his brother home. Traiano hesitated for a moment and stood in the centre of the car park, calling Alfio and Gino to himself. Rosario strained to overhear what they were saying, as did Maso, Rosario noticed. But they heard enough. Six motorbikes, twelve helmets, needed soon, to be kept in the garage under the gym. Then they all departed and the car park was left dark and deserted.

It was late, and Traiano got back home by motorbike in just under half an hour. Ceccina had just gone to bed and was waiting for him. He undressed and got into bed. She felt the scent of his sweat. Within half an hour he was exhausted and blissfully asleep.

Despite the fact that it was past eleven, it was Friday night and there was traffic. Rosario's idea had been to drop Enzo and Maso off at the top of the via Etnea, near the Borgo station, where they lived, and then drive himself home. However, as they edged their way through the traffic, it seemed that the bleeding lip was getting no better, and he was able to persuade both of them that it would be wise to drop Enzo off at home and then take Maso to the hospital where he could get his lip seen to. But Maso refused and said instead that the best thing to do would be to wake up Doctor Moro, and get him to see to the lip; that way there would be no waiting for attention, and no crawling through further traffic. Rosario conceded that this was best. Despite the lateness of the hour, the traffic seemed to be getting worse, as did the pain of the lip, and the worry that Maso would look deformed on Sunday, when the baptism took place, or even for life. They proceeded at a snail's pace for several more blocks down the Etnea until they reached the turn-off towards the Borgata station. By this time Maso was admitting to feeling the pain, and as they stopped and started in the traffic, Rosario found some paracetamol in the glove compartment of the car, which Maso took, washing them down with some coke, a small bottle of which was on the back seat with his jacket.

On arrival, Maso jumped out, while Enzo accompanied him. There was no need for Rosario to stop too, and besides which there was nowhere to park, so he rejoined the traffic. Before reaching the Etnea, he heard the ping of a message arrive on the mobile phone – but not his mobile phone. It was the phone in Maso's jacket, which in his hurry he had left on the back seat. Perhaps it was Maso messaging to say that he had left the jacket behind by mistake. The car was stationary in the traffic, so he reached over and took the jacket and found the phone. There was a message on the screen. Then he realised, his interest piqued, that this was not the phone he had shown to Traiano, the phone belonging to Enzo. There was another phone, a phone Maso was not supposed to have, for none of Calogero's men were allowed phones. Calogero was insistent on that point. He could not resist. He looked at the message on the screen, and he saw the number it had come from. He carefully put the phone back where he had found it, and then turned the car round, hoping that Maso would not deduce from the time of the message that he had seen it. He made his way back to the block where Maso lived, and there saw Enzo waiting in the street, who, when he drew up, took the jacket from him without thanks and turned away without a word of farewell.

On Saturday evening, something - pity, perhaps guilt - drove Rosario to phone his brother's flat and ask where he was. The answer he was given was that he was sitting in the bar in the square, drinking whiskey. Rosario came and joined him. It was late, but the bar was full of life. This was the hour when its clientele changed subtly, when the couples, the drinkers, faded away, and the buyers and the sellers moved in. In half an hour the place might become deserted, and then, in another hour or so, full once more.

He had not seen his brother since the feast of the dead, since the disastrous lunch when he had struck him across his mother's kitchen table. That humiliation, so minor compared with what he had had to put up with as a child, now placed in perspective, seemed hardly important. He came to his brother's table, and Calogero looked up; then he sat down opposite him, and the attentive barman, his eyes trained to know what the owner wanted, came over. As a gesture of solidarity, Rosario ordered whiskey.

Calogero looked at him with a look of implacable hatred.

'You come here like a vulture in search of carrion,' he said. 'What have you heard? You look like a man brimming with secrets.'

'You are the one with the secrets,' said Rosario placidly. 'You are the one who can never talk. I am not wedded to silence. But I have not come to quarrel. Merely to see you before the baptism tomorrow.'

Calogero regarded him.

'And the baptism after that?'

'My new nephew? I haven't had a chance to say congratulations. I was told by Traiano that it is a boy and you will call him Sebastiano di Rienzi. I am glad of it. I don't like it when illegitimate children are badly treated, poor things. How will Stefania react?'

'I do not care,' he said decisively. 'Perhaps Sebastiano may not be illegitimate for long. I could divorce Stefania and marry Tancredi.'

'You don't really think that, do you?'

'No, I don't. It would be a disaster. It would make some bastard of a lawyer rich and would destroy everything I have built up. I do not believe in divorce. Like Anna.'

'Don't joke.'

'I believe Anna was serious when she decided to end her marriage without resorting to divorce. Revenge, a dish best savoured cold, etcetera. One should never underestimate women when they are intent on hurting you. I have tried to placate Stefania and I have failed. The real problem is that she never loved me and I never loved her. Nothing can make good a loveless marriage, except acceptance of the state of lovelessness. She finds my coldness unforgivable, you see. But what did she expect? She knew me. I never deceived her. She made this mistake. She thought she wanted one thing, and then she discovered that she wanted another. Money and dresses and shoes and jewellery were not what she wanted after all. She wanted me, in the end. The one thing she cannot have. The one thing I do not have to give. Myself. As you rightly observe, I am bound by a code of silence. I have nothing to confide.'

'One person knows the truth. The person who was there at the time. I was there, but only part of the time. I saw. But I was too young to understand.'

'How is Carolina?' asked Calogero. 'The lawyer's daughter.'

'We spent the day together. We had our first quarrel.'

'Perhaps the first of many.'

'I want a quiet wedding. I want to live quietly, but she….'

'You must give her what she wants,' said Calogero. 'You see, she wants different things to you. You think you can go without, but she thinks in a more worldly manner. She has two elder sisters, doesn't she, and a pushy mother. It makes sense. Her establishment has to live up to their expectations; it has to outshine them. You, my dear little brother, on your own, are not so great a catch. You would have been for one of the girls of this quarter, your natural habitat. But for her, her mother, her sisters, you need a bit of padding out. You did not like my offer. They did. So you have to accept my offer because they make you accept it. That is why you quarrelled, I think: because she made you cross. She forced you to give up, to retreat. The first lesson in married life, even before married life begins. Always give way. Though I would add it is not a good lesson. I gave Stefania everything she wanted. And all she does is want more. She blames me for everything, but really, she should blame herself for not knowing what she should have known when she married me. It's intractable.' He sighed. Then he said, more briskly: 'I want you to come and meet Tancredi. Sometime soon. I owe her another visit. You can come with me. Traiano is going to be busy this week, so you can keep me company. Besides, she ought to meet some of the members of my family. She should meet you. You are respectable. She is very religious, just like you. We will go one evening next week. Early next week. Perhaps Monday. You have never been to Donnafugata, have you?'

He shook his head.

'Good, that is settled.'

Just how much was settled emerged the very next day, the day of the baptism. All the women of the party wore the same sort of close-fitting dress, which was clearly the fashion of the moment, coupled with towering high heels. Moreover, each one of them had elected to adopt a chignon, and some rather arresting dark red lipstick. How this fashion and colour co-ordination had happened was explained by Traiano. Ceccina's sister, Pasqualina the hairdresser, had come round early in the morning to do Ceccina's hair and make-up and that of Catarina too, and Stefania, somewhat to his amazement, had turned up as well. After working on the women, his sister-in-law Pasqualina had wanted to do something with Traiano's long dark curls, and had subjected him to a violent brushing and the creation of a pony tail.

Carolina, who was seeing all these people for the first time, was daunted by their lack of understatement. She herself could not compete, and she felt them looking at her, weighing her up, judging her. But it soon emerged, once Mass and the baptism were over, and they poured out into the square to enjoy the thin rays of winter sunshine, that Rosario's friends and relations were disposed to be welcoming and kind. While Catarina hung back, Ceccina and Stefania were very keen to pay her attention. This was the lawyer's daughter, about to take a degree in law herself, and become a lawyer. Of course, Rosario was a lawyer, with a degree from the same University, but the idea of a female lawyer was still a novelty to them. For Carolina was everything they were not. She was their equal in money, perhaps, but her money was respectable, and Ceccina and Stefania both knew that their own path to respectability was strewn with obstacles, even if Stefania might have advanced along it further than Ceccina.

Rosario had been holding her hand, as if to advertise their relationship, and to keep her perhaps by his side, to stop her wandering off, to keep her safe in this presumably hostile environment. But she was taken away by Ceccina when they reached the house – the house in question being Calogero's, lent for this occasion by Stefania – in order to look more closely at the baby, and the older child Cristoforo, accompanied by all the other children as well. As he relinquished her hand, Rosario watched her go with longing, and, as he had very much feared, he was approached by Catarina.

'Hi,' he said, wishing his sister Elena, who he could see at the other side of the room, would come over and rescue him, yet knowing he would have to speak to her eventually, knowing that it was best to get it over now, and that delaying it just made it worse.

'Hi,' she said with a slight smile.

'Look, I am sorry, about the summer, about not getting in touch.'

'No harm done,' she said. Her eyes looked across the room, towards the huge figure of Gino. 'I am with him,' she said. 'I wasn't for a time in the summer, but I was with him before and I am with him now, so…. She seems very nice. I hear you are getting married.'

'Everyone seems to have heard,' he remarked. 'Yes, we are. It is no secret. But in this place, everyone knows everything.'

'Not quite everything,' she said. 'Romances are known because we have nothing else to talk about, nothing else that we are allowed to talk about. God forbid we should let out any secrets, eh? Here's my new boss.'

Stefania was approaching. She had heard this.

'We have a new office and we have a new accountant. He has come from Palermo. He was recommended by Anna Maria Tancredi, who, as you know, is a financial genius. He has devised a new payroll, so everything is above board. Dearest Ceccina is now getting, I do not know how many hundreds a month, for being a consultant in our restaurant group. Yes, group, as we are buying a trattoria. It is not quite a joke, as she is an excellent cook and can advise on menus and recruitment. And Catarina is a cashier at the pizzeria, at least on paper, part time. Everyone has a job, everyone is paid, and everyone pays tax. My husband' – the word was pronounced with venom – 'just told me that you are going to meet Tancredi.'

She fixed him with a look. He felt trapped. Catarina murmured something and left.

'I am,' he admitted with difficulty.

'Exactly when?' she asked.

'Monday. Tomorrow. We have been invited there for lunch. I do not know why I have been invited.'

'I am sure Calogero has his plans, of which I know nothing and you know nothing either,' she said. 'But I will expect a full report. Do you understand me? You need to remember what you owe me. You need to defend the interests of your legitimate nephew and your legitimate nieces. He wants to give this new child his name.'

'I am not going to defend my nephew and my nieces by doing harm to my other nephew,' he said. 'And what do I owe you?' he added in a low voice.

'My silence,' she said with a smile.

'And what about my silence?' he asked.

'He would never harm the mother of his children, but he would quite happily harm you,' she pointed out.

'He would happily kill Maso, if he knew.'

She looked away.

'I know,' he said.

'What do you know?' she asked. When there was no reply, she said: 'How do you know?'

He told her.

'And you want Maso to be killed?'

'Of course not.'

'Well then,' she said. 'He knows the risks and so do I.'

'He is, what, eighteen, twenty? A stupid boy. You will get him killed.'

'All men are stupid boys, whatever their ages. If you were married to my husband, you would understand.'

'Your husband is my brother, I do understand.'

'You have as much cause to dislike him as I do.'

'True. In fact, more.'

'And like me, you cannot live without him, or more accurately, without his money or his power. This house will be yours. Carolina is already looking at it with greedy eyes. And the money he will give you will be in shares in the company. I arranged that. So, be grateful.'

'You arranged it, but he took the idea up and made it happen. He turned my lovely future wife into a greedy harpy. Into someone like you.'

She smiled brightly.

'All women are the same, all men are the same,' she said with a smile. 'That is human nature. And you are as bad as any of them. See if I am not right.'

His face went red.

'Do get Alfio to tell you all about his trip to Hungary. They are going on Wednesday, I think. For the dentistry, of course,' she said.

She left him, and he wondered about the dentistry in Hungary, but it was some minutes before he could follow this up. Anna had come into the room, and with her, her new man, Alfonso the photographer. He was lugging with him several cases; Anna explained that their lateness, which meant they had missed the ceremony of her granddaughter's baptism, had been caused by the Mass in Syracuse overrunning, by traffic on the motorway, and by Alfonso having to spend so long finding a parking place nearby, given the weight of the equipment he had brought with him. Maybe it was true. But even if it were, Anna surely enjoyed arriving late, creating an entrance for herself, her man, his photographer's equipment. She was wearing an architecturally structured dress that emphasised every pleasurable curve in her body. Her hair too was done up in a chignon. Her lipstick was carmine.

Leaving this scene, he went into the study, where he found the men of the party, or most of them. They were aware that Anna had arrived - how could they not be? But, for the moment, they were inclined to put this important event aside and listen to the strange tale of Alfio's teeth. Everyone was sympathetic. The dentistry in Hungary was world-famous, and in a week or two (they had booked two weeks) everything would be fixed, and his teeth would look rather different from the way they looked now. The only thing, apart from the expense, was the pain, of which he was very frightened. But Gino would be with him, and that would be a help. In addition, Gino volunteered, the drink in Hungary was good, and the food, though not as good as Sicily, obviously, was tolerable. But even so, it was a big adventure, crossing the Straits of Messina for the first time, flying to Rome, and changing planes there. Neither had ever left Sicily, neither could speak foreign languages, but several of the east Europeans who worked in the quarter had said that Budapest was beautiful, and the rumours were that the girls were wonderful. There was a brief pause while everyone savoured the thought of Hungarian prostitutes. Looking around them, Rosario realised that he was the only one who had no experience in this field. Gino said with seriousness that Alfio would be in such pain that he would have to go to bed early every evening. Alfio looked cross. The others giggled. Traiano announced that he would never go to Hungary, given its chief attraction. He looked to the door. He could hear his mother's voice. But she had arrived late, missed the baptism, so he saw no need whatever to go out to greet her. But Alfonso, Fofò, would be with her, and he was keen to see Fofò again. Rosario could see the indecision in his face.

'On Monday I won't be here,' Traiano said, suddenly talking business, 'and on Wednesday you won't be either,' he added, looking at Alfio and Gino. 'But there is Tuesday,' he said with meaning. 'I am going to Donnafugata on Monday with the boss and Saro. We may be there all night.'

Rosario saw the attention that Maso paid to this. He saw Traiano looking at him, cautioning him not to say anything. But Traiano was thinking of Tuesday, not Monday.

'You can tell us what she is like,' said Gino to Saro. 'Whenever we ask anything, Traiano says nothing of interest. But you may be more observant. Are you going to discuss the business?'

'My brother wants her to meet some members of the family, and wants to start with me,' said Rosario.

'You know the new gym is open?' said Traiano, changing the subject. 'We have all been given free membership. Caloriu wants to get it going as soon as possible. It's wonderful. Open 24 hours a day too. For those of us with first grade membership.' He took out an electronic fob and gave it to Rosario. 'Have mine. I will get another. Maso, show Rosario how it works.'

Maso seemed relieved by this.

'I can give you a tour,' he said. 'When would you like to go?'

'First thing tomorrow morning?' said Rosario.

'Nine o'clock?'

'No 5.30am,' said Rosario.

'For us that is last thing at night,' said Traiano.

118

'I will be in the street outside,' said Maso. 'Sunday night is a quiet night, so I will get some sleep beforehand.'

It was now impossible to ignore the presence of Anna, so Traiano went into the sitting room to find her, comforting himself that he would see Alfonso as well. Anna was there, overpowering in her mature beauty, looking round the room with proprietorial interest, her eyes taking in all the men, all of whom (with the exception of Gino) she had known professionally. She looked at her son, her face hard, unforgiving, signalling that while she was determined to love everyone, for her son she made an exception. Alfonso saw him, and his face lit up. Traiano placed a cold kiss on his mother's cheek, and a warm one on that of Alfonso.

Alfonso apologised for being late. He mentioned the equipment and where it would be best to set it up. Stefania presented herself, and advised the main bedroom, which was at that moment full of children. It was there that Rosario found Carolina surrounded by the children, sitting on the floor. Alfonso started to look for the best background and the best natural lighting.

'Are you enjoying yourself?' asked Rosario.

'I am thinking,' said Carolina, 'about how nice it would be to wake up in this room every morning. The view is lovely and the whole flat faces south. And the rooms are so big. I love it.'

'I know he has said we can have it,' said Rosario cautiously. 'But he may not be able to keep his promise. I mean, he has to find somewhere else, and it has to be somewhere Stefania likes, and she has very high standards.'

'They have a year to find it,' said Carolina. 'We could always put off our wedding until they do.'

'Wouldn't you live in the flat I already have?'

'You yourself said it was horrid,' she pointed out.

They were interrupted by Calogero.

'I see you have made friends with the children,' he said to Carolina. 'They adore their uncle. When they went on holiday with him last summer it was all they could talk about afterwards, their lovely Uncle Saro. But if you could let me have him, just for a moment....'

Rosario shrugged and followed Calogero into the hallway which was deserted. They stood by the airing cupboard. Traiano was waiting for them there.

'When you came out of church, after the baptism, you saw someone you knew, didn't you?' said Calogero.

'What do you mean? There were lots of people I knew.'

Calogero looked at Traiano. Traiano looked at the floor.

'There was a guy standing there and you saw him, recognised him, and nodded to him,' said Traiano almost apologetically.

'Yes,' said Rosario. 'I was surprised to see him there. It was Fabio Volta.'

Calogero drew in his breath.

'I thought so,' said Traiano. 'I thought I recognised him.'

'What the hell was he doing there?' asked Calogero.

'I don't know,' said Rosario.

'It was a rhetorical question,' said Calogero. 'The man was spying on us. Seeing who was there, maybe taking pictures… Whatever he was doing, it was nothing good as far as we are concerned. We ought to sort that man out. I have not forgotten what he did to you.'

'To me?' asked Rosario, surprised.

'Calling you in for questioning when you were just a little boy, trying to get you to say something to damage me. I have not forgotten. We need to teach him a lesson.'

'Boss,' said Traiano. 'You are losing it.'

He looked him square in the face.

'Don't damn well tell me I am losing it,' said Calogero in a low voice of controlled rage. He grabbed Traiano by the shirt front. 'You little pimp,' he added.

'Jesus,' said Traiano, removing his hand and walking away.

'For God's sake,' said Rosario.

He went back into the bedroom to get his breath back. Alfonso was there, the camera was set up, and the children were being photographed. This was rather a tedious thing to watch, but he admired Alfonso's patience in getting the children to pose: first the two daughters of the house alone, and then with their mother, and then with their brother. Then Ceccina with her two children, and alone with the newly baptised, then Traiano was called and posed with one child, then the other, then both, then both together with Ceccina. Then Traiano and Ceccina in each other's arms, in the window embrasure, with the dome of the church behind him. Then Rosario and Carolina, the engaged couple. Then it was time for anyone else who wanted to be photographed. Alfio came forward, and Maso.

'Where is your brother?' asked Alfonso. 'Is he here?'

'You know I have a brother?' said Maso.

'I think Anna told me,' said Alfonso. 'Would he pose with you? I like photographing pairs of brothers. You know, seeing the relationship revealed in the photograph. It is more interesting than married couples or engaged couples. When people are in love, it can be a little one dimensional. But between brothers it is usually more complex. I gather your brother is a bit special.'

'He doesn't like crowds. He does not like people. He doesn't like anything but screens, computer screens, phone screens.'

'But he likes you. Can you get him? Is he far away?'

'He is waiting for me outside. I could.'

Maso left.

'What about you and your brother?' he said turning to Rosario.

The question was answered by the entry that moment of Calogero and Traiano, both deeply discontented, yet both agreeing to be photographed. Rosario posed with each of them, and they posed with each other.

'Very psychological,' said Alfonso.

Then Maso came back with Enzo, who had been sitting on the church steps in the square.

'You had better leave us,' said Alfonso, on seeing Enzo.

In the rest of the flat, the party was dying down. People congratulated the parents of the newly baptised, kissed the baby Maria Vittoria, paid their respects to Calogero, thanked Stefania, and then left. Eventually, only

Anna was left, sitting on the sofa in the study, with Calogero opposite her, and her son next to her, while Stefania and Ceccina tidied the kitchen and the five children were glued to the television.

Anna listened to what Traiano was saying. There were just the three of them, there were no outsiders, no one who was not in on the secret, but Traiano was speaking to her in a low voice, and in Romanian, as if the words he uttered were too dangerous to be overheard, which of course, they were. She smiled as she listened to him, her eyes fixed on Calogero, who smiled back.

'Of course, what you are saying is true,' she said at last, when he had finished. 'There is no need for you to sound so desperate, so urgent, so worried. I will never do anything to harm my innocent grandchildren. Having their father sent to jail would harm them; and as you so rightly point out, if you two went to jail, so would I. We are all guilty in the matter of Michele Lotto. And in other matters besides. I know that. There is no need for you to blackmail me. Of course, you may think that I have been blackmailing you. As for Alfonso, you do not need to threaten his safety, because I will do as you wish. I owe Calogero a great deal. Indeed, I owe him everything: the house I live in, my safety over these years, and, of course, the service he did me in getting rid of Antonescu. And I do know how favours work. And I fully understand that if Stefania is angry, it is bad for all of us. But the thing is, that though you have made reparations, you have not made the reparation that she wants above all.'

Calogero sighed.

'Can't you get her to be reasonable?' asked Traiano.

'If you are reasonable, maybe she will be too,' said Anna. 'Cancel your trip to Donnafugata this week.'

Calogero sighed and nodded. It was pointless to remind them that Tancredi was vital for their success.

'We can send Traiano and Rosario on their own,' he said. 'It is necessary for the business.'

Anna nodded, seeing this as reasonable.

'And the other thing…..' she began.

'I have offered the other thing time and again. She won't have it,' said Calogero crossly.

Traiano giggled.

'Shut up,' said Calogero, shooting him a look.

'I will arrange that too. She does want it. She complains that you do not. And I know she is right. And do not tell him to shut up,' said Anna sweetly. 'I will tell her that you will not visit Donnafugata again, at least not until the child is born.'

Anna left the room to go into the kitchen.

'So,' said Calogero, 'You told her you would kill her beloved Fofò?'

'No, I said you would. She knows I like him. She knows you like no one.'

'Go to hell,' said Calogero.

'It is true. You want me to take Rosario to Donnafugata tomorrow?'

'Yes. Do your best. And if it is true that I do not like anyone, you will understand that we need to sort out Fabio Volta.'

'He is no threat.'

'He was hanging around. Why? He is too curious. Besides, that time, when my father died, shall we say that there is an unfinished account with him.'

'Yes, but....'

'No yes, but. It needs to be done. We need to show others that people like that will suffer. We need to show that too much curiosity is bad for you. Our affairs are our affairs alone. Volta has stepped over a line.'

'What have you in mind?' asked Traiano after a pause.

'I am not quite sure. You remember we had a meeting with him in that bar by the Cathedral. If we get Rosario to set up a meeting with him there, and you pop him as he crosses the square. Lots of people around, all very public, by the time anyone noticed, you would be long gone, lost in the crowd. You have been practising with that gun long enough. Time to use it.'

'Boss, can we do that? I mean, don't we need the permission of Palermo? They might not like it. The consequences…..'

'We can't be the poodle of Palermo forever. If we do it without telling them, they will respect us and fear us more.'

'They might decide we are loose cannons and kill us,' said Traiano. 'Does Antonio Santucci like you? No. Does he fear you? Yes. Did he blow up his own brother-in-law, because he did not like him and was jealous of him? I bet he did. Santucci will aim his rocket-propelled grenades at us next.'

'He may well do, but not in a hurry. And by the time he does that, I may have taken him out too.'

'Boss, this is too public a killing. You remember Perraino? He was a policeman but apart from his mother and his aunt, no one gives a damn. But when that man broke his jaw, it was public, so they had to give a damn; but when we killed him and cooked him and then got big Gino to crush his skull to dust, everyone could afford to ignore it because he is still officially alive. You remember we got someone to use his credit card all over Italy for weeks. No one liked Perraino except Tancredi and her sister. I am sure no one likes Volta and no one would really miss him apart from his mother and his sister, if he has one. We can invite him to the pizzeria one Saturday night, and then give him some cocaine, get one of the girls to sit on his lap, and do to him what was done to Perraino.'

'But is he such a fool?' asked Calogero.

'Then use Rosario to lure him to the gym, and drop him down the oubliette. But honestly, boss, it is risky. Is it worth the risk? I have a wife and children. So do you. I don't want to do twenty years in Piazza Lanza because of Volta. Besides, what do we know about Volta, what does he know? It might be worth finding out before we kill him.'

Calogero nodded.

'Besides, Alfio and Gino are going away to the dentist in Budapest. We would have to wait until they got back. But there is no hurry, is there?'

'None. We need to plan this carefully. And we need to find out what Volta knows.'

The women were coming into the room. Ceccina brought in the children, preparatory to going home, and Traiano kissed them and promised that he would follow in half an hour or so. Anna and Stefania appeared. Anna's calm announcement that she and Alfonso ought to go was the sign that negotiations with Stefania had concluded successfully. Calogero smiled and kissed Anna on the cheek. A moment later, Alfonso appeared with his equipment, and with Maso and Enzo. A few minutes later, Stefania and Calogero were alone.

He looked at his wife. He put his head round the sitting-room door, where his three children were regarding the television with rapt attention. He took his wife's hand and led her to the bedroom, locking the door.

Traiano accompanied his mother and Alfonso to the car, helping to load the photographic equipment. Maso and Enzo disappeared. While Anna took her seat in the car, Traiano and Alfonso exchanged a few words; he would come back with the pictures in a few days' time; he thought that they had been a great success, and was looking forward to developing them in his studio. They embraced, and then Traiano watched them go. He walked back towards his own flat. Crossing the square, he saw Rosario with Carolina, deep in conversation. He carried on, and arrived home. It was about to get dark. He knew he would see the boss later; but for now, he was free to go home, be a father to his children, and a husband to his beloved wife.

Chapter Five

At five thirty on Monday morning, it was dark, very dark still, and Rosario was a little surprised to see both Maso and his brother waiting for him outside the gym as agreed.

'Have you been to bed?' he asked.

'Yes, I have.'

'And your brother?'

'Him too.'

Maso, he saw, was a little bit depressed, perhaps by the early hour, perhaps by the darkness and the lack of sleep, perhaps by other things. He pressed his electronic fob against the pad by the door that led to the gym; it made a sound, and the door opened; they entered. As soon as they did so, the lights came on.

'It is the very latest thing,' said Maso. 'What they call an intelligent building. You do not have to switch on the lights; they sense you are here, and the lights come on. Traiano gave you his key?'

They walked down a corridor past the reception desk, and then down a staircase, into the basement of the building. There were three doors ahead of them, one marked with the sign for women, one marked with the sign for men, and the third marked with both. Maso applied his key to the pad of the latter.

'The only people who can use this room are ourselves,' he said. 'No finger prints, no keys for anyone else, no nothing. One of the managers comes in to clean every now and then, and he is related to Traiano's wife, and that is it.'

He led the way down a long corridor, and they came to another door, which also opened on the application of the fob to the pad. The lights came on. Before them was a room with lockers. Rosario was invited to pick one of the empty ones for his stuff. He took the one next to Maso's. Then Maso showed him the gym itself, which was accessible by a staircase, and through another door, opened by the same fob. He showed him the machines, doing his best to impress Rosario with his descriptions of how everything worked. The brother Enzo trailed behind.

'I'll show you something else that will interest you,' he said, as they returned down the stairs. 'This room was made possible by excavating some metres below the original floor level. They found this.' He led the way into the room with washbasins. At the end of this was what looked like a cupboard set in the wall, with a shiny metal door. 'We ought to keep this locked,' he said, opening it. 'Have a look.'

Rosario peered into the cupboard, which was empty. Before him was a shaft.

'What is down there?' he asked.

'It is hard to say,' said Maso. 'But when it rains, you can hear water flowing if you are very attentive. When the builders found it, they told the boss and he came and looked. It was the only time he came and looked. Otherwise, he is not interested. He has not been back. But he said that it is a well shaft that goes down to some sort of Roman structure, and that if we tell anyone, the archaeologists will never leave us in peace. Listen to this.'

He took a euro coin out of his pocket and dropped it down the shaft. They listened attentively. There was no sound.

'It is very deep. I tried with a coke can, and with a plastic bottle and with a glass bottle. No sound at all. And the water flowing could mean that it somehow is linked to the cloaca maxima of the Roman city. The boss calls this the oubliette. I had to look the word up. But whatever you throw down there you will never be troubled with again. So, the lesson is, don't leave the door open, and do not lose your footing.'

'And my brother was interested in this?' asked Rosario. 'What did you make of that?'

'Nothing at all,' said Maso smoothly. 'Nothing at all.'

They returned to the changing room. Rosario sat on one of the long narrow wooden benches. Maso stood before him, at a loss.

'On Friday when you dropped me off at home, when I went to Doctor Moro's,' he began.

'Yes?' said Rosario.

'You looked at my phone.'

'I did,' said Rosario. 'I am sorry. I shouldn't have. I wish I hadn't.'

'I am not supposed to have a phone. The boss does not like it. But....' He continued: 'She spoke to me very briefly yesterday, and she said that you could be trusted to keep quiet about it,' said Maso uncertainly.

'She is right. I can. I do not want to harm her, the mother of my nephew and my nieces. I will say nothing.' He looked at Enzo. 'Should he be here?'

'He can be trusted not to talk, because he can't talk, even if he wanted to talk,' said Maso. Enzo was sitting on the bench staring at the floor.

'Why has he come?'

'He wants to use the machines. And I thought a quiet time for him would be best...'

'You have taken a great risk,' said Rosario. 'Not with your brother, but with her.'

'Well, I did. Then last night she sent me a text message, saying she did not want to see me anymore, and that I was to erase all messages and her number from my phone.'

'You have been stupid, and she has saved you from your stupidity.'

'You are right, I should be grateful, and it did not go on very long; it was risky, and it could have ended badly, with me dead, or her dead, or us both dead, but....'

'He would not have killed her, she is the mother of his children,' said Rosario. 'Would he have killed you?'

'In a manner of speaking. Traiano gave me a good whipping one night just for catching me smoking. If I got whipped for that.... Well, you work it out. I am a bit depressed. I would like to have a girlfriend, but....'

'But what?'

'Well, there is him. Wherever I go, he goes. He follows me round like a dog. I can hardly ever leave him, except late at night. We spend 23 hours out of the 24 together. Yes, he is listening, but he knows this. He needs me. I love him, he knows that. Though I would like a normal life. But I have him instead. He needs me. The other guys would not harm him, but they do not understand him, and he needs me to protect him. My parents don't understand him. He fears them and hates them. I am the only one who ensures he is happy. But he puts girls off. I sometimes think he does it deliberately.'

Enzo did not react to this.

'Does he...?'

Maso shook his head vigorously.

'He did not like her, you know. In the past, if I was away from him, and he did not know what I was doing, that was OK. But he knew what I was up to with Stefania, because he was there in the flat, supposedly looking at the computer, but he knew, he sensed what we were doing, and he resented it. What about you?'

'Me? Well, your brother ruins your life and my brother ruins mine. Sometimes I think that people only want to know me because I am Calogero's brother. But, you know, someday someone will notice how kind you are to your brother and like you for that.'

'You think?' This seemed to cheer him up. 'I know he is waiting for me to take him to the machines. Is it alright if we do that while you do?'

Rosario nodded.

'Did she say anything about me?' he asked.

'Stefania? Nothing in particular.'

Rosario nodded again, relieved.

'Anyway,' continued Maso. 'I am grateful, boss. And thanks for doing me this favour. One day I will pay you back, I promise you.'

'How?' asked Rosario. 'Will you kill one of my many enemies?'

Maso saw that this was a joke, smiled and nodded.

'You just name them, boss.'

'I will make a list. And I am not your boss.'

Forty-five minutes later, having finished his time in the gym, he was in the shower, enjoying the plentiful hot water that he never got to enjoy at home. There was a slight knock on the wall of the partition that separated the shower from the next one, and he peered through his shampoo-blinded eyes to see Traiano smiling at him.

'Hi, handsome,' he said.

'Fuck off, handsome!' he said jocularly.

'I love you too,' replied Traiano. 'I see the other two are upstairs. I knew you were coming here, and I thought I would get to see you before you went to Church at 7am. You see. I know your habits. I always go to bed at about this time. I had better rush, as Ceccina will be waiting for me. Shall I pick you up in the car outside the church at about 9.30am? Great. Wear your smartest suit, if you have got one. I have a lot to tell you, but will tell you when we are in the car. You have got the day off work, haven't you? You won't need to take tomorrow off, in case you are wondering, as we will not be staying overnight in Donnafugata. See you.'

He was there at 9.30, on the Church steps, having gone to Mass, his daily habit, and having had a leisurely breakfast.

'Where's Calogero?' he asked, as he got into the car, noting Traiano's smart suit, a different one from yesterday.

'Not coming,' said Traiano shortly. 'He and Stefania are back again together, reconciled, thanks be to God, and what a relief for us all. I was beginning to think I could not take much more of it. He gave in. He acceded to her demands, thanks to the negotiating skills of Anna. He has promised not to see Tancredi again. So, Stefania is happy. She has won. Or

136

so she thinks. When the party ended, they retired to their bedroom and screwed like for the first time, while the children watched television.'

'He told you that?'

'He did not need to. I know. Instinct. But he did tell me that. He tells me everything. Sunday evening, when the children are occupied, that is when all couples retreat to the bedroom. In a few months, Stefania will be pregnant again. That is what she wants: her claim to be the mother of a great dynasty. Something that Tancredi will not be able to do at her age. You watch. I was on the way home to see my wife to do the same thing, when I saw you with Carolina on the church steps, having a quarrel, or so I thought.'

'What makes you think that?'

'Instinct. She has fallen in love with the boss's money and now you are wondering whether she is in love with you after all. You want to be loved for yourself. My poor Rosario.'

'As I said to you earlier this morning, fuck off!' said Rosario.

'OK. OK, I know that was not what you were talking about. You were asking her to come up to your flat, and she was refusing to do so because she had to go home and get ready to go back to Rome, or some other excuse. And you are now feeling guilty because you are eaten away with lust, and you do not like that side of yourself. Well, welcome to the real world. We are all eaten away with lust. But some of us are not eaten away with guilt as well.'

'You are married,' pointed out Rosario.

'And you soon will be. Only another eleven months. Patience, as I am sure don Giorgio says all the time.'

'Oh, fuck off!'

'One day I may well do that. Just fuck off back to Romania, and open an Italian restaurant. Change my name so no one can find me. The children can work as waiter and waitress, and Ceccina can cook. She is a very good cook. It would be a lovely life.'

'Is that what you want?'

He laughed.

'Maybe it's what Ceccina wants. Now listen, when we get to the first service station, we will stop, have coffee and I will make some phone calls.'

He did not ask who he wanted to speak to, or why it had to be from the service station. There was a payphone in the bar, and as he drank his coffee, he heard Traiano speak, and the replies coming down the line.

'Hi, handsome,' said Traiano.

'Hi, handsome,' responded the weary voice of Alfio.

'Are you alone?'

'Yeah.'

'Pity. But there you are. Listen, when are you scheduled to come back from Budapest?'

'Wednesday 22nd December. Yeah, day after tomorrow, two weeks.'

'That is pointless. Stay for longer. Christmas here will be quiet, it always is. Your teeth may need the attention. Come back in the new year.'

'Really?'

'Yes, think of all those whores you are going to bang once your teeth recover.'

'Now you mention it, it sounds like a good idea.'

'OK, great, now go back to sleep.'

'Hi, handsome,' he said a second time.

'Hi, handsome,' came Gino's voice.

'Did I wake you?'

'You did.'

'Is whoever you are with asleep, or did I wake her too?'

'She is asleep,' said Gino. 'You want to speak to her?'

'Who is she?'

'Come to think of it, her name escapes me at this moment. Polish girl. Works for you.'

'Marta or Beata?'

'Something like that.'

'Where is Catarina?'

'She told me to go to hell, so I did.'

'If it is either Marta or Beata, hell sounds better than what one was led to believe.'

'Did you call to ask me about my sex life?'

'Not directly. But now you mention it, I was thinking that you need far longer than two weeks in Budapest. I think Alfio does as well. In fact, he desperately needs it. So, take three, or four. Come back after Christmas.'

'It was Budapest that pissed off Catarina. She did not want me to go. Now that she has gone, I had better make the most of going there.'

'Exactly. So you are finished with her, this time?'

'Looks that way.'

'She was not your type. Anyway, that was the second or third time you finished, so this time make it permanent, that is my advice.'

'You always give good advice, boss.'

'All the best,' said Traiano, ringing off.

'Why are you getting rid of them?' asked Rosario.

'You will see,' he replied.

A third call followed.

'Hi, handsome.'

Hi, handsome,' replied Alfonso. 'This is a nice surprise.'

They chatted amicably for a few minutes, at the end of which it was arranged that they would call in at Syracuse on their way back from Donnafugata, by which time Alfonso would have the prints ready from yesterday's photos. They were to come to the studio, and he would meet them there.

After this interlude, they drove on in silence. They were now on the state road, half way between Lentini and Francofonte. Traiano glanced over from the driving seat, and noticed the way Rosario was playing with his mobile phone, the one Maso had given him, and at the same time looking out of the window abstractedly. Minutes passed. He wondered if he should say anything. Then, at last, Rosario began to type a text message. He paused a moment, then pressed send.

Traiano sighed.

'About time,' he remarked. 'So you didn't cancel her number from your phone?'

Before Rosario could reply, the phone pinged.

'There,' said Traiano. 'She was waiting to hear from you.'

The journey passed in silence with some desultory clicking of Rosario's phone.

'Well?' said Traiano at last.

'Why are you sending Alfio and Gino away?' Rosario asked, to change the subject as much as anything else.

'Aren't you glad? It gives you a bit of time to renew your friendship with Catarina, now her cousin and her boyfriend, or ex-boyfriend, or whatever he currently is, are out of the way. But in fact…. Your brother….' continued Traiano, in a different tone. 'He has been under a lot of pressure and has become a little unhinged. When someone is like that, you do your best to put dangerous weapons out of their way. Gino and Alfio are dangerous, they are tempting; we do not want Calogero to give them intemperate orders, shall we say. Gino in particular. He is a nasty character.'

'You always give the impression you like him.'

'I don't. I don't like many people outside my own family, apart from you and Caloriu. Maybe I pretend to like them, but I would not trust them an inch. Certainly not Gino. He is from Agrigento, and so he is not really one of us. I am glad Catarina has given him the push. She is from our quarter, and she is one of us. We need to recognise that the only people we can trust are the ones we have known all our lives. Like me and Caloriu, me and you. Alfio, maybe. Gino; not really. That Maso and his brother, I doubt it. The lawyer, never. We people from Purgatory are the lowest of the low, and that is what makes us so frightening.'

Rosario laughed.

'OK, so you are educated, but your father was a practised killer. That is the most important fact about you. The fact that you are educated, are a lawyer, that makes no difference at all. And even uneducated people like me and your brother, we are not stupid. Nor are Ceccina or Stefania. Look how well the boss is doing.'

'He is making money, yes.'

'What other measure of success is there? And people respect him. And people like Tancredi and Alfonso want to be his friends. That is not bad you know.'

'One moment you say we should stick to our own level, then you say we should be socially ambitious. Which?'

'I said we should only trust the people we have known all our lives. That is all.'

'But you don't trust them, not really, do you?' said Rosario. 'My brother uses people, then throws them away when he doesn't need them anymore.'

'He would never do that to me,' said Traiano.

'He would to me, without a moment's hesitation,' said Rosario.

'You underestimate him,' said Traiano. 'All he wants is what is good for you.'

'And what is good for me?' asked Rosario gloomily.

His gloom, his depression, was dispelled on the last leg of the drive by the careful instructions that Traiano gave him about what they were to do when they arrived at the house of Anna Maria Tancredi. He told him that he would like the house: the paintings, the books, the furniture, the olive groves and the orange groves, the swimming pool. It was quite unlike any other house either of them had ever known; perhaps it had impressed the boss. But the main thing about Tancredi, rather than her looks, her charm, and her infinite good taste, was her ability to make money for them. She was the linchpin. Everything depended on her, and they could not afford to offend her. The new office being set up under the nominal control of Stefania (though they both knew that Stefania was not the type to stay only nominally in charge) was going to be run by accountants provided by Tancredi, and what they were gathering to discuss was the business plan that she had drawn up. The boss would not be there, thanks to Stefania, but one hoped that Rosario's presence would delight her; and when she spoke, when they went through things, he would need to pay attention, so that when they went back to the boss, they could both give him an account.

They arrived. The gate was opened by Muniddu, who saw Traiano's suit and greeted him with a degree of reserve. Muniddu was still on gate duty, while Traiano had been upgraded from the garage to the dining room. There was a little resentment in his air. Nevertheless, Traiano did his best to assuage this, pausing to ask him how he was, to ask after his children and wife in Palermo, and to introduce the man he called 'my boss's brother.' Muniddu was respectful to Rosario, and pleased to shake his hand. From Traiano, he had a kiss on the cheek.

She was waiting for them in the hallway, heavily pregnant, looking a little tired, but her face animated, and, Rosario thought, charming.

'Caravaggio,' she said, allowing Traiano to kiss her cheek.

He explained the boss's absence. He was ill. He saw that she did not believe him; rather he saw how she remembered the last time and knew that such devotion was too good to continue; but she did her best to hide her disappointment; indeed, it was visible for less than a second, and only an acute observer like Traiano was able to see it. Then she turned her full attention to Rosario, taking his hand, looking at his face with care, as if to see any resemblance with his brother. There was none at all; that was clear. Rosario was taller, thinner, more angular, with a sharper, less attractive face, with somewhat untidy brown hair rather than those close cut curls which distinguished the boss. He was paler too, less healthy-looking, less at ease in his skin.

'It is so nice to see you,' she said. 'I have wanted to meet you for some time, to know the uncle of my son.'

'Being an uncle is a role I like,' he replied, at once wondering whether this was the right thing to say, bringing to mind, as it did Stefania's three children.

'And you, how are your children, Caravaggio? How was the baptism? I call him Caravaggio, because he looks like he has stepped out of one of the master's paintings. Caravaggio is my favourite artist, and as we know, he worked in Sicily.'

'She loves to flatter,' said Traiano. 'I think Alfonso has the same idea. He said I was good looking but in an unhealthy way.'

'Alfonso!' she exclaimed. 'I have not seen him for years, and indeed I doubt he would remember me. But what a man. So charming, so handsome, so talented. I have all his books, did you know? I found them the other day and I have put them all together so you can look at them after lunch. And how is he?'

'He was at the baptism. He took pictures. My mother wants to marry him.'

'Well, he is quite a catch, don't you think?'

'I do think. We are seeing him on our way back to Catania. He may have the pictures ready. I am keen to see them.'

'One day, we must all meet up. But listen,' she said, suddenly changing her tone, leading the way into the drawing room, dominated by the picture of the Immaculate Conception that immediately caught Rosario's eye. 'I have just had a phone call. A certain person is just passing this way, on his way to down to Pozzallo, he says, and wants to call in. Now, all these people who are just passing by… the other day it was the Cardinal of Palermo. They come to satisfy their curiosity about me. Well, I hope they are not disappointed. This man is using my late nephew as an excuse. He is a very senior policeman, called Colonel Andreazza. It is an informal visit, and he is coming in plain clothes. He is quite a young man still, even though a colonel. He knew poor Fabrizio. You may have heard that my nephew, who was a policeman, has disappeared. It happened in August. Calogero tells me that he is dead, and we accept that. The Romanian gang who killed so many others. Ah well. Anyway, this Andreazza is in charge of the investigation and wants to tell me in person how the investigation is going. I think it is a public relations exercise. I doubt there even is an investigation. I don't trust them, who does? No true Sicilian. Anyway, I have felt the need to invite him to stay to lunch. One does not want to give him the brush-off unnecessarily. One has to flatter their vanity. What do you say? I think it is better Calogero is not here. But you can meet him and see what you make of him.'

'Indeed,' said Traiano. 'It could be interesting. He works in Catania?'

'Yes.'

'Well, we always like to make new friends. This Colonel is unknown to us. But he may be interested. I doubt that he is coming purely to talk about Fabrizio.'

'I doubt it too,' she said. 'Too much of a coincidence.'

They made their way into the drawing room. The maid Veronica came with coffee, and Anna Maria gave her instructions about how many were coming to lunch. When they were alone, she directed them to their seats and pointed to several large files of papers, telling them to open them, and then talking them through the contents.

'It is all legal, don't worry,' she said to Rosario, seeing the look of uncertainty on his face.

She spoke, and her words were a revelation to Rosario. Also revealing, was the way that Traiano took all this in as completely normal, and asked some sharp questions. He had not thought that he was so able to grasp the extent of Calogero's organisation.

The income, she explained, was just under a million a month, but this would rise significantly over the next few years. The chief sources of revenue were the pizzeria, the two bars, the trattoria, and the rents from over a hundred properties in the Purgatory quarter and on the via Etnea. The office block and the gym were not making anything, yet, but would do so soon. Rosario cast his eye over the list of properties, noting his own, which was supposedly bringing in a rent of five hundred a month, which he had never paid. If the income was huge, the outgoings were pretty large. The single biggest one was to service the debt that Calogero had accrued, which was being paid to several banks, including Anna Maria's own. Then there was the payroll: all the people who worked in the bars and in the pizzeria, all those who did maintenance on the various properties. This accounted for several hundred people. Quite a few names jumped out at him: Traiano, Ceccina, her parents, her uncles, her aunts, Alfio, Gino, Maso, Enzo, and, to his shock, Catarina. Indeed, virtually everyone he knew seemed to be on the payroll. Traiano was being paid, he noticed, more than anyone: 12,000 a month, a suspiciously large figure. Most of the others were being paid in the hundreds, sometimes the low hundreds. Calogero was paying himself 20,000 a month, he noted. And there was provision too for himself, to the tune of 4,000 a month. For what, he wondered?

'As you can see,' said Anna Maria, 'the enterprise just breaks even, and in the future, as we buy up more properties for future development, we may head into negative territory, as we will have to borrow more. But this is a good time to borrow.'

'I see you are giving a generous amount to the Confraternity,' said Rosario.

'Money given to charity is never wasted,' said Anna Maria. 'The accounts of the Confraternity are something I would like to see. But I doubt anyone does apart from our friends in Palermo. Not even the lawyer Petrocchi.'

'The Confraternity is what keeps your mother,' said Traiano to Rosario. 'She has a pension from them. You may have noticed that she is not poor.'

This was said with a degree of bitterness that surprised Rosario. He realised that this bitterness was aimed not at his mother, but at his naivety about where the money came from. He noticed that Anna's property in Syracuse, was supposedly rented for a large amount. He was sure it was nothing of the sort.

'The Colonel will be arriving soon,' said Anna Maria brightly. 'I can't drink, but Caravaggio will have his usual Cinzano, I am sure. What will you have?' she asked Rosario.

He only drank wine, beer and mineral water, and he felt he ought to have some sophisticated reply on the tip of his tongue, some effortless riposte that would give the impression that he was used to having drinks before lunch in beautiful drawing rooms, where one discussed vast sums of money. But he could not think of what to say, and replied that he would have the same as Traiano.

She rang a little bell, Veronica re-appeared, listened to the order, and then came back with the drinks. Anna Maria drank mineral water from a heavy crystal glass. Rosario found this very alien. The only other household approaching this, he had entered, had been the lawyer Petrocchi's. But they did not have a maid who appeared at the sound of a bell. Or heavy crystal glasses.

'I see you like my Madonna,' she said to Rosario. 'I have had her a long time. She is Spanish. Like your Madonna in the Church of the Holy Souls in Purgatory, but whereas that is priceless, this is not. It is of the school of, or perhaps by some obscure painter no one knows the name of. Possibly the school of Murillo. But I like her. I bought her years ago. In fact, she was one of the first things I bought. I did not inherit her, she is mine. I have other paintings that I have inherited in my house in Palermo. They are, some of them, too valuable to move. When I came here to wait for the birth of your nephew, I brought the Madonna with me from Palermo. She looks after me. I know you are religious. That is what they call you: 'Calogero's devout brother.' Don't say you do not deserve the description; I am sure you do. Would you like to meet the Cardinal? I can arrange it. Do you ever come to Palermo? No? A pity. You must come. You can stay in my place whenever you like. Palermo is a lovely city, you know, and you must not let the bad things people say about it put you off. Perhaps you will come one day.' There was the sound of a car. 'Ah, our friend in plain clothes. This might be fun!'

She smiled. But she made sure the papers were cleared away before the policeman entered.

Colonel Andreazza was about thirty-five, of grave demeanour, perhaps prepared to visit the grieving aunt of one of his men. He was smooth-faced and well coiffured. Traiano studied him and immediately recognised the type. The Colonel was a pillar of society, at the height of his career, ambitious: he noted the neat and expensive clothes, the perfect shoes, the over tight jeans (surely a mistake, he should have been wearing a suit, but no, not a mistake, someone who was confident in meeting people like Anna Maria, someone who could wear jeans and get away with it wherever he went) the expensive shirt, the fashionable jacket, the English look – but Andreazza surely had a weak spot, and it would not take him long to find it. Hands were shaken: Colonel Andreazza was gracious, and devoted himself to their hostess with the sort of low sonorous voice one used with the bereaved. He shook hands with Rosario, then with Traiano, with an air of sudden consciousness. He knew, Traiano could judge, that he was meeting two figures, well, one really, of legend: the underboss of Catania and the brother of the boss of Catania. People he had heard about, but never met, never expected to meet, certainly not here, and, this was vitally important, Traiano could tell, people he wanted to meet. For Andreazza wanted something, even if he did not admit it to himself very often: white powder, money, prostitutes, or something at least that Traiano was sure he could provide. Perhaps he has already started on one or the other, or all three.

'You are married?' said Traiano with a friendly smile, having noticed the shiny and surely new wedding ring.

'Yes, for several years. But we have only just had our first child.'

They discussed the joys of children, marriage and fatherhood, sleepless nights, the lack of space where they lived (though they both, as it turned out, lived in three-bedroom apartments). Rosario watched the conversation, saw Traiano work his charm, saw the way Andreazza was drawn in at first warily, then eagerly. The smile, the teeth. He himself felt no reason to like the policeman, whom he thought far too smooth, almost effeminate.

'You knew Fabrizio,' Rosario said, when there was a pause in the conversation. He did not have to specify which Fabrizio he meant.

'Yes,' said Andreazza, with a sad smile, the necessary tribute to someone who they must assume was now dead. But the smile did not admit whether he liked him or not, mourned him or not. Rosario had known Perraino too, and loathed him, and he could sense that Andreazza realised that this might be the case, and was hedging his bets, all too aware of Anna Maria on the other side of the room, who presumably mourned her nephew, though not as much as one might expect. That story was well known. Did he know who the father of her child was, he wondered?

'Have you discovered anything about what really happened?' asked Rosario.

Andreazza seemed embarrassed for a moment. Traiano smiled broadly, looking away.

'We conclude the worst. His credit card was used all over the peninsula after his disappearance, to give the impression that he was alive, but that is an old trick. We think he was murdered and his body disposed of, and that it was part of a co-ordinated massacre arranged by the same people who shot the man on the beach at Cefalù and blew up the yacht off Favignana.'

'Rosario was at Cefalù, and saw the shooting happen,' put in Traiano.

'It was a big shock,' said Rosario. 'I was with my sister-in-law and her children, my nephew and two nieces. Luckily the children did not realise quite what was happening. We saw the assassins walking away. It was very odd. I heard the shots without quite realising what they were. And then we saw them walking away, and I realised by then what had happened, but I was sort of paralysed, and when they asked me for descriptions, it was hard to be specific.'

'It is often the case,' said Andreazza nodding his head sagely.

From her side of the room, Anna Maria said:

'Colonel, I have suddenly remembered where I have seen you before now. You go to Lourdes every year with the Knights of Malta, I seem to think. I go, or have been going, every year with the Cardinal and the Archdiocese of Palermo. Do you go, Rosario? Have you been, Caravaggio?'

Rosario confessed that he had never been to Lourdes, but very much wanted to go. Andreazza said he had planned to go again next year, with the Knights of Malta, but his wife having the baby made this look unlikely. Anna Maria agreed ruefully that babies constituted a disruption and an interruption, and she would not go next year either, or perhaps the year after that, but one day would go back. (This was the only reference to her pregnancy she made.) Perhaps she could take Rosario with her, and introduce him to the Cardinal. The Cardinal, she confided, was so amusing. And he loved young people. She was the oldest of his circle in Lourdes.

'You know, Caravaggio, you should come too, and bring your lovely young wife when it's possible to do so. It would do you good,' she said archly. Then she continued in a more serious tone. 'It is simply wonderful you know, the way they treat the sick and look after them. I always wanted my nephew to go as a brancardier, one of those strong young men who push the wheelchairs and the mobile beds, but he was far too flighty and pleasure-loving for that.'

'I used to be a brancardier,' said Andreazza. 'I loved it so much.'

Traiano smiled, relishing this public display of hypocrisy.

The maid came in and stood silently in the doorway. They rose for lunch. In the dining room, Anna Maria placed the Colonel on one side of her, and Traiano on the other. Rosario was opposite her. The first course was served: spaghetti alle vongole.

Rosario had never met a police colonel before now, and Andreazza sensed it. Andreazza also sensed the unspoken assumption between them, namely that the Colonel knew who Rosario was, and who his father had been. If Andreazza had spent nearly twenty years in the police, he had been a policeman before the Chemist of Catania had achieved his notoriety in death a decade ago. There was something about Rosario that acknowledged this: that he had been caught out, exposed, revealed as a fraud, and the Colonel was too polite, too correct and too kind to point this out to him. For what was he doing here, in this grand house, with this grand lady, in the presence of a Knight of Malta, with someone constantly threatening to introduce him to the Cardinal? He was, he realised, out of his depth, painfully so. He had no desire to get on in society. Traiano had the charm and the looks to gain an entry anywhere; Traiano was a criminal, and that perhaps gave him a certain reputation, but he, Rosario, did not even have that distinction.

'Colonel,' he said. 'Do you know much about the case of Salvatore Giuliano?'

'I do know a great deal about it, as a matter of fact,' said the Colonel with a smile, 'but not at first hand. He was killed in July 1950, long before I was born in 1975. But my grandfather was in the police during those years too; he knew all about it, and he told me everything he knew. He is dead now, sadly, but what he told me, I remember. You are interested in Sicily's Robin Hood?'

'Up to a point. I am more interested in why people are interested in him. I mean, my brother is obsessed with him. He carries his picture in his wallet. He loves him in the same way one loves a saint.'

At the mention of his brother, he saw the Colonel's interest was aroused.

'There was Giuliano the man and now there is Giuliano the myth, and the myth has obscured the man. The myth has absorbed parts of other myths, and made them part of its own story. The story of him and the Duchess; the story that he was on the side of the common people; the story that he was betrayed to his enemies and killed, like Christ; the story that he loved the poor, like Saint Francis. And, like King Arthur, he may not be dead, but overseas, in America, planning to come back and save us all, our once and future King, though if he is still alive, he must be very old by now. But the real Giuliano was a criminal, a bandit, a gun for hire, someone who was used by the politicians and who allowed the politicians to use him. Even the photographs of him, that show him looking so heroic: they were posed, they were calculated, everything was calculated. The person who first fell in love with Giuliano was Giuliano himself. And my grandfather said he was not very intelligent, he was naive, he was stupid, and he allowed the really clever people to use him. But he was vain, utterly vain. He was blessed with a certain measure of good looks, an adoring mother and sister, and perhaps this was what turned his head. Vanity – that is what is at the root of every criminal career.'

The others had been listening to this.

'What about him and the Duchess? Was that not true? Please tell me it was true. You'll break my heart if you tell me that was made up,' said Anna Maria.

'All made up,' said the Colonel. 'I am sorry to be the bearer of such bad news.'

'Women who live in lonely country houses, such as myself, constantly dream of bad but beautiful men coming in to rob us in such a polite and kind manner, taking our rings and wearing them to their dying day. Now you tell me it was not true, I have nothing to live for.'

'He was a mummy's boy,' said the Colonel. 'He loved his mother and his sister and no one else. The police were after him every step of the way, and he hardly ever saw them. If you go to Montelepre, the place he came from, they will tell you that he was the lover of every woman for miles around, and the putative father of numerous children, all sons. It is a load of nonsense. His main vice was vanity, and I doubt he ever loved anyone. My grandfather, who knew some of his associates, was of the opinion....'

The Colonel made a waving motion with his hand.

'Ah, you break my heart,' said Anna Maria. 'Such a handsome man, but as you point out, clearly aware of it. That is so often the way.'

Traiano looked at the Colonel, and smiled impudently. Andreazza looked away, momentarily embarrassed. Veronica came in and removed the plates. Shortly afterwards, an enormous platter of fried fish of all descriptions appeared.

'It is Monday not Friday, but it is the 6th December, and the day after tomorrow is the feast of the Immaculate Conception, so it is always a time of abstinence from meat before a major feast, as I am sure I do not have to remind you,' said Anna Maria, to a murmur of appreciation.

'The lemons are yours?' asked Traiano.

'Indeed. I am self-sufficient in citrus fruit and in olives and in olive oil. Not that I make the oil myself, you understand…. A man comes and does that for me; he harvests the olives and then gives me a huge container of oil that lasts all year. I will get Veronica to give you all a bottle before you go, then you can see how good it is.'

'Our wives will be thrilled,' said Traiano. 'Not Rosario's, as he has not got one just yet. But he is engaged.'

'Caravaggio, as you call him, always likes to embarrass me in public,' said Rosario, who seemed to be displeased by this mention of his engagement.

'The lemons are wonderful,' said Traiano. 'With your permission, us two married men should be allowed to pick a few after lunch to take to our wives as presents. A lemon is a romantic present, don't you think?'

'By all means, by all means… Go out and explore after lunch. Help yourself to whatever you can carry away.'

Once more Traiano regarded Andreazza with meaning.

'You are thinking of Goethe?' said the Colonel.

'Of course,' said Traiano, who had never heard of Goethe.

Rosario had heard of Goethe. He quoted:

'Do you know the land where lemon trees blossom;

where golden oranges glow amid dark leaves?

A gentle wind blows from the blue sky,

the myrtle stands silent, the laurel tall:

do you know it?

There, O there

I desire to go with you, my beloved!'

There was silence when the quotation ended.

'More talk of romance,' she said.

In the meantime, the fish was delicious, particularly the octopus, the prawns and the mussels. The conversation moved to the idea that the day after tomorrow's feast was a public holiday, meaning that no one had done any work today, Monday, but made the bridge between the weekend and the Wednesday. As if the people of Sicily needed encouragement not to work! It was their great weakness. People in Milan and Turin would not be taking today off, they were all sure. But here in the beautiful south, where there was better weather, where everything was so much nicer, could one be blamed for sitting long over the lunch table, particularly when the food was so good? In the north, they were not true Italians, but more Germanic, more like the Swiss…

Coffee arrived, and sweet little biscuits. Lunch had gone on long enough, and the Colonel expressed his regret, but he would have to be off soon.

'So soon?' said Anna Maria.

It was clear that she and the Colonel had some things to discuss in private, and thus the other guests got up from the table and went through to the drawing room. Rosario took up a book, while Traiano lay back on the comfortable sofa and shut his eyes, deep in thought. Some minutes passed, then the Colonel entered with their hostess.

'Well, it has been lovely. You are sure you cannot stay to tea at four? I have to lie down, because of my condition, but I am sure Caravaggio and Rosario will stay and amuse themselves for an hour or so.'

'I would love to see the lemon groves,' said the Colonel, looking at Traiano.

'Perfect,' said Anna Maria.

Anna Maria retired upstairs. Traiano gave Rosario a covert look. Rosario took up one of the books – the books of Alfonso's photographs – and pretended that he had no interest whatever in seeing the orchards, no matter how fine the lemons were.

'Let us go and look at the lemons,' Traiano said brightly.

Andreazza was swift to take up this invitation.

'Wait till we are out of sight,' said Traiano in a low voice, as they strolled through the garden.

They were soon sheltered by the high orchard wall, and looking round, seeing that they were not in view of the house any more, Andreazza pressed himself against Traiano and tried to kiss him. The smell of

Andreazza's aftershave and his clothing was overpowering; he moved his face away, but felt his lips graze his cheek.

'I am married, and so are you,' said Traiano, pushing him away, but not too roughly. 'Besides, you need to remember that I am carrying a knife, and I can use it, so don't get too carried away. Besides which, I am far too old for you.'

'How old are you?' asked the policeman.

'Seventeen next summer,' said Traiano. 'I married young, unlike you. You were very wicked stroking me with your foot under the table during lunch. It was my foot you were aiming for, not Rosario's? Thought so. Not our hostess's either. Though I am sure she found you simply charming. As do I. Charming and potentially useful.'

The Colonel nodded, unable to speak.

'What do you want?' asked the Colonel eventually.

'We should first of all establish what you want,' said Traiano. 'I suppose we have done that. I can get you what you want, very easily. There would be little risk involved for you. I would be the one doing the dirty work. There are lots of young boys in our quarter who will do as they are told and who are open to inducements. Teenagers, sometimes less than teenagers. Their mothers are dependent on us, the children never go to school, well, you can understand perhaps how easy it is to arrange. For them it is a way of getting on… as I am sure you have heard.'

'Is that how you first got on?' asked Andreazza.

Traiano looked at him with cold fury for a moment.

'Have you ever been stabbed?' he asked. 'It hurts like hell, as I know from experience. Please remember I am the one with the knife. You are unarmed. You are the supplicant here.'

In fact, the knife was in the glovebox of the car, but Andreazza did not know that.

'What do you want to know?' asked Andreazza in more accommodating tones. 'What do you want from me?'

'Good, you are being reasonable. And there is so much for you to gain. First of all, I want you to co-operate with us. Oh please, it is not that bad, and really you have no choice. We have lots of your colleagues working for us, as I am sure you know, though none as high ranking as you. You are quite a catch, Colonel. There are lots of things we can give you to make it rewarding for you. Trust me on that. Things much better than trying and failing to kiss me.'

Andreazza groaned in despair.

'Your secret is safe,' said Traiano with a cold smile. 'Let us look at these lemon trees, and pick some fruit for our wives. Now, I want the truth. What do you lot know about Perraino's murder?'

'That it was murder. That you did it. That there is no proof, and never will be.'

'If there is no proof, how can you possibly suspect us, or do you mean me in the singular?'

'You did it, or Calogero did it, or one of his thugs. He disappeared on a Saturday night, before the Romanians started their massacre. That was the clue. And he was last seen in Catania. The massacres all happened elsewhere. It follows the Romanians did not have a hit squad in Catania. Besides, you had the motive. He had locked you up some time before, hadn't he? And he had humiliated your boss's brother. He might have had something to do with it.'

'Rosario? You have just met him. Don't be ridiculous. As you say, there is no proof. Anyone could have killed him. He could have driven across Sicily that Saturday and been anywhere. His car. Where was that?'

'On the slopes of Etna, burned out. Anyone could have dumped it there.'

'So what are the police going to do?'

'Nothing.'

'Really? Nothing?'

'Worse than nothing. We are regarding this as a missing person's case. If it is a murder, and it remains unsolved, it is bad for the statistics. Of course, we know it was murder, but why give your boss the credit for such a crime? Besides, everyone loathed him. He was a troublemaker when alive. Now he is dead, we are not going to take any trouble over him.'

'And what do the police think of my boss?'

162

'We think he is clever. We think he is vain. We think he will overreach himself. We think that one day the people in Palermo will have enough of him and kill him.'

'What do they think of me?'

'They think you are the brains behind the operation, as well as the muscle, that you are cleverer than Calogero and that one day you may kill him.'

'That will never happen,' said Traiano, laughing.

'What would be interesting to know is what your boss thinks of you, and what you think of him,' observed Andreazza.

Once again that cold look crossed Traiano's face.

'It is not something you people could ever understand,' he said, dismissively. 'There is something else that is far more interesting. Are any of our people working for the police? Ah, you had to think of the right answer, didn't you? That tells me you know something.'

He waited.

'Volta. Fabio Volta,' said Andreazza.

'I know him. Is he a friend of yours?'

'My wife knows his girlfriend. They are friends. I know him. We are not close, but we know each other.'

'In short, you cannot stand the man. Tell me everything you know about Volta.'

'Volta was a policeman, and he has lots of contacts in the force still. I know him quite well, as we were colleagues once. The girlfriend is a policewoman. He is obsessed with your boss and wants to bring him down.'

'He is all talk,' said Traiano.

'He claims to have someone on the inside of your organisation,' continued Andreazza.

This caught Traiano's attention. He paused in the act of picking a lemon, and looked at Andreazza.

'But I do not know who. Sometimes he hints that he knows stuff thorough this source. Sometimes he hints that he is playing a long game, trying to find out about Palermo, Rome and Brussels, where the real power is, not Catania. This is all rumour, but it is what I hear. The person he has is near your organisation, but not in it. We are sure of this, because Volta has no idea who the police on your payroll are. So we think Volta is talking to one of the women or one of the lawyers. But he is talking to someone. Unless of course it is all a bluff, an empty boast.'

Traiano realised he had stumbled upon more than he had expected. He was quiet and thoughtful. The lawyers? Could that mean Petrocchi? Or Rossi? The women? Could that mean Elena, or Assunta, or Stefania, or Catarina, or his own wife? But what did they know? It all seemed too fantastical. He said nothing. He concentrated on the lemons, trying to find the nicest and juiciest ones.

'My wife will be delighted with these,' he said, having selected three of the fruit.

Andreazza began to look for lemons too. When he had found some, enough for his wife too, he turned and saw Traiano leaning against the orchard wall, an abstracted look in his eyes.

'Are you sure that Volta has a source close to my boss?' he asked. 'Are you sure he is not just boasting in an idle moment, wanting to give the impression that he knows more than he does?'

Andreazza shrugged.

'His girlfriend told my wife, and then regretted telling her, and begged her not to tell anyone else. Of course, she told me. It could be true. Or it could be as you say.'

'Where have you been?' said Rosario, with a touch of asperity, laying his book aside, when Traiano came into the room. 'Where is the Colonel? What have you done with him?'

'Too many questions,' said Traiano. 'I have been talking to the Colonel, as you call him, and getting him to do something for me, or more accurately for your brother. Right now, I feel extremely exhausted. Colonel Andreazza was hard work. Right now, if Ceccina was here, she would take me in her arms and tell me how much she loved me.'

He sat down next to him on the sofa.

'I am not Ceccina,' said Rosario.

Together they looked at the book. The photographs were of naked girls, all very young, all very blonde. Some of them were standing in waterfalls, some were coming out of the sea, all were wet, with slicked back hair, and water droplets on their beautiful tanned skin. Each one had a look of total and utter innocence on her face. The arms of each one hung down at the sides with palms turned outwards, emphasising their welcoming purity. Their breasts were small, perfect, their nipples inviting.

'They are beautiful,' said Traiano. 'Alfonso has an eye. Have you ever seen anyone as beautiful as that? Turn back that page.'

'Have you?'

'Yes, my wife.'

'Are you faithful to her?'

'Absolutely. Not looked at anyone else ever. Why would I? Ceccina is perfect. Not even in my imagination. Not even pictures. You are leading me astray.'

'There is another book, with pictures of churches in Noto. I just opened this one a moment before you came in.'

'Sure you did. You are a hopeless liar,' said Traiano. 'You have had so little practice. Have you ever in fact told a lie?'

'You know I have. To the police, when they interviewed me about my brother killing Vitale.'

'Have you ever told me a lie?' persisted Traiano.

'Never.'

'Would you ever?'

'No. Though I might tell you to mind your own business. Can I turn the page?'

'Sure. Would you ever do anything to hurt me?'

'What has brought this on?' asked Rosario. 'I have known you since you were three years old. I am your daughter's godfather. Sworn to protect and love her. What did you say about trusting the people we have been brought up with and only them? You were the one who hurt me, by shooting me in the leg. I am not capable of hurting you.'

Traiano sighed.

'Show me the book with the churches of Noto,' he said. 'I know you prefer churches to naked girls.'

'You know I like both,' said Rosario. 'So where is the Colonel?' he asked again.

'He came and he went; he made his excuses and said he had to leave. I will be seeing him again. I didn't like him. Did you? Well might you shrug your shoulders. As I say, he is a shit and a hypocrite, but a useful man to know. He makes me feel bad.'

'Bad? Why?' asked Rosario.

'He just does,' said Traiano. 'You do not want to know.'

But he was wrong there. Rosario had a strong desire to know. The house was quiet, the meal had been heavy, dealing with Andreazza had been strenuous, and the book was restful, and Traiano sprawled back on the sofa. He could feel the force of Rosario's curiosity. His face was impassive, but it alarmed him. One not in their organisation, one of the women perhaps, one of the lawyers perhaps was talking to Volta. But....

'We need this Andreazza,' he said at last. 'He is too good an opportunity to miss. He wanted to get me on my own; I wanted to get him on his own. I wanted to know about the Perraino case, and he wanted something else entirely. Well, I found out about the Perraino case; it is not a case at all; they are not doing anything. That interests us, as it is something they might otherwise try to pin on us. As for Andreazza, he is disgusting. One day I will take the greatest pleasure imaginable in sticking a knife in his guts.'

'You mean….?'

Traiano nodded.

'That is horrid,' said Rosario. 'I thought there was something a little bit strange about him.'

They were both profoundly silent for some time.

'I will be fine when we get home,' said Traiano. 'You should get married to Carolina as soon as you can manage it. It is the cure for everything. When I am with Ceccina, I forget business, I forget work, I forget my mother, I forget my father, I forget my childhood. I even forget Calogero.'

'I wish I could forget Calogero,' said Rosario.

Traiano shut his eyes. Why had he asked Andreazza if there were anyone on the inside of their organisation who was betraying them? Why had he asked? He felt himself fall into a troubled doze.

When he woke up, it was to feel that he had slept deeply, though he had hardly been asleep for any length of time. Generally, he was awake all night and asleep all day, but today had been different. He opened his eyes gradually, aware that he was in a strange place and that he could hear the sounds of someone turning the pages of a book. Then he heard the rattle of tea cups, and he was aware that there were two people in the room with him now, one of whom must be Rosario and the other Anna Maria. He opened his eyes. He felt a terrible heaviness of heart at the thought of what he had learned from Andreazza. Why had he asked that question? What would now happen? Who was Volta's contact? He thought he knew, but the knowledge he had was not the knowledge he wanted. He remembered the glances, the nod of recognition exchanged outside the Church of the Holy Souls in Purgatory after the baptism. He dreaded what was now going to happen. Gradually he opened his eyes wider and tried to rouse himself. He allowed himself a slight smile.

Seeing he was awake, Anna Maria said:

'We were talking about my nephew Fabrizio.'

She handed him a cup of tea, which he gratefully accepted.

'We?' he asked wearily. 'You and Rosario?'

'Yes. But also me and the Colonel.'

'Oh good. And what did he say?'

'That it was murder, and that he will use his best efforts to try and get the case moved from that of a missing person to that of a murder.'

'But there is no body,' said Traiano sleepily. 'I forgot to ask, what exactly does Colonel Andreazza specialise in? Not traffic, I imagine?'

'He is in charge of murder for the whole of Catania, for the province, for the whole east of Sicily, I think. So, if anyone can get the case moving, it is him.'

And if anyone can stall the case, it is him, thought Traiano to himself.

'Do you think Palermo had anything to do with it?' asked Traiano casually.

'I hope not. Why should they? Besides, Palermo has its own problems. Ever since don Carlo Santucci died so tragically with his friends off the coast of Favignana…' She looked at Rosario. 'Do you know the history of the Palermo family?' He shook his head, in a way that signified he did not know but wanted to know. 'It's interesting,' she said. 'Don't worry, it is all ancient history,' she added, looking at Traiano. 'But the sort of history you should know. It started before the Second World War. There were two brothers called Santucci, originally from Montelepre, who lived on the outskirts of Palermo, quite near a place you may know, the church that contains the body of Saint Benedict the Moor, the secondary patron of the city. A lovely place, with beautiful views, you should both of you visit, especially you, Rosario. These two brothers grew lemons, and exported them. As it happened, they were very tough men, and they soon controlled the lemon production of a vast swathe of territory, and the exportation of lemons as well, principally to New York. Every time, they say, someone had a gin and tonic in the Algonquin Hotel, they were using one of the Santucci lemons. Other lemon growers went out of business as their product rotted on the dockside, or was stolen, or their trees were burned, or some other bad luck befell them. Then the war came, and the Americans came and the contacts with New York were resumed, and after the war they went into the import and export of anything and everything, especially cars, but lemons as well, and wine and cheese. But it was the New York connexion that made everything they touched turn to gold. New York trusted them; the American troops trusted them, and the politicians trusted them because the Yankees did. At that time, after the War, the Americans were pouring money into anyone in Italy who was anti-communist. The Santucci brothers were certainly that. So they prospered. In the next generation, the two brothers each had two sons. There were numerous female relatives, but they counted for very little, until perhaps the present day. Two of those sons still live: they are the father and uncle of Antonio Santucci, who are called Lorenzo and Domenico. One of their cousins fathered Carlo Santucci, and Antonio married his second cousin, Carlo's sister, whose name I can never remember. You will know from history that when dynasties decline, they are, in the end, taken over by women and children. Carlo is dead, and there are only two active age adult males left in the family, Antonio and his nephew, more importantly his wife's nephew and his cousin once removed, Renzo Santucci. You met Renzo, you remember, here, Traiano. Carlo was the more clever and capable, and the more liked; Antonio was always in his shadow. And now, not only does Antonio feel under pressure, he also has to deal with his wife, his sister-in-law and his mother-in-law and all the other females lamenting the death of Carlo and, of course, Carlo's son, Renzo, snapping at his heels. So, you see, the family dynamic is not good. And it is affecting the business. My father was their banker too: goodness knows what he would have made of it.'

'I do not like Carlo,' said Traiano. 'The nephew I just saw that once, here, with you. He seems alright. But... as you say, dynasties decline. They become soft and they forget their origins, and they think they are great people who are entitled to respect, a respect they have never earned. They have an easy life, they become spoilt. Then the barbarians take over.'

'Quite,' said Anna Maria.

'Maybe Renzo has some sort of potential, but Antonio is past it,' said Traiano dismissively. 'But, of course, he is useful to us,' he added quickly. 'The link in the chain, to New York, to Rome, to Brussels. But as you imply, a weak link.'

'One can replace weak links to strengthen the chain. Lots of people will be thinking of that,' said Anna Maria. She smiled and looked at Rosario. 'It has been such a pleasure meeting you,' she said.

There was silence. Tea was over and it was time to leave. They gathered up all the files of papers, and, after saying goodbye to Anna Maria at the door of the house, walked towards the car. The papers were placed on the back seat. Traiano took off his jacket to drive, and placed that on the back seat as well. Muniddu appeared, to open the gate. He had been lying in wait.

Traiano, never one to neglect someone who might one day be useful, gave him a warm embrace. Not to seem stand-offish, Rosario shook his hand.

'How was it?' he asked.

'Fine. Good meeting. She is well, I am glad to see. I am looking forward to seeing the baby, and so is Rosario.'

'The Colonel?' asked Muniddu.

'Very interesting. Very useful. How are things in Palermo?' he asked.

Muniddu looked at him knowing that this question meant more than it signified.

'I am going back there. Did you hear? Don Antonio says he needs me. He is beefing up his security. Round the clock from now on. He thinks someone might be trying something one of these days. After his brother-in-law was murdered, he has become very nervous. And maybe the lady herself is going back for Christmas to Palermo too.'

Traiano and Muniddu looked at each other with understanding. Neither made any comment, but both understood. Traiano embraced him again, then he and Rosario got into the car.

'Nice chap,' he remarked to Rosario, as they prepared to drive off.

'Really?' said Rosario, who was now busy checking his phone.

'What have you been saying to Catarina?' asked Traiano. 'What has she been saying to you?'

'Never you mind,' said Rosario.

Traiano giggled.

'You are evil,' said Rosario.

'Why?'

'You put bad ideas into my head.'

'Those bad ideas were there all along,' said Traiano. 'They just needed a little encouragement to come out. When are you seeing Catarina?'

'Wednesday, the day Gino and Alfio fly off.'

'That was quick. If you have an ounce of gallantry, you will save that poor girl from that evil bastard Gino. She is one of our own, from the quarter. I like her. And she is clever.'

'I like her too,' said Rosario.

They drove on in silence, heading towards Syracuse. As they passed Noto on the motorway, Traiano remarked that that was where he and the boss had first met Anna Maria Tancredi.

'From what she said about Palermo,' said Rosario. 'It seems to me that things are entering an unstable period.'

'Yes, I agree.'

'A dangerous period.'

'Agreed. But for whom? For Antonio Santucci, perhaps. He is increasing his bodyguard. For other people the danger is an opportunity.'

'You mean for my brother?'

'For Calogero, and for me. It is a bit like when companies go bust or have a hard time, they become ripe for a takeover bid, sometimes a hostile takeover bid.'

'So, he is right to be afraid?'

'Why does it interest you?'

'If my brother is in danger, should that not interest me?' asked Rosario.

'Of course, you are interested in the money. Without that, no one would want to marry you, and without your brother, Petrocchi would not want you either.'

'Maybe.'

'You hate him, admit it,' said Traiano. 'But you never will admit it. You are too much of a hypocrite.'

'If you were his brother....'

'I'd hate him too? But I am more than his brother. I am his right hand.'

'You love him,' said Rosario sadly.

'Passionately.'

'He killed your father.'

'Anna did that. I never knew my father. I do not care about that. I care about my children and my wife and Caloriu. Anyone who threatened them, I would kill. And that includes Santucci. But not just Santucci, anyone.'

'You would resort to murder?'

'What do you think? What did your father do for you? What did your brother do for you?'

'I didn't ask them. They did it for themselves.'

'You are wrong. Everything we do we do for the people we love. But sometimes they are not grateful, because they do not love us. Ingratitude is the greatest sin of all.'

They had arrived in Syracuse and had driven to the centre of the island of Ortygia, where they were to meet Alfonso. By the greatest good luck, they found a parking place by the fountain of Diana, where the afternoon shopping crowds had long dispersed, and then they walked the short distance to the studio in via Roma, behind the Cathedral. It was nearly closing time, and the street was empty. Alfonso was waiting for them as they entered the brightly lit studio from the darkening street. Greetings were exchanged. Alfonso shook Rosario's hand; he kissed Traiano's cheek.

The studio walls were covered with the work of the master, and dominating the entire room was the photograph of Anna, naked, standing with the fountain of the nymph Arethusa behind her, at night, brightly illuminated. This picture, in black and white (most of the pictures were black and white) dominated the wall facing the entrance, and the eye was irresistibly drawn to the figure of the naked woman, her soft bosom, her wonderful and enticing vagina. That vagina in fact dominated the shop, and all the other pictures merely served to frame it. Rosario could not take his eyes off it. It reminded him, incongruously, of the way the Church of the Holy Souls in Purgatory, so full of baroque splendours, served as an elaborate frame for the picture of the Spanish Madonna; and how the picture itself drew your eye to the compassionate face of the Mother of God. But this was different. One was drawn to Anna's chief attraction, something that had been loved, worshipped and adored by so many men who had come in almost blasphemous pilgrimage. It was enough to make you forget God, the world, everything, if one could only have that.

'Nice, eh?' murmured Traiano behind him, referring to his mother's nakedness.

'She always makes an impact,' said Alfonso. 'Lots of people come into the shop just to see her. I tell them that the original lives just a few streets away. The police even came in. They said it was obscene, which of course it most certainly is not. I told them she was my fiancée, and they said that was alright. Amazing how their minds work.'

They went into the room at the back, which was the work room, and here Alfonso showed them what they had come to see, the pictures from the baptism. With great care, Traiano examined the ones of himself and the children, of which there were dozens, trying to decide which he wanted printed.

'There is always something so sad about family photographs,' said Alfonso.

'Why?' asked Traiano.

'Everyone looks so happy, and one fears there will come a time in the future when one will look at these pictures and say 'That was when we are happy, and now...''

'Why rush to meet that which we should most avoid?' asked Traiano. 'Why dwell on future disaster? It may never happen. Besides, you seem to overlook the fact that this family happiness has me to defend it. God help anyone who tries to harm my wife, myself and my children. I like this one. The suit looks good.'

He was pictures seated, legs apart, with Ceccina resting against his thigh.

'Nice smile,' said Alfonso. 'I thought that one was good too. It shows your character.'

Traiano was flattered that Alfonso thought he had any character to show.

The best family photos were rapidly picked out after that. Then they looked at the pictures of Traiano, Calogero and Saro; each had been photographed with the other.

'These, I think, also betray character,' said Alfonso.

In all of them, the boss was serious, withdrawn, handsome and menacing, his expression unchanging, whether Traiano or Saro were next to him. It was as if he cared for neither of them, but was unaware of them, even if Traiano were hanging on his arm and laughing. He looked at the camera with suspicion, as if it were a policeman come to interview him, or a prosecution lawyer come to question him. He looked like a cold, controlled man determined to give nothing away. But they had all known this – the camera merely revealed what they already knew.

Traiano, by contrast, was smiling and laughing, and not standing still, either leaning forwards or sideways or backwards, his arm around the boss's waist, his arm hanging round Rosario's shoulder, or trying to make him laugh by grabbing him by the arm. As for Rosario, trying his best to smile, to look at his ease, it was clear that he too regarded the business of being photographed as a risk, and was doing his best to conceal his lack of confidence.

'It is clear,' said Traiano, 'That the boss loves his brother and loves me, but does not want to show it, because he thinks that would betray weakness, and he wants to be thought a great and important man. But he is not such a good actor, and I know him better than that. As for Saro, it is plain that his brother and I both love him, in our different ways, but this makes him uncomfortable.' He turned to Rosario. 'You need to relax.'

Alfonso nodded.

'The best ones are these,' he said, leading them to another table.

In silence all three of them examined the pictures of Maso and Enzo.

'You cannot display these,' said Rosario at length. 'They are too raw. I mean they are good, easily the best, but they are too frightening.'

'I suspected they were, you know, more than just brothers,' said Traiano evenly.

'That crude reaction is exactly what I mean when I say you can't show anyone these. They are too intimate, too liable to misinterpretation by low minds.'

'I took dozens - these are the best ones,' said Alfonso. 'I think this one could win competitions.'

In it, Maso's huge eyes swam with tears as he wrapped his powerful arms around the almost foetal form of his brother who was not looking at the camera. Both brothers were shirtless. In another, Enzo's eyes, terrified, stared at the camera, as if it were a gun raised to shoot him, while his brother's forearms were raised to protect him.

'Despite what Traiano says,' said Alfonso, 'I think of these pictures as icons of brotherly love. The nakedness is just to emphasise their vulnerability. The pictures raise questions. Who is the most vulnerable, the most frightened of the world? The poor autistic boy (that is what I assume he is) who cannot look at the world, so terrifying does he find it? Or the brother who has to protect him, and fears he may in the end fail, that his brother, despite all his efforts, cannot be protected? It was quite interesting to see the way both of them bared their soul for the camera. This is the sort of thing all photographers look for, but only find once in a while.'

'And what about me?' asked Traiano. 'You are saying I did not bare my soul?'

'You did not.'

'Thank God for that.'

'Was it hard to get them to strip?'

'They only took off their shirts, but yes. Very.'

'Unlike Anna, eh?'

'That is just a picture of a beautiful woman. These are pictures that make you wonder what beauty is.'

'I was joking,' said Traiano. 'And about them sleeping together too. I don't dislike Maso. I just think he is a fool. A middle-class boy who has seen too many crime movies and who wants to be a criminal, as if it were a game. We were looking at your books earlier today,' he continued, changing the

181

subject. 'The one about Noto Cathedral, which we both liked, and the one about the naked girls standing in waterfalls. We liked that one too. You could perhaps give us their telephone numbers.'

Chapter Six

Calogero stood in front of the mirror in the bathroom, studying his face. It was nine in the morning. He could hear the front door slam, as his wife Stefania left with the children: Isabella and Natalia to go to school, Renato to the nursery, and she to her brand new office, a large open plan space, filled with potted palms, the top floor of the refurbished building that had the gym in its basement. He would perhaps go to the office later, but he knew there were more important things to catch up on and understand before he did so. He sensed that, though the front door was now closed, there was someone in the flat, and he knew who. In a few moments Traiano appeared in the mirror behind him.

There was silence.

'You have got up very early. You must have lots to tell me,' said Calogero, taking up his toothbrush.

Traiano nodded. He watched the boss brush his teeth.

'Why did you do it?' he asked at length.

Calogero waited until he had laid the toothbrush aside. He knew what he meant. From now on, the toothbrush, with its hard pointed but blunt handle, would always be the weapon that had finished off Antonescu senior in the Bucharest prison showers. As he put his own toothbrush down, Calogero had a moment of vision, of the hard plastic being rammed into his chest cavity, a relatively easy thing for a strong man to do. Traiano could perhaps do that right now, given that he was defenceless, here in the bathroom, just as Michele Lotto had been defenceless in Anna's bathroom. But he knew Traiano would never kill him.

He turned and faced him, and he put both his hands on the younger man's shoulders.

'I did it because Antonescu was a useless piece of shit. I did it because I could do it, and it was a useful exercise of power. I did it as a favour to Anna, and I did it as a favour to you. You are better off without him.'

'I suppose so,' admitted Traiano. 'Do you think Anna would ever betray us?'

'Is that what worries you? No, I do not think so, because in betraying us, she would betray herself. She would be an accessory to murder. Besides, why would she want to send her own son to jail for a very long time? Or me even? I am the one who keeps her, or have been up to now. No, Anna will never betray us, though she will make us pay a high price for her silence.'

'Perhaps not now,' said Traiano.

'What do you mean?'

'She is getting married, to Alfonso, she said so last night. She told me, and Saro was there too, and Alfonso as well.'

'We knew that. That is her idea. I wonder what Alfonso thinks. Can he be such a fool? Now, go into the kitchen and make some coffee while I get into the shower.'

'No, boss, she is really marrying him. Not what you call a white marriage. They are sleeping together, or planning to. They are going to have child.'

Calogero frowned as he turned on the shower. He was not sure if this was good news or bad. He prepared to take off his dressing gown. Traiano was still there.

'Coffee, now,' he commanded.

Fifteen minutes later they were in the kitchen, with the coffee.

'I am not so displeased,' said Calogero. 'Having given it some thought, it might make her more stable. It will be good for your little brother Salvatore. It might mean we have to worry about Anna a lot less. Is she giving up her profession?'

Traiano explained what had happened over dinner last night. After visiting the studio and looking at the pictures, they had gone to Alfonso's house in the via della Giudecca, a very beautiful flat, full of antique furniture and paintings, where Anna and Salvatore were now living. She had given up her old men. In fact, one of the old men had died, and several had become progressively less and less active, amongst whom was Alfonso's father, her future father-in-law. She had decided she wanted another child, and Alfonso, at the age of fifty, decided that he too wanted a child, and so they were determined to produce one together. Both, it seemed, were determined to give up any outside interests.

'I may have to give that property by the fountain of Arethusa to someone else,' said Calogero. 'Well, lucky Anna, snaring a man like that; a man too who, on the whole, is immune to feminine charm. But he is an artist. He has brought in a great prize. He is marrying his muse. When is this happening?'

'Some time after Christmas. But they are starting the attempt to create a child right now.'

'Babies, babies, everywhere,' said Calogero. 'Is Ceccina pregnant again?'

Traiano shrugged.

'It is still a bit early.' He had only just left his wife. He smiled as he remembered making love to her before the children woke up. 'What about Stefania?' he asked.

Calogero frowned again, remembering the experience of making love to Stefania last night.

'She may be already, and if not, she will be soon. She wants to go to New York for Christmas. That is a sign. She loves travel, and she is obviously calculating getting a holiday in before she is too big to go anywhere. I would quite like to go to New York too. Why not? And talking of all that, how is my brother?'

'He was exchanging text messages in the car as we drove to Donnafugata. With her. They are meeting up tomorrow, as soon as Gino is out of the way.'

'Did you sneak a look at his phone?' asked Calogero. 'Those mobile phones tell you everything.'

'I didn't need to. He told me himself that he was meeting up with her. But I did have a look when he went to the bathroom at the service station on the way back, when he left his phone in his jacket pocket. His messages to her are quite passionate. It made embarrassing reading. I did not know he had it in him. The things people say.'

'I am glad to hear that he does have it in him,' said Calogero. 'I sometimes wonder if he is my brother. Did you find out anything else, anything useful, who he is talking to?'

'Most of it was work related, or messages to Carolina. Nothing interesting at all.'

'Were you hoping to find something interesting?' asked Calogero.

Traiano shrugged.

'By the way,' he said, changing the subject. 'I told Gino and Alfio to stay in Hungary until after Christmas.'

'Why? You do not like them anymore?'

'No. Because I know, if you want to use them on a certain job…. well, that would be better put off till January at the earliest. There is nothing wrong with waiting. I have put your deadliest weapons beyond your reach.'

Calogero smiled.

'But you are still here,' he said.

'Yes, because what you need now is a very skilful surgery with a sharp knife, not a sledgehammer coming down on a walnut. You remember how Gino and Alfio got rid of Perraino? How they cooked him and then Gino crushed his skull and other bones? Brute strength, but not much brain or skill. And they are asking questions about Perraino.'

'Who is?'

'Tancredi.'

He explained what had happened yesterday.

'Well, we know he is not a missing person. But if they keep him as such, that would be good. We can talk to Palermo. Someone there can pull strings, lose the file, whatever it is they do. But if you have this Colonel under your control, there would be no need to involve Palermo. Good work with the Colonel. He could be a very valuable asset to us.'

'Do you think this flat is bugged?' asked Traiano.

'Of course not. How could it be? No one comes in here, no suspicious characters, apart from ourselves. No one reads the meter without me standing over them, or fixes the gas, or any other thing that could be used as a cover for planting devices.'

'Except Maso and Enzo.'

'Except Maso and Enzo. But Stefania was with them the entire time, and she knows that people must never be left unsupervised. Besides, don't you trust them?'

'I don't trust anyone apart from you, boss,' said Traiano. 'And you the same. When we were lying in wait for Lotto, you could have killed me, and I could have killed you. But neither of us did, and neither of us ever will. But others can betray us. What do we know about Maso? What do we know about his loyalty?'

'You do not think that Maso is a threat,' said Calogero reasonably. 'Here you are, sitting in my kitchen, drinking coffee, talking of the murder we committed, something you would not do unless you were sure that no one was listening. Unless, of course, you want to talk about Lotto to get me to incriminate myself, because you know someone is listening. But I doubt that, because you and I are equally guilty with regard to Lotto.'

'Yes, but I was not eighteen, boss, and you do not have the excuse of youth on your side. They would blame you more than me. But you are right, I don't think anyone is listening, but if someone were, and if I were suspicious, then I would think it was Maso. He is not from this quarter, he is not one of us. His brother is an expert at electronics. They have fitted this flat out with a computer, with Wi-Fi, and the office too. If someone wanted to spy on you, that is the way they would do it. And they have offered us all phones, even if we have not taken them, even if we have passed them on. Maso steals them, and Enzo wipes them clean, and then Alfio takes them to a phone shop in the via Etnea where they are packaged and sold as new. Nice little earner. What I am saying, boss, is that if some enemy wanted to get inside our organisation, they might use Maso to do so.'

'But it would not work,' said Calogero. 'I do not have a phone. None of us have phones. God forbid I catch any of you using a mobile or a computer.... If I did, I would teach them a lesson. There is too much chatter in the world. There can't be enough silence for us. Even this conversation is dangerous.'

189

'The police cannot touch you,' said Traiano. 'Lotto, Carmine del Monaco, Turiddu, Ino, these were all perfect crimes, crimes which had no real witnesses, no evidence trail. Oh, and Vitale. Stefania and Rosario gave you your alibi for that supposed crime, and they would never betray you, would they?'

'Stefania knows nothing,' he said. 'My brother knows, but, as you say, he would never betray me.'

'How does he know?' asked Traiano, a touch sharply.

'I told him,' said Calogero quietly. 'He forced me to admit it. It was when he came back from Rome. He said he knew about Vitale, because that night I came home and got into the bed next to him, I smelt of petrol. I told him that he was a hypocrite, because he was happy to live off the proceeds of murder. I meant my father, of course, but... he knew what I meant, and I knew what I meant. He lied for me about Vitale's killing. Having lied once, he has to keep on lying.'

There was a long silence. It seemed to Calogero that standing between himself and a jail sentence was the ability of his brother to keep on lying. The only comfort was that for a consummate hypocrite like Saro, having to admit one lied to the police to protect a murderer, even one's own brother, was a step too far. He was not worried. But it drove home to him the fragile foundation of his success.

Traiano was more perturbed. Everything would disappear, his wife, his children, his freedom, to be replaced by a jail sentence of great length, should the empire Calogero had created collapse. But Saro would never do that to him, or to Calogero, would he? He was Calogero's brother. He was the godfather of Traiano's latest child.

190

'Volta,' he said at length, 'is talking to someone.'

He recounted what he had found out from Colonel Andreazza. Calogero listened carefully and was silent for some time.

'Make some more coffee,' he said at last.

Traiano did so. Calogero collected his thoughts. When their cups were full again, Calogero spoke.

'I was annoyed to see Volta at the baptism on Sunday,' he said. 'It was intrusive, it was rude. But you were right, it is not a hanging offence. It was hasty of me to propose killing Volta. Besides, killing people like that is bad for business, it creates too much publicity, and it produces little tangible good for us. One could shoot him in the University Square, to teach him a lesson, and to show the world we can do that sort of thing, and are not frightened. But... on the whole, Volta dead would be more of a nuisance to us than Volta alive. Besides, getting rid of Volta is not really what matters right now. It is finding out who is talking to Volta. One assumes, one must assume, that this Andreazza was telling the truth. We would be foolish to ignore his words. So, we need to follow this up. Whoever is speaking to Volta may know very little, but they must know something for Volta to want to speak to them. Whoever it is needs to be silenced.'

They considered it.

'Whoever it is?' said Traiano.

Calogero nodded.

'Could it be Maso?' asked Calogero.

'It could be,' said Traiano. 'He is not one of us. It could be Gino, he is not one of us either. I would not miss either.'

'Neither would I,' said Calogero. 'The thing is this. You need to carry on as if everything were normal. Do not do anything out of the usual, anything that gives away the idea that we know we have a problem. Yes, yes, I know you know that. The other thing is, how are they communicating? They all know that I think mobile phones are not to be trusted. I doubt anyone would be so foolish as to send messages to Volta or emails or phone him up. I know that Maso can use his brother to steal phones, hack phones, whatever, but if there is nothing to know from the phones, what is the point of asking him? Besides, he may well take fright, if he is guilty, and that is the last thing we want. Or he may intentionally or unintentionally let something slip, and, well, our investigation would merely serve to bring about what we should most avoid. You will have to act carefully. One has to strike when they do not expect it, before they can do any harm. That would be a strong message to Volta.'

They had both assumed that Traiano would be the one who acted.

'I will, boss, I will,' he said. 'The first thing they will know is that they are dead, before they can tell Volta they are discovered. If not Maso, could it be one of the girls? I don't mean Ceccina or Stefania, but what about Catarina? What about Beata, the Polish girl, whom Gino was sleeping with? And probably several others as well. Andreazza said he thought Volta's contact was someone close to us, but not one of us. Certainly not someone who knows who our policemen are.'

Calogero nodded.

'Let everything carry on as normal. Try to find out a name through Andreazza. Or wait till someone makes a mistake. There is no need to speak to me about this again. Do whatever you have to do. Whatever it takes. I will never ask you for explanations or for justifications. Just do it.'

'Yes, boss.'

Suddenly the kitchen, the whole flat, felt claustrophobic. They both felt an overwhelming desire to get outside. Calogero said he wanted to go and see Stefania in the new office, and that Traiano should come with him. There were the papers to discuss, the ones that Traiano had brought from Donnafugata. They left their coffee, and went to the door, where Calogero put on one of his elegant overcoats. Traiano was dressed in his habitual short jacket.

'It is December,' said Calogero. 'You should at least wear a scarf.'

In the darkness by the door, there were several scarves hanging, some woollen, some silk. Given that Traiano's jacket was leather, Calogero took one of the silk scarves and put it round the youngster's neck. He made a playful attempt to strangle him.

'You can keep it, but don't lose it. It cost a fortune. Stefania bought it somewhere. Some famous designer. Real silk, nice pattern.'

'I'll treasure it, boss. Let us hope that Stefania does not notice you have given it to me.'

He laughed.

In the darkness of the front door they embraced for a moment. Traiano held Calogero tightly, and felt him tremble. Then they parted, opened the door, and stepped out into the stairwell and the reality of life in Catania.

It was always a pleasure to walk the streets of the city with Calogero. As a tiny boy, aged about six, Traiano could remember the pride and satisfaction he had felt as he had walked through Purgatory with the boss, then the age he was now, but already a person of great standing. And now, as they walked towards the Corso Sicilia, it was notable that nothing had changed. People looked at Calogero, people noted his presence, and many acknowledged it with a nod, or a smile or a word. And those who did not acknowledge him in this way, did so in another way, by pretending not to see him. Those, of course, were adults. The children had less guile about them. Of course, children were supposed to be at school on a Tuesday in early December. But in Purgatory, even on school days, there were usually rather a lot of children in the streets. Now, two or three small boys greeted don Caloriu, as they called him, with great enthusiasm at every street corner. He knew their names, and rewarded each one with a kind word, a stoke of the cheek, and, according to their age, a banknote: a five for the small ones, a fifty for the teenagers, and a ten for the intermediate ones. He told each one to give the money to their mothers, knowing, of course, that they would not do so. The boys looked at don Caloriu with awe and affection, and at Traiano with something like aspiration. He was what they wanted to be, the friend of the boss of the quarter. He, after all, was the source of employment for many. Greeting don Caloriu cheerily, they spoke to Traiano with the expectation that he was the channel of favour, and Traiano looked at them with a silent promise that one day he would use them to their benefit. And so, through the streets of Purgatory they came to the refurbished office block that he had bought that summer.

'One can see why she insisted on the top floor for her office,' said Calogero, looking up.

The street was narrow, pretty much blocked by parked cars. The garage entrance was cavernous, and there stood on duty one of the many relatives of Ceccina who was paid to survey the place, a man paid not to see for the large part. Next to the garage entrance, which disappeared into the void below, was the entrance to the gym. Next to that was the entrance to the upper floors. A smart young woman sat at a desk. She did not have to ask their names. They took the lift to the top floor.

'I meant to ask,' said Calogero. 'How much did you give her?'

The girl on the desk had reminded him of the other girl, the one called Catarina.

'Two,' said Traiano.

'Is that all she's worth?'

'Two now, two later, when she has snared him, which she will do tomorrow night. That is when they are meeting, as soon as Gino is out of the country. And then, when she has properly got hold of him, boss, when she is your sister-in-law, unimaginable wealth will be hers, or so she thinks. I don't suppose she would be wrong either. I was quite economical because I did not need to offer more. She is very keen, boss. She has longed to get hold of him since the summer, when she did get hold of him, but let him slip away.'

'She got hold of him?' asked Calogero with interest.

'Yes, she told Ceccina, and she told Stefania. She even told Elena, or at least Elena was there; no one knows how much she understood. You know how these women talk.'

'As long as they only talk about things like this, let them talk,' said Calogero. 'You explained to her what we wanted?'

'Yes. She understood. She is not stupid. She is from the quarter. One of us.'

The lift arrived, and they stepped out into the top floor, open plan, well lit, potted palms everywhere, vast windows with, on the one side, a view of the domes of the Cathedral and the abbey of Saint Agatha, and the mass of the Opera House; on the other, the delightful snow-capped peak of Etna, glowing in the winter sunshine.

'You see, my wife has taste,' said Calogero, with evident pleasure.

The said wife was waiting for them in a glassed-in section of the office, where she sat at a huge desk, looking at a slim computer.

'The place looks wonderful,' said Calogero, kissing her extended cheek. 'I should have come to see it before.'

'You get the pleasure of seeing it finished. Until recently, it was a complete mess,' she said. 'Hello, handsome,' she said, turning to Traiano. 'Nice scarf. Looks familiar to me.'

They sat in front of her desk.

'They have shown you the payroll and all that sort of thing?' asked her husband.

'We have been doing that for the last hour,' said Stefania. 'That chap over there' – she indicated a young man on the other side of the glass – 'has a gift for explaining things. I am very glad we have got him. He is a proper accountant, and everything will be above board. We should be grateful to the Bank of Donnafugata for giving him to us, and to him too, for moving here from Palermo.'

There was an edge to her voice as she said this.

'He is just an accountant,' said Calogero. 'Unless you think he is a spy too, for Santucci, perhaps?'

'He is just an accountant. Facts and figures. That is all. Let him spy, if he must. There is nothing to spy on.'

'And there is Rossi,' said Calogero, raising a hand to the rather shabby figure at another desk, who returned his greeting. 'You can rely on him, a real legal drudge. And he is terrified of me for some reason. Good hard worker. Nice of the lawyer Petrocchi to let him go.'

'Ah, the lawyer Petrocchi,' she said. 'I anticipate some difficulty in that quarter.' She looked at her husband and at Traiano. 'My brother-in-law has, as soon as his girlfriend went back to Rome, developed a new interest. Or rather a new old interest. I know this is true, because Catarina has been telling Ceccina, and Ceccina has been telling me, asking me if I know, asking me if you know.'

'That was quick,' said Traiano.

'My dear, what my brother gets up to in that regard, which I had always assumed was very little, is none of my business. Nor do I want it to be.'

'Don't you want him to marry Petrocchi's daughter?' she asked. 'We have all met her and she seems nice enough.'

'He can marry whoever he likes, even marry no one at all,' said Calogero. 'I don't care who he marries. The only thing that concerns me is the money aspect. The lawyer seems OK and I have known him a long time, but the wife… she is ambitious one could say, or greedy, perhaps, is more accurate. She expects us to sanitise our brother with a lot of cash, and with our house. I have agreed to pay that. But, if he were to find someone less demanding…. It would save us a lot of money. Signora Petrocchi is quite demanding, really, isn't she?'

'I wonder if he really is in love with Carolina,' said Stefania, 'or met her on the rebound from someone else. Or wants to marry her because she is the boss's daughter.'

'You attribute ambition to my pious and holy brother?' asked Calogero. 'Maybe Carolina is the more ambitious. Maybe they are well suited, both wanting to get on, both seeing each other as good opportunities for getting on.'

'Is he in love with her?' asked Stefania, looking to Traiano. 'He talks to you, doesn't he?'

'Of course, he talks to me. But he often clams up, you know. He is a huge hypocrite. My guess is that he loves sex as much as I do, but cannot admit it to himself.'

198

'You're vulgar,' said Stefania reprovingly.

'And honest as well. I think he loves them both, though for different reasons. I think he should give up the lawyer's daughter, though that is no business of mine. She is not one of us. Her mother sounds like a nightmare. Catarina is more down to earth. But Saro can't see this as he won't admit to himself what he wants. But are they in love with him? Surely that is the question you should ask.'

'Are they?' asked Stefania. 'Catarina seems keen, if Ceccina is to be believed, and Ceccina gets her information direct from Catarina.'

'Every woman in the quarter is in love with him,' said Traiano, with a smile. 'He is so sweet, so kind, so gentle, so nice, so unlike the rest of us, so un-Sicilian. But underneath all that, he is as ambitious as the rest of us; he wants what we want. All that going to Church, all that kneeling down and praying, all that wearing a cross around his neck and the image of the Madonna…'

'I wear a cross around my neck,' said Calogero.

'And you are no saint,' observed his wife.

'I wear a cross too,' said Traiano. 'And I am no angel. But Saro has that thing of the Madonna round his neck as well, just to show how ultra-holy he is. It will be interesting to see what happens now that two girls are after him. In the summer something happened between him and Catarina, and after that he had some experience which I think gave him a lot of confidence, and that spurred him on to make up to the lawyer's daughter….'

'How do you know all this?' asked Stefania. 'You are as much a gossip as we are.'

'Quite,' said Calogero. 'We are here for business, remember. I was thinking, my dearest,' he said with a smile towards his wife, 'that you should do as you suggested and go ahead and book us a week or maybe ten days in New York. It might be fun to go for Christmas. If we have not left it too late. Perhaps you should look and see what is on offer. Failing that, London… they say London is fun too. I am sure the children would adore either. Isabella and Natalia are getting to an age when travel appeals to them.'

She beamed. She was now so pleased she was keen to seem reasonable.

'We could leave it to January or February,' she said, 'as that is when the bargains are. But you never know. Last minute for Christmas may be best. And it gets you away from your mother.'

She smiled at her husband.

'How are you feeling?' he asked solicitously, a silent reminder to her of last night's lovemaking.

'Fine,' she said, with another smile. 'Go and talk to Rossi and the accountant about this property we are buying out by the airport. I want to talk to Traiano.'

Calogero did as he was told.

'Is Rosario mad?' asked Stefania, as soon as her husband was gone. 'Is he thinking of throwing away the lawyer's daughter in favour of Catarina? She is nice enough, but....'

'She is not a lawyer's daughter?'

'Quite. You must speak to him. We must not offend people like Petrocchi. He is important. I must speak to him. I must knock some sense into him. Men are such fools. Well might you look at me like that. Holy Mary. He is supposed to be your friend. Make sure he does not make this mistake.'

'OK. Is that all?' he asked.

'Of course not. Tell me what happened yesterday. How did you find that woman of Donnafugata?'

'If she was disappointed that Caloriu failed to show up, she hid it well. My guess is she does not give a damn about him, never did. He was just an amusement.'

'She should stop playing with other people's husbands,' said Stefania.

'Quite. She is a bad woman. She is now huge with the child. I think it is going to be born in February, isn't it? Of course, if you go to New York then he won't be at the birth, holding her hand, will he? Even if he wanted to be.'

'Believe it or not, I had not thought of that. And Saro, what did he think of her?'

'He was impressed, very impressed. The house, the furniture, the paintings... I could tell he liked it.'

'And her?'

'Ask him. You may like to know that my mother and Fofò are getting married very soon, perhaps in February too. And it is not a white marriage. Yes, I was surprised too. They have decided they want to have a child.'

'Well, if Anna is happy, we all benefit, particularly you, and particularly him,' she said motioning to her husband on the other side of the glass. 'And as for Fofò, Anna will find herself catapulted into the very heights of Syracuse society. What a career she has had! I am glad for her. I am glad it is all coming right for her.'

'I am glad you are glad,' he said. 'But there was a price to pay,' he added, thinking of his dead father with a toothbrush handle stuck into his chest.

Of course, she did not know about this, but there were other things she knew, other things that she pretended not to know. The source of all this wealth, this nice new office, the potted palms, the fantastic view, was the white powder that flowed into the quarter and out again. The white powder and the prostitutes, the pizza, the coffee, the drinks, the pastries and the tinkling glasses of Cinzano and other drinks, and the rent boys. All of which the boss left to him, so his hands would not get dirty, and so that his hands would not smell when he went back to his house and to his wife and his children. The rent boys... he had nothing to do with them. But now he must think of the needs of Colonel Andreazza. The house. He asked her:

'Are you still thinking of moving then, when Saro gets married?'

'Certainly. I really must talk to Saro. He needs a bit of advice, and advice from me. He must not let the lawyer's daughter escape. But I am thinking that perhaps we do not want to move out of the city. Perhaps we should try and stay here, indeed, stay in the same block. Above us are six flats, all of them tiny, all with better views, and it would be wonderful if we could buy out the tenants and restructure the whole floor, and make one big flat for ourselves. But we have a year to think about it. If Saro gets married, it will be in November next year. Though one should not get married in November, as it is the month of the dead.'

They wandered through to the other side of the glass partition to where Calogero was talking to the lawyer Rossi.

'We are buying the farm,' said Calogero. 'Or rather we are making an offer on the farm. The farmer is holding out for more. Let us hope he will come to be more reasonable.'

The plans were in front of them. The farm was not large, just a few hectares, with a few neglected fields, a few rundown buildings, all of which could be cleared for housing. Next to the plans was the map of the entire area, the area they planned to buy up, showing how the farm fitted into the overall picture. Calogero spoke while the others listened attentively: the farm, the apartment blocks, the disused factories and the factories still in use; the petrol station, the semi-abandoned ill-lit and quiet roads with their overgrown borders, the drainage ditches; and overhead, the never-ceasing noise of the aeroplanes. All this one day would be theirs. It would just take time.

'I have got complete confidence in you,' said Calogero, when they eventually left the office.

Half way through the afternoon, Rosario opened the locked draw of his desk, to which he alone had the key, and took out the telephone he kept there, pressing the dial key on the one number stored in the phone, and, after it had rung once or twice, immediately hung up. This was his signal to Fabio Volta that he wished to meet him in the usual place, at the usual time. Then he placed the phone back in the drawer, covered it with papers, and locked the drawer.

When the hour of the Angelus approached, he left the office in plenty of time for his meeting at the shrine of Saint Agatha. He must have had a sense of purpose about him, for when he met his sister-in-law at the entrance of the building where Petrocchi's office was, she immediately asked him where he was going.

'Just home,' he lied. 'I mean I was thinking of going for a little walk first, a bit of fresh air.'

'Then you have time,' she said, 'to have a drink with me. I am at a loose end. Your brother is with the children, giving them their supper and putting them to bed. You see, he is working his passage, as they say. He is keen to regain my favour. We will see how long that lasts. There are some nice bars along the via Crociferi that I have never tried, if you can walk that far, and if the hill is not too much for you.'

The hill was steep but short, and very soon they were in a bar opposite the Jesuit Church. They had the place to themselves. He resigned himself to a talk that he was sure he would not want, and ordered a beer. Volta would realise that someone had caught him. She ordered a crodino. He didn't like crodino. He didn't like beer much either, but he was sure that if he had a choice between the two, it would never be crodino.

'You look like a trapped rabbit,' she observed. 'And don't look at my drink with such disdain. Non-alcoholic is what I am sticking to.'

He nodded, he understood. She was pregnant, or might be pregnant soon.

'Your brother, if he were any good at personal relations, should have a talk with you,' she observed.

'He had many. They always ended up with him whipping me with his belt or threatening me with his knife.'

'In my family, we were all girls, so these awful tales make no sense to me,' she said. 'Giuseppina and I always got on so well. But let us leave his bad behaviour to one side for the moment. I am annoyed with Traiano. I know we have to put up with him, and I know why. But…. I feel he takes too many liberties. It is such a little thing that has annoyed me. Caloriu gave him a silk scarf that I had given him for his birthday. It is very beautiful and very expensive and I took some time choosing it, and now he has given it to Traiano. Well, he looks good in it, and it goes very well with his long hair and his leather jacket, but still. The way he flaunts himself. He has too much power.'

'But my brother, and by extension you, cannot do without him.'

'And neither can you. Remember how they always tried to turn lead to gold? Well, we get in the lead, and we turn it into gold; we get in the white powder and the other things and we turn it all into respectable money. Don't you want to be respectable? I do. And I want my children to be respectable.'

'Then maybe you should not have married Caloriu.'

'Too late for that now. Besides when you are born poor you do not want to remain poor. Caloriu was a catch, you know. Which brings me to you.'

'I am not a catch,' he said.

'You are nice enough,' she said. 'Considering.'

She remembered the nights they had spent together, the terrible sound he made like a bull being slaughtered; she had thought he would wake the children.

'Considering I am the son of a murderer, and the brother of a murderer.'

'No, considering that you are who you are, a man of average charms. And please remember that your father was convicted of nothing, and your brother has been convicted of nothing. It is all rumour, supposition and innuendo.'

'We both know that is not true,' he said quietly. 'We were both there the night Vitale died.'

'So, go to the police, put us all in jail, deprive the children of their father,' she said with anger. 'There is no evidence that would stand up in court. He was very clever.'

'Yes, he was.'

She sighed.

'It is not just the scarf with Traiano. It is the fact that he has become so friendly with Tancredi. Why was he there yesterday, why were you there yesterday?' She didn't wait for an answer. 'What did you find out that you can tell me, that would interest me?'

He told her what he had heard about the troubles in Palermo. This interested her. He also mentioned that Colonel Andreazza had been there, and had, he guessed, agreed to act as an informer for Traiano.

'Good. Now, on to you. You have heard it said that money has no smell and that it takes three generations to sanitise a family. The lawyer Petrocchi is respectable, though he came from nothing, and though many of his contacts are questionable, but he is rich and successful, so no one minds. But his wife.... There are solid middle-class credentials there. You marry the daughter, you gain the mother-in-law's contacts, the sisters of Carolina's contacts. In short, you move a decisive step away from your background. You will provide my children with some very nice cousins. You will dilute the taint in your blood, perhaps cancel it altogether. Can't you see how lucky you are to have a girl like Carolina? I confess freely that I am desperate to see you married to her. That is why I was so happy to vacate our flat for you to have it. And now Traiano tells me that you are showing interest again in that girl Catarina!'

'She is a friend of yours, isn't she?' asked Rosario.

'Yes, of course she is, but, Rosario, she works in a shop on the via Etnea. Carolina is a lawyer's daughter. You like Carolina.'

'Of course I like Carolina. She is my girlfriend. We are close. But please, Stefania, stop interfering.'

207

'I am only interfering because Traiano has interfered. I want you to listen to me, and not to him.'

'I will listen to myself,' he said resolutely. 'I don't want to be trapped in an unhappy marriage. I do not want to marry for money and status. I know you are not happy. Remember, I know about you and Maso.'

There was silence.

'Listen, I don't blame you. I am sure he is a nice boy and all that. And I do not reproach you. After all, I am as guilty as you. I know that being married to my brother is not easy, to say the least. If he found out, he would not kill you, but he would kill me, and he certainly would kill Maso.'

'It is no longer happening,' she said. 'Ever since your brother decided to give up Tancredi. Tancredi and her child. We are going away in February. That was decided today. To New York, with the children. He has never been and wants to go. Me too. The original idea was to go away for Christmas, but then this very afternoon, we got the summons to go to Palermo. Don Antonio Santucci has booked us, all of us, a suite in the Grand Hotel in Palermo. Four nights over Christmas. There are so many beautiful things to see in Palermo. The mosaics… Perhaps you should come too, as the children adore you so much. It would be nice. Of course, Santucci annoys me. He summoned Caloriu and assumed that the children and I would want to come too simply because Caloriu would command us to. Actually, I do want to go to Palermo, but I do not like the assumption. Of course, we have to take Traiano as well. They have booked a room for him too. You should come. I will speak to Caloriu. He will be busy with Santucci for a lot of the time, so we could do some sightseeing together.'

'I have never been to Palermo, so it would be nice,' he said. 'I would love to see Monreale. I need to get a passport. I have never had one.'

'For Palermo?'

'No. For the honeymoon, whenever that is. You need a passport for England, don't you?'

She nodded.

'You know,' she said, 'It is quite romantic to think that men would risk death in order to sleep with me.'

'Well, I think any lover you might have is safe enough,' said Rosario not quite gallantly. 'After all, if Calogero were to come after Maso or me he would be admitting that somehow or another he was a less than perfect husband.'

'Which is exactly what he is,' she said with a laugh. Then she said: 'Promise me you will marry Carolina.'

'I will marry Carolina, don't worry about that,' he said, with a sense of weariness.

'I had better go home, the children will be waiting for me,' she said, finishing her crodino.

She left him with his beer. The hour of Angelus was long passed. He knew that Fabio Volta would not have waited for him. He thought about Palermo, and the idea of going to see the mosaics and to meet the people his brother worked for. Volta would be excited by that. After all, it was not the little crimes of Catania that counted, or even the big crimes of Palermo. It was the people in Rome and Brussels. They were the ones that mattered, they were the sources of real power, they were the ones who gave his brother and the Santuccis their competitive edge. But this enormous structure of power impacted on him as well. Because of it, Stefania wanted him to marry Carolina, for her sake, for the sake of her children, for the sake of his future children, to help breed out the tainted blood of the Chemist of Catania. When he was younger, he had wanted to marry no one at all, to become a priest, to stop the propagation of the murderous genes. Let them end with him, had been his thought. Which way should he turn? He took out his phone, the one Maso had given him. He pressed Carolina's number, and heard the other phone that Maso had given him ringing in Rome. She picked up, he spoke. At the end of the conversation, he looked at the time they had spent talking: thirty-six minutes. Then, his beer long finished, he left the bar and began the sad, slow walk down to the via Etnea.

The conversation had gone well, at least at first, and she had said how much she was missing him, how she had wished she had come back to Sicily for the Immaculate Conception, in order to see him; or failing that, that he had come to Rome. He had mentioned Stefania and he had been depressed by the way she had spoken about the flat, about the advantages of living there, about Stefania and Calogero moving out, and how they should get married and move in the moment it was available to them, in case the current occupants changed their mind. She had already thought about furniture and furnishings. This depressed him further. She seemed more excited about the flat than about him. She had never wanted to see the place he lived in at present. He had tentatively suggested that they live somewhere else, but she had been dismissive of this. Then he had mentioned the Christmas trip to Palermo. Should he go? Of course, she would be coming to Catania at exactly that time. Naturally, he expected her to be adamant that he should not go, but that he should be here in Catania with her, though he was disappointed by the pause as she worked out what was the best option. Her conclusion was that he should go to Palermo with his brother and sister-in-law, as it would not do to offend them, considering that they were doing so much for them. As for the people he might meet, that did not matter, as he would be there to keep the children company, and he loved the company of little Renato and Isabella and Natalia. At this point he had said something he should not have said, which had resulted in a puzzled silence on her part, a puzzled and perhaps wounded silence. He had said that if he went to Palermo, if he did not see her, as he had so hoped to see her, it would not be his fault if something went wrong. She said at length that she did not understand him. He reflected that this was probably true.

In the via Etnea, he paused outside the department store in which Catarina worked. It was still open. Perhaps she was still there, working on the second floor, if he remembered rightly. All the shops were open, brightly lit, as Christmas was approaching. It would be the most natural thing in the world to go and look in the shop, to pretend to do one's Christmas shopping, to study the clothes, the china, the scented candles, to pretend that there were people one loved whom one wanted to buy things for, and stage an accidental meeting. Besides, he needed some socks, and he really ought to consider buying a new suit. He went in.

The via del Canale was a road that bisected the area that Calogero wanted to buy. This area was known as the Furnaces, as, many years previously, it had been a place where bricks were made. But that industry had long ago ceased. Like the canal itself, more a drainage ditch really, after which it was named, the via del Canale twisted and turned: on one side grew high reeds and bamboo, which hid the course of the waterway, which had many years ago ceased to have any useful purpose and was clogged with rubbish, sediment and wild growth. On the other side of the road were plots of land which were fenced and gated, the fences consisting of old oil drums filled with stones, wooden pallets turned on their side, rusty sheets of corrugated metal and barbed wire. Behind these barriers were a series of smallholdings, yards filled with abandoned cars, rubbish yards, store places of goods that had long been forgotten. The road itself had been paved in years gone by, but not repaired for decades, as it saw very little traffic. For this very reason, the seclusion of the spot, cars would come at night and park, and couples would use the place for their pleasures, evidence of which littered the sides of the road: old cigarette packets, cigarette stubs, screwed up tissue paper, and shrivelled used contraceptives. All the street

211

lights were broken, and the only illumination was provided by the glare of the nearby city and the airport reflected in the night firmament.

The six motorcycles arrived at about 11pm, and drew up at both ends of the deserted road, the riders dismounting and hiding their vehicles in the bushes and undergrowth as best they could. There were twelve of them, each dressed in unremarkable dark clothes, each wearing a motorcycle helmet; but there was one of the gang to whom they looked for guidance; that guidance had already been given. Six from one end, and six from the other, they approached the parked cars. The smashing of the windscreens was quite easy, given the number of large boulders and bricks that were to be found at hand. The screams of the girls inside and the shouts of the men rapidly died away when they realised that they were facing six toughs. The girls, they let run away, once they had robbed them of their bags; the boys were not so lucky: they were subjected to a good kicking, as they hurriedly tried to dress themselves; they too were robbed, and the final indignity was the use of the lighter, an old fashioned one with a huge flame, which was used to burn off the eyebrows of each boy before he was allowed to run away.

In the noise and hullabaloo that this created, some cars tried to make a dash for it, but were stopped, their drivers robbed, their female companions allowed to escape. Finally, at midnight, the operation was over. No less than eight cars had been abandoned by their owners and had their windscreens smashed. It was now only left to force open the petrol tank caps of the cars, and set the cars on fire. At just past midnight, the six motorcycles left the via del Canale, the night sky now bright with flames from burning cars. Within ten minutes they were back in the city centre, where the motorcycles and the helmets were abandoned. Then they walked to the gym, and went down to the room they used. All the wallets and purses and phones that they had stolen were laid out on the bench in the centre of the room. The cash was extracted, the wallets, cards and purses were thrown down the oubliette, never to be seen again. Then Traiano ordered each one to throw their outer clothes into the showers and turn on the water, and then to dress in their original clothes from their lockers. Afterwards, when they were dressed, Traiano sorted out the loot, giving the phones, which included several very expensive ones, to Maso, who immediately left for home where his brother would be able to wipe them. The money was shared out between the other ten. By quarter to one, the operation was over, and each one went to the bar of his choice to establish an alibi. Out in the suburbs, people were woken up by the terrible sounds of police sirens and the noise of a fire engine being driven at speed.

In the Purgatory bar, now rather crowded given the lateness of the hour, thanks to the women who worked there and the men who came to see them, Traiano sat with a Cinzano, conversing with Alfio and Gino.

'I liked one of those wallets,' Gino was saying.

'You will never see it again,' said Traiano. 'They are all gone forever. Down the chute. They may turn up all washed clean in the fountain by the fish market. By which time they will be ruined.'

'How?' asked Gino.

Alfio explained.

'Under the city there is a river, buried by the lava; in fact, there are several rivers, or so they say. No one knows how many. They come out by the fish market, near the fountain, and they are connected to the ancient drainage system. That chute goes down to some river – you can hear it when it rains – or some drain: so the wallet you liked has long been washed away. Everything is cleansed with water. The credit cards and the leather wallets will last, and goodness knows where they will turn up, if ever at all.'

'You are clever,' said Gino.

'And you are brutal,' said Traiano.

'I know,' said Gino. 'I certainly beat up those guys.'

'You did. Nice one.'

'And you burned off their eyebrows.'

'I did. It hurts, a lot, or so they say. And people with no eyebrows never complain to the police. They look so stupid. They feel a loss of face, you could say. They have to wait for the eyebrows to grow back before they can even go out of doors. As for the cars, they will be loath to report them destroyed. But the insurance companies will notice and they will refuse to insure anyone in the Furnaces ever again. The place will get a reputation. That is just what we want.'

'So what is next?' asked Alfio.

'Next is you and Gino go to Hungary where you get your teeth fixed and screw prostitutes to your heart's content. Then you come back after Christmas. Next is, I, with the other boys, do a few more trips to the Furnaces and make them live up to their name. That petrol station will be an excellent target. Next is we get the immigrants to move into the abandoned and empty flats, some of which we own. Talking of which, next is, I go to Palermo with the boss for Christmas and stay at the Grand Hotel. Four nights, lots of meetings.'

He smiled. He could see the jealousy cross their faces.

'Are you going to meet…?' asked Gino.

'The boss is going to meet Santucci and his father and uncle and the other people in the family. They have a big gathering at Christmas, just as they do on the feast of Saint Lawrence, their patron saint. The boss is a member of the honoured society. They want to meet his wife and children. It is a family gathering, and I am going to keep the boss company. Everyone there has some sort of bodyguard. That's all it is. There is no question of me being admitted to the honoured society. I am far too young. You have to be a certain age; and you have to be Sicilian. I will get older, but the name Antonescu may never sound more Sicilian than it does at present. I doubt I would be admitted into the honoured society before either of you.'

This was a lie, but easily said. He was very keen to go to Palermo, and to make a good impression, not on Santucci, whom he hated, but on those around him. And Tancredi had promised to push his cause. He would be in the honoured society long before Gino and Alfio ever were, he was sure. He would much rather have spent Christmas with Ceccina and the children, and he had told her that when he had announced his absence. As he had expected, she had been furious. Firstly, she had wanted to go too. Then, when told it was strictly business, she had asked why Stefania and the children were going. He had left her sulking earlier that evening. Luckily, he had told her after making love to her, not before.

'In February, the boss is going to New York with Stefania and the children. He was going to go at Christmas, but now he has put it off.'

'Will he meet people there?' asked Gino.

'I doubt it. But that would be interesting.'

Maso entered the bar. He shook hands with the three of them.

'You did well,' said Traiano, catching the barman's eye. Maso ordered a drink, having a little conversation with the barman about what type of beer was best. Having created an alibi, he said quietly: 'Enzo has wiped the phones. He did it at once. Nothing can now connect those phones with their previous owners. All sixteen of them.'

'I am going away tomorrow,' said Alfio, 'So on Thursday, take the phones to the man in the phone shop and tell him I sent you. See if you can bargain a little with him to get a better price than last time. Then keep the money, putting half aside for me, and give it to me when I get back.'

Maso nodded. He sipped his beer. His eyes wandered over the various girls in the place.

'You can spend some of your share now,' said Traiano. 'That one there has already noticed you looking at her.' He called her over with a look. 'Hi, gorgeous,' he said.

'Hi, boss,' said the woman, one of the more mature females who worked in the place.

'What is your name again, gorgeous? Are you Marta or Beata?'

'Beata,' said the woman, a little crossly. He assumed that this was not the one that Gino had slept with the other day, who must have been Marta. He found the two names confusing. Marta, he remembered, was rather younger and blonder. Beata was at least thirty.

'Handsome here wants to spend a bit of time with you, Beata, and he is too shy to ask.'

'Boss, I….' began Maso.

'What?' asked Traiano.

'I need to get back to my brother, I told him I would not be away for long.'

'You won't be longer than two minutes with Beata, I guarantee. Besides, you need an alibi. Your brother will not notice you are gone.'

'Would you like a drink?' asked Maso.

'Crème de menthe, please,' said Beata.

'Have they got it?'

'They should do, ask,' she replied.

He went to the bar and asked for a crème de menthe. The barman looked at him:

'For Beata? Nice. Lucky you.'

He took the drink back to her. Beata accepted it with thanks. He sat down. She sat on his knee. He felt her soft warm bottom against his legs. She drank her crème de menthe with dispatch, and then stood up. He regretfully laid aside his beer.

'It will be here when you return,' said Traiano.

He followed Beata out of the room, like a man going to execution. When he was gone, the other three giggled. There followed some ribald comment, and surmises about how long the encounter would take. They took bets on when Maso would be back. Traiano gazed at the silent television, high on its stand, which was tuned to a local news channel, to see if anything was being reported from Catania. A drugs bust in Trapani; a shooting in Augusta; a series of armed robberies in Messina, a major car accident near Syracuse. On the whole, a very quiet night in Catania, though. That was good. There was no need just yet for the thing to get into the papers, onto the websites or on the television. The damage they had done would perhaps be more effective if it were to start as a creeping malaise.

He looked away from the screen. There was Rosario standing in front of him.

'Up so late?' he asked.

'I saw you through the door,' he explained. He shook hands with Alfio and Gino, and let Traiano kiss him. 'I was wandering around. There is no work tomorrow because of the holiday and I could not sleep just yet.'

The barman's eye was caught and drink came. Another beer.

'I see you are still wearing the scarf,' he observed. 'Stefania told me all about it. She is cheesed off.'

'That is nothing to do with the scarf or how much it cost, nor the fact that it is pure silk. It is because her husband loves me more than he loves her.'

'You are probably right,' said Rosario. 'But she has been pacified because we are all going to Palermo for Christmas. And they are going to New York in February.'

'We all?'

'Stefania wants me to go, and I want to go. To spend time with the children and also to see the mosaics at Monreale.'

'Ceccina was furious, but I told her it had to be. She can go to her mother with the children. But what about Carolina?'

'She wants me to go. Very keen. Wants me to meet all the right people, perhaps,' he said bitterly.

'She is ambitious,' said Traiano, absently. 'When Maso comes back,' he said turning to Gino, 'challenge him to a fight.'

'I have to take a plane this very day, this coming afternoon,' objected Gino. 'I will look like a criminal if I am covered with bruises.'

'You are a criminal,' said Traiano.

'He has to look like his passport photo,' said Alfio. 'We only just got the passports too. If they look at him and then the picture, and the two are not the same....'

'Did it take long to get the passports?' asked Rosario with interest. 'I am getting one. I would like to travel and soon.'

'You can go to most places just with an identity card, you know,' said Alfio.

'Boss,' said Gino. 'I do not want to have a fight with him. He is a tough little fucker! He came close to a draw with you. I would win, but only just, maybe. Yes, I know, those are the best type of fights. But really, right now... Besides, he is not a bad kid. I know you do not like him. But he is a good kid. And he is useful. I think you should lay off him a bit. He might get resentful.'

'So what, if I do not like him?' said Traiano. 'I don't like many people. That is my privilege. And if I want to punish little Maso, then that is my business, not yours.'

'Boss, boss, boss,' soothed Alfio, placing a hand on Traiano's arm.

Traiano pushed the hand aside and stared at Gino. Gino stared back.

'Fuck you!' said Gino levelly.

'No, fuck you!' said Traiano.

Alfio groaned.

Rosario was aghast.

'If you won't fight him, fight me,' said Traiano.

'Fists? Knives?'

'Fists. It will give you your best chance of beating me, but you won't,' said Traiano. 'Let us go back to the gym and do it there.'

Gino stood up. He placed his glass on the table and trembled slightly. Despite his strength, he knew no one had ever beaten Traiano, apart from the boss, the real boss, himself. He did not quite trust himself to place the glass down without it rattling. Traiano stood up, still looking Gino in the eyes, sensing his fear. Then he laughed, leaned forward and kissed Gino on the mouth. The others laughed as well with amusement and relief.

'You are such a good actor,' said Gino, relieved.

'And you are such a bad one,' said Traiano.

'Why do you do it?' asked Rosario.

'To see the look on his face,' said Traiano. 'Ah,' he said, seeing Maso return. 'How long was that?'

'Just under twenty minutes,' said Alfio.

'More like twenty-two or three,' said Traiano. 'Where the fuck have you been?'

'You know where I have been,' said Maso defensively, reaching for his beer.

'You took your time,' said Traiano.

'I like to,' he replied.

He said hello to Rosario and shook his hand.

'I am going but will be back soon,' said Alfio, who had caught one of the girl's eyes.

'He can't even wait till we get to Hungary,' said Gino, indignantly.

'Sex maniac!' said Traiano, crossly. 'Unlike the rest of us. Talking of which, I have to meet someone. You can go back to your brother, Maso; and you can wait for Alfio, Gino. And you can come with me, Rosario.'

They went out into the square where it was cold. The façade of the Church, the masterpiece of the great architect Stefano Ittar, was floodlit, and despite the fact that it was now two in the morning, there were little boys playing, kicking a ball in the open space. Traiano stood on the steps of the Church parvis, with Rosario next to him.

'We are meeting someone here,' he said. 'We may have to wait a bit. Have you had a good night so far?'

He shrugged.

'Tomorrow, you are seeing Catarina?'

'Yes. But I saw her this evening too. I went to her shop. We went to have something to eat.'

'How did that go?'

'I feel depressed,' said Rosario.

'You will get over it,' said Traiano.

A child was approaching them. It was one of the boys that Traiano and Calogero had met yesterday.

'Hi, handsome,' said Traiano, enfolding the boy in a warm embrace which ended with mock strangulation. 'Have you spent that 50 euro the boss gave you yesterday?'

'No, boss. He just gave me ten.'

'Did he? A mistake. Let me correct it. There's fifty. Give it to your mother. She will be pleased with you. Where is she? Does she know you are still here?'

'She is working,' said the boy, looking at the ground.

'Never mind,' sympathised Traiano. 'My mother worked strange hours too. How old are you?'

'Twelve.'

'Remind me of your name?'

'Paolo or Pavel, but I prefer Paolo. My mother is Polish. She is called Beata. I am waiting for her to come out of the bar.'

'Yes, I know her. I think she may be busy for some time yet.'

'Have you got a job for me, boss?'

'I may do and soon. You know who this is, Paolo?'

He indicated Rosario.

'Our boss's brother.'

'Yes, shake his hand.'

'You are growing tall,' observed Traiano. 'One of these days I will fix you up with a girl.'

'Don't be disgusting,' said Rosario.

'Would you like that?' asked Traiano.

Paolo nodded.

'OK. I will see you soon. Look out for me. And remember you met the boss's brother. Now go home to bed.'

Paolo left them. Someone had entered the square, someone in a large overcoat and a baseball cap.

'Were you serious?'

'About what? Fixing him up? I am a pimp, Saro, or had you forgotten? But here comes another reminder. Why are you getting a passport? Is it something to do with feeling depressed?'

'Maybe.'

The figure in the baseball cap was now in front of them. To Rosario's surprise, but not to Traiano's, it was the police colonel, Andreazza. Rosario shook his hand, and so did Traiano. They walked towards the street that led to the pizzeria.

'Is it open?' asked Rosario. 'Now, at two in the morning?'

'Tomorrow is a holiday. I told them to keep it open for us. Others might pop in and out while we are there. It will be quiet, it will be discreet.'

The pizzeria was open, and empty. They took a table which was in full view of the window, though Andreazza was careful to make sure his back was to the window.

'What did you tell your wife?' said Traiano casually as they ordered drinks.

'That I was on duty,' he said.

'And are you?'

'I am on call. I was on duty until thirty minutes ago.'

'Is it a quiet night?' asked Traiano.

'Yes, an average night,' said Andreazza. 'No more than the usual sort of things you would expect on the eve of a public holiday. Some cars burning out somewhere near the airport. Vandals, hooligans, nothing serious.'

'Arrests?'

'No more than usual. You seem interested. Why?'

'Just wondering, that is all,' said Traiano, 'what it is you police get up to.'

The waiter came with the drinks. They ordered pizzas. Rosario was surprised to realise that he was so hungry. He was never up this late, but he was curious to know why the policeman was here, and felt no inclination to go to bed. His curiosity was immediately satisfied, as he saw Traiano look up towards the street doors, which were made of glass, as someone entered.

'Hi, handsome,' said Traiano to the stranger. 'You know our boss's brother, don't you? No? Rosario, this is Giorgio. Giorgio, this is Marco.'

Marco, it seemed, was Andreazza's name.

Hands were shaken. The young man was well built, wearing a combat jacket, jeans and a woolly hat. The waiter approached, and Giorgio ordered a pizza and a beer, taking off his hat, to reveal dark, closely cut hair. He had a strong jaw. Traiano invited him to join them. Rosario was alert, for this was unusual. He could see that some sort of meeting was being fixed up. There was desultory conversation, in which Giorgio revealed the traces of a Balkan accent and an inability to smile. They spoke, the four of them, about the team, the Elephants, the Etneans, the Reds and Blues, about how tragic it was that the team was bottom of the A Series, and what Marco Giampaolo, their coach, needed to do about this, if they were to avoid relegation. The conversation became long and involved, as often it did when such important matters were discussed. Andreazza had been at the match in the summer when Catania had beaten Juventus, away in Turin, 2-1. He described it shot by shot, pass by pass, recalling the beloved memories; Giorgio had watched it on the television, as had Traiano and Rosario. Giorgio expressed his huge envy at Marco's luck in being there. The pizza came, and was eaten; more drinks were ordered. Traiano looked through the glass doors once more and swore under his breath. Then he gestured to the person he had seen in the street to enter.

It was the boy Paolo.

'I thought you had gone home,' he said severely. 'Didn't I tell you to?'

'I did,' said the child. 'But no one was there, so I came out again.'

'Have some pizza,' said Traiano patiently. 'Then I will take you home.'

There were plenty of untouched pizza slices left on their plates. The child slid into the bench, and did what lots of children did: he sat on Traiano's lap and began to eat off his plate. He was clearly hungry.

'You are just like Salvatore, my little brother,' said Traiano. 'He eats like a horse.'

Rosario noticed that under the table – he could see from where he was sitting, but assumed that Marco and Giorgio could not see that he could see – Marco was stroking Giorgio's thigh, and Giorgio was talking and listening as if it were someone else's thigh entirely. He noticed too that Traiano had observed this, for Traiano seemed alert.

'I should take this boy home, and we should all go to bed,' said Traiano with decision.

'No, let's have another drink,' said the policeman.

More drinks were ordered, but at a look from Traiano, Giorgio got up to go.

'It is late, and I need to get home, though I live very close. My place is decorated in red and blue. It is great to meet someone else who cares about the Elephants as much as I do. Can we exchange numbers?'

'Sure,' said Marco.

Numbers were exchanged. They got up to shake hands.

'Nice work,' murmured Traiano to Giorgio.

The drinks came.

'You are too heavy,' said Traiano to the child. 'Go and sit on someone else.'

He went and sat on Andreazza's lap, and began to eat the scraps from his plate.

Rosario, full of pizza, began to feel drowsy. He could no longer keep up with the conversation. They were talking about the coming collapse of the Berlusconi government. It struck Rosario that he had never heard a more boring topic discussed. Governments were always collapsing. He yawned. He would rather discuss football, though in truth he did not care so very much about that either. He felt he was getting more and more tired, and eventually he nodded off, his head leaning against the wall.

The thing that woke him was the sound of the waiter switching off the pizza oven, the harsh, metallic noise made by the gas taps as they were carefully and forcefully closed; then came the raking out of the oven, or what he imagined was the raking out of the oven. Then the sense that, apart from the waiter, he was alone. His back was stiff, his limbs ached, but before he could ask the waiter where the others had gone, Traiano appeared holding the boy Paolo by his hand.

'Where have you been?' he asked. 'How long have I been asleep?' He looked at the child. 'Paolo, are you OK?'

The child did not answer.

'Where is Andreazza?' asked Rosario.

'I was just showing Paolo the private room at the back. Now I am taking him home. You have only been asleep for a minute or two, though perhaps it feels longer. Andreazza has gone to join Giorgio, round his place.'

'Are we going there too?'

'Don't be stupid,' said Traiano a touch tartly. 'Unless that has suddenly become your thing?'

They left the pizzeria. Traiano held on to Paolo tightly by the hand. They came to the Church square, where they paused. Traiano looked at the boy.

'Did you enjoy your pizza?' he asked.

Paolo said nothing, but stared at the ground.

'If you are not grateful, I will take off my belt and slap you here and now. Well, maybe not here and now, but the next time I see you. That hurts, a lot. Trust me. Understood? I was whipped at your age, very regularly, and it did me the world of good. I will come round and whip you. So watch out. We do not like ungrateful children. And remember, not a word about what you have seen tonight. Silence is our first rule. Don Calogero demands it. Remember the fifty I gave you. Here are two more.'

He put two clean notes into the boy's pocket. The boy seemed to revive at this.

'Now give me a kiss, and give Saro a kiss, and go home to your mother and stay there, OK?'

The boy did as he was told and disappeared.

'What is the matter with him?' asked Saro stupidly.

'He is up too late, that is what. His mother should be whipped. You know her? Beata, the one who drinks that revolting drink, crème de menthe. Maso screwed her earlier this evening. God knows who she has screwed since then. I feel sorry for the child. I know what it is like to be a prostitute's son. But we have all got to do nasty things, like being polite to that Giorgio.'

'You do not like him?' asked Saro, surprised.

'I try to have nothing to do with people like that. Anyway, to please the police, we have to get our hands dirty so that we can get on with our other illegitimate things. Giorgio is being very useful to us right now, screwing the Colonel, or whatever it is he likes. He did well. I told him to come to the pizzeria, not looking like a prostitute. Well, he did that, and he did not talk like a prostitute either. Good for him. There will be money in that for him; and the Colonel, the nasty shit, will be a useful friend to us. He was nervous about coming here. I was glad you were here. That reassured him. You are respectable. I am not. But that is the trouble with the respectable, they have to brush shoulders with people like me. So, tell me all about Catarina,' he said, changing the subject. 'I have got time. It is still too early to go to bed, and I do not want to wake Ceccina before I have to. Hopefully she will have forgotten that I have to go to Palermo for Christmas. Let us go to your place…'

They left the square. All was silent, apart from the Purgatory Bar, where Beata the Polish prostitute, among others, was still entertaining clients. The tinkle of glasses and the subdued laughter from within was barely audible. In a cold and empty one room flat a few streets away, the very flat that had once been the home of Anna the Romanian prostitute and her son, Paolo lay in bed waiting for his mother to return.

Chapter Seven

Fabio Volta worked in the City Hall, just between the Cathedral and University Squares. From the room he occupied, from whence he dispensed advice to his employers, one could see the famous Elephant, the symbol of the city. The Hall was a vast building, full of offices, full of politicians and their employees, of which he was just one. He normally kept his office locked, as it contained sensitive information, namely all the dirt he had collected over the years about the political opponents of the party he worked for. He had been out of the room for just a few minutes, paying a visit down the corridor to colleagues, and had not thought to lock the door. Now this had happened. Someone had come in and placed an envelope, with his name on it, on his desk. He had opened it. It contained a blank piece of paper and a single bullet sellotaped to the paper. His blood had frozen as he saw it. He had been standing as he opened the envelope. He had, with difficulty, managed to sit down, controlling his breathing, feeling his bowels turning to ice.

For about quarter of an hour, he had sat there, looking out at the square, focussing his eyes on the elephant, his mind blank, unable to think, the terror of death upon him. This, he knew, was what they wanted, to create terror, to engender fear, so that their quarry would make a mistake. It was necessary to keep calm. One must not, like a hunted animal, break cover, come within their sights, allow them to release the dogs, whose chase would have but one result. They wanted him to panic; holding onto this one thought, he managed to calm himself.

Who had sent the bullet? There could only be one answer. It had to be Calogero di Rienzi, and it had to be connected with the event two Sundays ago when he had turned up to watch the baptism of the new child of Traiano Antonescu. He had gone out of curiosity, to see who would be there, and because he wanted to get a sense of the people who formed part of Calogero's inner circle. That must have annoyed Calogero. But... would it really have provoked so severe a reaction as a death threat? And was this really a death threat? To kill him, to gun him down in the street, to blow up his car (the preferred method of Calogero's father) would be more than just an ordinary crime. To kill him, a former policeman, a current political researcher, campaigner and adviser, would create headlines. He was someone who specialised in organised crime; it would be seen as organised crime fighting back, giving a warning, advertising their power, showing that no one was safe. To do that, Calogero would need the permission of Palermo. Had he got that? Palermo was very cautious, and would surely have reined the hothead in, tried to talk sense to him. Indeed, the idea of Calogero threatening death, in a fit of pique, was something that would warn Palermo that their man in Catania was hardly a safe pair of hands. No, this was something else, a threat, certainly, but essentially a bluff, a move to frighten him – it had succeeded – and perhaps a move to get him to make a false move, to show his hand. After all, what had he got on them, after so many years of looking? Very little. He had only one asset, and that a questionable one, for he knew very little: Rosario di Rienzi.

Right now, the natural thing to do was to set up a meeting with Rosario, particularly as, only a few days ago, Rosario had sent him the signal, and been prevented from meeting. He should send him a missed call. But that was surely what they were hoping for. He was being watched, perhaps; no, he was certainly being watched, because someone had come into the building or was already in the building and had placed the envelope with the bullet on his desk. They would now be watching very closely to see whom he contacted, whom he met. It was important he gave nothing away. But he needed to meet Rosario. The only question was how.

He pondered for some time, and then realised he had a meeting with his boss. There were a few minutes to go, so when he left the office, he locked it, though that seemed a useless precaution now, and went down into the courtyard for some fresh air.

There he saw the police colonel, Marco Andreazza, a man he did not much like, who had married a girl of some importance, a few years ago, by whom he had recently had a child. But he had to be polite to Marco Andreazza, as they had once been colleagues, and as his own girlfriend, Rosa, who was in the police, was friendly with him, and even more friendly with his wife.

'Congratulations!' said Andreazza, with a broad smile, holding out a hand.

Volta frowned, then realisation came. He had quite forgotten Rosa's pregnancy.

'Oh thanks,' he said. 'It wasn't planned, so a bit of a surprise, but we are both in our thirties, so, you know, an unexpected blessing. We haven't told anyone yet…'

'Rosa told my wife who naturally told me,' said the Colonel. 'Good news travels fast. You cannot repress it.'

'And how is your little one?' asked Volta, unable to remember whether it was a girl or a boy.

'Very noisy. I try to work at nights as much as I can. But my wife really likes motherhood, so that is nice.'

Volta nodded.

'What do you know about this crime wave at the Furnaces?' he asked. He had already discussed the matter with Rosa, and wondered what Andreazza would say. 'Eight burned out cars is a lot even by the standards of our province, and all in one street, and no one reporting it? And then the petrol station going up in flames a couple of nights later. And with Christmas coming.'

'Well, the Furnaces is a bad area,' said Andreazza. 'People should keep away. Arson could just be the sort of things teenagers get up to. But there are certain types of people who don't like couples who park in cars.'

'Like the Monster of Florence?'

'There have been no murders thank God, and let us hope that does not happen here. You know there are squatters in the flats around there? And people camping out in the wastelands of the Furnaces? They say they come from Libya, or via Libya, from Africa and the Middle East. Not very many of them, but their numbers will grow. They are marking their territory. They don't have papers, so we cannot deport them, and if we do, they come back. This lot here are new. Already, some people are helping them; others would say encouraging them. It is a big headache for the Mayor already, I would guess, and will become worse. The Left and the Greens will make hay with this, won't they? One lot will say we are not doing enough to make them welcome and look after them, poor things; and another lot will protest about Italy being overrun by foreigners. A lose-lose situation.'

'A good analysis,' said Volta.

'I feel sorry for these immigrants. They are fleeced in Libya by people smugglers, and then they get here, to the land of plenty, and live in squalor, and they become a political football between left and right. They say the government will collapse; but if the left get power, how will they handle this? It is as if it is an engineered crisis, designed to give us all hell.' He paused. 'Oh well. Rosa and my wife are always meeting up. We should join them some time. You look well.'

They shook hands and parted. He did not think he did look well; he felt the blood had fled from his face when he had opened the envelope. He thought to himself that, in paying him the compliment of looking well, Marco Andreazza had played a false card.

The meeting with the boss was pretty straightforward. He was there to discuss the possible involvement of organised crime in the recent happening in the Furnaces. The explosion of the petrol station had quite literally shaken a lot of people and made a lot of noise; the noise and the flames had led to a completely unnecessary but temporary closure of the airport, thanks to the initial assumption that the explosion had been terrorist related. This had made the national news, and made the local administration look incompetent, reinforcing the national prejudice that Catania and Sicily could not run themselves. However, it was now thought that whoever had blown up the petrol station on Friday 10th December had also set fire to the cars in the via del Canale on Tuesday 7th December. It was otherwise too much of a coincidence, and they all knew that coincidences did not happen. The presence of immigrants in the area, newly arrived, was very bad news. They would get the blame, and the Mayor would get the blame for their presence. The presence of immigrants was a weak point for the Left, who were sympathetic, ideologically, to open borders, and a weak point for the Right, showing up their inability to enforce immigration law. And as for the Church, constantly making reference to the need to welcome the stranger, that made matters hard for both Right and Left, both of whom chased Catholic votes, and both of whom were desperately keen not to offend the Archbishop of Catania.

But it was all clear to Fabio Volta. This was the work of di Rienzi's gang; not Calogero di Rienzi in person, who, as a teenager, had murdered Vitale and burned down his shop around him, so was familiar with arson, but his gang of teenage thugs. And why? The answer was twofold. It was a project by Palermo to embarrass the government of the day, to be used as political leverage when the next election came. If Calogero's men were doing this, the order had come from Palermo and ultimately from Rome, and perhaps even from Brussels. An immigration emergency would generate emergency funding. And what was in it for Calogero? The land of the Furnaces, some of which he owned, and all of which he aimed to buy. That much was obvious, but he said nothing during the meeting about it, except tangentially, because everyone there accused him of being obsessed with

Calogero di Rienzi. He would explain this all later to the boss when they were alone, though he was beginning to think that the boss regarded him as equally obsessed. But the general idea was aired that all this was the fault of organised crime, and organised crime was sponsored by Palermo, Rome and Brussels. And the police were doing nothing about it.

But even in that room, the police had their defenders, and he, as a former policeman, now living with a policewoman, who would, within less than nine months make him a proud father, was inclined to be fair to the police. There was no evidence whatever of criminal involvement by di Rienzi or his proxies. He was far too clever for that. Moreover, there was officially no crime at all, as no one had reported the criminal damage to the cars. The police had traced the owners, of course, all of whom had come up with the improbable story that their cars had been stolen and that they had not been near the via del Canale that night or ever. Of course, people might not want to admit to nocturnal visits to the via del Canale. It was a little bit embarrassing to admit you had been surprised and robbed while in the midst of fornicating in a public place. Even though fornication was a popular pastime, no one wanted to admit to it. He sighed. How had it happened, this case of his child, Rosa's pregnancy? How, in this day and age, had such a contraceptive failure happened? He had left it to her, and she had taken the responsibility, granting him this favour, and then this had occurred. His mother, always wanting him to get married, and have children, would be happy. They had not told her yet. But they, or rather Rosa, had told Andreazza. Another mistake on Andreazza's part, he realised. It betrayed the fact that he knew more than a man ought.

As the meeting ended, he sent a message to Rosa, suggesting that they meet for a sandwich at lunchtime in one of the bars. Her reply was immediate and enthusiastic. Of course, they were both in their mid-thirties, it was now or never, she wanted a child, she wanted a husband, so who could blame her? With his policeman's mind he was swift to convict. It had been no accident; she had perhaps decided to precipitate things. And she wanted to get married. He knew she did. He knew his mother wanted him to get married. Of course, they wanted him to get married. One could read their minds. The funny thing was that all of a sudden, he wanted to get married too. The bullet in the post had depressed him. He wanted someone

238

to love, he wanted to feel loved. And it would be nice to have a child, be a father, achieve something on the domestic front, when he seemed to achieve so little professionally.

At half past noon he was in the bar opposite the Collegiate Church of Our Lady on the via Etnea. She came in, and they kissed.

'Hi, gorgeous,' he said. 'Feeling well?'

'Hi, handsome. Yes, never felt better.'

They found a table, and sat down. Food was ordered. He placed the envelope on the table. She looked at it, and opened it.

'Jesus,' she said, with a sharp intake of breath.

'Don't worry, don't worry,' he said. 'It is not a joke, but it is not as serious as it looks.'

The food arrived, two rather anaemic cheese and salami sandwiches for him, and a rice ball for her.

'I need you to tell me the answer to some questions,' he said, looking at her, noting her alarm and distress. 'We need to trust each other, as parents of our child, as a future husband and wife.' This was the first time he had mentioned marriage to her, but she did not seem to register this. 'You know that police colonel, Marco Andreazza?'

She nodded.

'You know his wife?'

'You know I do. She is one of my best friends.'

'I think that Andreazza knows something, that he has found out from his wife, that she found out from you, that you were told by me.'

She looked at the bullet again.

'Oh my,' she said. 'I am most terribly sorry. I didn't know that she was not to be trusted, that he was not to be trusted. Oh my…'

'What did you tell her?'

'That you were investigating Calogero di Rienzi and that one day you were confident that you would nail him.'

'Well, I have said that often enough in public, I suppose,' he said. 'They all think I am obsessed with di Rienzi, which I suppose I am. Did you say anything else? Did you mention any names?'

'I said that you had said that you were sure you would nail him because you had someone on the inside helping you.'

'Did you mention any names?' he asked gently.

'No,' she said. 'You never mentioned any names. Will you ever forgive me?' she asked.

'I have already done so,' he said with a smile. 'But you see what this means? By the way, Andreazza, whom I do not particularly like, and never have, knows you are pregnant. You told her, she told him. You see, anything you tell her, gets back to him. Well, that is to be expected. One thing this reveals, then, is that Andreazza, husband and wife, talk to teach other. But do you see what else it reveals?'

'That the Colonel is talking to them,' she said.

He nodded.

'They sent this bullet to flush me out of hiding, to make a mistake, to make me reveal who the source is. If you were to tell the wife who the source is, she would tell him, and he would tell them, and the source would be dead in twenty-four hours. They sent the bullet to make me nervous. But it reveals that they are nervous, very nervous. They know there is a source in their midst, and they do not know who this source is; they might suspect, but they cannot be sure.'

'You are not thinking…. surely?'

'I confess, it did pass my mind,' he said. 'One thing is sure. Andreazza is a prick. A complete and utter prick. He thinks very highly of himself, but he has put himself in their power, perhaps, and made the mistake of revealing that he is working for them. I saw him today, and his very insincerity gave him away. And I am sure he delivered the envelope with the bullet. But never mind the bullet. That is not serious, I feel. What is serious is that I need to warn my source, and that they are looking at me, waiting for me to lead them to the source. I do not want that source harmed. In the meantime, we can cause them a little headache. Andreazza said that you were seeing his wife soon.'

'Tomorrow night.'

'A month ago, we had some interesting intelligence. It wasn't secret at all, it just required someone with a sharp eye to pick it out of the mountain of information that travels around the modern world. That person was me, funnily enough. I was googling the name Antonescu, restricting myself to articles in Romanian, which is an easy enough language to work out. Back in October, one Trajan Antonescu was murdered in prison in Bucharest. I did a little further research and discovered that Traiano Antonescu is this Trajan's son; we know that because the younger Trajan, as he is properly called, recently got himself a proper identity card, which gave details of his parentage, and his father's date of birth. Antonescu senior was the victim of an organised hit, I think, made to look like an average prison brawl, well, average for Romania. Now who would want this small-time criminal dead? His wife, Trajan's mother, the prostitute who used to work for Calogero di Rienzi. She must have used her powers with Calogero to have it done, and maybe the son objected. In fact, my source told me that the son did object. Perhaps little Trajan is getting his revenge by telling me all about Calogero's doings? What do you think?'

'Neat,' she said.

'If Andreazza is working for them, then he will get his wife to pump you for information. And you can be most unwilling but let something slip. Then let us see what happens. At the very least, suspicion and dissension in the camp of Calogero.'

'At worst....Can you live with that?' she asked.

'Can you?' he answered.

There was silence between them.

'Are they watching now?' she said.

'Yes, but this is a bar we rarely come to, so if they are, they are watching not hearing. And what could be more natural than us two having a bite to eat in our lunch breaks? The thing is, if I am being followed all the time, how to meet with my source without exposing him?'

'Somewhere they cannot follow,' she said. 'Somewhere where they could not go.'

'But where?' he said.

Halfway through the afternoon, Rosario received the call he had been waiting for. The phone in the locked draw of his desk registered a missed call. At the hour of the Angelus, at six, when it was already dark, he was at the shrine of Catania's most distinguished citizen, the martyred Saint Agatha. But no one else was there. The Cathedral was full of dark shadowy presences and isolated pools of light, illumined statues and confessionals, glowing side altars, from one of which came the sacred words of the Mass. But there was no one who looked like Volta to be seen. He went up the grille that protected the Saint's relics, and looked into the chapel. He knelt on the step, pressing his forehead against the grille. His eye was attracted by a faint movement in the darkness inside the chapel. Someone was trying to attract his attention. He stood up, in order to get his rosary beads out of his pocket, a perfectly natural thing to do. Then, moving to the side of the chapel, he knelt down and pretended to say the rosary quietly to himself.

'They let me in the back way,' came Volta's whispered voice. 'I think I am being followed. There is a man called Marco Andreazza, a police colonel, who has told your brother that there is an informant speaking to me. You are that informant, of course, but they do not know your identity. You are in danger. But I have done something to throw them off the scent, but you must be very careful. We must not meet again.'

'Are they following me?' asked Rosario in a whisper.

'Who knows? Perhaps, perhaps not. They may not trust one of their own to follow you. You are his brother and perhaps beyond suspicion. Besides, they may think that you know nothing.'

'I met Andreazza at Tancredi's, and he has been to the quarter. Traiano fixed him up with a male prostitute.'

'Ah, that is interesting. He is working for them. That is his reward. Interesting information. It does not surprise me. How are you, by the way?'

'More or less fine,' he replied. 'I am going to Palermo for Christmas, with Traiano and my brother and his family. To meet the San Lorenzo crime family. I may find out something there.'

'Remember, Rome and Brussels, that is where the power is.'

'I remember. I have all the information about the Furnaces. They want to buy it and develop it for housing, get the zoning changed and reroute the aeroplanes.'

'They may very well succeed,' said Volta. 'Keep your ears open. Remember not to act in a way that is in any way out of the ordinary. Pretend all is well. Is all well?'

Even in the whispers, he had picked up something.

'I am thinking of breaking it off with Carolina.'

Volta had been in the same position, hiding in the narrow space between the altar and the wall, for over an hour, which seemed longer. He twisted his body in order to relieve his aching back, and get a better sight of Rosario kneeling on the other side of the grille in the dim light.

'Why?'

'She is too middle-class. She likes money too much. I think she likes the fact that my brother is rich, more than she likes me. It is a bit disappointing in so religious a girl. Makes me think she is not so religious after all. But the real reason is that I have met someone else. Well, not met, met again.'

'Ah,' said Volta. 'I have no advice to give. If you have met someone else, that means a lot. People who are in love do not meet someone else.'

'I think you may be right.'

'I am getting married,' said Volta. 'My girlfriend is pregnant.'

'Congratulations.'

'That is what Colonel Andreazza said. I suppose it is for the best. But it was not what I was expecting. I should have realised that she wanted children and to get married, even though she never mentioned it. I feel a little taken in.'

'You mean…?'

'Yes. I don't blame her, but she went ahead without asking me, and, well, now I am catching up with what she wants. She is a good girl and I love her. I suppose I needed a jolt.' Volta sighed. 'Listen, you had better go, and we cannot meet here again. After Christmas, when you get back from Palermo, send a missed call and then come to the police headquarters, at least an hour later, saying that you want to report the fact that you have lost your identity card; make sure you take your passport, or vice versa. I will instruct the person on the front desk to show you to a private room where we can talk. OK?'

He nodded, made the sign of the cross and left. Twenty minutes later, one of the spies that Traiano had set upon Volta, saw him come out of the Archbishop's palace at the back of the Cathedral, where he had been for over two hours. He then watched him walk to the bus terminus beyond the city gate, at the other side of the park, and catch his bus home. The spy boarded the bus, and made sure that Volta went home; then he phoned his relief from a call box, and waited for him to keep watch on the door for the rest of the evening. He then left, to give his report later that evening to Traiano.

Meanwhile, Traiano had got up, having spent the day asleep, and was busy with the most enjoyable part of the day: feeding and bathing his two children, putting them to bed, and then watching them go to sleep. Then, after that was done, watching television for an hour or so with Ceccina and enjoying desultory conversation, until going to bed with her for an hour or so, then, while she slept, getting up again, going down to the quarter and meeting up with the boss.

'Is my mother pregnant, yet?' asked Traiano as they lay in bed together.

'Why ask me? Why don't you ask her?'

'She speaks to you. She is always ringing you up. She never speaks to me. Of course, I could speak to Alfonso. He and I are such friends.'

'I don't think she is just yet. Give him time.'

'And Stefania?'

'That may take time too. After they are back from New York. She won't want to ruin her holiday.'

'That is not till February. And what about you?'

'Do you want me to be?'

'It would be nice, yes.'

'This house is a bit small.'

'I can sort that out. You leave it to me. Are you?'

'Ask me again in a week or so,' she said.

'What?' he said, sensing there was something she wanted to tell him.

'All the people in the top floor of the block Calogero lives in are moving out?'

'Yes. They may not realise it, but after Christmas we are chucking them out, and then the whole top floor and the roof terraces will be Calogero' s and, more importantly, Stefania's.'

'And the flat they occupy at present? Which is so much nicer than this one?'

'Just be patient,' he said. 'He is going to give that to Rosario when he marries.'

'No, when he marries the lawyer's daughter. What if he does not marry her?'

'For such an innocent person, Saro gets himself into difficulties. What do you know?'

'That he has been to bed with Catarina.'

'He did not tell me that. I will tease him about it.'

'Don't, it's cruel.'

'I am cruel. Anyway, it is what boys do, tease each other. Catarina is ambitious. Maybe she will be living in the big flat in a year's time, not you.'

'We deserve it more,' said Ceccina. 'You have done so much for Calogero. Even sacrificing Christmas with me and the children, to go off to Palermo with him. It is the least he could do.'

'That again,' he said. 'I had better get up and do my work,' he said.

'Don't go just yet,' she said.

'Then I'll stay,' he said.

An hour later, having washed and dressed, he was in the Purgatory bar. The chief spy, a boy of thirteen, Tonino Grassi, had submitted his report. Volta had spent the day in his office, except to come out at lunch time for a sandwich with a lady in police uniform, whom he kissed affectionately, and to visit the Archbishop's palace behind the Cathedral, where he had spent more than two hours at the end of the day. Then he had taken the bus home. On the reception of this report, Traiano's first reaction was a strong desire to give the boy a good whacking. Volta was an ex-policeman, and clearly knew he was being followed after having received the bullet. He must have slipped into the Archbishop's palace, pretending to have some appointment and then left it by another door. There would, he assumed, be doors that led into the Cathedral, and doors that led into the Cathedral Museum, and possibly a back door that led out to the via Dusmet or the via Porticello; then he could have re-entered by the same way. This was infuriating, considering that today, the day he had received the bullet, was the day he was most likely to make a mistake. He could easily have met someone, undetected. He could have met that someone and warned them. He pondered the time when he had entered the Palace: shortly before 5pm.

It was still early, not quite 9pm, so he walked quickly to the street off the square where Rosario lived, pressed his button and walked up at the click. The front door was open. He saw the disappointment on Rosario's face as he walked in.

'Who were you expecting?'

'No one. I have to go out, that is all. Meeting someone at 9.30pm.'

'Is that when she finishes work?' he asked. 'The days before Christmas, late hours in shops, I suppose. When do you finish work?'

'Half past five.'

'So what have you been doing since then?' asked Traiano casually.

'Nothing much,' he said, without the slightest hesitation.

The answer was perfect. The question betrayed the fact that he was under suspicion.

'Are you breaking up with Carolina?' he asked. 'There was something that Ceccina said just now....'

'I think I will have to. I don't know what to do. Catarina and I. Well, it does not seem fair to Carolina. There is no point saying anything over Christmas. Perhaps my mind will be clearer then. When we get back from Palermo. I don't want to offend her, or her father. If I do this to her, how can I go on working for her father?'

'You would work in Stefania's new office. Plenty to do there.'

'I might just go away altogether,' he said miserably.

'Well, you are getting a passport,' said Traiano. 'Use it.'

'You are a great help.'

'Yes, I am.'

'I feel that I have been dishonourable.'

'That is a feeling I have never experienced.'

'It is depressing.'

'I imagine it must be. Are you being careful?'

'You mean…?'

'Yes. My mother is trying to have a baby, Stefania is trying to have a baby, and so is Ceccina, and no doubt all three soon will. But let's hope Catarina does not join them.'

'She says there is no need to worry.'

'And you trust her?'

'You are saying I should not?' asked Rosario. He thought that moment of Volta's girlfriend.

Traiano shrugged: 'Trust no one is a good starting point.'

'There is no danger just yet,' he said miserably. 'We have talked about it, but…. Not done it yet.'

'Yet. But you have tidied up your flat. The last time I was here, this place was a mess.'

'I thought just in case she wants to come up,' said Rosario.

'She will if you invite her.'

'I did.'

'And?'

'I may invite her again. She perhaps does not want to look too eager. Carolina has never been here, and that makes me feel bad.'

'I despair,' said Traiano cheerfully.

They went down to the square. He watched Rosario make his solitary way out of the square. He felt the need to speak to Catarina quickly, to speak to her before Rosario arrived, to ask her what the hell she was playing at, and why, why she had not done what was asked of her, what she was paid to do. But women, he knew, did not like to be hurried. If she were going to co-operate, she would do so, in her own time. If she were not, no amount of shouting down a phone or threatening messages delivered by pigeon would help. Besides, did it matter now? Two thousand euros down the drain, but she could always pay off that debt later by rendering some other service. He sighed, and turned his steps to the bar, knowing the boss would soon be in for their usual evening talk. Of course, they would not discuss Saro. On that topic the boss wanted to hear nothing further.

As Rosario expected, there was nothing to be served by making any decision before Christmas. He could not bear the thought of discussing things by phone. As a result, in the days before the feast, his phone calls with Carolina became more and more perfunctory. She was returning to Catania from Rome by aeroplane on Thursday 23rd December, the very day that they were to drive to Palermo; there was an overlap of a few hours, but her first moments would have to be spent with her parents, and it was agreed without discussion that he would go to Palermo without seeing her first. Their return from Palermo was scheduled for the Monday, the 27th December, so it would be a long Christmas weekend. Carolina was staying with her parents until the New Year, for a further week, so they would meet then. In the meantime, there was the excitement of Palermo and Christmas to deal with. Everyone apart from himself seemed to be thrilled by the prospect. The two older children, Isabella and Natalia, were excited beyond measure by the prospect of staying in the Grand Hotel, and wondered constantly about the palatial nature of the place. The excitement of Christmas was compounded by the fact that it was Natalia's birthday too on the day itself. And to be in the company of their beloved uncle added to their joy. All the children were extremely fond of Saro, and he of them, though this was not something from which he derived much joy at present; their happiness merely served to underline his own lack of it. The children were to travel with their parents in one car, and he and Traiano in another car.

They arrived in Palermo in the early afternoon, having stopped on the way for lunch. Calogero and Stefania were shown up to a suite on the first floor, and the three children were given the room next door; Rosario and Traiano were accommodated in less grand rooms on the floor above. After unpacking, which did not take very long, Rosario prepared to go downstairs to find his sister-in-law and the children, knowing that like him they wanted to go out almost straightaway. He went to the next room to tell Traiano that he was going out, and on walking in, found his brother lying on Traiano's bed, his jacket thrown to the floor, looking up at Traiano, who was leaning against the window. There was perfect silence between them.

Calogero looked at his brother, his eyes gradually focussing, as if he were a complete stranger.

'I am going down to Stefania,' Rosario explained.

'She is unpacking my stuff and her own stuff and the children's,' said his brother, with an air of detachment. 'Traiano and I have things to discuss.'

Traiano looked at Rosario, and shrugged.

Rosario withdrew and shut the door behind him.

'This happened….?' asked Calogero.

'A week ago,' said Traiano.

'Sometimes you are so stupid I would like to hit you,' said Calogero evenly.

'Well, hit me. You have done so often enough in the past,' said Traiano. 'But are you sure I am the stupid one? I think it is Volta who has made the mistake. I sent him the bullet, and he worked out where it had come from and who brought it. He was meant to. And immediately he broke cover. As I thought he would. He went to the Archbishop's palace. Into the Cathedral the back way. And then later that evening, the person we were talking about went into the Cathedral the front way. Someone saw him, one of our children on the lookout in the Cathedral square. It all fits. I asked him what he was doing, and he said nothing in particular. If his visit to the Cathedral had been innocent, he would have mentioned it. It is too much of a coincidence.'

'But no one saw them talking?'

'No…'

'So, no proof.'

'A supposition that is as good as proof. They met somehow. Not sure how, and not sure it could be detected, but they met. And then what Colonel

Andreazza told me soon afterwards, which he got from his wife who got it from Volta's girlfriend....'

'Ridiculous information.'

'Exactly. A bad miscalculation on his part. Now if he had said that Maso was the spy, I might have believed him. He had access to your flat, and he knows, or at least his brother knows, all about electronics. That all fits. I would have fixed Maso without a second's hesitation. Or if he had said Alfio, or even Gino; in that case I would have laughed until I was sore. They lack the imagination to do any such thing, and besides, why would they ever betray the one who gives them the good life they crave? They are followers, not leaders. But he said it was me. On the surface it makes sense. But he does not know our history, our shared history. If you go down, I go down. We are both as guilty as each other. Alfio and Gino are guilty too. But there is no evidence.... And besides, who would ever believe me? But you see what all this means? Volta is panicking. He knows we know and he very much suspects that we know who. That person wants to take us away from our wives, our children, the life we enjoy. The idea of spending one's life in Bicocca and Piazza Lanza is not appealing.'

'We have discussed this. We have decided. I don't need to hear any more about it,' said Calogero. 'Do as you judge best. You must defend yourself and your interests; and in so doing you defend me and my interests too.'

'That is because our interests are the same,' said Traiano. 'They always were.'

'Has that girl said anything? Has he said anything to her?' asked Calogero, after a pause. He meant Catarina.

'Not yet,' replied Traiano.

There was a knock at the door. Traiano opened it, to reveal don Antonio Santucci.

'So this is where you are hiding,' he said with a smile. 'Your wife sent me up here. She and your brother are taking the children out to explore our beautiful Palermo. My wife is in my suite, telling her woes to whoever will listen. Your wife does well to escape while she can.'

Calogero got up, and took Santucci's hand, and then kissed his cheek. Santucci took Traiano's extended hand, and kissed his cheek too. The atmosphere lightened.

'While the women are out of the way,' said Santucci, 'while we have our chance, someone you know is in her flat not so very far from here. I saw her yesterday. She is enormous with child. You would think she were about to give birth any day now, though it will be February she told me. She was going to stay in Donnafugata until the birth, but now she has changed her mind. She made me promise to let you know she was here. I have the address. And she spoke a great deal about you, young man,' he said, turning to Traiano. 'Her opinion of you is high, and I value her opinion. Naturally. As you both know, she is the one who has the ability to spin straw into gold, or to change white powder into gold dust, or whatever the turn of phrase should be. I like her as a person, and as a business partner, she is without equal. I like your suit,' he said, looking Traiano over.

Traiano smiled. If Santucci, who considered him no more than a Romanian pimp and knifeman, could act, so could he.

'Thank you so much, don Antonio,' he said. 'But you should see what my boss will be wearing. You would have thought he was coming for three weeks, the clothes he and his wife packed.'

'I expected no less,' said Santucci. 'Everyone has heard about the fashion sense of our Catania colleagues. My wife too has felt somewhat under pressure to make a good impression. The younger members of the family are looking forward to meeting you; and not just them. My father and my uncle are here. Of course, you know we had a bereavement in the summer, my brother-in-law Carlo, killed by, well, let us not say who, at Favignana, along with several of his friends. His son is here, my mother-in-law too. Of course, you met Renzo at Donnafugata. They are not at all at peace about the matter.' He sighed. 'It is sad to lose beloved family members, but…. You have to move on.'

'You do indeed,' said Calogero.

'And your brother has come?' asked Santucci. 'Is he a promising young man?'

'Not in the least. He is here to help with the children and take the women to Church.'

'Ah, how nice.' He turned once more to Traiano. 'That nice man, Muniddu, is here too, on duty, keeping an eye on things for us all. When we are all together, it generates a little bit of nerves. He is on door duty. I trust him with our security. I am sure he would like you to say hello. It would please him so much. Now you have risen in our organisation, to be the underboss of Catania, while he….. But as I say, I trust him completely and so can you. And the other doormen. They are all our people.'

'Of course,' said Traiano. 'Naturally, I never go anywhere defenceless, so you can rely on me too. And my boss has never lost a fight in his life, have you boss?'

'Never,' said Calogero with a broad smile. 'No one has lived to tell the tale.'

Santucci brushed this boast nervously aside.

'We shall be in the bar when you are ready. And then we have dinner at about seven – a buffet – for the benefit of the children. Then later, we will talk.'

He smiled and left.

'Prick,' said Traiano, when he was safely out of earshot.

'I leaned on him; she leaned on him; perhaps her leaning on him was the more decisive. But now that he has agreed, in principle, not to object to your membership, you should perhaps stop hating him. It is a bad idea to hate people. It clouds the judgement. One needs to cultivate indifference. Judgement and decisions require a coolness of mind.'

'He looks at me as if....'

'Yes, he is a fool. Of course, you are a druglord and whoremaster, you are a pimp, but he has allowed that to cloud his judgement. So, I think he is a fool, which is far worse than being a pimp. Of course, he grew up rich. He had never had to fight, never had to use his hands, never had to get covered in blood like us. His hands have never been dirty. That is why he has to rely on paid help, people like your Muniddu. That is a useful contact to have. Keep that one warm. He trusts Muniddu. That might be his undoing. I am, of course, thinking several steps ahead here.'

'You mean…?'

'Why not? His uncle is old. His father is old. He killed his own brother-in-law.'

'How do you know that?'

'He was not on the list that I gave him, the Romanians' shopping list. He killed him. What better way to hide a murder than to slip it into a massacre? As we did with Perraino. That was a man who deserved the epithet you used more than any other.'

'I wish I had been there,' said Traiano. 'If it comes to Santucci….'

'You get first refusal. I promise you that. Though it may not be for years, and someone may beat you to it. We shall see. What did that policeman have to say about the Perraino case the last time you saw him?'

'He won't stay a missing person forever, but he will be for some months yet. They can sit on it, shuffle the papers around, lose them, delay the process, which is pretty long drawn out anyway, but sooner or later, it will turn into a murder enquiry.'

'Good. Delay is crucial. The more of it the better. It means that when it is a murder enquiry, people can legitimately ask why it took so long. We can get some journalist onto that story. Whichever way, the police will look stupid or corrupt or both, and that will deflect from the real story; and by the time they get round to that no one will remember who Perraino was, or who might have wanted him dead. I am beginning to forget why we wanted him dead?'

'Will his aunt forget him?'

'Ah,' said Calogero. 'Perhaps not. Or his mother for that matter. They had Carmine del Monaco killed, after all. But time is a great healer. I am not worried about Perraino. Now, let us get ourselves changed and go down and meet these people from Palermo. And let me phone Anna Maria Tancredi.'

Downstairs, the bar was the preserve of the male part of the San Lorenzo family. The two patriarchs were there, the father and the uncle of Antonio, Lorenzo and Domenico, as was Antonio himself. The eldest member of the next generation was there, another Lorenzo, whom everyone called Renzo, and who was saying goodbye to his girlfriend, someone wearing a very tight dress and towering high heels, who had great difficulty walking out of the hotel and into a taxi. Renzo thought he was a grown up, and tried to act like one, while conscious that he was only pulling off a less than passable imitation. This was the first time he had been fully admitted into the circle of the adults, and he had been allowed in because his father was dead, blown up at Favignana, and he was there, supposedly, to safeguard the interests of his side of the family. He had other siblings, in the large room set aside for the women and the children, where they were playing games with his Uncle Antonio's children, under the watchful gaze of his grandmother, Antonio's mother-in-law, and his Aunt Angela, Antonio's wife, along with the other grandmothers, Antonio's mother and aunt. So many women in the family and so few men! And one man less in particular, his beloved father Carlo!

261

He and his uncle were the sole adult males between the ages of seventy and eighteen descended from the founders of the family; his grandfather and his great-uncle, now deceased, had been great friends and first cousins of Antonio's father and uncle; and his Aunt Angela and Antonio had united both parts of the family by marriage. His father, Carlo, had not liked Antonio overmuch, who had been jealous of him, but Renzo himself loathed his uncle with a passion, with harsh words having been exchanged, and on one occasion people had had to step in to keep them apart. His Aunt Angela, of whom he was fond, had tried her best to broker a peace between them, and he had decided that this was best accepted on his part for reasons of state, if for no other reason. But he did not like his uncle, and he did not like the way his uncle had taken over the family business in the absence of his father, to his detriment and to the detriment of his siblings and his mother. It was up to him to right this balance, to make sure that what was theirs should be regarded as such; but he felt his youth and his inexperience weigh heavily upon him. His mother and grandmother counselled caution, and advised him that his time would come. But he chafed under restraint. He was twenty-five, and he was one of the richest men in Sicily for his age; he had all the money he could possibly want, and all the freedom. He had the girls he wanted, the fast cars, the cocaine, the alcohol and the parties. But he wanted so much more. He wanted what had been his father's, a place at the table, a place at the heart of the family. The more playthings he had, the more he wanted real power.

Having said goodbye to the girlfriend, and placed her in a taxi, Renzo nodded to the doorman, whom he recognised. The doorman nodded back. Renzo had been to this hotel many a time and knew that there was something about this doorman that was different, and that he had seen him before, and that he was one of his uncle's men, not one of the normal staff of the hotel. He knew, or at least he sensed, that his uncle lived in fear of assassination, which, given what had happened to his brother-in-law Carlo, Renzo's father, and others, last August, was only natural. So this man, Renzo could see, was the bodyguard, or at least one of the bodyguards. He paused on the steps to have a cigarette, to admire the palm trees and the passing traffic along the via Roma, wanting the bodyguard to see who he was, to get used to the idea of him. He hoped to catch his eye again, to enter into a conspiracy with him. As he smoked, someone came out of the hotel and spoke to the bodyguard. He did not turn, but he heard what was said.

'Hello, handsome,' said the stranger.

'Hello, handsome,' replied Muniddu.

'You have been promoted?'

'So have you, I hear. Well, I am no longer with Anna Maria. She is here by the way. The boss wanted more people around him.'

'I had heard she was here,' said Traiano. 'We will be seeing her. When do you finish this evening?'

'When everyone goes to bed and they shut up shop. But I am here all night. I am sleeping on the top floor.'

'I never go to sleep until very late. We will meet up, OK?'

'OK.'

Traiano went back into the hotel. Turning round, Renzo threw away his cigarette and followed him in.

'Hi,' he said, extending a hand to the stranger. 'I am Renzo. Remember? We met at Donnafugata.'

They shook hands and went into the bar together.

That evening, Rosario and Stefania and the children had walked the length
of the via Roma and arrived at the city centre, where they had admired the
great church of Our Lady of the Admiral and its mosaics, with the fountain
outside; then they had visited the Jesuit Church and the Theatine Church
nearby, and then saw the Opera House; they then walked up the Corso
Ruggiero VII to the Politeama, and then returned exhausted to the hotel.
There, the ladies of the Santucci family were waiting for them: the wife,
mother, mother-in-law, and aunt of don Antonio Santucci. The children
were also there: the various youngsters, four in all, belonging to Antonio,
and the younger siblings of Renzo, the children of the murdered Carlo. To
this little group, Isabella and Natalia were added, along with tiny Renato,
while Stefania and Rosario sat down, worn out, and a waiter brought them
tea. Stefania was smartly dressed, her shoes were not made for walking,
but very fetching, and as a result her feet were hurting. Rosario was in his
suit, but felt so tired, and the room was so hot, he took his jacket off. He
was the only adult male present. All the other women were dressed in
black, still in mourning for Carlo. Ever since August, it was clear,
mourning had been the focus of their lives, the late Carlo, the centre of
their attention. Antonio's wife, Angela, asked Stefania with solicitude if
she had ever lost anyone close. She admitted she had not, and that she was
lucky. The wife, along with her mother and mother-in-law, turned to
Rosario; he condoled with them on their loss, as seemed only right, and
they for their part acknowledged his own sad loss and resulting grief. It
took Rosario a moment or two to realise they were referring to his father,
blown up by his own bomb, now over ten years ago. He had been twelve at
the time and had never mourned the man nor liked and admired him, and
never truly known him. Any possible grieving process had been sorely
disrupted by the revelation that his father, the Chemist, had been a bomb
maker blown up by his own bomb, and therefore the father he had thought
he had known, he had in fact never known. The dead man was, in his
death, revealed as a stranger to him.

Then something extraordinary happened. One of the old ladies, with a slight smile on her face, looked at Rosario, and said:

'You have a look of your father. I knew him, and at the time I knew him, he was about the age you are now. Do you know how I knew him? This was over thirty years ago, perhaps more. He used to teach in a school. The school Carlo went to here in Palermo. A very nice school. Your father was about your age, as I say, and Carlo must have been seventeen, and your father came to the house to tutor him in chemistry. This would have been....'

'My father was over thirty when I was born, so this would have been about thirty years ago,' said Rosario.

'That is about right,' said one of the women. 'Carlo was forty-seven when he was taken from us.'

'I remember saying to my husband, when I read about your father's death, that we had known him, though my husband said he had no memory of it. But he is forgetful these days, and was forgetful even then. I remember everything,' she said proudly. 'I remember him and Carlo spending hours together working on Carlo's chemistry.'

'I never knew that my father ever lived in Palermo,' said Rosario. 'I assumed he was always in Catania.'

'You are very lacking in curiosity,' said Stefania. 'I was a girl when he died, but of course, my husband talks about him a great deal. He was born in Catania, but his father or grandfather was from Montelepre which is near here. When he was a chemistry teacher, which he was not for very long, he taught here in Palermo. But I had not realised he had known don Carlo.'

'Did they know each other after he stopped teaching him?' asked Rosario.

The old lady smiled: 'I never asked,' she said. She looked at him as though he had missed something important, not just about the conversation they were having, but about life itself. There were things one did not ask; there were things one knew about and chose not to acknowledge. Carlo had been murdered, but from the way they spoke, one would have imagined that he had died peacefully of cancer or some other slow, debilitating illness. Indeed, from the way they spoke about him, it was almost as if they believed he had done so, and not left this world in a spectacular explosion off Favignana. All of them were so adept at believing only what they chose to believe that they had come almost to believe the lies they told themselves. But this young man had failed to realise the smoothness of the repeated lie, the lie that all was normal.

Another old lady, the mother, the mother-in-law, or the aunt, he was not sure which, and they all looked alike in their black dresses, with their carefully set hair, now raised a subject that interested them, even if it was the one subject he would rather not discuss.

'Your sister-in-law told us that you are getting married next year, next autumn. Congratulations!'

They fell on the prospect of a marriage, the subject of an engagement, with all the appetite of birds feeding off delicious carrion. In this one thing, Palermo was jealous of Catania. Catania had had the pleasure of three marriages in a relatively short time: the boss himself, married at seventeen; the underboss married at the tender age of sixteen, and now the boss's brother getting married while still in his twenties. They wanted to know all about it, for the only prospect they had was Renzo, and the idea of him marrying soon was not one they considered feasible. So, in the meantime, they would make do with Rosario, and subjected him to minute questioning, and then listened to Stefania as she gave them the details they craved. Rosario answered, then listened, and wondered. His wedding, which might never come off, was the object of intense forensic scrutiny. He wondered what Carolina was doing now, what she was thinking; he wondered about Catarina; he clutched his cup of tea and felt tiredness and boredom sweep across him.

In the bar, the two old men, the brothers Santucci, Lorenzo and Domenico, Antonio's father and uncle, were sipping vermouth with such placidity that it was hard to tell that they were actually conscious. They were both old men, older than their years, and had passed responsibility for the family business to the younger generation, to Antonio Santucci and his brother-in-law Carlo, the son and nephew of their deceased business partners and cousins. Then Carlo had died, God rest his soul, Carlo who had been the cleverer and more energetic of the two. And now they were condemned to watch Antonio mess everything up, with Renzo, his wife's nephew, snapping at his heels. The two old men had no grave illusions about Antonio's worth. He had not been brought up the hard way, in the outskirts of Palermo, as they had been; he had inherited wealth and influence, power and position, and never earned it. They had spoilt him. Carlo, thanks to the foresight of his parents, had been less spoilt, but had spoilt his own son. Renzo, good Lord, what a child! Brought up in luxury, a crown prince, given everything he had ever wanted from the earliest age, he was even worse than Antonio and promised to be worse still with every year that passed. To this had their family sunk; for this they had made sacrifices, fought battles, won over the right people, killed the wrong ones, so it could all be thrown away by Antonio and Renzo. If only Carlo had lived, that was the one thought that tormented them.

As for this man from Catania, who they were meeting once more, they had first met him many years ago in Messina, when the lion had roared at noon. They liked him. In fact, it was more than liking, it was love, as in at first sight. He knew how to behave. He was not loud, not full of himself; he was almost self-effacing, and yet conscious of his self-worth, conscious of his standing without feeling the need to get others to acknowledge it. The contrast he presented to Antonio and, even more so, to Renzo was painful to behold. They had spoken with him, they were pleased with him, he had come up the hard way, as had they themselves. They remembered his father, whom they had both known. He was a serious man, like his father. He would, they sensed, go far. Indeed, he had already come far.

Having spent time with the two old men, who, despite their placidity and lack of physical energy, had clearly not lost their mental powers, Calogero now found himself in conversation with his friend and rival Antonio. They did not like each other, they knew that. Antonio was jealous; and they both knew that as well; moreover, Antonio was annoyed that his own father and uncle seemed to like this newcomer more than they liked him. But, for once, he was prepared to put all this behind him.

'I know Anna Maria is well,' he said conversationally. 'But how is your wife?'

'She has been placated,' said Calogero. 'She and I are going to New York in February, with the children; that is when Anna Maria gives birth. I have to put the Atlantic between us, but I have agreed to do so, and Stefania has, if not forgiven me, at least agreed to overlook my fault. Besides, she is hoping to give birth herself next year. It is early days, but....'

'Congratulations. A new child will change everything. I was hoping to go down that route myself, as neither of us is too old, but since August, since the blessed Carlo went to heaven, there has been no chance of anything. I was thinking that by now they would all have moved on, but as you will see when you meet them, they are enjoying their grief for all it is worth. They do not seem to share the worry that the very people who came after Carlo might come after the rest of us.'

'There is little chance of that, surely?' said Calogero easily.

Antonio ignored this.

'We are very safe here,' he said. 'The booking was done discreetly, and, until I cancelled them, I had other bookings at different hotels. And our men are all over the place. I mean on the door, behind the bar… we own the place. Security is tight. Not that I am nervous, but one likes to take precautions so then one can relax. We are in an enviable position. Naturally, many resent it. The Romanians, or whoever the Romanians were working for. But the Americans, the Colombians, all these other interests, all these finely balanced interests, work together in our favour. Not a grain of the white stuff enters Sicily without our knowing it. And then from Sicily to other markets. Import, export, that is what we do so well. Did you know that all the lemons in every bar and restaurant in New York come from Palermo, or through Palermo? Lemons one way, American cars the other way, but the thing that really counts is the white powder. The other things make us rich, but the white powder makes us even richer; and not just us, you too; and the people in Agrigento, the people in Trapani, the ones from Messina, they are all arriving tomorrow. You came first, as a special favour; and because you are new to the business, relatively speaking. You will meet the other guys. I wonder what you will think of them. You will like them, I am sure. Such nice guys. As for the Romanians or whoever wishes us ill, if they come back, we are ready for them. Besides, New York is on our side. New York is what counts. Of course, some people want us to diversify, to go into other things, but that would be suicidal. Cocaine is clean; it attracts a better class of customer. These other things, like heroin and crystal meth, we can leave those to others; the police and the politicians do not like those sorts of things. But with cocaine, they are very forgiving. And people trust us. Our product is good. Long may it continue. And it will continue. We have all the muscle we need to make sure it arrives, it is distributed and paid for in the proper manner. All over Sicily. It is like clockwork.'

Calogero smiled. It was on the tip of his tongue to ask, if everything was so well, then why, in the summer past, had he taken the trouble to murder his brother-in-law? And having done so, had he found that the problem he had sought to solve had in fact only grown worse? He looked over to where Traiano was talking to Renzo.

The glance at his nephew was enough for Antonio to find unburdening irresistible.

'That boy is spoilt rotten, he drinks too much, he sniffs too much cocaine, and he spends too much time chasing girls. He had a job, after he left university, not that he ever went, but as soon as the blessed Carlo died he wanted to get a foothold in the family business. He manages a car show room. Except he does not. He just does so on paper and he makes trouble for the real manager who has to correct all his mistakes when he bothers to turn up to work. Which is not often. He should have got a job in the office, overseeing the import and export of stuff, looking at the accounts, getting a feel for the business, starting at the bottom, working his way up, winning the respect and admiration of our employees. But would he? Not he. He wanted to walk into a top job, and he is twenty-five. The concept of earning a top job is beyond him. And I am sure he will just get worse. And because he is my nephew, well, my wife's nephew, and Carlo's son, he thinks he is entitled to everything he has.'

'Didn't Carlo take him in hand?'

'Carlo idolised all his children,' said Antonio bitterly. 'He never stopped talking about how wonderful Renzo was. The sad thing is that Renzo came to believe it. That was one of Carlo's weak points.'

'And you?'

'What can I do?' asked Antonio helplessly.

'I know what I would do. I would take my belt and beat him to within an inch of his life. Again and again until he learned the meaning of fear. It works. Look at him, look at Traiano. He would have turned out rotten if it had not been for the firm hand he received from me. And my brother as well, and all the boys I employ. My father beat me. It was the making of me. Does Renzo get into fights? No? Pity. He needs to get into a few fights and lose them. He cheeks you, you say? God forbid he should do that to me. Maybe he will never learn. Maybe you need to do something more drastic.'

'We are not used to the tough methods of Catania here in Palermo,' said Antonio.

'I noticed. You use guns. Too impersonal. The knife is better. And on one occasion you used the rocket-propelled grenade. That is like playing a game. You need to see the whites of their eyes, you need to smell their fear. They need to know what it was that caused their death. But that young man may drive his fast car into a wall, or take one drug too many, and that way go to join the blessed Carlo, as you call him. After all, he has brothers; and you have sons....'

'And if they turn out the same?' said Antonio gloomily.

There was silence as he contemplated this awful prospect. Noticing that the two men were now silent, Traiano approached, with Renzo. Renzo, for once, was quiet and respectful. He had heard of don Calogero di Rienzi. He was very much disposed to like him. Calogero and Traiano were men from the slums of Catania, with barely any education, who had nevertheless made reputations for themselves and made themselves rich. He had asked Traiano when he had left school, only to be told that he had never left, since he had never gone in the first place. (This was not strictly speaking true.) Moreover, it was clear that the boss of Catania and his underboss both lived relatively modest lifestyles, knowing that money was not meant to buy luxury, but power. But more than this, though the law of silence meant that no details could be known, it was clear to him that their reputation rested on their physical strength, and their determination to use it. Where was Michele Lotto the wild Romanian? Where was the policeman Perraino? Where was Carmine del Monaco? Where was Vitale?

These were the names of those who had been killed or had disappeared, and whose fates, in no way, could be attached to Calogero or Traiano, but, everyone knew... They did not have to boast of the men they had killed, so daringly too; their reputation had established itself. They had blood on their hands, and he respected that. His uncle, by contrast, sat behind a desk, and made phone calls to killers, or so he imagined, and how could one respect that?

He shook hands with Calogero, feeling his uncle watching him, knowing that this was somehow a test. After all, his uncle was the boss of Palermo, the most important boss in Sicily, or at least he had been since August, since his lamented father's demise. But he, Renzo, had a claim to his father's inheritance. He wanted to compete with his uncle. He wanted to meet Calogero as an equal, but as he extended his hand, he felt almost a shame at his lack of experience, at his own weakness. He felt, as he placed his hand in Calogero's, a sense of his own crushing inadequacy. If only he could learn. He surveyed Calogero. Like his underboss Traiano, he had a sense of his own invincibility; he looked like a man who would never be frightened of anything. Indeed, he looked like one who had seen lots of frightening things and never once turned aside from them. His wide apart brown eyes looked at Renzo searchingly. Renzo felt himself examined, judged and found wanting.

Renzo looked at Calogero's clothes, the immaculate white shirt, the beautiful silk tie, the perfectly cut hair, the smooth skin of his face, the glowing healthiness of his skin. He was aware of the broad shoulders, the muscular arms, hidden by the well-cut jacket of his suit, which also hid, he was sure, the knife he was reputed to carry at all times. He took in the perfection of his shoes. His own appearance, he knew, and even that of his uncle, left something to be desired. Their ties were not quite right, their collars a little askew; their shirts just the wrong shade, their jackets and trousers a little creased, and their shoes, though expensive, too flashy. He felt his shoes needed a polish as well, and that his hair was untidy – it was the sort of hair that could never do as it was told – and that his skin was not looking its best thanks to his poor shave, the late nights and the smoking, as well as the stuff he shoved up his nose.

He felt the eyes of don Calogero survey him with pity. He was not, he surmised, a healthy specimen.

'You smoke,' said Calogero. 'I do not allow my men to smoke. And I like them to be physically fit, for every eventuality. Look at Traiano. He has never smoked, and he is very fit and very strong. He has never lost a fight. By which I mean fights for fun, as well as fights that were the real thing. Do you like fighting? Bare knuckle, boxing, that sort of thing? You could take lessons. It is useful.'

Renzo felt humiliated. He wished he knew what to say. Even his uncle, he could tell, felt the need to say something to uphold the family honour, but could not think what.

'The guys from Agrigento and from Trapani, do they fight?' asked Calogero. 'It would be fun to challenge them. And we could take bets. Perhaps if the management allows us a room to ourselves. What an idea, what a good idea,' he continued. 'When the women go to church at Christmas, we could do some fighting. I would be prepared to bet thousands on Traiano coming out on top. We could have a competition, four ways, to find the All Sicily champion. Draw lots, and have Trapani versus Agrigento versus Catania versus Palermo.'

'My chief bodyguard could perhaps defend the family honour,' said Antonio. 'I think you know Muniddu?'

'Yes, I do,' said Traiano. 'He would not be a problem.'

'He is a knucklehead,' said Renzo contemptuously. 'He might be able to punch people, but he has no brain. Without a brain, you are no use to anyone. He is just a bodyguard. What this family needs is someone with a brain to make money. Someone who can use computers, someone who knows about accounting and banking.'

'And that would be you, would it?' asked his uncle.

'It certainly would not be you,' answered his nephew rudely. 'Everyone knows we are not making as much as we should.'

'Everyone?' asked Antonio. 'You know nothing. Who have you been talking to?'

'I know nothing? Ha! You have allowed Catania to walk all over you. If my father were still alive, these, these provincials, would still be in the stinking gutter they came from.'

'As an insult, that is not very original,' said Calogero quietly. 'You make me laugh.'

'Are you laughing at me?' shot back Renzo.

'Traiano,' said Calogero. 'Are we laughing at him? I think we are.'

'Damn you both!' said Renzo, with venom.

'You should apologise,' said Antonio.

'Damn you too!' said Renzo.

He stood up and left the bar. There was a brief, shocked silence.

'I will make him apologise,' said Antonio.

'No,' said Calogero. 'I will.'

He got up and left the room.

Chapter Eight

To take command, that is what one had to do. He had done it as a small
boy on the square outside the Church of the Holy Souls in Purgatory,
where he had made himself the leader by force of personality, by the power
of his fist, and through the promise that nothing was too brutal for him to
contemplate. He had done it as he had grown up on the streets of
Purgatory, making himself master of the place. He had done it with his
business ventures, and would, one day, be the richest man in Sicily and
lord of anything he chose to look at. He had done it with all his followers,
who obeyed him unquestioningly. The only people he had not done it with,
the only people he had never quite completely submitted to his will were
his immediate family: Stefania had constantly to be placated; his mother
and sisters were not frightened of him, and neither was his brother Rosario.
But the reckoning with all of them would come. And there was also Anna
Maria Tancredi and Anna the Romanian prostitute, who remained accounts
to be settled in some yet to be defined way. But now, lying in bed in the
Grand Hotel, in his silk pyjamas, he could savour another victory.

Stefania had got up early, as had the children, as had their uncle,
determined to have breakfast and to be away to Monreale, to see the
mosaics, in the morning light, and to have lunch there. Calogero luxuriated
in the double bed, with a cup of coffee and a croissant, savouring their
absence, while Traiano sat at the end of the vast bed like some contented
pet cat.

'You saw him last night?' asked Calogero.

'I did. The bruises are horrible,' Traiano said with relish. 'His testicles
look like a pair of aubergines, all swollen and purple.'

'He showed you?'

'He was frightened he would never be able to have children. I reassured him on that point.'

'He insulted you too.'

'He knew that. He thought I had come to add to his woes.'

'Did you?'

'Only a bit. I wanted to make my investment. Naturally, he wants to see you this evening. Yesterday, he told his mother, by phone, that he did not want to come down for supper and that he did not want to see anyone. But Muniddu went up, saw him, and told Antonio. Antonio did not go up and see him, but according to Muniddu, he was perturbed.'

'As well he might be. He just lost control of his family to me.'

'I saw Muniddu last night, late, and that was what he thought. Your boy Renzo had been trying to corrupt all the family retainers with girls and cocaine. Muniddu had heard about this and was hoping, I think, for his turn last night.'

'Young Renzo will now know better. The retainers, as you so quaintly call them, will not respect him in return for girls and white powder. They will respect him if he works hard and is clean living. And they will respect him if he takes revenge for his father's murder.'

'Muniddu and I talked, and he said the same thing exactly. The men liked Carlo. They don't like Antonio. Carlo was tough. Antonio is too much of a slippery customer.'

'Do they know?'

'They suspect. They think it was mighty convenient that when the Romanians struck, they took out only the people Antonio would have liked to have seen gone. If they were given confirmation, and if Renzo shows he can act responsibly, a takeover is possible. We shall see. Now, if you can arrange it, let us go and meet Anna Maria Tancredi for lunch.'

Before lunch, in the bar, as he sat with a Virgin Mary, and with Traiano next to him, Renzo entered. He approached, walking with the deliberation of one who is covered with bruises, pale, determined, like a pilgrim who has come over many miles to seek the truth, and who is now about to find it. He stood before Calogero, with his eyes cast down to the ground, like a penitent, prepared to seal the abject submission he had made last night.

'Hi, handsome,' said Calogero lightly.

'Don Calogero, what I did was wrong. You pointed that out to me. I have been very foolish. I now want to know that you will forgive me.'

'I am naturally very forgiving,' said Calogero. 'To those who deserve it.'

'I will try my best never to displease you again,' said Renzo.

'I hope so. It would displease me to have to kill you,' said Calogero.

'I will act only as you want me to act.'

'I hope so. An alliance would have great benefits. You have much to learn. I have much to teach. You need to act like a man, not a child any more. I want you to listen to me in future. You will soon, I feel, be in a position of great authority. You will need good advice.' Calogero stood up. 'Remember that from now on, you belong to me.' He embraced him, and felt him flinch as he touched his bruises under his clothes.

After he had gone, Calogero said: 'You must cultivate that Muniddu. You spent hours with him at Donnafugata, didn't you? You see, nothing is wasted. He likes you? You like him? Good. When the time comes, he will do us and Renzo a great favour. Keep him sweet. And that police Colonel you met at Anna Maria's? Is he being kept sweet? A Colonel – now that is useful for us. I am very pleased.'

Brilliant winter sunshine bathed the cloister at Monreale. It was the perfect way to spend Christmas Eve. The Cathedral had been magnificent, more wonderful that Rosario could have imagined. He had always wanted to see it and now he had. Then, leaving Stefania and young Renato, he and Isabella and Natalia had made the long steep and exhausting climb onto the roof of the Cathedral, and from above the apse seen the view of the plain of Palermo, the place that had so fascinated the Byzantines, Arabs and Normans. Stefania had enjoyed the same view sitting in the cloister, of mountains, blue sky, sparkling sea, buildings, orange and lemon groves. Rosario and her daughters joined her, and the two girls took charge of the baby, while the two adults sat next to each other, enjoying the peace of the cloister, distracted only by the distant voices of the children.

'I am so glad to have seen it at last,' said Rosario. 'It was worth the wait. But I must come back, as there is so much else to see. I doubt we shall have time this time to see the Castle of the Normans and the Palatine Chapel. And it is not just here. There is so much else I would like to see, in Trapani, in Agrigento, in Caltagirone, in Piazza Armerina. When I was a

279

child, we never went anywhere. My father travelled and we stayed at home. Of course, I lived in Rome, went to a good school there, but.... I now feel the desire to travel more. Did I tell you I have got myself a passport?'

'You did. I assumed for your honeymoon. You want to go somewhere like Egypt, or Thailand, or England?'

'I would like to go to all of them,' he said.

'Yes,' she said. 'You want to escape. But you can't escape. None of us can. You least of all. You went to Rome, and then you came back. You didn't need to come back, but you did.'

'You persuaded me to.'

'I played my part,' she said. 'But the person who convinced you was yourself. You could have run off to the jungles of Brazil and become a missionary. But Catania drew you back. I am not reproaching you. I am glad you are here. Very glad. It is nice to have you here with me. I did think of divorcing him for what he has done with Tancredi, but that would be pointless too. He might even marry her, which would be a bad outcome for me and the children. The children adore him; one day they may be less enamoured. Though that will be something they will learn for themselves. I will never turn them against him. It would be counter-productive; they would only turn against me. One can rebel against Calogero but never win. So, one has to live with him in every sense of the word: live with him, put up with him, submit to him.'

'I know,' he said, sensing her ulterior meaning, 'that marrying to please your family is a thing that people do. Marrying to spite your family is a very bad idea. Did you marry to please your family?'

'My parents were delighted,' she observed. 'I was pregnant. The shame of it! But marriage corrects that. He was rich too. And you know, everyone admired him. Even me. They still do. Except me perhaps. I think I may be pregnant again.'

'Congratulations.'

'It is his way of apologising for Anna Maria Tancredi. It is my way of outflanking her. My four against her miserable one. Poor children. Yes, you should marry to please your family. And Carolina should marry to please hers. Her parents are dazzled by Calogero, despite themselves. And they like you too. But the fact that you are his brother gives you special weight. And Calogero himself and I too are keen for it to happen, for our children to have some nice cousins.'

'And if I do not want it?' he asked.

'Who else is there for you?' she asked.

'The whole thing is inevitable,' he said.

He sounded resigned. He felt resigned. The rest of his life lay before him, as set out by his family. There might be consolations along the way, but this was not the life he would have chosen for himself. He felt an overwhelming desire to break it off with Carolina when he went back to Catania, but he was not sure he had the courage to do so. It would anger and upset so many people. The person he really cared about, and this surprised him, was the lawyer Petrocchi, who had helped him so much in the past. It would seem so ungrateful. And Carolina herself would be so upset. And he would have to find another job too, as he could hardly continue working for Petrocchi after treating him and his daughter in this way. But if the police were suddenly to arrive and take Calogero away in handcuffs, then he would be free to live his own life. He remembered his meeting with Volta, scheduled for after his return.

'What if Calogero were ever caught?' he asked Stefania.

She laughed.

'What ideas you have. He will never be caught. You and I know that better than anyone. It was a long time ago, but you saw the way the police had nothing on him over the case of that man.'

'Vitale?'

'Was that his name?'

She was right. They had never had any evidence against him. And that was because, he and she knew, they had both lied about the case, or, in her case, would have lied if asked.

'And this policeman Perraino?'

'He was with me in Giardini Naxos when that happened.'

'No, that was when Turiddu supposedly hanged himself. When Perraino disappeared off the face of the earth, he was in Donnafugata, I think. With her.'

'They will never catch him,' she said. 'Even if he were responsible for all these crimes. And what about the illegal matters, the drugs? No one would dare ever give evidence against him. He has complete impunity. And besides all the illegal stuff is done by Traiano. And if he were arrested, the other thugs would take over. He is unstoppable. And besides, do I want my father's children to go to jail? Frankly, no. And it is not as if any of these people who have died were in the least bit innocent, is it? And the thing you need to understand, and surely you do, is that your brother is a sadist, surrounded by masochists, with the possible exception of your mother and sisters. He dominates people though fear, and they love being frightened of him.'

'I am not.'

'It would be good for you to convince him that you were,' she said. 'And now, let us gather the children and go for lunch somewhere in the sunshine, not that gloomy hotel.'

Anna Maria extended her cheek to Calogero with a dry smile.

'You find me like a beached whale,' she said, alluding to the fact that she was lying on the sofa, and had not risen. 'But in the pink of health and expectation. You too look well. It is nice that you have come to our capital city at long last. And you too, Caravaggio. We are having fish to eat, as it is a fast day, a day before a major feast. When I last saw you, Caravaggio, we were also having fish, as it was the day before the eve of the feast of the Immaculate Conception. But I got bored in Donnafugata, and wanted to be in the city. I brought the picture back with me.'

The Immaculate Conception, of the school of Murillo, if not by the master himself, dominated the splendid room. In the distance, they could hear the traffic, through the windows they could see the mass of the Politeama. Calogero examined the picture in this, to him, unfamiliar setting.

'Not as nice as your Velasquez, I know,' she said. 'And not as valuable either.'

'Just give the command, and I will steal the Velasquez for you,' he said. 'But you would never be able to hang it on your wall. Just as when I stole it, I had to keep it in a cellar.'

She laughed. She reached into her pocket and drew out a key.

'Go down the corridor, to the last door. This is the key. It never leaves my side. There is a light switch and there are no windows. In there you will find something that no one ever sees, and which was given to my father in 1969, for him to take care of. After all, he was a banker and people trust bankers. Well, he died and he left it to me. Go and have a look.'

They returned some ten minutes later, stunned.

'You like it?' she asked. 'I am so glad. I feel sorry for it, locked in a dark room, with no one to appreciate it. It was made for an altar, for people to pray in front of, for people to love and honour. But now it has an audience of one. Sometimes I go in there and say a little prayer to baby Jesus and to the two saints, Saint Francis and Saint Lawrence. The clue of the painting's fate is in that title. The man who stole it was not really a great art connoisseur, any more than you were when you stole the Velasquez. He wanted it because of the Saint Lawrence. You see, the San Lorenzo crime family.... The clue is in the name. So he stole it, then did not know what to do with it. Therefore, he entrusted it to his banker, my father. He was young at the time. He was one of the original ones of the San Lorenzo gang. He was a mere boy in 1969, but now he is long dead. But you have met his grandson, Renzo; his son was Carlo, blown up off Favignana. Carlo's father died without telling anyone where the painting was. Hence the ridiculous story that it was eaten by pigs. Who on earth would feed a Caravaggio to the pigs?'

Sitting next to her on the sofa, and taking her hand, Calogero asked:

'Will it one day belong to our son?'

'Perhaps. Or I might give it to the Cardinal, so it can go back to the Church. But maybe our son would like it. He would be a unique child, owning his own Caravaggio.'

Calogero smiled joyously.

'Lucky, lucky boy. The child of fortune, our little Sebastiano.'

'Yes,' she said, thinking for a moment of his wife and other children, but determined not to let the thought destroy the beauty of this moment. 'But what is this you have just done? My phone has been ringing all morning. You have been in Palermo less than twenty-four hours, less than a day, and already, you have shaken things up. Just before you arrived, Carlo's widow – we are old friends – was on the phone, almost crying for joy. It seems that she and Renzo, always a difficult boy, well, she spoilt him, are now all sweetness and light. He told her that not only would he accompany her to Midnight Mass, but he also wanted to go with her on Sunday as well. For years, she has been begging him to go to Church, and he has refused. And when Carlo died in August, she begged him to come to all the Masses for the repose of his soul, and he refused. And now… it is a complete volte face. And it gets better. He has ditched that frightful girl he was seeing, and

285

told his mother he is turning over a new leaf. She is ecstatic; and she told me that it is all because you gave him a good talking to.'

Calogero shrugged modestly.

'The boss had a word. He can be very persuasive,' said Traiano.

'Indeed, Caravaggio, he can,' said Anna Maria happily. 'Look how he persuaded me. And you too. But far more serious than Renzo's reformation, which may not last, there is the matter of his uncle. He was here earlier. Antonio is not happy.'

'So I imagine,' said Calogero.

'You spoke to the errant nephew, and he feels he ought to have done so. The women of the family – his wife, his mother-in-law, Carlo's widow, his own mother, his aunt, that family is full of women – they all feel that he should have been the one to sort the boy out, and then you came and showed how it was done, so he feels he has failed, and that he has failed them. Oh, my dear, you are so clever: you have pulled the carpet out from under Antonio Santucci. You have given all the people who dislike him, and that is almost everyone he has ever met, the excuse they were looking for. Now they will loathe and despise him and think that they have an excuse to do so. He cannot control his own family. And the men who work for him. Renzo should have looked upon Antonio as his substitute father, but he never did. Antonio clearly did not win him over. But you have. Ah, poor Antonio.'

'Poor Antonio,' echoed Calogero. 'I very much fear that his long-term prospects are not good. He may feel undermined, and he may become dangerous. But this is not a new thing. He was jealous of his brother-in-law

Carlo. He may well become jealous of his nephew. Ah well, what can we do?'

'A great deal, as you know,' said Anna Maria with meaning. 'Perhaps you will have a clearer idea when you go to New York in February. I will be here, giving birth, and you will be there, reflecting, relaxing, and making plans.'

'My head is zinging with plans already,' admitted Calogero.

Traiano did not stay for lunch, as he had made an appointment with Muniddu; they met at a trattoria on a small, sloping street off the via Roma. It was very crowded, and that made it ideal for secret conversations. Muniddu was there, waiting for him, he was glad to see - a sign that he was eager to see him, and willing to take this risk, as, after all, his own boss might be suspicious about this contact with people he might easily see as rivals.

They talked over the spaghetti al ragu about their wives and children, the sort of conversation that they had had at Donnafugata earlier that year. Muniddu, like Traiano, was excessively fond of his children, who were older than Traiano's and two in number. Traiano intimated that a third might be on the way for him, and Muniddu congratulated him, expressing his own desire for a third, if it could be managed. This led, inevitably, to the question of work and pay. He had been bored at Donnafugata, not liking the countryside, finding it too quiet, a position with which Traiano completely concurred. But it had been easy work, and he had been well paid for doing very little. Now, when the lady had decided she wanted to be back in the city, someone else had the job of looking after her, and the boss, don Antonio, had taken him on as one of his bodyguards, of which he had half a dozen, who were there to guard him round the clock. This was what he had wanted ever since don Carlo had been blown up. The death of his brother-in-law had made him very nervous. He felt his life was in danger, so never went anywhere without two armed men with him. Which was all very well, thought Muniddu, but, if they were going to get you, they were going to get you. Even if don Carlo had had several armed men with him, it would not have saved him. As for the rumours that flew about, regarding that murder… He was silent.

Their saltimbocca arrived, and Muniddu continued. Of course, as a bodyguard of the boss, and as the one he trusted the most, one was well paid, but what one missed were the major jobs. He hadn't had a major job for several years now. A major job made a huge difference. Traiano nodded in agreement. They both knew that a major job could earn you up to fifty thousand euros, perhaps more, depending on the target. Muniddu sighed, recalling the old days, before his time, when the two Santucci bothers, Lorenzo and Domenico, had been young, and their cousins, also Santucci, now deceased, had been extremely active. There had been lots of major jobs in those days.

'Whoever killed don Carlo Santucci and his friends on that yacht off Favignana,' began Traiano.

'That was the Romanians, and they are all dead,' said Muniddu mechanically.

'Whoever did it would have been well rewarded,' said Traiano.

'Some of our guys seem to have a lot of money,' said Muniddu quietly. 'Don Antonio has been very generous to some.'

'The boy, Renzo, tell me about him. Antonio, I know.'

'Ah, Renzo,' said Muniddu with an unexpected smile. 'He was such a sweet boy; when I first started working for the family as a driver, I used to pick him up from school. What a sweet child he was. He still is. The trouble is that he went to school and learned nothing. He never has had any experience on the streets, either, knowing how things work, knowing how people work. Anyway, I knew him as a child, but now he barely knows me. He does bad stuff. I have heard the rumours. And he has this girlfriend who does not look like a good girl at all to me.'

'Not any more. He has dumped her.'

'Good. He is a good kid, or at least I want to believe he could be. But he needs educating. Someone should take him in hand. Perhaps someone has already done so? Your boss, I have observed him, I have seen him, at Donnafugata and here. The next few days will be crucial to his ambitions. The people are coming from Trapani and from Agrigento, from all over the eastern end of Sicily and from Messina too, and they will be looking at him very carefully, weighing him up, judging him, thinking about the future. They do not like Antonio. I can tell you that, because I am not saying anything you do not know. But Antonio is guaranteed by his father and his uncle; though they will not live forever. Renzo's the coming man, if he can only be a man, if you know what I mean. He needs experience, education, to be taken out on jobs, to learn how to command people, to get a reputation for himself. Your boss, the way he stands in a room, you know he is used to command, used to being obeyed, and people want to obey him, want to win his favour. When did he first do a major job?'

'Just after his father died. When he was sixteen.'

'His father, yes. That helps. He has that reputation behind him, just as you have your boss's behind yours. He trusts you completely?'

'Of course.'

'And you have done major jobs for him?'

'Several. The first one when I was fourteen. He trusts me. And right now, we are on a series of practical jobs for him. Last week, that petrol station that blew up just outside Catania? That was us.'

Muniddu was full of admiration.

'I saw it on television. The noise was incredible. They say everything shook for miles around. They shut the airport. And the police?'

'Accident investigators are looking at it. We know who they are. The police tell us who they are. That man who came to Tancredi's, the Colonel, he is one of ours now. I handle him. I give him what he likes, and he is useful to us. Not just information, but things like having crimes categorised as accidents, murders as missing persons. Very useful. But as you say, Renzo needs advice, and my boss will provide it. And so will you. My boss will tell Renzo that you are just the person to help him. But as you say, a lot depends on Trapani and Agrigento and the rest. And nothing will change while the old men live. But if I were don Antonio, I would be worried about the future,' said Traiano.

Muniddu understood. A plan had been formed, one that would not bear fruit for many years, perhaps, but which was nevertheless ready to go when the time was ripe.

'Do please give my warmest best wishes to don Calogero when you see him next,' he said.

The old men, the two brothers Santucci, knew exactly what was happening over these Christmas days spent in the hotel. They sipped their drinks, they ate their food with deliberate slowness, savouring every bite, and they watched things unfold. They knew that their cousin Carlo had been the brains of the family; they knew that Antonio was not a natural leader of men, and that the inheritance was not safe in his hands; they knew too that Antonio had been jealous of Carlo, because he, Antonio, had been less confident, less liked, less talented and less gifted. This they regarded as a weakness on Antonio's part. They watched the children of the family play in the large rooms of the hotel, unaware of the family drama around them; they watched the women; and they watched Renzo, the only other adult male in the family. Renzo could, perhaps, make something of himself; but it was far more likely that someone would make something of Renzo; indeed, someone was already doing so, and that man was Calogero di Rienzi.

They had known his father and respected him. The Chemist, as he had been known after his death, had been a man of the greatest discretion. So too was his son. They knew his achievements and the way that his reputation had grown; indeed, had they not commissioned the murder of Carmine del Monaco? Had they not spotted the talent in Calogero? And now that talent was in front of them, here, in Palermo, a most expansive talent, and there was only one way to stop him.

They summoned Antonio, who came, reluctantly, late on Christmas Eve, while Calogero di Rienzi and his family, and the women of their own family, and Renzo, surprisingly, were all at Midnight Mass. They sat in one of the suites with a bottle of whiskey. It was already clear to the old men that Antonio was depressed, irritable, and a little bit drunk.

'You need to act,' they told him.

'Act? Act how?'

'First you need to tell your wife and your mother-in-law to shut up. To stop talking about Carlo. They never stop. Carlo's wife, well, that is to be expected, but no one cares what she thinks. She is not important. But this endless chorus of grieving women....'

'An endless chorus of grieving woman? This is Sicily, for God's sake. You might as well tell the cicadas to stop singing in summer. Or the lemons to stop growing on the trees. You think I have not told them? I have tried everything. They simply do not listen to me.'

'They do not respect you.'

Antonio shrugged and reached for more whiskey.

'If women do not respect you, will men? You need to control Renzo.'

'He's out of control. I have tried. He is a brat, you know that.'

'Then you need to punish him.'

'How? Shoot him, arrange a car accident? Are you crazy?'

'Perhaps,' said the uncle and the father, speaking as one, 'You do not realise the gravity of the situation.'

'What exactly is it that you are trying to say to me?' asked Antonio coldly.

There was silence in the room for some time. The uncle, Domenico, made as to speak, but Antonio's father, Lorenzo, raised a hand slightly to silence him.

'My son,' said the father, 'The situation is grave, indeed critical; unless something is done right now, it may be too late to redeem matters. If you think I am being melodramatic by saying that the clock stands at five minutes to midnight, believe me I am not. Your uncle and I know how power works; it is a lesson we learned many years ago, with our two cousins, Carlo's father and uncle. This is a history you have heard many times, perhaps, and you may think we are foolish old men; but it is a history you have not understood. Power came to you because of your family connections, but it is now fleeing from you because those family connections are not enough to ensure that you keep it. They gained it for you; but you have to take decisive action to keep power in your grasp. We are old and we may not be here for much longer. For now, you gain deference because of us. You are my son, your uncle's nephew. But that sort of deference does not last; it wears off; people forget whose son you are, whose nephew you are, and they look at you and ask what you have ever done to deserve respect, and they begin to doubt that they should defer to you. You never did what we had to do. You have never wielded a knife or used a gun. You have never seen the whites of your enemy's eyes. You have risked nothing. Look at what people see: a hen-pecked, spoilt, pampered middle-aged man with a sense of entitlement. Not even your nephew - who should love you - loves you. The men who work for the family, what do they think of you?'

'You think they prefer Renzo?' he asked. 'That lousy kid?'

'That lousy kid, as you call him, may grow up and surprise us all. But they certainly preferred Carlo. And they will not have forgotten that Renzo is Carlo's son.'

'You were never fair to me when I was growing up,' sniffed Antonio. 'You preferred Carlo. You always preferred Carlo.'

'And do you wonder why?' asked his uncle bitterly. 'Don't you understand that your father and I are trying to save your life?'

'Have you gone mad?' asked Antonio.

'We are realists,' said his father, in tones of kindness he did not feel. He sighed. The business they had built up, now to be lost by the succeeding generations. 'You have made some mistakes, my son. You killed Carlo, and you made an alliance with Calogero di Rienzi. It should have been the other way around. You failed to identify the threat, the real threat. It was never Carlo. You were jealous of him, but he would never have threatened you in the way di Rienzi does. Yes, yes, we know about Carlo. You did not ask us, we were horrified when it happened, but what is done is done. But it remains a terrible mistake. You thought killing Carlo would solve everything. But Carlo was never the problem. The problem is you. And Calogero di Rienzi turns up here, and people see him, and they fall under his spell – he is careful that they should – and then they look at you.'

He sighed.

His uncle was blunt: 'If it had been me or your father, if we were still running things, Calogero di Rienzi would be dead by now. He has come, he has made a bid for your power, and you have done nothing, and that way you lose power.'

'What has he done?' asked Antonio miserably.

'It is subtle,' said his father.

'You hardly notice,' said his uncle. 'Like when someone robs your house of a valuable painting, and for days you do not notice it is gone, then you do, and everything is changed, everything is ruined. Power is fleeing from you. You need to prove yourself to the ones from Trapani, the ones from Agrigento, that you are in charge not Calogero. You need to kill him, and kill him now. You need to show you have not lost your nerve. Kill Calogero and everything falls into place. And kill that Romanian while you are at it as well.'

Antonio took a gulp from his glass. He was unable to talk. He shook his head miserably. His father looked on in silence, as did his uncle. They understood. He had lost his nerve. They looked at each other.

'Well then,' said the father to his brother. 'You leave us with no alternative. We will have to negotiate with the visitor from Catania.' He looked at his son. 'You sob like a girl for what you cannot defend like a man.'

But his simmering anger suddenly vanished. It was time to be practical.

Midnight Mass was very well attended, as it always was. The people of Palermo had crowded into the city centre, and every church was full. The women of the Santucci family, accompanied by their children and by Renzo, had gone to the Cathedral. Rosario, more practical, knowing that the sermon at the Cathedral, with the Cardinal celebrating, would be long and boring, suggested that they go to the large church at the Four Corners, that of the Theatines, which was the most heavily and delightfully decorated in the entire city. Here, he and Stefania and the children managed to get seats. Traiano and Calogero stood at the back. Here in the shadows, they leaned against the marble balustrade of one of the side altars, and conversed, during the sermon, in low voices.

'If you want to strike, it can be done,' Traiano was saying. 'Muniddu is his bodyguard, one of several, but eager to change sides. He did not say anything specific, but he gave me plenty of indications. It would cost us a bit, but really it would not be that much. More than fifty, less than a hundred thousand. Then we would have his co-operation. He drives the car sometimes.'

'An accident? Is that what you are thinking?'

'Yes. Muniddu knows his movements. I am sure that the man goes around, visits people. One could arrange an ambush. Shoot him in the street. The right people would know it was us, but most people would assume the nephew, or the Romanians, or just some internal grudge in the San Lorenzo family.'

'Messy,' said Calogero. 'The father, the uncle, might object, though I am sure the nephew Renzo would be delighted. But the father and the uncle, even if they do not like him much, would still feel the need to avenge him. Is he frightened someone will take a pop at him? I mean all these bodyguards....'

'He is very frightened.'

'Fear is a sign that you have lost the game. Why hasn't he taken a pop at me? Too frightened.'

'And the others might object, the ones from Trapani and Messina and Agrigento. He is their guarantor, as he is yours. The peace of Palermo. He protects you, supposedly, he does not gun you down. Taking you out would destroy the whole system.'

'Yes,' said Calogero thoughtfully. 'We cannot do anything without the nod from New York. Anna Maria could arrange that. One other thing, which is connected. Do you think my sister is attractive?'

'Assunta?'

'No. Elena.'

'I have never thought about it,' admitted Traiano. 'Elena is nicer than Assunta, that is for sure.'

'That is not hard,' observed Calogero. 'Nicer in looks or in character or both?'

'Both, I would say.'

'Good. Tell Ceccina to become her friend, will you? The girl needs to get out more. She hasn't got a boyfriend as far as I am aware. She needs to get away from my mother. I feel that she is an underused asset for the family. What do you think of Renzo?'

Traiano was silent.

'Well?'

'I was just admiring how your mind works so effortlessly. How you plan ahead. Renzo has nice teeth, have you noticed?'

'Yes. I think they spent a huge amount on having them fixed. I was careful not to knock them out. Talking of teeth, when are Alfio and Gino back?'

'After Christmas. Are you thinking of them doing the job on Antonio? You promised it to me. Or there is Muniddu.'

'He knows you. You have another job that is equally delicate, remember, the one we are not talking about. As for the Santucci job, when and where will be known in a few days' time. Things may develop.'

The sermon was over. The choir began to sing the Creed, something that Traiano always enjoyed. They stopped talking.

They were back in the hotel, tired but elated, shortly after one thirty in the morning. No one, however, was intent on bed. Rather, they piled into the ballroom, where they feasted on a buffet that had been laid out for them, and drank champagne. The ones from Messina, from Trapani and Agrigento were there, the ones who had not seen Calogero before now, and who were only too eager to see and talk to the man they had heard so much of. They in turn had brought their womenfolk and their children; indeed, they had taken over the whole hotel, and the ballroom was filled to capacity, with the noise of excited children, the chatter of women and the serious conversation of men. Calogero stood in the centre of the room, immaculately dressed as ever, like a monarch receiving tribute. To one side, sitting in an armchair, by now seriously drunk, was Antonio Santucci, contemplating the wreck of his fortunes.

One by one, pair by pair, the men approached Calogero. The ones from Trapani wanted to talk about the business of selling and distributing pizza;

they wanted to hear about the Purgatory quarter and the property developments he had in hand. They wanted to congratulate him on his immaculate suit, his perfect shoes, his wonderful shirt and his lovely tie. The ones from Agrigento wanted to talk about the girls he had in the quarter, so discreetly maintained, and the others of the male sex who catered to human weakness; they congratulated him on being the great son of a great father, on having such delightful children and such a beautiful wife; they alluded to the way he enjoyed the high opinion of Anna Maria Tancredi. The ones from Messina were charm itself, telling him how much he should visit one of their hotels in Taormina, the very hotel he and Stefania had stayed in for their honeymoon. They alluded to the way he had vanquished all of his enemies, without quite mentioning how he had done so, referring to his firmness, his decisiveness and bravery. At all of this, Calogero smiled, keeping his reserve.

And finally came the two old men, the brothers Santucci, Lorenzo and Domenico. They were direct. They needed to talk, they said. It was Christmas Day already. Perhaps they could meet at 5pm. Anna Maria Tancredi would need to be involved. They should meet at her flat. Calogero nodded. He knew that they expected everyone to drop everything if they summoned a meeting; and he also knew that they knew he would be happy to do so. He would come. Perhaps they were planning to assassinate him. The brothers were inscrutable. They had assassinated many men in their time. Or perhaps they were planning to negotiate their surrender. He glanced to where Antonio Santucci was sitting. He guessed he was to receive the terms of their surrender.

The women were not talking to the men, but among themselves, as was their wont. Men's business was not their preserve. Antonio's wife, Angela, the sister of the murdered Carlo, and her sister-in-law, the murdered Carlo's wife, Renzo's mother, were deep in conversation with Stefania. It seemed that Calogero had worked a miracle. In the first place, thanks to his influence, Renzo had come to Church, something that he had adamantly refused to do for years, which was so sad for them, and such a bad example to the younger children. Secondly, he had got rid of that horrible tarty girlfriend of his. What a relief that was! To think of Renzo spending time with a girl like her, when what he needed was someone mature and sensible, someone who would guide him through life. He was almost twenty-six and he needed not a girlfriend but a prospective wife. Stefania nodded. Her mind began to work. Renzo did not realise it, the mother and aunt continued, but he was quite a catch, as they had money, and therefore were prey to fortune hunters. They fell to abusing the fallen girlfriend, and Stefania continued to nod vigorously, remembering that her own mother-in-law had probably used just the same language about her once upon a time.

The truth was, the ladies averred, that Renzo had lost his way after the death of his father. It had been such a shock to all of them, but particularly to a young man at such an impressionable, such an important, age. Just when he needed a father, he lost a father. But now he had met don Calogero, they were all hopeful once more. Don Calogero would be the perfect father figure for Renzo. Others had tried but failed. They meant, by this, the broken man sitting on his own. But don Calogero would succeed. Stefania smiled at this. Her husband was certainly charismatic, she thought.

Traiano stood at a little distance with Renzo.

'How are your testicles now?' he asked.

'A little less swollen,' said Renzo. 'I can, as you can see, stand.'

'That's the spirit,' said Traiano admiringly. 'Never let pain get you down. Good training.'

They were both gazing at Calogero, who, now the line of people wanting to speak to him had dissipated somewhat, came over to join them. He noticed the devoted, almost slavish look in Renzo's eyes. Stefania, seeing him approach the two of them, also joined them.

'Nice suit, boss,' said Traiano.

'Best in the room, boss,' said Renzo.

'Well,' said Stefania. 'Almost. There is a handsome man over there wearing a nice suit. See him? Is he one of the ones from Trapani? I was talking to his wife earlier. He flies to Rome to buy his suits. You can tell. When we go to New York… soon Calogero will have hundreds of suits. But maybe London is best.'

'Not Milan?' asked Renzo anxiously.

'Is that where you get yours?' she asked kindly.

'I bought this in a shop on Corso Ruggero VII, I think. But it comes from Milan, or so they told me.'

'Yes,' she said with a trace of uncertainty.

'Next time we go north, we can take Renzo and Traiano with us, and we must not forget Ceccina as well, then you can have the pleasure of fitting him out with whatever he needs,' said Calogero. 'My wife has a great eye. She is very observant. You saw how she spotted that man from Trapani, who is, I must say, very well dressed and very handsome. Who knew there was such talent in Trapani? But do not think for a moment that Stefania spends all her time on clothes, mine or hers. She knows the importance of making a good impression. But she is also running the family office in Catania, working on the legal side of things, dealing with the accounts, the payroll, and all that. Which is wonderful, as that is just the sort of thing I do not like. And Traiano here is deeply involved in the practical side of things, as he might have told you. It would be nice to have you over to learn a few tricks of our trade. I am sure your uncle…'

'He knows nothing,' said Renzo bitterly.

'When all the children have gone to bed, and the others,' said Calogero. 'We will talk. We will tell you about what we are doing in the Furnaces, near the airport.'

The children were now falling asleep on the sofas, and the women began to gather them up and take them to bed, then headed for bed themselves, knowing that the real reason for this Christmas gathering was to allow the men to talk. The two Santucci brothers, Lorenzo and Domenico, also went to bed early, as they were old, and they knew the really important talking was to be done at 5pm, later that day, in Tancredi's flat. Antonio Santucci, demoralised and drunk, left without saying a word to anyone, which was noticed by all. The rest gathered round, the waiters left them, and they surveyed the wreckage of the bottles on the tables. There were eleven of them in all: Calogero and Traiano, Renzo, the sole representative of Palermo, three from Trapani, two from Agrigento and three from Messina. The bosses spoke, the underbosses kept quiet; no one wrote anything down, for it was an informal meeting, and not everyone present was a member of the honoured society. Indeed, the three senior members of the society, Antonio, his father and his uncle, were all absent, which lent the gathering an informal, almost irresponsible air. The important meeting was scheduled for the feast of Saint Stephen, the 26th December, but this meeting was perhaps just as important and would set the scene for that meeting.

First and foremost, the topic was the white powder, snow, cocaine, and the way it entered the island, the way it left the island, the way it was distributed, the problems encountered, the solutions adopted, the police who were being paid not to notice. They spoke of new markets, and old markets that were expanding. Someone mentioned that they had the whole island as well covered as McDonald's did. Wherever you went, places that sold cocaine were as frequent as the golden arches, said the man Stefania had noticed, the one from Trapani: driving from Trapani to Agrigento there was Castelvetrano, Marsala, along the way, one could get off one's head by the time one got to Agrigento, if that was what one wanted.

Other products were mentioned – weed, and crystal meth. These could be safely left to the others, the people they despised, the Albanians, the Romanians, the Maltese, as long as they paid protection for their factories and their networks. The white powder was different, that was theirs, that was their lifeline to New York. As for the girls and the rent boys, this was a minor matter, and easy to run in the lower echelons of the organisation. As long as they all had passports from funny places like Ukraine and Moldova, and were therefore nervous about their legal status, which gave one a hold over them, they caused no trouble.

Trouble was what they feared the most. Trouble was what hung over them all tonight, on this holy night of Christmas. One could see that not all was well with the Santucci family: Carlo dead, the two old men retired, not just for the night, but retired in all senses, and Renzo still young. And the Santuccis were their lifeline to New York; they were the providers of infrastructure in the trade. And now all this depended on don Antonio, now gone drunkenly to bed. Eight of them presently looked towards don Calogero; Renzo and Traiano already looked towards him for everything. The current situation could not go on. They all knew this. Calogero certainly did. But he knew too that the uncertainty worked in his favour. At 5pm, later that day, all would be decided. Until then, he reasoned, let them look for salvation, and thus be even more grateful when it arrived. For trouble was the one thing that they did not like.

The meeting broke up some time after three in the morning. Taking the last few bottles of champagne with them, and other bottles besides, the eleven men gradually drifted upstairs. Calogero went up to Traiano's room, carrying a bottle of champagne, a bottle of Cinzano and three glasses, with

Traiano and Renzo following him. When they reached the second floor, he said:

'Tonight, someone might come and try to assassinate me, though somehow I doubt it. But it is wise to change rooms just as a precaution. Don't be alarmed,' he said to Renzo. 'I doubt your uncle has the guts. Let's not allow it to stop us having a drink together and enjoying ourselves. Anyway, I will sleep in Traiano's bed, and he will sleep on the sofa by the door, in case anyone tries to come in and surprise us. For if they want to kill me, they would almost certainly try to kill him too.'

Traiano took off his jacket, and placed his gun and his knife on the dressing table, where they would be within easy reach. Renzo looked on these weapons with fascination. The boss too took off his jacket and placed his knife under the pillow. Then he opened the champagne. Renzo accepted a glass. Traiano poured himself a tiny measure of Cinzano.

'Have you killed a man?' asked Renzo.

'One, no. Several yes. But the key thing of our organisation is that one ever speaks about these things or boasts about them. There are several people who are, shall we say, no longer with us, and everyone who thinks about it knows that they did not disappear or die without a cause. And the cause was that they became inconvenient to me, or inconvenient to my friends. Isn't that so, Traiano?'

Traiano nodded.

'It is a question of ruthlessness and swift action and determination. You make your mind up and you act. Your uncle cannot make his mind up, I think. Because if he could he would have acted by now. He controls lots of men. One of them would have stepped out of the crowd tonight as we left church and pumped me full of bullets, or stuck a knife between my ribs.'

'Is that how it is done?'

'Shooting someone in a crowded place? Only if you want to send a message, make a claim. A public execution is a way of asserting your power. Your uncle is losing his power. It is fleeing from him. People are washing their hands of him. I am sure even now, the phone lines to New York are busy. And tomorrow, I am meeting the Santucci brothers, Lorenzo and Domenico, with Anna Maria Tancredi, and we will hammer something out.'

'Are you going to kill my uncle?' asked Renzo.

Calogero smiled.

'Traiano would like to. He hurt his feelings. But I think someone else should pull the trigger or wield the knife.'

'Who?' asked Renzo.

'He means you,' said Traiano.

'Why me?' asked Renzo.

'You would like to?' asked Traiano.

Renzo was silent a moment.

'Perhaps,' he said. 'But why me?'

Calogero looked at him.

'Revenge for the massacre of Favignana,' he said. 'Carlo and Antonio did not like each other. Carlo was murdered by Antonio, because Antonio knew that Carlo was plotting to kill him, through the Romanian gang led by Michele Lotto, who is now dead himself. It is all supposition, but it was your uncle's men who killed your father. Only your uncle, apart from the state itself, had access to rocket- propelled grenades. I do not think that the government blew up that yacht, not for a moment. Why would they? But Antonio… and now he has lost his nerve. He has seized power and having done so finds he cannot wield it. And so he must lose it. And because life is very unforgiving, someone must pull the trigger. And that someone is you. Though not just yet. We will wait a bit, perhaps years. But one day.'

'If I kill him, won't they know it was me?'

'Yes, they will. They will know that Renzo Santucci avenged his father against his uncle Antonio Santucci. And they will admire you for it. One should do it in a way that makes it clear that the killing was not what they call a senseless act, but there was reasoning behind it. One should dispose of him on an exploding boat, or through a rocket-propelled grenade. The killing would be an announcement: that Renzo has arrived, that Carlo is avenged, and that Antonio deserved to die.'

'Might he not get his revenge in first?'

'Are you frightened of him?' asked Calogero.

'No,' said Renzo, after some consideration.

'You are untouchable. If he kills you, every one of your father's employees comes after him. As for arranging an accident, he would not dare; it is too difficult, too many people involved, and they would ask why, which would entail a confession of guilt on his part. The murder of Carlo haunts him, it must; he did not realise it at the time, but in killing Carlo, he signed his own death warrant. But, as I say, not just yet. We need to train you up. We need to get you to Catania. We need to get you to build up relations with the men who work for your family. Come back with us to Catania, and stay for a few weeks, and get some flavour of active duty.'

On Christmas morning, the hotel was full of crowds of very excited children, all of whom were opening presents while their mothers, grandmothers and aunts looked on, sipping coffee and eating croissants. Because the men had all stayed up late last night, they were not to be seen; even Rosario, who had gone to bed relatively early, was not in evidence. He was talking on the telephone to Carolina, telling her about the Grand Hotel, the Midnight Mass at the Church of the Theatines, the wonders of Palermo, their trip to Monreale, and all the food and drink they had had to eat. He realised, as he spoke of these wonders, that he sounded like a provincial, a person who had never stayed in any hotel, let alone a grand one; someone who had never drunk champagne before now, and someone who was unacquainted with haute cuisine – all of which was true. A sense of sadness crept over him as he spoke to her. He had so little to offer her by way of wealth, prestige and experience. He was no one, and only in the Grand Hotel because of his brother, who, he had noticed, had not addressed a single word to him over the entire Christmas holiday so far. He was not capable of adapting himself to this new life, in the way Traiano was. Or even in the way Calogero and Stefania were, both of whom gave the effortless impression in their different ways that they were utterly used to such luxury, such expense. He thought, as he spoke to Carolina, of his mother, who was always so cold and withdrawn. She had always been frugal, and would be shocked by all this extravagance, and perhaps would be right to be so. Assunta would be angry that she had not been invited, and so would Elena. But was this what he wanted? But it seemed Carolina wanted it, for she was talking of their honeymoon and wondering whether Palermo rather than Taormina might be the better destination, given that it would be winter, and there was so much more to see in Palermo. Rosario's heart sank. He imagined the consummation of love, the end of the long wait, taking place here; not in this room on the second floor but in one of the suites on the first floor. It all seemed so false, so unlike what true love should be.

He got up, and dragged himself into the bathroom. After he got out of his shower, at the very late, for him, time of eleven in the morning, Catarina phoned him to wish him a happy Christmas. She did not ask him about the hotel or the food or the drink, but asked him how he was. That, he sensed, was the right question. He asked her how she was, sensing too that this was the right question. She was no better than OK, she replied. She was with the family, helping her mother, getting things ready for the huge Christmas dinner; then she paused. Alfio had phoned her from Budapest, where Christmas was not going so very well. His teeth were causing him considerable pain. He had not realised that dentists could be such torturers. They had not been able to do much by way of eating and drinking as a result; but they had been to the various hot springs, which was enjoyable, and there were lots of nice things to see. Then he had put Gino on the phone, and she had realised that Alfio had spoken first to see the lie of the land. Gino was, in tone at least, penitent, cognisant of the fact that they had not parted on good terms. He had had one of his teeth, as he put it, 'corrected.' It had hurt like hell. Like her cousin Alfio he had had no idea that dentists could inflict such pain. This had amused Catarina. If one spent one's life avoiding the dentist, then such reckonings would inevitably come. Gino said that he had had his teeth cleaned as well, and gave a lengthy description of the process, clearly under the illusion that this was something that had never been done before now to anyone else. But apart from the correction and the cleaning, his teeth had been pronounced fine, and now looked white and shiny, though not too white, not too shiny so as to look unnatural. Gino then went on about all they had done, the hot springs they had visited, the buildings they had looked at, the boat trip on the Danube, the visit to the parliament building, which had been very interesting. Through his silence, he made it clear there had been no other activities. He passed her back to Alfio, who told her that they were sharing a room, had gone to bed early most nights, and that Gino snored. She had known this. Then Alfio passed her back to Gino, who had said, for the first time in his life, some sweet things, at the end of which he had proposed marriage.

'And?' asked Rosario.

'I couldn't answer there and then,' she said. 'Not on the phone. They are back for New Year. I told him that I would tell him then.'

'I understand,' said Rosario, though he didn't.

After the conversation was over, he got dressed, and went downstairs in search of coffee. There was a light buffet laid on in the dining room; the main feast would be that night at eight. He kissed all the excited children, and then made the rounds of the ladies, kissing each one on the cheek, including the new arrivals from Trapani, Agrigento and Messina, who seemed to expect it. He listened to their conversation, talk of clothes and children, car journeys and food, the niceness of their rooms and the bathrooms, the Mass last night, and what they had bought their husbands and children, and what their husbands had bought them. He felt an even greater depression settle on him. If Catarina married Gino – did he care? He thought he did. And if she refused him - and why would she do that? - would it mean that she wanted to marry him? Did he want to marry her? Or did he want to marry Carolina? Or would it be best if he married no one at all?

In other parts of the hotel, important conversations were happening. The two Santucci brothers were calling in at the various rooms, taking what they called soundings. They were listening to Messina, to Trapani and to Agrigento; they were making phone calls to the various employees of the Santucci family, all of whom were surprised to hear from them on

Christmas day, indeed surprised to hear from them at all. The two brothers were retired; that they should be intervening so actively in affairs now was a sign that there was a crisis. Or rather there was no crisis, the brothers insisted: there was just decisive action to head off a crisis.

At four in the afternoon, they summoned Antonio and his wife Angela, Carlo's sister. And at a few minutes to five they were ready to go to Anna Maria Tancredi's with a deal ready.

The man who had occasioned all this trouble in the meantime slept on peacefully, lying in Traiano's bed, while Traiano slept on the sofa, and Renzo, not to be outdone, slept on the floor. The three of them began to stir at about half past two in the afternoon. At three, tea and coffee were called for, and a waiter brought up a tray; he came with Stefania in tow, who had intercepted him in the lift, and had wondered where her husband had got to. But there they were, like three drunken students after a particularly hard party. Calogero assured her he was fine, and had not wanted to come in late and disturb her. He would be down soon to pick out a new suit and shoes. Renzo and Traiano wished her a polite good afternoon. Their spirits were all high. No one had tried, let alone succeeded, in killing him in the night. Antonio Santucci had lost his nerve. Calogero di Rienzi had won. Stefania did not realise this, but she sensed something important was happening. She said she would pick out the suit herself, and the shoes.

By a quarter past four, Calogero was back in his own suite, getting ready. At four thirty, Traiano and Renzo joined him, both of them immaculately dressed, and watched their boss pick his tie, and tie his shoelaces. They were to accompany him to Anna Maria's in a show of unity and strength. They were all freshly showered, freshly shaved, hair neatly combed and brushed. They made their way downstairs out of the hotel. In the lobby, they saw Rosario. Traiano smiled at him, but Calogero ignored him. They went out into the street and turned left, northwards, towards to Politeama and Anna Maria's flat.

The Santucci bothers were already there, in the drawing room, which Calogero alone entered, Traiano and Renzo being shown into another room where the television was. Calogero came in and sat before the two brothers. Anna Maria was on the sofa. It was the elder of the two, Domenico, who spoke. He was Antonio's uncle. Antonio's father, Lorenzo, said nothing, perhaps, one surmised, because this was too painful for him.

'The Santucci family, as very few people know, is the most influential in Sicily, and respected beyond the shores of our dear island. In New York, in Rome, in Brussels, the name Santucci means something. People respect it, they know it guarantees certain things. You yourself, don Calogero, have benefitted from this. But when the centre grows weak, the periphery suffers. I won't give you a detailed history of how this happened. But suffice it to say that we two and our two cousins got on very well indeed. We worked together, always together, unity was strength. But in the next generation, Antonio and Carlo had difficulties from the start. Their inability to work together was the cause of all our woes. We need someone strong in charge. I have to tell you that Antonio has already left for his country house outside Castelvetrano.'

Calogero bowed his head in acknowledgement.

'It is a beautiful place, and there he wants to concentrate on his hobbies of making wine and producing olive oil. The house needs work, and his children and wife will join him there in due course. But he himself left a few hours ago. He is no longer here. He will be in Castelvetrano, where he will do no harm, and no one will do him any harm either.'

Once again, Calogero bowed his head, signifying agreement. He did not study the father's face or the uncle's, but he knew what they must know: that this agreement was with them. As long as they lived, Antonio was safe; but when their day was past, then Antonio would have to look after himself. They had bought him time, no more, and how much time, who could be sure?

'Antonio will be from now on a sleeping partner in our family enterprise. Anna Maria will be able to explain to you everything you need to know about that. The olive oil, the wine, the citrus fruits, the cars, the whole import and export business. That is all run by managers and bankers and accountants. Paid people. On the whole, they do it well. And then there is our very profitable sideline. In that sector, we have some pretty tough people working for us, and we have some pretty tough people who are on the outside, perhaps wanting to get on the inside: the Romanians, the Albanians, the Russians, people from Calabria, people from Naples. But this is our thing, not theirs, though we know it needs to be defended. You were the one who took care of Michele Lotto. You are the one who we see as fearless and without pity or mercy for anyone who threatens our position, your position. We admire that. That was what we were, before we got old and decided to retire. Poor Antonio did not have the necessary steel, or the necessary judgement. We think you have both.'

Calogero bowed his head in acknowledgement of the compliment.

'Our cousin Renzo is still young. His brothers younger still. Antonio's children are teenagers. But their time will come, perhaps. Renzo needs to be prepared for his role. That is why we are proposing a period of regency. You take over from Antonio, you educate Renzo until his time comes. The people from Trapani, Messina and Agrigento are happy with this. After all, they rely on Palermo for their product, for regular deliveries. They think you can guarantee this. You have the necessary force of character. They think that if anyone causes them any trouble, they can look to you for a solution. For the foreseeable future, the whole cocaine operation is yours. Think of it as a farm. We are renting it to you. It brings in millions every year; all you have to do is make sure 50% comes to us; the accountants will let you know how.'

'That is very generous, a very generous arrangement,' said Calogero.

Half now, he thought. The rest later. He looked at the uncle, Domenico, and then the father, Lorenzo; they knew what he was thinking. In ten years' time, he would fight it out with Renzo. He was sure he would win; he wondered if they thought he might lose.

'We have assured certain parties that you are the man for us,' continued the uncle. 'To tell you the truth, the pressure for a change of management came from below and comes from above as well. Our political friends in Palermo want to meet you. Our friends in Rome want to meet you. And our friends in Brussels as well. In January you may have some travelling to do. Needless to say, these people keep their friendship with us, their membership of the honoured society, very secret.'

'I keep secrets too,' said Calogero.

The two old men nodded.

Calogero then spoke.

'I have a small favour to ask,' he said.

'We have heard,' said Antonio's father. 'The answer is yes.'

'For Traiano and for Renzo.'

The two youngsters were brought in. Renzo kissed the cheeks of his grandfather's cousins. Traiano kissed their hands. Finally, Calogero kissed their cheeks. All was settled. The two youngsters were told that they would be admitted to the honoured society.

'Now,' said Antonio's father, Lorenzo, with a touch of sourness to Calogero, 'Your important meeting is tomorrow; then you will discover just how hard you have to work and how much there is to do.'

'One last thing, one little favour, don Lorenzo and don Domenico,' said Calogero humbly. 'It is really something for Renzo rather than me, but it is important. The names of the trigger men who carried out the massacre of Favignana.'

Lorenzo and Domenico looked at each other. The man from Catania missed nothing. They nodded. They had expected this. They had requested these names from Antonio earlier. Out of this jacket pocket, the uncle, Lorenzo, took out a sheet of paper, already prepared. On it were two names.

Chapter Nine

The feast on the night of Christmas, at which about twenty-five adults and twenty-five children were present, began at 8pm and carried on till well past midnight. There were endless courses, various palate cleansers, and the same courses repeated: the usual bacchanalian tedium of the exceptionally heavy Sicilian banquet. Rosario found himself surrounded by children and old ladies. It was only when the first meat course was arriving, after the lobster had been taken away, that Traiano joined him, taking the temporarily empty seat next to him.

'How are you?' he said. 'I am missing Ceccina and my children. Other people's are delightful but only up to a point. Are you missing Carolina?'

'I wasn't thinking of her,' said Rosario. 'We spoke earlier today. And Catarina rang me. She said that Gino asked her to marry him, over the phone from Budapest.'

'Really?' asked Traiano.

'You seem a little surprised. It seems he realises that he should not let her get away.'

'And what are you doing about it?'

'What should I do about it?'

'Ask her to marry you, instead of that monster.'

'Is he a monster?'

'No, but… oh well, she can marry whom she likes. As can you. Have you noticed that there's been a bit of movement round here?'

'Yes, I noticed… I am not sure what I noticed, but clearly a lot has been going on. This is a business meeting, right?'

'Exactly. And Antonio Santucci has left. He has been replaced, overthrown, removed, whatever you want to call it. And the man of the moment is your brother. Though perhaps I should not tell you this. People were not happy with Santucci, least of all his nephew. And his father and uncle saw the way things were going, and decided to make a change before things fell apart, before change was forced on them. This is big for your brother, and big for me, and for all of us. Potentially big for you. Calogero will now be in an expansive mood. He has settled everything the way he likes it. He has even made his wife happy and his mistress happy. I think Stefania is pregnant too. So, everything in the garden is rosy. Except you.'

'Me?'

'He hasn't talked to you once, has he, since we got here. He has not talked to you, but the way he would see it, and I know how his mind works, you have not talked to him. He feels… well, you know how he feels about you.'

'How does he feel about me?' asked Rosario with a frown.

'Oh Saro, how difficult you make this. If only Ceccina was here, she would know what to say. He feels you hate him. I am sure you do not. But he feels you do. You need to go and show him you do not. He is vain in the extreme. You need to flatter his vanity. You need to let him know just how important he is to you and that you will do exactly as he says from now on, and enjoy it.'

'You mean I should act like Renzo? I did notice that. That guy is like his lapdog. That happened very quickly, didn't it?'

'Your brother has a way of winning people over. It is what he does. But he can't seem to win you over, and that is what hurts him.'

'He will never win me over,' said Rosario. 'Never. I would like to see him in jail for his crimes.'

'Why are you so hard and unforgiving?' asked Traiano. 'All he ever did was love you. And if you want to see him in jail, which I cannot believe for a moment, where do you want to see me? Look, never mind Calogero. You need to do this for me. Tomorrow morning, I will come and get you, and you can come over to his suite, late, and we will all have breakfast together and become fast friends.'

'Is that what he has suggested?'

'No, that is what I have suggested. It is my idea. And I want you to do it, and you will do it, because of me, not because of him. You may not love him, but you do love me, and I love you. You are my daughter's godfather. So do it for me.'

'I can't,' said Rosario after a long pause for thought. 'But you are right, I owe you a great deal because of our friendship, and I know you love me. So why don't you do this for me? Leave here, right now, leave these people, go back to Catania, pack everything up, and go to Romania with

Ceccina and the children, change you name, disappear, and lead an honest life from now on. Leave my brother, leave this life, leave everything, start again.'

'Are you saying I should leave before the law catches up with Calogero?'

'If you want to think of it that way. But think of it this way: leave before your character is ruined for life. Leave while you still can.'

'That moment has passed,' said Traiano.

'Then I can't help you,' said Rosario.

'And I cannot help you,' said Traiano sadly. 'You are ruining your brother's triumph. And you are making me very unhappy.'

'I cannot help it,' said Rosario.

They ate on in silence. The meat was cleared away; the vodka sorbets arrived. Traiano went back to his original seat. After a moment, Stefania appeared by his side.

'He told you?' she asked.

'Yes,' he said, wondering whether she was referring to her probable pregnancy. 'Congratulations.'

'There is no need to congratulate me, congratulate your brother. He is very pleased with himself. But this means that things will change. We are going back tomorrow evening, you, me and the children. He and Traiano will stay on, I am not sure how long for. He has to have a meeting with all these people, though the main work is done. Then he has to see all the new employees, and then…. Well, he mentioned spending time here, and then perhaps going to Rome briefly. My impression is, not that he ever tells me anything, that he may be spending a lot of time away from Catania from now on. More time here. That does not please me. Tancredi is here, after all. I am not stupid.'

'Who would he see in Rome?'

'Not the Pope. And what else is there in Rome? The government, the ministers, the parliament. He won't take me, that is for sure. He is taking Traiano. He said it was strictly business and that they would go by train rather than fly, and I would not like that. He has a point. The train is very uncomfortable and takes all night. Why would he put himself through all of that?'

Rosario knew why. It was because rail tickets were less traceable than air tickets. Rail was discreet. You could buy the tickets with cash quite easily. You took the train to Rome when you did not want to leave a record of your visit. But who was he seeing? How he would love to know. This would be the great information that Volta had sought so long. It was pointless asking Stefania. She would not know. But Traiano might.

'What shall we do tomorrow, before we have to leave?' she was asking.

'Perhaps you could do something with the children. I might well stay here and spend a bit of time with my brother. I have hardly seen him. I feel a bit guilty about that.'

319

'I suppose you better had. And speak to him about your wedding. The more he repeats his promises, the more he will feel forced to keep them. And now he has got what he wants, he is going to be richer than ever, so make sure he does not plead poverty.'

He nodded and finished his vodka sorbet. The first of the sweet courses was about to arrive: huge, towering cakes decorated with sparklers, which delighted the children. He was deep in thought for a few moments. He got up and went to look for Traiano, when he found him, he said:

'I have thought about it. You were right. When is a good time tomorrow?'

'Once Stefania goes out with the children, and before we have our meeting. I will come and get you.'

Traiano seemed relieved.

He did not sleep well. The vastness of the Christmas banquet, the huge amounts of alcohol, the noisy gathering, meant that when he went to bed, he took with him a heavy stomach, a dizzy head and ringing ears. In fact, he hardly slept at all. In the middle of the night, he sent a text message to Catarina, asking her why she was even considering marrying Gino if she was not considering marrying him. As soon as he sent the message, he regretted it. The answer, to his surprise, came almost immediately: "I have to marry someone", she declared, the bare words eloquent of a despair she felt, and one he shared. "If Gino asks me, and no one else does… " And then, "Are you asking me?" He thought for a long time, before replying that he did not know. Her reply was cutting, namely that he was not very gallant. In misery, he abandoned the conversation. He dared not send a message to Carolina.

For years, he had not only not had a girlfriend, but had had no thought or prospect of marriage. Now he had two women he could marry, two who wanted to marry him, perhaps. How had he got into this mess? And he had complicated things by making love to his sister-in-law who, in her turn, had allowed herself to be tupped by Maso. How he had got into this labyrinth, he did not know, but the really difficult question was how he was to escape from it. What could he do? And in the morning, he had to see his brother. He dreaded that, he was not quite sure why. He loathed and feared Calogero. He wanted to send him to jail for a very long time – he felt a momentary annoyance with Volta whose investigations never seemed to yield any fruit at all – but he would see Volta when he got back, and maybe, just maybe, some progress could be made. Who would Calogero see in Rome? That was the key question, the one thing Volta would want to know. He pondered his last interview with Volta. Volta's girlfriend was pregnant, which was a bit of a shock to Volta. Perhaps Volta's mind was not quite on the quarry that had obsessed him for the best part of decade? Had Volta allowed himself to be distracted? He had told him to be careful, that they knew there was someone on the inside. He knew suddenly what he had to do. He had to get further in.

He fell asleep late but woke early, and was almost impatient by the time Traiano appeared at his door, in his dressing gown, to take him to his brother's suite. There was Calogero, lying in bed, in his silk pyjamas, with Renzo sitting at the foot of the bed in his white hotel dressing gown, amidst the splendour of coffee cups and pastries being dispensed by a uniformed waiter, from a trolley. Rosario sat on the immense bed as well, and there was silence while they waited for the waiter to withdraw, which he did, with a hint of hurry and confusion.

Once the man was gone, Rosario looked at his brother, and resolved to play the part that was expected of him. He took Calogero's hand and kissed it. Then he leaned forward and kissed his lips. Then he spoke, slowly and deliberately, aware that the other two were listening intently, as was his brother.

321

'Don Calogero,' said Rosario. 'I need your fraternal advice. I need your guidance. My father has been dead these many years, and who should I ask for guidance, apart from you? Shall I marry Carolina Petrocchi; or shall I marry Catarina? Or should I marry no one at all? I know now that the only thing that matters is pleasing you. Traiano has spoken to me about this. Traiano is younger than me, but he is cleverer, and he has a more pronounced sense of gratitude. I have not always been grateful for what you have done for me. I am sorry for this. Now, tell me what to do and I shall do it.'

Calogero was silent a few moments, as if savouring his triumph.

'Marry Carolina,' he said at last. 'She is my choice. And Stefania's. That is the best from the point of view of the family. We need Petrocchi's firm on our side. As for Catarina, she is rather rebellious, I think. Best leave her to that brute Gino, who will know how to handle her.'

Rosario nodded. But he knew at that moment with absolute clarity, that the girl he wanted to marry was Catarina, not Carolina. But he brushed this aside.

'I want to work for you,' he said. 'When I marry Carolina, maybe I should leave Petrocchi's and let her work there, and come and work for you in the new office.'

Calogero stared at him.

'Things are in flux, right now, but will soon be clearer. I was just discussing this with Traiano and with Renzo. I will have to stay here while you and Stefania and the children go back to Catania. There are meetings to be held. Traiano has stuff to do in Catania as soon as the holidays are over and will take Renzo with him to show him our lovely city, which he has hardly seen, and also show him our various businesses. I am meeting the Santucci employees here, then some people that Anna Maria will introduce me to, and then I will have to go to Rome. I am going to get Muniddu to accompany me, as I know I can trust him.'

'Good idea, boss,' said Traiano.

'Why not take me?' asked Rosario.

Calogero studied him.

'Muniddu is a bodyguard. He would deter anyone who tried anything funny. And if someone did, he would make sure they regretted it. I am going to Rome discretely. Stefania wanted to come, but discretion is not her strong suit. She wanted to go because she loves Rome, she loves the shops.'

'I love Rome, I love the churches,' said Rosario.

'You know, boss,' said Traiano, 'Taking Saro would be a great cover. Two brothers, wanting to spend time together, making a pilgrimage to Rome, to pray and light candles. No one would doubt that Saro was there to pray, and you would sort of shelter under the umbrella of that.'

'But a touch hypocritical as well, don't you think?' said Calogero innocently.

'Muniddu could trail along in the background,' said Traiano. 'He knows how to do that. And when the time came, Muniddu would be able to take you along to see the person who wants to see you.'

'Which may not be until after New Year,' said Calogero. 'He is probably on holiday until then. We have to take Muniddu if only to guard the suitcase.'

The other three looked puzzled.

Calogero laughed.

'You don't think I am going empty handed, do you? I am going in the manner of a provincial vassal, with a suitcase stuffed full of cash. Lots of it. A donation to party funds. He likes cash, or so I am told. Anna Maria has tried to get him to accept money via wire, but he prefers the weight of cash. The people here, all of them contribute, as do we. Where is the suitcase we brought?' he asked Traiano.

'In a very safe place,' he replied. 'Trust me.'

'I do. Do we have any spare cash lying around? Yes? Go and get it.'

Traiano was not long. He came back with a rucksack. He placed it on the bed. Calogero opened it, and revealed that it was full of 500 euro notes.

'If I take the train up to Rome from here, when we get the signal, perhaps Saro could get the train the same night from Catania; the two trains join up, don't they, when they cross the straits of Messina. Then we could arrive together. I could share a couchette with Muniddu until Villa San Giovanni, and then Rosario could swap with Muniddu. The only question is when. Muniddu can tell you, Traiano, and you can then tell Saro. Be prepared, my brother, to drop everything at a few hours' notice at best.'

'But who are you meeting?' asked Rosario.

Calogero smiled beatifically.

'Tell him, Traiano, but whisper it.'

Traiano leaned forward and whispered something in Rosario's ear. Calogero watched his brother's eyes widen. Then he turned to the rucksack, and rummaged through its contents.

'I want you to buy Carolina something nice when you get back to Catania. Something she will treasure. There must be some jewellers Stefania can recommend. Does your dressing gown have a pocket?'

He counted out twenty of the 500 euro notes, rolled them up and put them in Rosario's pocket. He then gave the rucksack back to Traiano.

'Put it back in its safe place. That is the tips for the staff when we leave. Now, I must get ready for the meeting later today, and so must you.' He looked at his brother. 'Thanks for coming to see me.'

The three left him.

Ten minutes later, Traiano was back. He put his head around the bathroom door. Calogero was brushing his teeth, and caught sight of him in the mirror.

'You tried and you failed,' he said. 'So do not blame yourself, blame him. It is all his fault. What name did you tell him?'

Traiano approached and whispered. Calogero laughed.

'Great imagination. Perhaps it will be him. Perhaps not. We shall see. I will only know who it is when I am called in to see him.' He rinsed out his mouth. 'My brother is not skilled enough at this game. He made several very silly mistakes. No one with an ounce of skill would ever ask whom I was meeting in Rome. It is his hunger to know that gives him away. In this business, you never ask, you just wait to be told, and you are told the minimum you need to know, as knowledge is dangerous. Stefania never asks questions. I will get her to make sure the engagement is announced. He will buy her something nice at the jewellers and that too will make it public. Make sure he spends that money. Then when he vanishes, it will be clear why. It will be because he did not want to get married after all. You have worked out what to do?'

'Yes. I have it all worked out.'

'Good. When he goes back to Catania, he will try to see Volta. Watch him like a hawk.'

'Volta?'

'Yes. Watching the other one would be a bad idea. It would arouse suspicion. But you know that. When are Gino and Alfio back?'

'Today or tomorrow.'

'We may need them. We will see.'

'For…?'

'A job here.'

'Anyone I know?'

'Things will be clearer tonight,' said Calogero. 'After the meeting.'

The meeting was at noon, and all the men were to disappear for the rest of the day at that point, while the women went out to lunch and then dispersed. Shortly after the hour of noon, Rosario, Stefania and the three children left in a car; the drive would take about three hours, and they resolved to stop half way at Enna. Prompted by her husband, glad to have her brother-in-law alone to herself and her children, they spoke only of his forthcoming marriage. He mentioned the money Calogero had given him. She spoke of what he should buy and where he should buy it. And as they progressed along the motorway, he thought that he could easily break it off before November, or even extend the engagement beyond that, given that the house might not be ready in time.

Monday 27th December was supposed to be a working day. After the long stay in Palermo – it had only been a few days, but had seemed to be a never-ending bacchanal of eating and drinking – he was resolved to live a somewhat cleaner and more restrained life. He got up very early, as he liked to do, and was in the gymnasium at 5.30am, when the place was absolutely deserted, which was just as he liked it. Indeed, the only person ever present at such an hour was Traiano, who knew he liked to visit then,

327

and sometimes was there. After the gym, he was in the Church of the Holy Souls in Purgatory for Mass at 7am, and then he walked towards the Etnea, where he had a cup of coffee and a cornetto in his usual bar, opposite the office, and then went to the office, which was rather empty for that time of day. The peace and quiet was reassuring. He checked the locked drawer for the phone which he used to communicate with Volta. He had his passport and his driver's license in his jacket pocket, and he knew what he needed to do with these. In an hour or two he would give Volta a missed call, then wait for an hour, and then head to the police headquarters to report the loss of his identity card. In the meantime, with little to do, he would ring Carolina.

He rang and made an appointment to see her after work. He intimated that there was a surprise in store. After the call, he felt rather deflated. Then, sensing the boss had arrived, he went to call on the lawyer Petrocchi; they had a pleasant conversation. Petrocchi particularly wanted to know what had happened at the Grand Hotel. He told him about the food, the drink, the rooms, the quality of the sheets, the women and the children, and how he had seen the brothers Santucci and don Antonio; in other words, he had seen the carapace of ordinariness, but seen nothing of the important stuff. Except....

'My brother and I are better friends than we have been for some time. And Calogero is feeling expansive. The younger Santucci, Antonio, has withdrawn, and the nephew has changed sides, and the two old men have sanctioned it. Calogero is in Palermo seeing people, and then going to see other people. People in Rome.'

'You mean.....?'

'It looks that way. One could tell by the way he and Traiano and this Renzo were acting. It is my guess...'

'He has done well for himself,' said Petrocchi. 'He always meant to. I always thought he would. Whatever you do, you must never offend him. He is now a very powerful man, if what you say is true.'

'Sir, we are better friends than ever. He gave me a very nice present. You know him, money is what he likes, and you can judge your standing against his generosity. I am meeting Carolina after work, and buying her an engagement ring. It is high time we got round to it.'

'Excellent. And we need to talk about your promotion in this firm. As my son-in-law....'

They talked. Once more he felt a sense of deflation. He was not cut out for the business of lying.

At a little past ten he was back at his desk. He unlocked the drawer, and gave Volta a missed call. He noted the time. A little less than an hour later, he left the office; within a few minutes he was at the police headquarters in the San Nicolella square. He told the officer on the door that he was there to report the loss or theft of his identity card. He presented his passport. He was given a piece of paper stating his purpose and was sent to the requisite office on the first floor. That turned out to be the wrong office, he was told on arrival. He was sent to another part of the building, and told to wait on a bench. He did so obediently. After a few moments his name was called, and he followed a policewoman, who led him to a small room. There sitting behind a table was Volta. He stood up and smiled.

They spoke for an hour or so about Palermo, about the Grand Hotel. Volta made notes of all the names of the people that had been there, most of whom Rosario had memorised. He listened to every detail attentively, asked questions, got him to go over things several times. Then leaving the notes aside, they discussed personal matters, in a way they had not been able to do for years. Volta spoke of his wedding plans, of the coming child.

Rosario spoke of his own wedding plans too. The wedding had been spoken of as taking place in November 2011, but he was thinking that it might be better scheduled for January 2012, because it was not good to get married in the month of the dead, or in December which was Advent, but January, this time next year, once Christmas was over, might be best. But, as he told Volta, and Volta alone, he did not want to get married to Carolina at all, and the longer the wedding was postponed the longer he had to break it off, but really, he wanted her to break it off, to have that burden. He knew he did not want her, and he was sure that she did not want him; it was like an arranged marriage, brought about through family interests, interests he did not share. He felt she would break it off, if, by this time next year, Volta could bring Calogero down; because he was sure she only wanted him because of the fact that he was Calogero's brother; certainly, that appealed to her mother and even to her father. But if he were merely the penniless brother of a presumed criminal under arrest, then the engagement would crumble with Calogero's fortunes. And he would be free.

Volta listened to this attentively.

Rosario confessed that he felt guilty for the way he was deceiving Carolina, deceiving her father, and deceiving her mother; though, of the three, he felt least for the mother and most for the father, who had always been so kind to him. As for Carolina, she was deceiving herself, so he did not feel so bad. And really, she had revealed traits of character that he did not much like. They were not sleeping together, had never slept together, and that was a relief. He would feel very guilty if that were the case. If she were ever to suggest it, he had the perfect excuse in his religion and hers. But that made him feel like a hypocrite, which, he admitted, he was. Calogero knew that. About that, he was right. After all, did he believe in justice, or did he just want to settle accounts with his brother? Was this altruistic, or was it revenge?

'It could be both,' Volta said. 'It may not be possible to bring him down by this time next year, you do realise that?' He saw Rosario nod. 'Of course, when he is arrested, and investigated, we will take in the whole lot. Some of them will squeal. That will bring him down. It will all collapse like a house of cards. The Colonel, Andreazza, he will cut a deal. Anything to save his name, anything to keep him out of it. Then we have Traiano on some very serious charges. That boy....'

'What boy? You mean the guy who likes football, Giorgio, the one from Ukraine?'

'He is over eighteen. I mean the one called Pavel or Paolo.'

'Oh. But... I didn't see anything. You think....?'

'I am sure of it. You saw enough. That boy has a mother. She might be a prostitute but she will have some sense of morality. She can be turned easily enough, so can the child, and that means so can Andreazza. I know Andreazza knows little, but he can accuse Traiano of pimping, and then we can turn Traiano. You can turn Traiano.... Then the whole thing collapses. But the key piece of evidence is seeing your brother with this person.'

He tapped the piece of paper on which he had written the name that Traiano had whispered in Rosario's ear.

'For that, I need to go to Rome.'

'Do you trust him?' asked Volta. 'Does he trust you?'

Rosario knew what he meant. Was he being strung along by Calogero? Was he being deliberately deceived? Had he managed to deceive Calogero, or had Calogero deceived him?

'Time will tell,' said Rosario.

'Be careful,' counselled Volta.

'I can look after myself,' said Rosario with confidence.

Volta doubted this, but did not say anything. If Rosario was confident, then why should he deny him his chance? And not just his chance, but Volta's own chance, to bring down Calogero and the whole gang and the political contacts in Rome. He was already visualising the fallout from this. He would be nothing less than a national hero if the whole thing worked out as he hoped it would.

'You know who this man is?' he said, tapping the paper with the name, the name that was somehow too important to mention.

'Of course.'

'A name that points to the rotten heart of our democracy, the corrupted heart,' said Volta. 'This man is the lynchpin of his political party, little known to the public, on the face of it an unimportant government figure, but, the man with the influence, the man with the power. The power behind the throne. And now we know why he is the power behind the throne. Unless of course Calogero is spinning us a line.'

'You mean Traiano. He gave me the name.'

'How clever is he?'

'Very, I would say.'

Volta sighed and looked at Rosario. He knew at this stage that he ought to advise caution, the very greatest caution. The enemy was sly and successful. All the people who had caused them difficulty in the past were now dead. There was nothing that Calogero di Rienzi and Trajan Antonescu would not do, he was convinced, to safeguard their own interests. He was sure of this, as the evidence of the past was clear. Nothing. They would stop at nothing. Were they deceived by Rosario? Would they show Rosario any pity if not? He could not be entirely sure. But this was their best chance. The risk was surely worth taking; and yet he knew it was not his risk.

'Be careful,' he said.

'I have known them both all my life,' said Rosario. 'I have always been careful.'

'We won't be able to meet here again,' said Volta. 'And I am going to leave in the back of a police car, lying down too. We do not know who is watching. Next time we meet, it will be here.' He gave him a card with a name and address on. It was very distinctive, a laminated bright pink card. 'You have to give me a missed call, and then wait an hour and present yourself at this address. Ring the bell and go up to the flat. I will be there waiting for you.'

'Whose flat is it?'

'It is someone I know from of old. She is a prostitute. High class. Nothing to do with your brother. I will get into her flat by entering another building and walking across the roof terraces. They are modern apartments, and have flat roofs. She is quite well known. Her name is Silvia. If people see you ringing her bell, they will assume that you are there to see her and not me. If I need to see you, I will call and see you at Silvia's within the hour. It is only a fifteen-minute walk from your office. Until then.'

There had been quite a lot of trouble to sort out in Palermo, and Calogero was not back in Catania until the end of the week, in time for the New Year celebrations. Traiano and Renzo came with him. The first that Rosario knew was when he went to the gym and found Traiano there on the Friday morning, on the feast of Saint Sylvester, the last day of the year, 31st December.

'You have been coming here all week, have you?' asked Traiano, as Rosario came in and put down his bag. It was five thirty in the morning.

'Working off all that food and drink,' said Rosario.

'Did he tell you about the food and drink?' asked Traiano, turning to Maso, who was also there.

Maso shook his head.

'So how has it been without me?' asked Traiano. 'We came back last night very late. I have yet to go home and wake up Ceccina and give her a nice surprise, and then get the children up. But I wanted to say that we are holding the New Year's dinner tonight at my house. Ceccina will cook. You know what a wonderful cook she is. Your brother will be coming, and Stefania and the children, and also Renzo and we have invited your sister as well - not Assunta, Elena.'

'The lawyer Petrocchi has invited me,' said Rosario. 'I have to be there at eight in the evening, and no doubt it will go on till past midnight.'

'It won't be the same without you, said Traiano sadly. 'How is Carolina?'

'Quite well,' he said guardedly.

'While I have been away, Maso here has been giving the tenants above your brother notice to quit. Sometime soon we can begin the restructuring of the entire floor for your brother and Stefania, and then you will get their place.'

'Is what you are doing legal, Maso?'

'Yes, it is,' said Traiano, preventing Maso from answering. 'I mean he is just asking them to leave. Nothing wrong with that.'

'And they have all said they would?' asked Rosario.

Maso looked at Traiano. Traiano looked at Maso, and Maso answered Rosario.

'One has refused,' he admitted.

'He will have to be persuaded,' said Traiano. 'The rest were eager to go. The places need restructuring; we were able to offer them financial inducements to leave or to sell, or to go to other properties. The place will look wonderful, the whole floor, a magnificent roof terrace, and the boss will at long last put a lift in.'

'Nice,' admitted Rosario. 'And how was Palermo after I left?'

'Good. We had a little trouble, as expected, but the boss cleared it up. He did what that fool Antonio Santucci was unable to do. Confront a few people, well, two in particular, stamp his authority on the operation, and take decisive action. As he always does. He is going to be spending a lot of his time in future in Palermo.'

'And you will look after things here?'

'Yes. Along with Stefania. By the way, did I tell you? Gino is back, and Alfio. They came over to Palermo, but they are now back here, and Gino told me that Catarina is marrying him, sometime next year.'

A sense of terrible disappointment swept over Rosario. It was visible in his face. Traiano looked at Maso, giving him the nod to go.

'You should have moved while you had the chance,' said Traiano. 'If you really liked her.'

'I did like her. She didn't like me. At least she didn't like me enough in that way.'

'Well, there is always Carolina,' said Traiano. He sat down on the bench next to Rosario. He was wearing his smart suit still, one of his smart suits, and the silk scarf that Calogero had given him, the scarf that he clung to and wore always, like a fetish. 'Carolina may be the girl for you after all,' he continued. 'But you should have told me that you lost your identity card.'

'What?'

'If you had told me, you would not have had to have gone to Police Headquarters and wasted a huge amount of time. We could have got someone we know to get you a new one just like that. I know people there from when I had trouble with my identity card, before getting married. You did not have to go and queue up with the common herd.'

'How did you know I was there?'

'Someone said they saw you and mentioned it. As the boss's brother, you are remarkable, you know. People spot you wherever you go and they talk about it. Just like if you go and see a high-class prostitute on the other side of the city, they will know about that too. Why go all that way? We have that sort of thing here, you know. You speak to me, and I will arrange it, maximum discretion. Top quality too. Your best friend is a pimp and you do not use him. You should.'

'The other side of the city is more discreet,' said Rosario, blushing. 'Was I seen there too?'

'No. No one is following you, dear Saro. Why should they? You never go anywhere, except perhaps when you do. It is just you had her card in your wallet, and someone noticed it, that is all. It is rather distinctive. You were buying coffee, and they saw it in your wallet as you were taking out your cash. I believe Silvia is very highly regarded, but a specialist.... Don't worry, I will not tell Carolina. And when you are married, you will find better things to do, such as stay at home. I did when I married. Talking of which, it is time for me to go home. Happy New Year!'

'Before you go,' said Rosario, stopping him. 'When is Calogero being summoned to Rome?'

Traiano sat down again.

'He doesn't know. When they call him is the only answer. But it is going to be soon, and it will be with little notice. I mean, with just a day's notice. You need to be ready to go not quite at once, but with alacrity.' He looked around, to check that no one was listening, to check that they were quite alone. 'Keep a case ready. Tell Petrocchi that you may have to be unexpectedly absent for a few days in the new year. You are here at this time every day?'

'Yes.'

'Good. As you know, I am up all night. Make sure you are here every day, and I will be here too and keep you informed.'

Rosario nodded.

For a moment Traiano held him in a warm embrace. Then he jumped up and left. As he expected, Maso was outside waiting for him.

'You heard?' asked Traiano.

'Eight in the evening,' confirmed Maso.

'You know what to do?'

'I think so. Take my brother to his flat, using the key you gave me, and see if we can get inside his computer.'

'Good. And the other thing I asked you about?'

'Enzo says he can do it.'

'Really?'

'Yes, it is quite easy. You route the computer through a series of servers –'

'Whatever. Technology bores me. Just make sure that when I ask you to do so, you can send emails that look like they come from him and his computer, from whatever place we choose.'

'Yes, boss.'

Seeing there was nothing else, Maso left. Traiano watched him go. He liked the way Maso did not ask questions. He called him back.

'There will be a big reward,' he said. 'One that you will like a great deal.'

'Thanks, boss,' said Maso, leaving once more.

He walked the short distance through the deserted and dark streets to his own house, opened the street door, and then walked up to his flat. Opening the door, he savoured the warmth and smell of home. He carefully removed his shoes, and walked down the corridor to the bedroom he shared with his wife. He was aware of his sleeping children, and as he carefully opened the door, of the sleeping presence of Ceccina. He undressed, carefully hanging up his suit, and then quietly got into bed with her. She stirred. He put his arms round her. She murmured a few tired words of welcome. She turned towards him, whispering that she was glad he was back, and they kissed. The kiss was like water in the desert, like the taste of food after many days of starvation. The warmth and softness of the marital bed was heaven itself after the gorgeous luxury and loneliness of the Grand Hotel. How he had missed her, how she had missed him! She did not have to ask him how he had enjoyed Palermo, for she knew.

'Catarina has said yes to Gino,' she said, knowing this was big news.

'More fool her. He is a monster. But they will be happy enough. Though not as happy as us.'

'Why didn't she catch Saro? Why didn't Saro catch her?' she wondered.

'They both hesitated too long. Besides Saro asked Calogero for advice and told him he would do as he said. And Calogero told him to marry Carolina. Which is what Stefania wanted.'

'Are they reconciled?'

He wondered if she meant Calogero and his brother, or Calogero and his wife.

'Everyone is reconciled with everyone.'

'Will Saro be happy with Carolina?'

'They are ideally suited,' said Traiano. 'But there is no passion there, just duty.'

Conversation ceased while passion took its course.

'They are all coming here tonight,' he said later. 'Stefania and Calogero and the children, and Renzo and Elena.'

'I was told,' she said. 'Is Renzo nice?'

He thought about this.

'Not really.'

'Is he handsome?'

'Not really. But he is rich. He likes the boss, he likes me, he has never really been to Catania. He would do anything for the boss, even marry Elena, just you watch.'

'Well, she wants to get married,' said Ceccina. 'And she always feels she has been overlooked in the past. If he is very rich, and he has more than Saro, more than Assunta, more than us, I am sure she will be very happy.'

'They will have plenty. And so will we. Just you wait and see.'

He kissed her again. There was plenty of time before the children got up. This, just this, was what he lived for, the company of his wife, the knowledge of the children asleep in the next room, the safety and comfort of his family.

Afterwards he slept, and he awoke to see the light of the last day of the year fading. It was the night of Saint Sylvester. He could hear already the crackle and the bang of fireworks being let off in the streets, in the square, from people's windows. It was not quite five in the afternoon, and the noise would only grow as the night and the excitement advanced. The flat was full of the smell of delicious food. Ceccina must have been cooking all day, while he slept. He recalled last night; being in Palermo, the long drive home, the conversation with Saro in the gym early in the morning, then coming home to Ceccina. Now he could sense the children in the flat, and he knew he had to get up to see them, not having seen them for a week. He rose, put on his dressing gown, and went to find little Cristoforo and Maria Vittoria. They were having their bath, and cried with delight on seeing their father. Ceccina left him to bathe the children, while she returned to the kitchen. Afterwards, when the children were bathed and dressed, and when he too was bathed and dressed, he went to join her. Everything was as it should have been in the kitchen. The lentils were cooking nicely. This was important. You had to have lentils if you were to have a prosperous new year. He was sure they were going to have a very prosperous new year.

There was a television in the kitchen, and he switched it on idly for the six o'clock news. The set was tuned to a local station, and the first item was not how the island was gearing up for the celebrations of the night of Saint Sylvester (that came second). The first item was two murders the previous night in Palermo. Two bodies had been recovered from the harbour; expensively dressed, they were identified, not as members of the San Lorenzo crime family, but as the manager of a company that exported lemons and the manager of a company that imported cars. Both these companies were owned by the same holding group, which was owned by

342

various shareholders, among them Antonio Santucci. The murder ha an unusual aspect to it. Both men had been tied together, and thrown into the sea; one had been shot in the head, the other had been pulled down by the corpse and drowned. Their pockets were stuffed with five euro notes. The television showed legions of police standing around looking concerned at the place where the bodies had been recovered. There were also shots of the Santucci house, where a spokesman announced that Antonio was away for New Year, staying at his country house, tending his vines, and had been absent for some time. Then, as Traiano was sure there must be, there were the usual talking heads: a politician from Palermo lamenting how this savage and cruel murder would tarnish the city's reputation; a grieving relative of one of the men, saying that he had been one of the best and kindest of men; and finally, worth waiting for, surely, Fabio Volta. Traiano watched with a sneer of contempt.

They gave Volta considerable air time. This murder, said Volta, sent a message, as evinced by the money in the pockets of the victims, who were clearly accused of selling out their masters. The two men were well known upper ranking operatives of the San Lorenzo crime family. (No law against libelling the dead, thought Traiano.) Their murder signified a rearranging of the power structure in the family, a change of management, a change of personnel. This had to be directly connected to the events of August, when several leading members of the San Lorenzo crime family had been blown up off the island of Favignana. Whoever condemned these men to death was showing that the new lords of misrule were not to be messed with, which was, Traiano reflected, an excellent analysis. Then there was the policeman in charge of the investigation, making an appeal for witnesses and speaking of the search for the weapon.

There would be no witnesses, Traiano knew, none at all. It had been very late and very dark when the cars had drawn up at the water's edge. The two tied up men, the trigger men of the massacre of Favignana, had been taken out of the car boots and led to the water's edge. Both had pleaded for their lives. Both had looked up at Renzo, and then at Calogero, speaking of their families, speaking of how they had only been carrying out orders. Neither, clearly, had gone into the meeting in the Grand Hotel expecting to be accused, tried and sentenced by the boss and the new boss, and by their

343

peers. Neither had come up with anything compelling despite spending six or seven hours locked in a storeroom in the basement of the Grand Hotel. Both, Traiano had noticed with disdain, had soiled their expensive suits. Calogero had weighed the gun in his hand, looking bored and disappointed by their performance. One of the men started praying. Calogero handed the gun to Renzo and whispered something to him. Renzo nodded. The two men looked up, thinking that perhaps Renzo would show them mercy, whereas Calogero, they both knew, never could, mercy being totally foreign to him. They had known Renzo as a child. He still was a child. But they were wrong. Renzo aimed at the praying man and pulled the trigger. The aim was effective enough. It blew off his jaw. Then the two were tied together by the other men, their former colleagues, and tipped into the sea. There was a great deal of struggle and movement, which was watched with interest. Finally, the two were still. The living, after the slightest of pauses, got into their cars and drove away, Calogero, Traiano and Renzo, to Catania. The murder weapon (Calogero had no gun) was currently in the bottom draw of a chest in his bedroom. Good luck finding that, he thought.

'My sister is coming soon, to do my hair,' said Ceccina, above the sound of the television, now talking about the night of Saint Sylvester. 'I told her to do yours too.'

'You know how she hurts me when she pulls my hair around,' said Traiano. 'It really hurts. But if you want her to make me suffer…. What are you wearing?'

'My blue dress.'

'The new one?'

'Yes.'

'Nice.'

'What are you wearing?'

'What I am wearing now. I was wearing a suit all week.'

'The jeans are nice. Is that shirt silk?'

'No, it is linen. An old one of the boss's. He gave it to me. It was made in India, he told me. But this scarf is silk. I really like it.'

'You hardly ever take it off. By the way, the Te Deum is at 7.30pm. We ought to go. We will have time. Calogero will be there, and so will Stefania and also Petrocchi and daughter and wife and your beloved Saro.'

'Why do you call him that?'

'I know you love him.'

'I do. You are right. Are you jealous?'

'Of course not. And don't forget that tomorrow there is the Veni Creator in Church. We cannot miss that either.'

'I would not dream of doing so. But let us leave it as late as possible. Let us go at noon. Anyway, when have I ever missed anything like that? I have even been to the supplication to the Madonna of Pompeii every year since I met you.'

She smiled at him.

'You are so good,' she said. They kissed. 'Next year, I don't mean just yet, but in nine months' time, we are going to need a bigger house.'

She said it lightly. They kissed again. He held her tight. She was touched to see that there were tears in his eyes.

They were all in good time for the Te Deum. For once he sat with his wife and children, holding the baby, at the front of the Church, and so did Calogero; whereas it was the usual practice for the women and children to sit and kneel in the chairs at the front, whilst the men stood at the back, or around the doorway, or even out in the square, while only the notably pious males sat with the women and children. One such was, of course, Rosario, who knelt with his head bowed before the service began. Sitting behind him, Traiano studied the back of his neck, aware too that Calogero, some rows back was studying not his brother, but him. When it was over, there was a great deal of excited chatter in the brightly lit church and much lighting of candles in front of the Madonna and the other saints. Rosario turned to find Traiano at his side, holding his goddaughter.

'I spent the whole day asleep,' he said. 'You?'

'At the office,' said Rosario.

'I have made a good resolution. To save my soul.'

Rosario looked at him sharply.

'What has happened?'

'Nothing has happened. Well, a great deal has happened. Ceccina is pregnant.'

'Congratulations!'

'I have to think of my children. Ceccina has been speaking to me, it is not just you. But from now on I know I need to listen. Have you seen the news on television? No? Make sure you do. Your brother is watching us. Don't do anything unusual. Act as if all was as normal. Remember, on workdays you go to the gym every day at 5.30am, don't you? We can talk there.'

He looked up at the Spanish Madonna, as if he were saying a prayer, made the sign of the cross, and then drifted away. Rosario stood where he was. Outside, the flashes and bangs of fireworks were growing more and more insistent.

The balcony of the lawyer Petrocchi's flat overlooked the via Tomaselli and the darkened trees of the Villa Bellini. Beyond that the domes and towers of the city were illuminated, and as midnight approached, the noise of fireworks became tremendous; as the hour struck, as 2011 began, the ships in the port all blew their horns, as did every car in the street. The noise was deafening. Holding Carolina's hand, Rosario said to her that this was now the year of their wedding; he saw her smile, and he kissed her. It would also be the year of his brother's downfall, he promised himself. And if she still wanted to marry him after that, then she was a better woman than he suspected.

He had seen the television news. He had gone home after the Te Deum and watched the local channel, and seen Volta. By his calculation it was clear that his brother and Traiano could have been present in Palermo just at the time of the crime. The fact that Traiano had told him to watch the news seemed to indicate as much. It was tantamount to a confession. He realised that he and Volta were now very close to success.

The party at the lawyer Petrocchi's had been a large one, he had seen on arrival. He had not expected this at all. There had been two other families present, so they had been a dozen in all. The two other couples and their children, who were roughly his age, had looked at him with a curiosity they had felt hard to disguise. They had engaged him in conversation, as one would a foreigner from some exotic and distant land. They had treated him not as a Sicilian and a man from Catania, but as someone whose customs and values were completely different from their own. It was only when he mentioned that he had been to school in Rome, that he made references that established he was a devout Catholic, and that he had also been to university, that they softened towards him, realising that he was, after all, one of them.

Rosario realised that these two families were the lawyer Petrocchi's, and more importantly his wife's, canaries down the mineshaft; that he was being tested for his launch as their son-in-law. It was necessary to see if he could pass in good society, a type of society, he freely admitted to himself, of which he knew very little. He supposed, as the conversation lost its stiffness, as they gradually realised that he was another human being, not some animal to be viewed as in a zoo, that he had passed the test. He would do.

On the whole he found good society slightly boring. Unlike the sort of society that he was used to, the men and women talked freely among themselves, rather than the men talking among themselves and women doing the same, and the two not mixing. The subjects were not dissimilar. There was lots of talk of religion: the Pope, the Cardinal, the Archbishop of Catania, Saint Agatha and her feast, Padre Pio and his shrine (which seemed to be the only place they had all visited); they all spoke of the

Spanish Madonna and how they liked her a lot, and they did so as if to pay him a compliment. There was a lot of talk of Rome, the one place they all loved, and Milan, less loved, and Naples, not loved at all, except, of course, for the shrine of Saint Januarius. But if Naples were little loved, Palermo was even less so, and it was at this point the subject of the double murder of early that morning, or late last night, of the two bodies in the harbour, came up, as he was sure it would. Indeed, he could tell that they were all eager to discuss this one thing, and to discuss it not just among themselves, but with him, the brother of the presumed criminal. He was Calogero's brother, so he must have some inside insight on the matter. Only he did not. He knew exactly what they knew, having seen the same news report; but of course, this was not true. He knew a great deal more. He knew the cruelty without which organised crime could not flourish. The manner of the two men's execution struck him as chillingly cruel, designed to warn others, and no doubt carried out in a way that made others fear that the same fate awaited them. He understood perhaps what they never could, that cruelty was a drug on which the cruel became dependant. He detected in them not horror at the thought of cruelty, but admiration and interest in the proceeds of crime. He realised they were rich, and that they deferred to him as someone as rich as themselves, perhaps richer, perhaps destined to be very rich. The talk was of Padre Pio and the Madonna, but the hunger was for euros.

He felt the intoxication of flattery without letting it master him. This was what Stefania wanted, to be with rich fashionable people and to be accepted as one of them. This was what Calogero wanted too, he supposed, if not for himself, then for his children. And how easy it was to be accepted, after all, he reflected. Money sanitised everything. Money was the true God they worshipped, even if they did not realise that it came from the sheer might of the killer and the torturer. And the ridiculous thing was that the aura of money was so insubstantial. He himself was poorly paid, and had very little by way of savings, and yet, because of Calogero, the magical aura of wealth had settled on him. And tomorrow, Calogero could lose it all. And then where would they be? He would be a simple jobbing lawyer without any family behind him, and with a brother on remand for trial, his assets no doubt frozen. When that happened, and he was confident it would, all the people round the table would be horrified. He wondered how horrified Carolina would be; how horrified her mother would be; how her father would react. For it was in the lawyer Petrocchi, who had not been born rich, that he had the greatest confidence.

In fact, he had spoken to the Petrocchi earlier in the evening when they had had a moment alone.

'It is possible that my brother may lose everything and quite soon too,' he remarked.

'You must have your reasons for thinking that,' observed Petrocchi drily. 'Let us just hope that if he falls, he does not take us with him.'

'You mean the Confraternity, sir?'

'That survived Garibaldi and the fall of the kingdom; I think it can survive the fall of Calogero and his friends. No, what I meant was let us hope he does not take you personally with him, or me. Of course, we are not criminals, we are lawyers; I don't mean that the police are going to come for us. I just fear that when the police come for him, he does not kill whoever he thinks responsible first. Of course, I am assuming that the police will come for him. Perhaps not. Perhaps the others will come for him. His is a dangerous game. People get greedy and they do not have the law to protect them. That chap who was killed off Favignana in the summer. Who did that? Not the police, I imagine, but his friends who had turned into secret enemies. These people eat themselves in the end, but it is my hope that they do not take too many innocents with them. Though they invariably do.'

'I may have to be absent at short notice, sir, at some point over the next few days.'

'Very well,' said Petrocchi. 'I hope you know what you are doing. You have been in the office between Christmas and New Year, so do take a few days off. Just drop me an email.'

'Thank you, sir.'

The party ended shortly after one in the morning, and he, as the future son-in-law, was the last to leave. Carolina accompanied him to the street door. As the lift closed on them, they embraced and kissed. There was more kissing in the deserted lobby of the block of flats. He was not certain that he loved her, or that she loved him, but his flesh betrayed him, and his cheeks became flushed.

'By this time next year,' she said. 'We will be married.'

'Yes,' he replied. 'By this time next year, Calogero will have lost all his money.'

She looked at him in disbelief.

'What makes you so sure?' she asked.

'He is in a dangerous position,' he said.

'How dangerous?' she asked.

'I don't know. But you are marrying me, not him.'

She looked at him with puzzled eyes. He had noticed that she had not said the thing she ought to have said. She had not said that Calogero's money, or the potential loss of it, could make any difference to her, and that she loved him for himself.

They parted, and he stepped out into the via Tomaselli. The sound of fireworks had died down. He took out his phone. Several people had sent him messages wishing him happy new year. There was one from Ceccina's phone, in other words, from Traiano, which simply said: 'I love you.' He texted back what he knew he ought to: 'I love you too.' Some things were best said by text alone. But he was glad that Traiano loved him, as he assumed this meant Traiano would never hurt him, that he had nothing to fear from him. Catarina had texted him too. He replied: 'I am miserable.' He wished he had the courage to add 'without you'. A moment later the phone pinged. 'Meet?' was the message. 'My place, 15 minutes', he replied at once before he could stop himself or regret it.

The party at Traiano's had been a great success. The food had been simply wonderful, and everyone had complimented Ceccina on her efforts. Renzo had been deeply impressed, as what they had eaten tonight was better than anything he had ever been given by his mother, grandmother or aunts. Also impressed had been Elena, who had been surprised and excited in equal measure to be invited. She was friends with Ceccina, everyone was, and she had been a visitor when the baby had been born, and had brought a nice present. She had come to the baptism. But her feelings about Ceccina were tinged with jealousy. Ceccina had a nice house and two nice children, while she, Elena, was still at home with her mother. While Elena had always admired her mother for her stern fortitude as a widow and her relentless courage in dealing with her two brothers, nevertheless, it was clear that life with her mother was not joyful, and living in the house she had been born in was rather dull. Ceccina, who had started so dubiously (getting pregnant at the age of fourteen) had landed rather well; in addition, Elena had always found Traiano uncomfortably attractive, particularly in the epoch before he had taken to wearing smart suits, and he had always worn jeans, shirt and leather jacket. However, these feeling were wearing off, and she felt this new affectation of his, of always wearing the silk scarf Calogero had given him, even indoors as now, rather tedious. And it was undoubtedly true that Traiano, though always polite, never paid her any real attention at all. She was barely there for him.

Some men had paid her attention, it was true, though there was always the question of her brother to negotiate; one wondered what they knew about Calogero, and whether the thought of her brother put men off, or worse, attracted them in the first place. She was in the settled habit of blaming Calogero for her lack of happiness in love. If she had not been the daughter of a criminal and the sister of a criminal, she thought crossly, she might have been able to meet and hold onto a nice man by now. Not that she was old, but Assunta, though her senior, was married, and she should be getting married about now, or so she had always calculated. And whatever happened, she had to keep up with Assunta; and she had to find a better husband than Federico, though that, she reflected, would not be hard.

She disliked Calogero because he paid her so little attention; she disliked Stefania for being pushy and materialistic, or rather being more successful at these activities than herself. And she very much disliked Rosario because he made her feel guilty. He had been a bullied child, and she had done nothing to stop it and nothing to comfort him; and now it was too late to repair the relationship. But as for Calogero, this evening, he had seemed more forthcoming, more concerned for her. He had, for some reason that she could not quite fathom, turned on the charm. She was a little suspicious. This was attention that she had not expected; after all, the females of the family counted for nothing. It was the boys that counted. Calogero's obsessive love for Rosario, which had shown itself in such a variety of cruel ways, was because he was a boy. He had no real feelings for his mother and sisters. He seemed fond of his daughters, but she was sure he did not care that much for Stefania. But here he was, being nice to her. She wondered what he wanted.

How different, how very different, was the visitor from Palermo! On the whole she did not care for people from Palermo, because they had a tendency to look down on people not from their city, and people from Catania in particular. But this young man, Renzo, the same age as herself, was politeness itself and very well brought up. One could tell that he came from a good family, a rich family too. He carried himself with confidence along with a certain degree of modesty. He seemed very eager to defer to her brother (most men made a habit of this) and even Traiano, and he was very polite to Ceccina, helping to clear the various dishes. He seemed charmed by the children, all five of them, and told her that he himself came from a large family, having three younger siblings and four younger cousins. He told her that his father had died in August, which had been a terrible blow, and that he was doing his best to take responsibility for the family affairs, and that Calogero was being a great help to him. He mentioned that he had met Traiano for the first time a while back, and also Rosario. It was quite as if he were advancing a claim to be an old family friend and ally.

She liked him, though he was not particularly handsome, but he did at least have good teeth. He had a very nice wristwatch, she noticed, though apart from that, he was not particularly smart. He had a gold chain around his neck, which she could see through the opening of his shirt, but he was a bit skinny and his clothes hung about him a little awkwardly as they did, for example, around her brother Rosario; he didn't have the smoothness of Calogero or Traiano, men who spent hours fussing over their wardrobe. She did not mind this. If she were to take him over, and how one's mind ran away with one at moments like this, she would surely have no trouble smartening him up, getting him to tuck his shirt in properly, getting him to wear better shoes, certainly the type of shoes that went with the jeans he was wearing. He was not beautiful, but he was improvable, a project for any woman who liked projects, and what woman did not?

They spent most of the evening talking together, and the more they talked, the more interested she became. He was still young, but mentioning the children – Cristoforo and Maria Vittoria, Isabella, Natalia and Renato – he expressed his delight in them and spoke of wanting children of his own one day, but not one day in the distant future. He alluded to marriage and family as if they were prospects that were not so very far ahead. He seemed to suggest that as his father was dead, he had control of the family money, though lots of dependants, but he certainly had enough money to marry on. He had had a girlfriend until recently, but was now single. She had not been right for him, and his mother, grandmother and aunts were very pleased they had broken up and that he had seen sense. He wanted someone older and more mature. She nodded vigorously as he said this. At the same time, she wondered if he saw her purely as a sympathetic listener. Her heart sank that he might think so. She was glad she had paid attention to her makeup before going out, and had resisted the temptation not to make an effort, given that she had expected a purely family gathering.

They talked about Christmas. It had been dull, in Catania, with Calogero and Stefania away, she said, though why she said this, she did not know. Their absence or presence made little difference to her. Renzo spoke of the Grand Hotel, but only in passing. The main thing had been the family gathering, the first since his father's demise. He spoke of the beauty of the Midnight Mass in the Cathedral and the Mass on the Sunday after Christmas. Palermo was a city of beautiful churches, but so, he had heard, was Catania. He was looking forward to seeing the famous shrine of Saint Agatha. She noted this: a good boy who went to church.

They spoke of her work, and she complained of the boredom of the routine in the office she worked in, where she was a junior accountant. It was a useful skill, he said, book-keeping. He spoke of his work, as the manager of a car show room, though he was rather vague about the details. Dealing with customers, dealing with employees, dealing with people in general.... One needed a lot of patience. She agreed with this.

After midnight, the children were put to bed, and Stefania made to take her three away. She could see that this was her cue to leave as well. Renzo turned to Calogero and asked his permission to walk his sister home. Calogero said that he was planning to do that himself (this surprised her; he had never done so in the past) but he would be delighted if Renzo were to do it for him. So they got their coats and he walked her the short distance home through the quarter. When they got to her door, he offered her a chaste kiss on the cheek and they exchanged telephone numbers. He spoke of the next day, now already begun, and promised to message her. She went upstairs to bed, very happy, and he walked back full of thought.

Meanwhile, all the women and children had gone to bed. Calogero sat on the sofa with Traiano next to him. The bottle of whiskey with the unpronounceable name from Scotland was before them, along with the bottle of Cinzano.

'What did you think?' asked Calogero.

'The way he held the gun? As if it were something dangerous? The face he made as he forced himself to pull the trigger? The look of terror on his face? The way he winced?'

'All of them.'

'He will learn. You will teach him. You have already taught him. When you gave him the gun, it was a test. He passed the test. The first time is always hardest. As for your sister, he seems to like her.'

Calogero smiled.

'How is Andreazza?' he asked.

'Busy. I forget you have never met him.'

'And never will. Let us keep on giving him what he wants, as long as he keeps Perraino as a missing person, not a murder victim. Are Alfio and Gino busy tonight?'

'Spreading disorder. Good night for it. All the police are at home drunk. And Andreazza is exactly where we want him.'

Renzo arrived. He eyed the whiskey bottle.

'Please have some,' said Calogero warmly, realising that he was waiting for permission, and glad that it was so. 'Tomorrow, we will give you a little tour of our city, or at least of the part we are interested in. We will drink all night, then sleep all day, and then get up, as it gets dark, and do mischief. How does that appeal?'

'Very much,' said Renzo.

Dawn had not yet come, but it was some moment very early in the morning, and he was looking at her, by the light that came through the inadequate curtains of his cold and dismal flat. Looking at her, he was aware that she was looking at him, and that she was making efforts to stir.

'Don't go,' he said. 'Don't think of going.'

'I have to, you know that,' said Catarina. 'He will wonder where I am. He is not completely stupid. I must not take silly risks.'

'I know, I know....'

'I am engaged to be married and so are you,' she pointed out. 'I shouldn't be here. You should not be here either.'

'I know, I know. Tell him you have changed your mind. And I will tell her that I have changed mine.'

'It is too late for that,' she said. 'You know how things work here. Your brother has arranged things. You promised him you would marry the lawyer's daughter.'

'I don't want to marry the lawyer's daughter.'

'You mean you do not want to sleep with her; or rather you do not want to sleep with her as much as you want to sleep with me. But you want to marry her. She is a better catch for the family.'

'And is Gino a better catch for you?'

'Given that if we married our life expectancy would be very short, yes. He is OK.'

'Is OK good enough?'

'It has to be. We must make the best of what is on offer. Look, we have enjoyed ourselves. Isn't that enough? We have got it out of our system. But now we have to play the game, and we did not make the rules. It certainly makes me sorry, but that is the way it is.'

'But don't go just yet,' he said.

She relented, against her better judgement.

'Tell me that you like me,' he said.

'You think I do not?'

'If they were all in jail, Calogero, Traiano, Gino, Alfio, and the rest of them....'

'Which will never happen,' she put in.

'It may be closer than you think,' he said. 'But if they were in jail, Carolina would not want me any more, that is for sure, and Gino and Calogero and the rest of them would be powerless. We could then be together.'

'Yes, but they will never be in jail. It is too close knit. They will never betray each other. There is no evidence against them. It is not that they have committed crimes and gotten away with it, but there were no crimes in the first place, for the most part. Turiddu killed himself, very convenient. That policeman who arrested Gino, Alfio and Traiano, has disappeared. There is no evidence he was murdered, nor is there likely to be. He vanished. The rest is speculation. They plan their crimes like this. They do not leave traces behind them.'

'There are certain things so bad that they must come out, like the corruption of children,' said Rosario.

'The corruption of children is standard round here,' she said. 'It is normal. No one is shocked by it. What are you talking about? Oh, I think I know. That curly haired boy who runs errands for Traiano and Gino and Alfio, and more than errands from what I guess? Paolo? His mother is Beata who drinks that vile drink, crème de menthe? You think she does not know what her son gets up to? Of course she does. He brings home the money, and so she tries not to think too much about how he earns it, I suppose. But she takes the money. We all do. Even you. No one can resist the lure of hard cash. Do not be so naive, Saro. If you didn't care about money, you would go and live in a monastery.'

'Maybe I shall,' he replied with a trace of crossness.

'You have just screwed me twice,' she pointed out, 'and you talk of being a monk? You need to work out what you want. You have got what you want, haven't you? You had it before Christmas when Gino was away.' (This was true; he had slept with her before going to Palermo, on several occasions, though he had not admitted this to Traiano.) 'And now you have had what you wanted again. Now think of something else.'

She began looking for her clothes. He watched her put on her bra, and sighed deeply. He had said the wrong thing.

'Look,' he said.

'Don't explain. You can't explain,' she said sadly. 'And when you try to explain you only succeed in making excuses, weak ones.'

'Could you be pregnant?' he asked.

'I told you, I took precautions, so you did not have to.'

He remembered the case of Volta.

'But if, by any chance you were…'

She turned and looked at him. It was pity in her eyes, he thought. She let him embrace her. Then she pushed him away.

'I have to go,' she said.

He watched her dress and, after she left, he felt black misery engulf him. Everything he did was wrong. This was no way to start the new year. He had to prove if only to himself that he was still a good person. He had to show that he did not care about his brother's money, only about truth.

Chapter Ten

'How was it?' asked Traiano.

It was Monday January 3rd, the first working day of the year 2011. It was just after six in the morning. The city slept. Rosario had been in the gym, which was completely deserted. He now stepped into the changing room to find Traiano there.

'How was what?' he asked.

'The weekend, of course. We did not see you. I was sort of expecting to.'

'I felt a little depressed,' said Rosario. 'I kept myself to myself.'

'I imagined that you were with Carolina.'

'I was expected at her place yesterday, but I could not face going,' said Rosario.

Traiano had taken off his black leather jacket and hung it up. He had also taken off the silk scarf of which he was so fond, from which he was inseparable, and hung that up.

'Did you spend any time with that prostitute, the one with the pink card?' asked Traiano.

'As I said, I was depressed.'

Traiano smiled.

'I know what depresses you. Your brother.'

'Perhaps.'

'Don't take off your shirt just yet,' said Traiano.

'I need to have a shower and then go to the office.'

'You need to talk to me,' said Traiano. 'The office can wait. Everything can wait. What I am going to say is important. Come and sit next to me. I am sick of this life, and I want you to help me get out of it. Calogero is going to Rome tonight and you are going with him. If I go to the police, I have to take something with me. What I can take with me is the evidence that you will see with your own eyes in Rome. They will be grateful for that.'

Rosario looked at him for a long time. Traiano stared back.

'It is what Volta wants,' said Rosario. 'If we give it to him, you go free, you go somewhere far away with a new name, and Calogero goes down.'

'Volta,' said Traiano. 'I knew about him from the day of the baptism. I saw you exchange looks. That was when I knew. That was when I realised I had an escape route. I told you twice that I knew about Volta. Neither time did you seem to pick it up. I told you I knew that you had gone to police headquarters to report your missing identity card, and I told you I knew about the prostitute. Both were excuses for meeting Volta. I had to be sure. I had to be sure that, not only were you seeing Volta, but that you were not going to change your mind and run away. If you were jittery, just one, let alone two of those hints would have been enough to make you get the first train out of here, all the way north, and you would not have stopped until the Alps were between yourself and Calogero.'

'I hate Calogero. What he did to me. What he has done to you. What he has done to everyone he has touched.'

'I know,' said Traiano. 'And you are determined to destroy him, whatever the cost.'

'It will be a new life for you and for me,' said Rosario.

'Yes. I know you just want what is good for me. You remember the message I sent to you wishing you a happy new year? You remember what it said. I love you. That is all. I do. I love you, passionately. Almost as much as I love Ceccina and the children. You are the best thing in my life, I think. Look, take off that shirt and get into the shower. We will talk later. You had better not be late. Just act normally. Calogero expects that.'

Rosario stood up and nodded. He was trembling with excitement. He began to pull the sports shirt he was wearing over his head. The process momentarily blinded him as he struggled with the tight and sweaty garment.

Traiano was quick. He had always told himself, promised himself, that he would be quick. Celerity was merciful. He wrapped the silk scarf around Rosario's neck; there was a very slight protest, as if this were a joke. But it was no joke. The noose tightened. Rosario lost consciousness. He fell to the ground. Glad he could not see his face, still covered by the shirt, Traiano knelt on his friend's chest, feeling his own heart break, keeping the scarf tight, until he was sure life was extinct.

Still not able to uncover his face, he dragged the body towards where the washbasins were. There was a horrible smell which he recognised only too well, the smell that resulted from the bowels of the corpse opening. He untied the scarf, and set it aside, knowing that the scarf would forever be the reminder he needed of the loyalty he had to the boss, and the repayment he had given the boss for the death of his own father. Opening the cupboard that hid the oubliette, he heaved the dead weight of the body over the edge, and gradually lowered it, head first, then released the ankles. The corpse disappeared. It was gone. He knew there would be nothing to see. Closing the cupboard, he went back to the bench and sat down, in an attempt to get his breath back. He hung up the treasured scarf. After a moment, he went to the door of the changing room. There was Maso, waiting, as arranged.

'How long have you been here?'

'Five minutes, as you said, boss.'

'Good. Now go to Rosario's flat. Steal his computer and his credit card. You know how to get into it, don't you?'

'I did it the other day.'

'Take the computer home and use it to buy a rail ticket to Rome, one way, in his name, OK? Now go. You still have the key. Don't worry, he is not there, but don't get caught. I will see you later. Not a word.'

'Right, boss.'

He was gone. Traiano returned to the changing room. He went to Rosario's locker, which was open. It contained his phone, his wallet and his day clothes. After checking the wallet for anything useful, he took the entire contents of the locker and threw them down the oubliette, including the phone, after their master. He then looked at his watch. It was not even half past six. He left the gym, knowing that even if anyone did see him, no one would remark on it, as he was often there at that time. He walked home to his wife and children. Taking off his jacket and the scarf, he took off the rest of his clothes and got into bed with Ceccina. She stirred happily, feeling his warm embrace. After a few moments they were as one; and then he slept.

At about nine that evening, having refreshed himself, Traiano was at the Borgo station. There, Maso was waiting for him, summoned by child messenger. In the station, where the crowds were thinning out dramatically, Traiano laid down a suitcase, for which he was sure some passing tramp would be grateful. It contained the things that Rosario had packed in readiness for going away. It was a large suitcase, and the dismal flat now looked even more cheerless than before. From the Borgo station, he and Maso went to where Maso lived, which was not far away. There they entered, aware of the sounds of a television from the sitting room, where the parents sat, and made their way to the room which the two boys shared. Enzo did not acknowledge his arrival in any way.

'Show me the computer,' said Traiano.

Maso explained. The computer held a series of documents, none of which seemed to be interesting. Traiano nodded. There were the email and the social media accounts. Traiano sat down and studied these last two. Some of the emails were connected with work. Many of them were from Carolina. Some of them were from Catarina. There were even some from his sisters, and some from don Giorgio. The social media was equally bare, showing a life of a man who had few real friends. He had posted numerous pictures from the various accounts associated with famous Italian shrines, particularly Assisi.

Traiano considered.

'OK. You get him' – he indicated Enzo – 'to do what you said he could do, to make it look as if the emails he is sending and the things he is posting come from Rome.'

'He has done that. Any message or log in will give the trace of a Roman server.'

'OK. He is in Rome. Let him post that his phone has been stolen. In Termini station. If anyone needs to get hold of him, they can't and had better email him or message his Facebook. Do that now.' Traiano watched him do it. 'Now go to the email. Aha. 'Why aren't you answering your phone?' from his girlfriend. Answer that, pretending to be him. Got it? But read her other emails first and his replies to her.'

'I did that this afternoon, boss. I know how he writes to her. And how she writes to him.'

'Send an email to his work. He has had to go away suddenly. For the girlfriend, the story is different. He is in Rome, and he is thinking of going to Assisi for a few days of prayer and retreat. He's having a crisis. Look at what he writes, get a feel for him and fill it in. Use your intelligence. Spin it out. In a few weeks he can tell people, via email, that he is not getting another phone, and he is leaving the country, and he is going to become a missionary somewhere. You do it all. I only want to know if someone called Volta emails him. The rest does not interest me. I leave it to you. This room is awful. You need to tidy up. By the way, you can move into

367

Rosario's flat after a decent interval. It is small but it is better than this. I will clear it with don Calogero.'

'Thanks, boss.'

Traiano noticed that Maso did not ask any questions. That was a good sign.

'Don't make him too active on the internet,' he cautioned. 'Very soon he won't need to be active at all. Oh yes, and try to close his bank account or at least empty it. You have the card.'

'Yes boss.'

Traiano prepared to leave. After he had done so, Maso reflected that the only person, apart from his silent brother, who knew of his affair with Stefania, was now dead.

Towards the end of January, Anna Agostini, as she would shortly become, was in the bar opposite the Cathedral in Syracuse, where she had just been to Mass. It was Sunday, the thirtieth day of the month. With her, was the child Salvatore. She stood at the bar, sipping her cappuccino, the child next to her. This was what she always did after Mass on a Sunday. Her soon-to-be husband had been with her, but had left to go to the studio and would, after whatever his business was there, join her for lunch at their house. She liked this little period of peace between the sacred mysteries and the matter of lunch. In her mind, she was preparing for the wedding, due to take place next week, when February came, when Calogero and his family would be away. They had chosen that very date, the first Saturday in February, for that very reason – so that Calogero would not be able to come; she wanted a quiet wedding. It was all arranged to take place in a side chapel of the Cathedral - the one at the back on the right. There would be few people there, just themselves and the witnesses, as well as Traiano and Ceccina, who had been invited and had said they would come. Then there would be drinks, no photographs – why would you want them when you married a photographer? – and then the guests could leave, and married life begin. She contemplated this new beginning with satisfaction.

It was a cold day, and the bar was full of people who might otherwise have gathered in the square outside, had it been sunny. There was, as always on these occasions, the smell of wet wool and wet fur, the smell of rain on coats, the splash of water on the marble floor from the umbrellas. She herself was warm and dry having taken refuge before the brief squall. She sensed that the men who came in all saw her at the bar, noted her, looked away, and then could not resist looking once more. How men looked; how their eyes sought her out. To hell with them all, she thought. Let them look. She belonged to no one but herself, and her children and her future husband, and the child who would be born some nine months after the wedding, she hoped. She was that one thing she had never imagined she would be: respectable.

One man was a little more persistent that the rest. She had not seen him here before: a pleasant looking man in his thirties. He looked at her across the bar, and she looked back at him, and she understood. Her look was not inviting, but the man was not to be put off. He approached.

'I know who you are,' she said, as he stood next to her, not looking at him, but looking at her coffee cup and her son.

'You do?' said Fabio Volta.

'Of course, I do. The way you stand there, wanting something from me. You have been annoying Ceccina, annoying Catarina, even annoying Assunta and Elena. They all told me. So now you have come to annoy me. I have been expecting you. You had no luck with them, so now you are trying your luck with me. Why you should expect to succeed with me when you failed with them, I do not know. Your enemies are my friends, and your friends are my enemies. You cannot seriously expect me to help you.'

'I don't think you are quite right,' said Volta. 'You hate Calogero as much as I do. But let that pass. I did not succeed with Assunta or Elena because they know nothing. They have chosen to know nothing. Their mother, I am sure, is the same. I did not even try with her. As the widow of her late husband, she knows what is really important. She would never speak. The two girls, well, I was a little surprised, but perhaps I should not have been. Assunta never liked Rosario. He told me that himself. When Calogero tortured Rosario she did nothing to stop it, she pretended it was not happening. Thus Rosario disliked her, and she hated him, because he made her feel guilty about what she had failed to do. Assunta refuses to believe the truth. Her brother was the guilty one, not the victim. So she denies that he is dead. And Elena is too busy with her new boyfriend from Palermo. She does not want to be disturbed by the thought of the injustice done to her brother, by her other brother too. Some tragedies are too much to contemplate. They insist that he is alive and well, and has gone away, they care not where. But you, signora, you always liked Rosario.'

Now she looked at him. He had caught her attention.

'He is dead? You are sure?' she asked, in a low voice. 'I thought....'

'You thought what? You mean you hoped. You hoped he had done what he did the last time, that he had run away. And no doubt you had heard, through Catarina, through Ceccina, just why he might have run, and where he has run to. Yes, there have been emails, sent from Assisi. Yes, over the new year holiday he slept with Catarina, a big thing for a boy like Rosario, then could not face the guilt of it, could not face his virginal fiancé, could not face his boss the lawyer Petrocchi who had always put such confidence in him, and decided to run. That was what the emails, put together explained. I have seen them. Catarina showed me. Carolina Petrocchi showed me. Don Giorgio showed me. The emails were very convincing. But… they are fake, they are fraudulent, they want to convince you that someone who is dead is in fact alive. As don Giorgio, who you trust, pointed out to me. The email he sent to don Giorgio contained a stupid error. It was clever, the sort of email Rosario would send to don Giorgio but it made a factual error. In it, Rosario spoke about his sin with Catarina, and how he had always confessed his sins to don Giorgio in the past. Only he never had. He used to confess to a priest at the Cathedral, and never to don Giorgio. Don Giorgio knew that, but I did not, and the person who was writing the emails supposedly from Rosario did not either. An easy mistake to make.'

'But someone in Assisi is sitting there sending out emails in Rosario's name?'

'No. The emails look as though they come from there. The earlier ones came from Rome. That is, they are sent from here to Rome and back to here. It is a simple operation. You do not have to be a computer genius.'

'If they made the error you say they made, they are not geniuses at all,' she observed.

'Then you accept that he is dead?' he asked.

She looked at him sadly.

'What does it matter what I think?' she asked. 'I shall not see him again. I am sorry for that. He was always a nice boy. You know whose son this is?' she asked, indicating little Salvatore. 'His father is dead too. I just take it day by day and try not to think too much. Yes, Rosario must be dead, but what good does it do to think about it? We cannot change the past. Rosario was always going to die. He did not heed the warnings. He did not give Calogero what he wanted.'

'And what does Calogero want?'

'Love of course.' She looked at him. 'You should heed the warnings too.'

'I am doing so,' he said. 'I am not entirely stupid.'

'You are if you think you can fight him. You can't,' said Anna. 'No one can. Did you speak to my daughter-in-law?'

'Yes, she knows nothing.'

'A wise girl. Did you speak to Stefania?'

'Yes, eventually. She did not want to see me, but I eventually forced myself on her. I had a bit of leverage. Something that Rosario told me.'

'She would not have liked that,' observed Anna.

'I went to see her at the office she has. She would have liked to have thrown me out, or called security, but realised she could not.' He paused, realising that Anna had not asked what it was Rosario had told him about his sister-in-law. Usually, people were curious. But Anna clearly realised that knowledge like this could be dangerous. 'I told her that I suspected, indeed, was sure that Rosario was dead. She furiously denied this could be true. She told me I had no proof. I agreed that I had no proof but I said she was deluding herself if she believed he had not been murdered.'

'Murdered for talking to you,' Anna pointed out.

'That was not the point she made. She seemed to assume that her brother-in-law had been killed for some other reason, that it was more her fault than mine. Whichever way, she did not, under any circumstances, wish to admit that he was dead. Denial. Anyway, she threw me out. But I have at least made her think, even if she now has to suppress her thoughts. Calogero has committed fratricide.'

'Every man who kills, kills a brother,' said Anna. 'You think she will now leave him? Never. But you should be careful. You are married?'

He explained his own situation.

'Think of that child,' she said. 'Now go, and do not come and see me again. I am sorry about Rosario, believe me, but there is nothing I can do.'

The flat where Maso lived with his brother Enzo and his parents was near the Borgo Station, at the upper end of the via Etnea. Here the two parents lived their perennially depressed lives with two adult children who never spoke to them. One, it was true, never spoke to anyone apart from his brother, imprisoned as he was in his own silence. The brother never spoke to his parents because he despised them, and he was hoping, very soon, that he would be able to move out, into the flat that had been Rosario's. But this was of itself problematic. The flat in Purgatory was very small, really only a single room with a kitchen and a tiny bathroom. It was up four flights of stairs. The flat he presently lived in, at parental expense, was larger and more modern and had a lift, although the two boys spent their entire time, when at home, in the large room they shared. To decant from that room to the flat was proving difficult. Maso's developing idea was that he should move into the flat and leave Enzo; that way they would both have more room. Enzo's equipment, all his computer stuff, took up a lot of space, and if Maso moved out, Enzo would be better off. But Enzo did not see it this way. If Maso were to move to the flat, then he would come too. They had always been together and they had to stay together. Besides the flat was marginally bigger than the room they now occupied. If it were still too small, would the boss not eventually give them another flat, a larger one?

That was undoubtedly true. Maso already knew that the boss was moving to the upper floor of his building, into a new space made up of six former properties, and that Traiano and his family would have the boss's old flat; and that meant that Traiano's current flat would be free for Gino and Catarina when they married. But eventually, given the amount of properties the boss owned, something better would come up for him and Enzo. Or so he told Enzo. When such a bigger flat came up, then they could live there together. But in the meantime....

Enzo suspected that this might never happen, and that Maso really wanted to get rid of him. He wanted to be alone. He said this, he articulated the idea, that Maso wanted to break the bond between them. Maso tried to explain that living in separate places would not mean they were no longer together much of the time. They would just be apart for some of the time. They would have separate bedrooms, which given their age, was right.

'You will be able to do what you want to do, and I will be able to do what I want to do,' he said.

This seemed reasonable to him, but it elicited a pained response from Enzo. He understood what his brother meant too well. Maso would be able to screw his whores in peace, and even get a proper girlfriend, which would be a prelude to getting married and leaving him definitively. Indeed, that is exactly what Maso wanted to do, in the long term - have a normal life. He also wanted to get away from his brother, his untidiness, his habit of sitting in front of the computer with his trousers open, masturbating, as if no one else was in the room. He wanted a place of his own where he could bring people back. He loved his brother, but he wanted to be free.

This argument had continued for several days. Quite often Enzo shouted with inarticulate hatred; sometimes he wept, shivered and groaned in fear, curled on the bed. On these occasions, Maso, wracked with something that felt like guilt, as well as with the fear that he would never escape, climbed onto the bed and held him tightly, while his brother continued to groan and cry.

Then Sunday came. The parents, who were used to these sorts of sounds coming from the room of their alienated sons, went out to Church as normal. A few minutes later, at the very time Volta was in Syracuse talking to Anna, the doorbell rang. Maso went, wondering who it could be. It was Stefania. She had entered the building as the parents had left, and had been lying in wait, for just this moment.

He was taken aback to see her. She stepped into the apartment. He took a few steps back, but not quickly enough. Her hand stung his cheek.

'You little bastard,' she said. 'You told Rosario, and Rosario went and told Volta.'

She hit him again and again. In vain, he tried to defend himself, both with words and by raising his hands to his face. Enzo, in the bedroom they shared, heard her voice. He crept out and looked up the corridor, and peered round the door at the end. He recognised her, the boss's wife, whom he had worked for, and with whom his brother had retired to the bedroom, locking the door. He hated her. She was the one he wanted, the one he wanted to be with, rather than his own brother. He wanted to move to the flat in Purgatory so he could be closer to her and sleep with her. Now she was screaming and shouting at him. He looked, saw, understood and withdrew.

He hadn't told Rosario, he reminded her. Rosario had seen his phone with a message she had sent. She was the one to blame. But Rosario had promised him he would tell no one. But it seems he had. He had told Volta. So it did not matter where Rosario was now, she didn't care, and she didn't worry about him. But Volta knew.

'Does Volta know about you and Rosario as well?' asked Maso.

That, he noticed with satisfaction, shut her up.

'You men,' she said with something like viciousness.

But she knew and he knew that Volta knowing was a problem. Volta had no reason to keep quiet.

'He won't kill you, he will kill me,' she said, speaking of her husband. 'His honour will demand it.'

They were both silent for a while.

'What are we going to do?' she asked.

'You mean, what am I going to do?' he asked. 'I am the one in greater danger.'

It struck him that Saro was dead perhaps because of Stefania, not because of Volta.

In the bedroom, Enzo became aware that they were now talking in low voices. This worried him. He waited until he could wait no longer. He left the room on silent feet and approached the end of the corridor once more. As he expected, they had forgotten his presence, as they had the last time. Peering into the room, through the open door, he could see what was happening. She was on the sofa, her dress pulled up and pulled down, her knees apart, and his brother was on top of her, his trousers round his ankles, his shirt riding up, showing his bare hairy arse, and they were moving, together. It was like, and not like, the pornographic videos that he watched. His brother was doing it with that woman. Enzo sat on the floor, out of sight, his hand in his mouth, hearing the sound they made, willing himself not to scream. The brother he loved, loved another. The brother he loved was leaving him for another, had left him for another.

After a time, after the sounds that came from them like animals in pain, there was silence. Then they began to speak in conspiratorial whispers, but he could hear what they were saying.

'You have to kill him,' she said.

'Your husband?'

'No, Volta. Don't be ridiculous. Kill Volta. It is the only way. Then no one knows and we are both safe.' There was a brief silence, while this sank in. 'Besides Calogero will want Volta dead. Go to Calogero, go to Traiano, and say you want to kill Volta. They will be delighted.'

'Will they? Won't they be suspicious?'

'Are you frightened of killing someone?' she asked. 'Are you a man for this but not for that?'

'Oh Jesus!' he said.

There was more silence.

'Look, go to Traiano,' she counselled. 'Tell him you will kill Volta. Tell him you want to do it, to prove yourself, and you want the money or whatever it is they will give you. You have got a hold over Traiano, haven't you?'

'OK, OK,' he said. 'Now go, before my parents come back. Mass does not go on forever.'

Enzo heard her get up and adjust her clothes. She went to the door, and it closed gently behind her. A moment later he heard his brother heave himself up from the sofa. A moment later, he was in the corridor, carrying his shirt which was screwed up into a ball.

'You,' he said, seeing his brother sitting on the floor. He aimed a vicious kick at him, and then headed to the bathroom to wash and change.

The night before Calogero was to fly to Rome with the family and then onto New York, was the night they discussed the murder of Volta.

Calogero had long wanted to get Volta out of the way, and had seen him as an unsettled score. Now, now that the Santucci family was effectively under his control, he did not have to ask anyone's permission. He could have it done. The children were in bed, and so was Stefania. They would fly out tomorrow at midday.

'Let him do it,' was all he said. 'If he wants to.'

'But will he do it well?'

'You trust him?'

'He is very keen. He has been trustworthy in the past.'

'If he makes a hash of it, if he gets himself arrested, can he be trusted to stay quiet?'

'Yes. There is the brother. The parents. He would not want to put them in danger, or indeed himself.'

'But why does he want to do it?' asked Calogero.

They were sitting together in the kitchen.

'He sees it as an opportunity. He wants you to give him a bigger flat than Rosario's, so he and his brother can live there comfortably. He wants to earn respect, and a bigger flat. My guess is that he wants mine when I have yours.'

'It is a fair price. He and his brother, that's an unhealthy relationship.'

'You bet. But he sleeps, I think, with that whore Beata, the one who drinks crème de menthe. So, he is sort of normal, apart from the brother.'

'Beata with the son called Paolo? The one who….'

'That's right.'

'Colonel Andreazza is an evil bastard.'

'But a useful one to us,' said Traiano. 'Indeed, essential.'

'You told little Paolo that, did you?'

'Yes. You are giving them a better flat, remember? They are very grateful.'

'And you told little Paolo….?'

'That one day we would kill Andreazza. But only when he is no longer useful. I wonder if that has occurred to the Colonel. Hope so. It keeps him alert. And in a year or two, when Paolo is too old for him, we will find someone else.'

'Does Maso know what to do?'

'I have coached him.'

'Good. So when I come back from New York…'

'It will all be done. No worries.'

Traiano stood up to go. They looked at each other. Traiano wondered whether Calogero would mention it. He had not done so before now. There was no reason why he should now. He could tell that Calogero knew what he was thinking. He wondered for a moment, but the moment passed. Rosario was not to be mentioned. He would, in fact, it seemed clear now, never be mentioned between them.

A few moments later, Stefania felt her husband get into bed with her.

'What has kept you up so long?' she asked.

'Business,' he replied, turning towards her. 'Sweets dreams,' he added.

Friday 4th February seemed to be the ideal date for the murder. On a Friday, people were more relaxed, looking forward to the weekend. Moreover, the police were always slower to react on a Friday, as their investigations never quite got into gear until the beginning of the following week, by which time many clues would have been blown away with the wind. It would not be a difficult job, Traiano had assured him, as Volta was a fool. He had been warned, and had not fled; and, despite the fact he was an ex-policeman, he made no attempt to vary his journey home nor his other habits.

This was to be a murder, not a disappearance. It was to be a display of power. This man had annoyed so many people, so he was to be killed in the open, fearlessly, to show who really ruled the city of Catania. Maso was there early, but not too early, waiting by the stolen motorbike and helmet, dressed in jeans and a black fleece, done up tightly, wearing a woolly hat. All these, he would dump when the deed was done, and change his clothes. It was February, but the idea was to dump the bike and the clothes in the sea north of the city, at a quiet place where some new clothes would be waiting for him, and then return to the city by bus.

The waiting was nerve-wracking. He knew he had to prove himself. He knew too that he had to get rid of the one man who had the knowledge that could get him killed. He knew he had been a fool to get involved with Stefania, but, oh God, he felt his blood surge at the memory of what had happened on his parents' sofa. He desired her so much, he wanted her so much, and he was sure, when he had done her bidding, that she would never refuse him again. In addition, there hung, on this, his promotion in the organisation. If this went well, - and why should it not? - then he would be able to look Traiano in the eye, and he would not be inferior in any way to Gino or to Alfio. They were all men who had proved themselves, and he would too.

The place chosen was the archway that led from the Cathedral Square to the park outside, the short tunnel that was always full of passing people, and which was the route out to the bus terminus, where Volta took his bus home every evening. The small boys had been watching him. This was his invariable route, the fool. He deserved to be killed. The tunnel was ideal, full of people, relatively narrow, blocking, or at least reducing, the chance of escape.

The weapon he had chosen was the knife. The choice had been his. At home, in the bedroom he shared with Enzo, he kept both his gun and his knife, and he had considered both carefully. He liked both, but he knew the knife was the better weapon for a man to use. It elicited greater skill. He knew exactly what to do. He would approach Volta, who would not recognise him until it was too late (he was sure Volta did not know him, but he knew Volta and had been studying them all from afar). He would put his arm round the man's neck, and then stick the knife in up under his ribs to his heart. Then he would watch the eyes understand for a moment what was happening, and then see them become sightless. Then he would put away the knife and calmly walk away, take the motorcycle and be gone, lost in the evening traffic. The thing was to keep calm.

He watched the faces coming towards him, leaning casually against the wall besides the little shop that sold postcards and souvenirs. He could pass for a young man waiting for someone, well, he was waiting for someone; waiting perhaps for his girlfriend. Once more he thought of Stefania, her rage, the way her rage had turned to lust, and the way they had gone at it like animals on the sofa. Oh Jesus, how wonderful it had been. She had enjoyed it too. Of course, the boss liked making babies, but he was not so keen on making love, or so she had told him. Strange. Of course, the boss would kill him if he knew, but some things were worth risking death for.

As now. Walking across the Cathedral Square was the figure of Volta, in the light of early evening. He was wearing a thick coat, but it was open, and he could see his white shirt. That was good. He felt his heart pound as Volta approached, clearly full of thought, clearly thinking of going home, a home he would never reach, walking towards the end of his life, without realising how close that end was. He was doomed; he would never leave the city, never make it to the bus terminus, but die next to the postcard shop and under the little shrine of Saint Agatha.

As Volta entered the arch, Maso stepped forward, uttering his name.

'Fabio Volta,' he said.

Volta looked at him curiously.

Maso put his left arm round Volta's neck, as if in friendly greeting. In the right, he held the knife. He pressed it against the flesh. Volta's eyes registered understanding, swiftly succeeded by blinding anger. Here was one of Calogero's men come to kill him. He felt the knife. He saw Maso's eyes, staring into his. With his right hand he grabbed Maso's genitals, and squeezed with all his might. The pain of having his balls crushed was excruciating, and Maso felt the breath leave his body. The knife for some reason had not gone in. He felt his hand weaken. With his right hand, Volta held onto Maso's balls with a deadly grip, inflicting searing pain. With his left he seized the knife, and drove it into Maso's side. He watched his expression turn from one of pain to one of shock and the sudden realisation that everything had gone wrong. Volta pushed Maso away, and saw him stagger, grasping the knife that was now stuck in his side. He leaned against the wall. His eyes were fixed on Volta and now becoming glazed. He slid to the ground. Volta watched him with contempt. Then he turned to the small crowd that had gathered, asking someone, anyone, to call the police.

It was Monday morning, some three days later, that Calogero, Stefania and the children returned from New York to Rome, and then onward onto Catania. Traiano had decided it would be best if he were there at the airport to meet them and to break the bad news. He had decided not to attempt to contact the boss in New York, knowing how much Calogero hated any form of written or electronic communication. Besides, he had seen no reason to ruin the last weekend of his holiday. Bad news could wait.

Both the boss and his wife, as they had flown back, were in a buoyant mood. Stefania had loved New York. The cold of winter, the skating in Central Park and the Rockefeller Centre, these had delighted her, as had all the tourist things she had done with the children. The shops too had been marvellous, and Calogero had told her to spend as much as she wanted and to have it all shipped back home. So she had.

She had watched him like a hawk, knowing that this was the time when Tancredi was to have her child; she had watched him for any sign that he was in touch with her, or someone close to her; she had watched to see if anyone was sending him the news of a successful birth. But there had been no sign. She herself had asked friends in Catania to let her know if anything happened, and sure enough, several had done so. She knew that Tancredi had given birth to a boy, to be called Sebastiano, but it seemed her husband was still ignorant of this. This reassured her. He had, of course, seen other people. In Rome, he had disappeared for several hours, leaving her and the children; and the same had happened in New York. But he had given no sign that these meetings were anything to do with Tancredi and the child.

As they approached Catania, she sensed that his patience would be rewarded and that, when they landed, someone would tell him just what he was surely pretending not to want to know, namely that he had a new son. And so it proved. Traiano was waiting for them as they came through the doors. And it was clear to her that Traiano was eager to see them, but nervous. He was wearing his jeans, his trainers, his black leather jacket, and the long silk scarf that he had given him, that she had first given her husband, and which he seemed never to take off.

There were kisses and warm greetings. The children were delighted to see Traiano. They loved him.

'Before we go into town, there is something I need to tell you,' said Traiano with a touch of desperation.

'There is a lot I need to tell you,' said Calogero. 'But it can wait till we are all in the car, surely?'

Traiano's face, unusually, told a different story. In the Arrivals Hall, there was a coffee bar.

'Go and have a cup of coffee,' said Calogero to his wife. 'Take the children.'

She did as she was told.

'Maso is dead,' said Traiano, as soon as she and the children were out of earshot. 'Instead of him stabbing Volta, Volta stabbed him. Volta was wearing a stab-resistant vest under his shirt. His girlfriend, the policewoman, insisted he do so. He got away with a pinprick, but he stuck the knife into Maso, who bled to death in the ambulance, just as they were arriving in the hospital. Friday night, bad traffic, lazy paramedics. Volta was arrested, but they have let him go and dropped all charges. I thought that was best. I got Andreazza to see to it. The last thing we need is a trial of Volta where he is given a platform.'

He looked at the boss. The boss was thoughtful.

'Maso was not to be trusted after all,' he remarked. 'We are better off without him.'

'It is the idiot brother I am worried about,' said Traiano. 'The parents are harmless, but the brother is strange, and he may blame us.'

'Us? We are not responsible.'

'But how does his mind work?'

'What harm can he do?' said Calogero. 'Listen. I saw our man in Rome. I saw people in New York. They are all very pleased with us.'

He described briefly how he had been admitted into the office of one of the most important men in the capital, and how he had kissed the dry papery cheek of their ultimate guarantor. And in New York, he had made contacts, spoken to people, had dinner, heard all the things he had wanted to hear. Then he asked about Tancredi.

'She had the child last week, all went well,' said Traiano.

'I will try to get over to see them next week,' said Calogero happily. 'Don't worry about Maso. He was an idiot. Look, you go and get the car and bring it round to the front. I will marshal this lot and all the luggage and see you there. OK?'

'Yes, Caloriu,' said Traiano.

The boss raised his hand and stroked his smooth cheek.

'Well done,' he said. 'I have missed you. Next time I go to New York, you will have to come too.'

He walked over to his wife and children. His wife looked up at him from her telephone with a serious expression.

'Was he just telling you this?' she asked.

He glanced at her phone. It was an article from a Catania news site.

'Yes,' he said shortly.

'The guy whose brother fixed our computers?'

'Seems so,' he replied, his look cautioning her not to discuss it in front of the children. 'He was a bad boy, it seems,' he added.

She looked at him. She felt terrible shock and grief. Had her husband done it? Had he known? Surely not?

'Look. Let us go to the car, Traiano is bringing it round.'

Traiano was bringing it round. He realised, as he approached the pick-up point outside the door to Arrivals, that he had not told the boss about his mother's wedding, that Saturday, the very day after the death of Maso. It had been a small occasion, but a nice one. He had complicated feelings about his mother, but he loved his little brother Salvatore, and he was very taken with his new stepfather. Alfonso had looked splendid in the new suit he wore. He always looked splendid. Of course, Alfonso was very keen to marry Anna, but he was also clearly loved Anna's son, himself. How delightful and flattering was that? Oh, what fun they would have over the years to come.

He saw them waiting there, as he slowed and drew up. There was the boss, in his stunning overcoat, and there was Stefania, easily the most elegant person in the airport. And there were Isabella and Natalia, such pretty girls, and sweet little Renato. They didn't know they now had a new sibling in Palermo. How would that work out? Rome was happy, New York was happy, his own wife was pregnant, his mother soon would be. The future stretched before them. So much money, so much power, so much to look forward to. And there, behind the boss, now waving to him, was Enzo the idiot brother, a look of incoherent hatred on his face. And he was holding a gun. They had not noticed him. Traiano froze. He was so close to them now; he wanted to shout, but he was in the car, and the windows were up. The boss saw the expression on his face and looked puzzled. Enzo raised the gun, determined to destroy the person who, in his twisted logic, had taken his brother away from him. And he pulled the trigger several times; Traiano heard the pop, pop, pop of the gun and saw Stefania's body tense, then slump and relax forever.

Printed in Great Britain
by Amazon

32368037R00216